WITH OR WITHOUT YOU

SHARI LOW has published twenty novels
over the last two decades. She also
writes for newspapers, magazines and
television. Once upon a time, she got
engaged to a guy she'd known for a
week, and twenty-something years later,
they live in Glasgow with their two
teenage sons and a labradoodle.

ALSO BY SHARI LOW

The Story of Our Life
The Other Wives Club
A Life Without You
One Day in December
Another Day in Winter

Non-fiction
Because Mummy Said So

Shari Low

WITH
OR
WITHOUT
YOU

HEAD
of
ZEUS

First published in the UK in 2018 by Aria, an imprint of Head of Zeus Ltd
This paperback edition published in the UK in 2019 by Head of Zeus Ltd

9 7 5 3 1 2 4 6 8

A catalogue record for this book is available from
the British Library.

ISBN (PB): 9781788549905
ISBN (E): 9781788541411

Typeset by Divaddict Publishing Solutions Ltd.

Printed and bound in Great Britain by
CPI Group (UK) Ltd, Croydon CR0 4YY

Head of Zeus Ltd
First Floor East
5–8 Hardwick Street
London EC1R 4RG

WWW.HEADOFZEUS.COM

To J, C & B – Everything, Always.
And to my aunt, Margaret Wallis, a wonderful woman who
will always have a special place in my heart.

HOW IT ALL BEGAN

I think we've all had those moments in life.

The crossroads.

The should I, or shouldn't I?

Will I, or won't I?

The moments when you know that you have to make a decision that will affect the rest of your life. Do you take the new job? Do you buy the new house? Do you sell up and move abroad? Do you cut off the toxic friend who detracts from your happiness? Do you start a family? Do you tell a forbidden love exactly how you feel and damn the consequences?

Do your choices affect the other people in your life? If you move a chess piece, does it change the game for other members of your family or your friends?

The seeds of inspiration for this book were sewn during a conversation I had with my husband last summer. On a beautiful, balmy night in Florida, we were chatting about a moment in time, almost twenty years ago, when we'd considered going our separate ways. In the end, the parting was brief and we stayed together. Two decades later we have an incredible family and I couldn't imagine finding more happiness in any other life.

But what would have happened if we'd made a different decision?

We speculated long into the night. Although I do confess to paying absolutely no attention to his theory that he may have become a rock star and married a supermodel. He'd look terrible in leather trousers.

Next morning, I woke up and couldn't shake the thought.

What if your whole life was determined by one decision?

By the end of that day, the outline for this novel was writing itself in my mind.

This isn't my story.

It belongs to a character who'd been living in my head for a while, just waiting for her world to come along.

Liv is a twenty-eight-year-old nurse who works in palliative care. She has been married to Nate for almost six years. It's 1999 and the dawn of the new millennium is only minutes away.

Her moment of decision?

Should she stay in a marriage even though she feels there's something missing?

Or should she walk away from the man she has loved for many years?

How can she possibly be sure of the right thing to do?

If Liv leaves Nate, will she regret it in ten years' time and mourn the loss of the man she will come to realise was the love of her life?

Or will she go on to find another great love and discover that there's a different happiness out there, one that she could never have imagined?

Or, if we're getting really deep and philosophical, would the outcomes be the same no matter what choice she made?

Perhaps our lives and loves are predetermined, our paths mapped out, and it doesn't matter what twists and turns we take on the road, we still end up exactly where we're meant to be.

Think about the crossroads you've had in your life. Did you say yes? Or no? Leave? Stay? Move forward? Or reverse right back to the situation you'd come from?

Would you have wanted to know how each scenario played out, so you could have made an informed decision? Or is it better to step into the unknown and take a chance on happiness, on love, on life?

I didn't have the answers, so there I was, wondering, thinking, visualising.

I wanted to know what would happen to Liv over the years from then until now, whether she opted to stay or decided to leave.

So I started with the choice, the moment of decision and split the view...

Two parallel lives.

But which one would be the happy ever after?

PROLOGUE

The Last Minute of 1999

There were sixty seconds left of the twentieth century.

Hogmanay. The biggest night of the Scottish celebratory calendar, when we eat, we sing, we dance, and we welcome in the New Year with the people we love. The music was blaring, the revellers were dancing up a storm, and glasses were being topped up with champagne, as I leant close to my husband's ear.

'I wish you'd had an affair,' I said, my voice cracking. 'It would be so much easier to do this.'

Nate smiled, leaned in and kissed me, but not with any grand passion. That was part of the problem. We'd been together since midway through uni, and then married the year after we graduated, and since the day we'd danced up the aisle we'd had five years of contentment.

Contentment.

I hated that word. Imagine the obituary. *RIP Liv Jamieson – a contented life*. Worse, who wanted to be content at the age of twenty-eight? I wanted passion and excitement and maybe the odd little bit of danger, but contentment? It was like a scarf of boredom that got tighter with each passing year, until I could barely breathe.

I loved Nate, but – clichéd as it was – I wasn't *in* love with him anymore. There was no one else, no drama, no big scandal or cataclysmic event. Just a gradual drifting apart. A disconnection. And, in a twisted demonstration of our compatibility, he had reluctantly admitted that – while he wasn't as far along the road of acceptance as me – he knew there was something missing too.

I loved him. He loved me. It just wasn't enough.

Nate pulled back and pushed a stray curl of my red hair back from my face. 'An affair? What if I told you I've had Kylie Minogue living in the loft for the last year because we're having a torrid fling and she can't get enough of me?'

'I'd say please tell her I'll let her have you – as long as she's willing to trade you for her entire wardrobe.'

Nate's brown eyes creased at the side as he laughed. It was my very favourite thing about him.

We'd tried. We really had. The previous January, just a day into 1999, we'd talked, and we'd agreed to give it everything we had for a year, determined to reignite the spark between us. We'd had weekly date nights. Lazy Sunday sex. Weekend breaks to quiet country cottages and busy city hotels. A fantastic holiday to Bali where we'd taken long moonlit strolls along the sands. We'd hung out with our gang of mutual friends and we'd laughed, celebrated, partied, and discussed it long into many nights.

Yet, much as it destroyed us to admit it, we were still in that 'best friends' zone. My heart didn't flutter when he entered a room. His gaze made me smile, but it didn't make my libido throb with lust. And neither of us could shake the feeling that there was something – or someone – else out there for us.

So we'd decided to call it a day. To wish each other well, split the CD collection and move on. That makes it all sound so simple, when the truth was that a piece of my heart felt like it was being surgically removed by a jackhammer.

Nate wasn't 100 per cent sure. He didn't like change. Preferred familiarity and stability to the unknown. But he said he loved me too much to make me stay in a marriage that didn't make me happy. And if he were honest, our marriage wasn't making him happy either, not like he should have been. I wanted more for me, for him, for both of us.

Tonight was our last night together. It seemed apt. Fitting. The final day of the century, a chapter closing, and a whole new world out there for us to explore. And if I kept telling myself that this was a positive move; the right thing to do, it squashed the part of me that was terrified.

I saw his lips move again. 'Liv, are you…?'

I missed the last bit. It got carried away on the wave of noise that suddenly engulfed the room.

Ten…

The lead singer of the band was counting down the seconds to midnight. Every year we headed to Lomond Grange, a gorgeous stately manor hotel on the edge of Loch Lomond, about forty minutes from home, to bring in the coming year. Despite our sadness, we hadn't wanted to bail out on the people who shared our lives, so here we were. One last hurrah. On the dance floor, our closest friends, Sasha and Justin stood next to Chloe and Rob, all of them with their champagne glasses in hand, party poppers at the ready, expressions oozing excitement, braced for the big moment.

Nine… Nine seconds until my marriage was over.

A wave of sorrow.

Eight… 'What did you say?' I asked him.

Seven… Seven seconds until my marriage was over.

He had to lean right into my ear so I could hear him. 'I said are you absolutely sure?'

Six… A stomach flip of doubt. We'd discussed this to death. Yes, I was sure. Of course I was. So was he. We'd agreed.

Five… Five seconds until my marriage was over.

'Yes. Why are you asking now?'

Four… 'I think…' I could feel his breath on the side of my face. 'I think I want to give it one more try.'

Three… Three seconds until my marriage was over.

A sick feeling of panic rising to my throat.

Two… 'But Nate, we both know it's time to move on.' We did. Didn't we?

One… 'One more try, Liv. We owe it to each other to give it more time.'

Noooooo. This wasn't the deal. We'd tried. It hadn't worked. We weren't right for each other. It was time to move on, to take different paths.

A deafening cacophony of sound erupted in the room. Happy New Year. Streamers shot in the air. Bagpipes bellowed out a chorus of 'Auld Lang Syne' to say goodbye to the past and welcome the twenty-first century.

We were entering a new millennium.

But was I going to spend it with Nate…

… Or without him?

WITHOUT HIM...
FROM 1ST JANUARY
2000...

I

One Minute After Midnight

1st January 2000

It felt like one of those arty black and white prints, where a couple stands in the middle of a room full of people, the crowd's expressions rapt with excitement and celebration, while the man and the woman in the centre face each other, lost in the moment, frozen in time, oblivious to all around them.

Everyone who looked at the picture had a different perception of what those two people were thinking, of what was going on in their lives that was so startling that it completely detached them from their surroundings.

Now I knew.

The bloke had just told his wife that he wanted to call off their separation.

And the woman wanted to cry. Or scream. Or fall into his arms. To be honest, she wasn't 100 per cent sure.

Actually, that's not true. She was 100 per cent sure about what she should do, she just wasn't 100 per cent sure she had the courage to go through with it.

'Nate, I...'

Before I could answer, the others crowded around us.

Sasha smothered me in kisses. 'Happy New Millennium gorgeous!' I hugged her tightly. 'You're going to be great without that boring fart,' she whispered in my ear. Sasha came from the 'in your face' school of life. She said what she thought, was completely fearless and, with her Morticia Addams hair and vampish make-up, you just knew that she was never going to be fluffy or dippy. It made some people run a mile from her, but I loved that she made no apologies for saying what she thought and living her life the way she damn well pleased. She'd supported my decision to call it a day with Nate right from the start, which sounds brutally harsh, but as one of my two closest friends, I knew she was only taking that stance because she truly believed it was the right thing for me.

'He wants to try again,' I hissed.

'No surprise there. I knew he'd change his mind.'

She had a point. In his working life as a PE teacher, Nate was organised and structured, but outside of the professional environment, my horizontally laid-back husband liked consistency and tended to avoid anything that could involve drama or uncomfortable situations. He'd have stayed married forever despite knowing it wasn't right, just to avoid the hassle of splitting.

Chloe moved in next and wrapped her arms around me, hugging me tightly. 'Happy New Year!'

If Sasha was Morticia, Chloe was her arch-nemesis in the fight for good, always looking for the positive in any situation and giving everyone the benefit of the doubt.

If I ever decided to switch sexual preferences, then Chloe would be my perfect woman: funny, caring, smart, and tough enough to handle just about any situation. Having a friend like her could make a girl feel inadequate, but she would find that thought hilarious because she had absolutely no ego or awareness of her brilliance at all. She was beyond beautiful too. Thanks to the genetic mix of her Jamaican mother and her Irish father, she had a stunning Afro, piercing green eyes and the most banging, curvy body I'd ever seen. My 36B's and apple-shaped figure just couldn't compare.

'Are you okay?' Chloe's mouth was still at my ear, so her words couldn't be overheard, and neither could my reply.

'He's just said he wants to try again.'

'I knew it! Say yes. Please say yes. You two belong together.'

Chloe and Sasha hadn't agreed on anything since the day we all met, so the difference in their opinions wasn't exactly a newsflash.

Chloe and I had got chatting on the first day of our nursing training at Glasgow uni and instantly clicked, and been delighted to discover we were only one room apart in the halls of residence. Sasha, who was studying business and planning to be a teacher, was in the room between us.

We'd all bonded over a mutual appreciation of home-made cocktails and prayer that a balanced diet of cheap pasta and late-night snack-runs to the local takeaway wouldn't damage our digestive systems for life. Over the next four years, we'd spent every day together, and many boozy nights contemplating the thought that cynical, dry, prone-to-bitchiness Sasha could ever be put in a position of responsibility for our future generations.

I wanted to pull Sasha and Chloe to one side and have a conversation that would involve swear words and vodka, but, as always, Sasha's boyfriend, Justin, the ultimate party animal, was leading the party celebrations and he didn't allow interludes for heart-to-heart chats. He popped open yet another bottle of champagne, more New Year exultations were exclaimed and drinks were poured. Nate's words had completely ambushed my mind, and the last thing I felt like doing was partying, but I didn't want to dampen the mood for the others. I just wanted to grab Nate, sit down with him and talk it through. Or run as fast as I could until the pressure that was building in my chest subsided. Or drink until I couldn't remember the problem. Instead, we all ended up back on the packed dance floor, swinging our bits to one of the many Steps songs that made me want to stick a fork in my hand to distract myself from the pain in my ears.

Halfway through, Nate signalled that he was heading to the bar. By the end of the song, I'd had enough. I decided to head back over to the table and saw that Nate was already there, his arm slung over the back of the chair next to him. He was watching me come towards him and the expectant expression on his lovely face told me that he wanted an answer I wasn't ready to give.

I couldn't face him. Not here, not now.

I needed a delay tactic. I considered giving my mother a quick call to update her on developments, then immediately dismissed the idea as madness, because Ida is… let's just say 'one of a kind'. If you crossed a Glaswegian housewife with the theatrical flair of Liberace, the need for attention of the average boyband lead singer, the self-obsession of a reality TV star, the self-awareness of a plant, and added unbridled shamelessness in the face of an audience, then dipped it all in a big vat marked 'propensity for drama and martyrdom', then you might get close to the gloriously eye-rolling, toe-curling, oh-dear-God-I-seriously-don't-think-we-can-be-related, Ida. However, she has a huge heart, is never dull, keeps everyone around her thoroughly entertained and is great at a party. She'd tell anyone who would listen that she'd almost been a star. Glasgow's Cilla Black, they'd called her back in the day. But she'd met my dad, Sonny – Glasgow's James Dean, she said – when they were both twenty-two and gave it all up for love. I've no idea where the pendulum of truth swung in that version of events, but it was the one she'd stuck to, and repeated at least weekly since I was a child.

I hadn't told her about the impending split because she adored Nate and I knew she'd insist we should stay together. She and my dad had been married until the day he died ten years ago, although I was sure there must have been bumps in the road. Ida's insatiable need to be centre of attention could be absolutely infuriating. And my dad… well, he loved a drink and wasn't

14

one for grand gestures or articulating his emotions. But they'd stuck with each other, and right up until he passed away, they'd still held hands while they were wandering round Marks and Spencer on a Saturday afternoon. Although, that was probably because my dad was just trying to keep one of my mum's hands occupied because it slowed down her shopping speed. Ida could hold an Olympic record for purchases attained in a 100 m dash.

Nope, I couldn't call Ida. And I couldn't trust my own bank of worldly experience either. My job as a palliative care nurse was to be with people at the end of their lives. How many times had I heard someone say that they wished they hadn't left someone they loved, wished that they'd tried harder? It was probably just as often as I'd heard someone say that they regretted not leaving a situation that made them unhappy, so those two arguments cancelled each other out.

Bravery. That's what I needed. Unfortunately, my current emotional reservoir was experiencing a severe drought of courage, so I settled for cowardice. I made a sharp detour and headed for the ballroom exit, finding it difficult to walk in my fishtail dress and crippling heels. Whoever designed these items clearly hadn't thought through trivial practicalities like walking, bending, and making swift detours to avoid tense conversations with your husband.

The light in the bathroom was so bright it made me squint for a second. That's probably why I noticed it – the shoe slightly sticking out at a weird angle under a door. Someone else with sore feet feeling the need to kick off their pain-inducing footwear. I used the bathroom, washed my hands, looked again. Puzzled, I crouched down to check it out, and realised that it was still attached to a leg and presumed the owner of both was sitting on the floor.

'Hello? Are you okay in there?'

No answer.

'I don't want to bother you if you want to be alone, but just let me know you're okay?'

Still no answer.

I pushed gently on the door and realised it was open, but it was stuck against something.

Another nudge on the door. It still wouldn't budge, but more importantly there was no reaction from the person inside.

I kicked off my shoes, and planked on the floor, getting a better angle of vision. Definitely someone lying behind there, and for the first time I noticed a couple of spots of very red blood.

Bugger.

I darted into the toilet next door, stood on the seat, then the cistern and pulled myself up higher so my weight was supported by my arms with one foot on the toilet roll holder. Ironic, since I couldn't do a pull-up at the gym to save my life. Apparently, my biceps had an extra store of strength for emergency situations.

My aching arms held me long enough to peek over the partition and see the top of a head, auburn hair, blood everywhere. Bugger. Bugger. Bugger.

I jumped down, just as two giggling women, wearing at least half of the free world's sequins, barrelled into the room.

'Call an ambulance!' I blurted, 'There's someone in here who's hurt. Tell them her head's bleeding and she's unconscious.'

'Oh Christ, Edna, you'll need to do it – I can't see ma phone without ma specs. I'll go get help.'

At that, Sequins Number One about-turned and dashed back out, while Edna Sequins punched 999 into her phone. 'Ambulance!'

While she was giving details, I scanned the room. This kind of shit may happen regularly on *Casualty*, *Grey's Anatomy* and *Holby City*, but I can honestly say that apart from the occasional call from my overdramatic mother claiming her latest dose of the cold could be morphing into a sure-fire case of Ebola, I'd never been thrust into an emergency situation while off-duty. Now wasn't the time for contemplation – it was the time for getting in there and holding something on the wound that was currently oozing blood at a really worrying rate.

Paper towels. Thankfully this hotel was the upmarket classy kind that had a basket of thick, good quality paper towels beside each sink.

Edna Sequins ended the call. 'They're on the way.'

'Okay, I'm going to climb over,' I said, entirely unsure as to how exactly I was going to achieve that. I'm the woman who's knackered after five minutes in a step class.

First things first. There was no way this dress was going to allow any form of flexibility. I unzipped it and dropped it to the floor, revealing my all-in-one, suck-it-all-in, control underwear, then jumped back up on to the barrier separating my cubicle from the neighbouring toilet.

'Do you know what you're doing, hen?' Edna asked.

'Yes. I'm a… nurse,' I gasped, mid-climb. I didn't add that I worked in palliative care and it had been years since I'd done my rotation in A & E during my training. This didn't seem like the time to give a run-down of my CV.

Eventually, I dragged myself to the top of the cubicle partition, pushed my upper body over, then swung my legs across, somehow managing to get one foot on the cistern. It gave me enough balance to climb down, squeezing into the space not already filled by an unconscious woman. An unconscious woman whose head and face I could now see were saturated in blood. This didn't look good at all.

It took me a few moments to detect a pulse in her neck. It was there, but it was faint and irregular. With this amount of blood loss, she needed to get to a hospital soon.

At least she was breathing, and I was managing to stem the blood with the posh paper towels. As I kept up the pressure on her wound, I could see that it was just her left leg that was blocking the door. Without letting go of her head, I managed to play some kind of Emergency First Aid Twister, move her leg, then climb over her to make enough space to yank open the door.

'Oh Mother of God!' Edna Sequins exclaimed as soon as she got full view of the situation and the poor woman on the floor.

She didn't get a chance to react further, as the door flew open and in rushed Sequins Number One followed by a paramedic crew. Wow that was quick.

'They were already here,' she blurted. 'They'd been called 'cause some eejit had passed out but he was just pissed… Oh my God!' she exclaimed as she took in the scene, echoing her friend.

'That lassie's a nurse,' Edna announced.

'Aye well she's clearly no' a model in that outfit,' her pal retorted. Only in a fifty-mile radius of Glasgow could I be dealing with a life-threatening emergency and still be subjected to pass-remarkable comments about my sartorial appearance. Although, granted, it wasn't my best look.

The paramedics, a male and female, swiftly moved past her and took charge. They fired a ton of questions at me and I answered them all. There wasn't enough room to fit us all in the cubicle, so I maintained pressure on the wound, while the paramedic who'd introduced herself as Jenny, attached a blood pressure monitor and took her readings. She then applied a dressing to the wound and set up an IV, while her partner shot back out the door, returning with a stretcher. As he came back in, I heard him ordering someone outside to keep everyone out of here.

In what felt like a week, but was probably only a few minutes, the paramedics had lifted her on to a stretcher and were heading out the door.

'Well done, love,' Jenny the paramedic said as they raced towards the door.

'What do you think?' I asked.

She knew exactly what I meant.

'Blood pressure is on the way up, pulse is getting stronger. Barring complications, I think she'll be okay. She's lucky you found her when you did.'

And then they were gone.

Lucky? If Nate hadn't been waiting for me at the table, and I hadn't bottled out of telling him that I didn't want to change my mind about separating, then I wouldn't have detoured, and I wouldn't be slouched on a toilet floor in my underwear, covered in blood.

But much, much more importantly, I wouldn't have discovered an unconscious woman with a serious head wound.

I didn't much believe in spooky stuff like cosmic messages and signs from the universe. But even a sceptic like me would have to acknowledge that, in some weird way, the forces of serendipity were definitely, absolutely, proving to me that I was doing the right thing.

It was time to go my own way. Whether Nate agreed or not.

2

Sasha's 30th Birthday

October 2000

'I know I'm supposed to be doing the whole "supportive boyfriend" thing, but I'm seriously considering feigning tuberculosis to get out of this party tonight.'

I laughed as I pulled his tie to bring him closer to me, then kissed him on the lips. He automatically scanned the surrounding area to make sure no one could see us. Relationships between doctors and nurses were frowned upon by the hospital, by many of the staff, and – prior to the moment that I clapped eyes on Dr Richard Campbell – by me.

I'd met him on the 4th of January, my first day back at work after the millennium. The hangover had subsided, but I was still feeling tender and a bit emotionally bruised and battered. Statistically, I was still at least 90 per cent sure that I'd done the right thing in refusing Nate's plea to try again. Okay, maybe 75 per cent. Once reality set in, it, my confidence had definitely wobbled.

I'd already moved out and into Chloe's spare room, previously inhabited by her shoe collection and an exercise bike that doubled as a clothes-horse.

Oh, and I'd faced the toughest challenge of all, the family equivalent of tossing an emotional grenade into a volatile situation and then feeling the full effects of the world-ending turbo-blast. Yep, I'd told my mother.

When I'd called to break the news – cowardly, I know, but a call had less potential for dramatic reactions than doing it in person – she'd sobbed for a full five minutes, then wailed, 'But how am I supposed to live without him?' I suspected she'd been listening to her Michael Bolton *Best Of The Eighties* collection. She'd followed that up with, 'He was the son I never had!'

I'd let her rant and weep for another ten minutes before I told her I had to get to work, which invoked a large sniff and a disapproving, 'Well, if you haven't got time to deal with *my* pain...'

Once again, her disappointment at my career choice oozed from every word. She was beyond devastated that a childhood of acting classes, dancing lessons, vocal training and preparation for a star slot on *Top Of The Pops* hadn't resulted in me becoming a performer. Or an actress. Or Madonna. Stand by someone's side as they took their final journey? Meh. Specialise in pelvic thrusts, have millions of fans, occasionally flash your tits in order to stir up publicity? Now there would be a daughter to be proud of.

Still, I loved her and she was the only mum I had, so Glasgow's Cilla Black and I were in it together. Even if she was in a big fat huff with me.

I'd rung off and headed into work early for my first shift of the New Year – I'd worked Christmas to let the nurses with children be with their families, and had a day shift on Hogmanay, so I'd managed to wangle three days off in a row. It sounded good, but it was just three whole days to ponder whether I'd made a huge mistake. I'd rather have been in work.

I was hoping to catch Chloe down in General Surgical before I started. She'd been on that ward since she'd finished her training, but she was waiting for news on her transfer request to A & E.

'Hey honey,' I greeted her, coming out of one of the private rooms. 'Here's your keys. You left them this morning and I'm double shift so I won't be home until late.'

'Ah, thanks. I'll come find you at lunchtime and see if we can get our breaks together.' We both knew the chances of this were slim. There was no such thing as a fixed schedule when it came to hospital wards. I was about to turn and go, when she stopped me. 'Listen, that woman you helped at the hotel the other night. The head wound…'

'Yes?'

'Did she have auburn hair? About twenty-five?'

I nodded. 'Why?'

'I think I've got her here.'

'Really?' It hadn't even crossed my mind to check if she'd come here, because I'd assumed that she would go to the nearest hospital to the hotel. We were miles away – however, we were the west of Scotland centre of excellence for neuro, so on reflection it probably wasn't so much of a stretch.

'Yep, cerebral haemorrhage, so she was transferred over here for emergency surgery. There are no free beds in neuro, so they brought her up here an hour ago from ICU.'

'Holy crap, that's a tough week. Is she okay?'

Chloe nodded. 'I think she's going to be fine. She's got a mother of a headache, but she's pretty much out of the woods. Do you want to see her?'

'Of course.'

I followed Chloe to the last ward on the left. Four beds. Two of them inhabited by elderly women who were deep in conversation. In the bed nearest the window, there she was, looking much better than last time I saw her, despite a heavily bandaged head, drains, and some bruising on one side of her face. I hung back, just outside the doorway.

'Is that her?' Chloe asked.

'It is.'

'Okay, wait here.'

She went over to the bed and spoke to the patient, and I knew she was asking her if she wanted to meet me. It was absolutely the right thing to do because it was entirely possible that revisiting any aspect of her trauma could upset her. Thankfully, her face immediately broke into a grin, followed by a couple of very definite, but gentle nods.

Chloe beckoned me over.

'Francine, this is Liv.'

'Hi,' she answered, with no sign of recognition at all, which was only to be expected given that last time I saw her she was out cold. 'Nurse says you're the one who found me in the toilets.'

'I did.'

'Thank you so much. I've been told that if I hadn't been found when I was that the outcome could have been very different and I could have... have...' She didn't finish the sentence and she didn't have to.

'You're very welcome. I'm just glad that you're okay. Can you remember what happened?'

'Not really,' she answered. 'But I think it was my shoes.'

'Your shoes?'

'Yeah, they were brand new and way too high. I couldn't walk in them. I'd already gone over on my ankle twice, so I think it was down to the heels, combined with a few glasses of champagne and some really bad luck. I'm guessing I fell over and my head met with the cistern.'

Just one of those completely random fluke accidents. If Ida were here, she'd be harrumphing her breasts and coming out with some morbid cliché like, 'Aye, you just never know the minute...'

'They told me you climbed over the cubicle to help me?' she said, her grin even wider now.

Ah, so she had full facts. She was, in truth, surprisingly alert and sharp for someone who had had brain surgery three days ago. 'Yep, I did that too,' I said, returning her smile.

'That's amazing.'

'You wouldn't be saying that if you'd seen me. Did they mention that I did it in my extra large knick-knacks because I couldn't climb over in my fishtail frock?'

Her chuckle interrupted the conversation between the two elderly dears in the next beds, who were now listening intently... as was a new arrival to the scene.

'Well, there's a mental picture that may stay with me for the rest of the day.'

A man's voice. My face-flush was instant, and deepened when I turned to see a doctor, standing directly behind me. I've always maintained that real-life doctors don't look like the strapping hunks on medical dramas, and generally that's true. Richard didn't have the chiselled jawline or the piercing blue eyes that would make patients and staff melt at his surgical shoes, but he did have slightly unkempt black wavy hair that curled over the stethoscope that was slung around his neck, somewhat tired, potentially intoxicating green eyes, and a cheeky grin.

If this guy was in *Grey's Anatomy*, he'd be the tall, medium-attractive one who played the heart-throb's sidekick, but who always got the girl because he had a twinkling eye, a great smile and the kind of charm that could take a patient's mind off most non-life-threatening ailments.

His comment was perfectly delivered, more amused than leery, bringing much hilarity to everyone in earshot, and much mortification to me.

'Richard Campbell, neurosurgeon,' he said.

'Liv Jamieson,' I replied. 'Palliative care. Late for work and about to dash off,' I added, before turning back to Francine. 'I'm so glad you're okay – and that I got to meet you.'

Her infectious smile was back. 'You too.'

Over the next few weeks, Francine made it back to full health and was discharged. Meanwhile, the good doctor and I would bump into each other with slightly suspicious regularity, until Chloe confessed that she was trying to set me up with him because I 'needed a happy distraction to stop me moping about

Nate'. She was right. After Francine had been taken to hospital in the early hours of New Year's Day, I'd told him I definitely wanted to go through with the split. It was the right thing to do. We'd agreed not to call each other for the first couple of weeks and we'd both stuck to that. So far. The 75 per cent certainty about my decision had dropped to 60 per cent, and if it went below fifty I was calling him.

Richard called me before that happened, at the beginning of May, when I was five months into life as a singleton. In a stunning pivot of hypocrisy about the whole doctor/nurse relationship disapproval, I'd accepted his suggestion of a date. It had taken a while, but I'd eventually relaxed and realised that the best thing to get over the end of a relationship was the distraction of a cute doctor with a cheeky sense of humour. I loved that he was a charmer and took nothing, except his work, seriously. I loved that it was easy and it hadn't strayed into deep and demanding. Most of all I loved that he was the complete opposite of Nate in every way.

Our shifts clashed, so we didn't see each other more than twice a week, but it was enough. It was uncomplicated. Fun. And not to be crude about it, but the sex...

'Chloe, he talks the whole way through,' I blurted, in the kitchen after the first time he spent the night.

'In that case, I'm so glad I was working. I'd have had to play a bit of Vengaboys at full blast to block the sound. Did it freak you out?' she went on.

'A bit.' Okay, so here's the thing. I could add up the total of my sexual partners on one hand. Two of them were short-term things when I was a teenager. Another was an unfortunate one-night stand, thanks to vodka overload during Freshers' Week. I spent the next four years at uni avoiding some guy called Jeremy who'd been intimate with my anatomy.

Then there was Nate, for eight years.

All in all, I wasn't exactly widely experienced in such things.

'But did you like it?'

'More than a bit,' I replied, as she roared with laughter.

'Who'd have known you had an inner slapper?' she'd teased, before she headed off, clutching a cream cheese bagel.

That seemed like so long ago now. Five months, three days to be exact. Not that I was counting. Okay, I was, but only to take my mind off the fact that nerves were twisting my stomach into a knot the size of a melon.

Tonight was the first time I was going to introduce Richard to the rest of the group. It had seemed like a good idea at the time. There would be a huge crowd at Sasha's thirtieth birthday party, so there would be less scrutiny and interrogation. And yes, Nate would be there. That in itself wasn't a problem. Since I'd moved out, we'd met up once a month or so. He'd definitely wobbled about the split in the early stages, but as the year had gone on, and after he'd bought out my share of our mortgage and we'd split everything we owned, I could see that he'd come to accept it was the right thing. Last week, we had agreed to file for a quickie, 'no fault' DIY divorce. It would be through in just a few months. Done. Over. Just like that. There was definitely still some sadness, but it was outweighed by relief that we could both move on.

Our friends still socialised with both of us, although not so much in couples now, for obvious reasons.

It was odd, given that we'd been a group for so long.

We were in our second year at uni when Sasha had introduced me to Nate (studying sports science) and Chloe had fallen in love with a guy called Connor (sports management). Meanwhile, Sasha's boyfriends had changed more times than I could count, until one night, a few months after we'd all burned our books. Chloe and I were in placements in the same hospital. Nate and Sasha were both doing their teaching post-grad. And we'd hit the town to celebrate Connor's new job in the sports division of a marketing company. We were in a packed, city-centre, trendy club when a good-looking DJ with a microphone jumped on the bar top and got the whole place hyped up by making them join in with House Of Pain's 'Jump Around'. The place went wild.

'Urgh, he totally loves himself,' Sasha had drawled, somewhat unfairly, as clearly the DJ was just doing his job. 'But I'd still shag him,' she'd added, with a wink.

That night she did indeed get naked with him, and they'd been together ever since. He'd had an instant connection with Nate, and, straight away, they'd become gym buddies who trained together a few times a week. It turned out Justin's gig at the club was a part-time thing to make some extra cash as he'd just left college and started work on the bottom rung of a finance company. He'd packed it in when he and Sasha got serious, preferring to spend his weekends enjoying his nightlife, rather than working it.

Nate and I were married that year. Sasha and Justin made the perfect, hard-core party-loving, up-all-night couple. And Connor had proposed to Chloe. We were a happy little trio of couples, until Chloe had contracted a spectacular case of frozen feet, decided they were too young to commit for the rest of their lives and called it off with Connor. About two months later, Connor met an American volleyball player at a tournament at the Kelvin Hall, and hightailed it off to Chicago where he'd begun the process of living happily ever after, right around the same time as Chloe realised she'd made a huge mistake and had said goodbye to the love of her life. She'd been miserable ever since, no matter how much she tried to move on and get over him.

Rob, her last boyfriend, was a perfectly acceptable replacement. They'd been together for a year or so, but I knew her heart wasn't in it. This was clearly evident in the fact that she wasn't fussed when he'd announced a few weeks ago that he was taking off for Ibiza to sell timeshares. The truth was, she was still pining for Connor, the one she sent away.

I could honestly say that over the last ten months, I hadn't been pining for Nate.

There had only been a few events that we'd both been at, mostly birthdays or Sunday brunch, and it had been fine. It really had. I hadn't mentioned Richard, and he hadn't spoken of having met someone new either, but around the start of the summer I'd sensed in his behaviour that he might have finally moved on and I'd guessed another woman had something to do with it. It wasn't a surprise when I'd heard through the official communication channels of the Sasha grapevine that not only had he been seeing someone, but he was bringing her along to Sasha's birthday party tonight. Apparently they'd met at the gym Nate and Justin had been training at three nights a week for the last seven years. According to Sasha, Justin said she was 'nice', which could mean anything from 'drop-dead gorgeous' to 'indistinguishable in a crowd'. These guys could come up with a dozen different adjectives for a goal in a football match, but 'nice' just about covered everything else.

It was fine. We were all adults. We could do this in a mature and respectful manner. Unless she was indeed drop-dead gorgeous in which case I reserved the right to bitch about it for the next fortnight.

I'd been planning for a while to introduce Richard to the group tonight, but the fact that Nate was bringing his new girlfriend made me even more determined that yes, he was coming, and no, he wasn't faking bloody tuberculosis to get out of it.

After my shift, I dashed home, showered and poured myself into a size 14, trusty, black dress and decided to forgo my super strength, girdle-style knickers. Richard wasn't a fan. Said that removing them took up valuable energy required for the next stage in the process. Bugger it, I would just have to breathe in all night and hope there was nothing irresistible on the buffet.

By the time Richard arrived, I was on my second glass of Lambrusco and starting to feel a tad light-headed. I blamed Chloe. If she were here, I'd be fine, but her shift didn't finish until eight and then she was going straight to the party. She'd been taking on loads of extra shifts since she'd split with Rob. I poured a third glass. Come on, no one met up with their ex and his new partner, or introduced their new boyfriend to their ex, on just two glasses of plonk. Maybe a bottle and a straw would be a better idea.

'Right let's go then,' I chirped, with completely fake enthusiasm, before my last shred of confidence deserted me and I ended up staying in with a bottle of wine and watching reruns of *ER*.

Okay, I could do this.

I could.

It would be fine.

We were all adults.

The mantra went over and over in my head all the way there.

'Nervous about introducing me to Nate?' Richard asked in his usual forthright way.

'No, not at all.' It was a lie, but I didn't want my anxiety to reignite his fake tuberculosis plan, so it was better to play it cool.

As always, Sasha had gone full on with an elaborate celebration. Somewhere along the line, she'd transformed from a fellow student with a partiality for Pot Noodles and being both funny and offensive when fuelled by cider, to a business studies teacher, who had a real, grown up, fully functioning life. She knew things that I'd never understand, like how to get red wine stains out of carpets and how to maximise and spend the points on those supermarket loyalty cards. That kind of adult stuff was all a blur to me.

We were greeted at the door of the restaurant with glasses of champagne, and I tried to ignore the slight lurch this caused in my stomach, courtesy of a flashback to the last time I drank expensive bubbly stuff, in a posh hotel at New Year.

That already seemed like a lifetime ago.

'Liv, you're here!' Sasha said, throwing her arms out and hugging me, making balancing the champagne a feat of dexterity.

'I am! Happy birthday, gorgeous!' I said, giving her a kiss. Gorgeous was an understatement. She was the perfect, stunning vamp in a figure-hugging, red Hervé Léger dress. She always did know how to make an impact.

If her outfit hadn't taken my breath away, the decor in the room would have sealed the deal. Curtains of white lights were draped in every window, swing music was playing in the background, glittering chandeliers dropped from the ceiling, and the leather banquettes surrounded dark wood tables with magnificent centrepieces. It was beyond beautiful.

Sasha's non-too subtle cough and head tilt in Richard's direction snapped me back to the present company.

'This is Richard. Richard meet Sasha.' They shook hands, but before Sasha could chip in with any kind of sarcastic comment or intrusive question, I jumped back in with, 'First, I've to tell you again that Ida said she's absolutely gutted that she's not here.'

'Och, we'll miss her,' Sasha said. Sometimes it felt like Sasha was closer to my mother than I was. Two Alpha, rebellious personalities that had clicked the moment they met. The first time I took Sasha home, Ida had insisted we venture out on a pub crawl, which culminated in them doing a duet to 'Suspicious Minds' in an all-night café, over cream-piled lattes surreptitiously infused with vodka. To Ida's horror, Sasha's party had coincided with a Mediterranean cruise she'd had booked for months. She'd consoled me with, 'Oh, darling, I know it won't be the same without me, but try to enjoy yourself even though I'm not there.'

'I'll try, Mum. It'll be tough though.' Her mournful expression told me she took every word at face value.

Justin appeared at Sasha's side, clutching a bottle of Bud and already swaying slightly. He was always first at the party and last to leave, but Sasha adored his hedonistic, wild ways. They'd never be voted 'Most Likely to Appear as a Cookie-Cutter Family in a Toothpaste Advert', but they'd be too busy whipping up fifty folk for a shindig at an hour's notice to care.

Justin had now climbed the ladder at one of those slick, work-hard, play-hard finance companies where they all socialised together outside of work too. If it were the eighties, they'd be called Yuppies. Now they were just called – according to Sasha – overpaid, self-indulgent, egotistical twats.

I hugged him too, before a gentle dig in my back reminded me that I hadn't made the second introduction.

'Justin, this is Richard.'

Richard shook Justin's hand. There was no time for awkward silences or sizing up, as Sasha immediately slipped into tornado mode.

'Right, we're at a banquette over there. Guard it with your life. I've invited everyone from Justin's work, because, you know, I'm a saint, and they're spreading around the room like toxic waste.'

'Consider it done,' I assured her.

She wasn't listening, already training her interrogation techniques on Richard. 'Excellent, but before we go over there, I need a few personal details.' I should have intervened. I really should. But there was no point trying to halt the inevitable, and if he was going to be around Sasha there was no better way to start than with a baptism of fire. Besides, I was pretty sure he could handle it.

'Shoot,' he said, laughing.

'Where are you from?'

'Manchester.'

'Age?'

'Thirty-four.'

'Are you now, or have you ever been, married?'

'Nope.'

'Do you have a criminal record?'

'No.'

'Shame,' she said, regretfully, before going on, 'How are you on mind-numbing conversation and acting interested in the face of acute boredom?'

'I'd say well-practised, possibly to expert level.' Not only was he handling this brilliantly, but he looked like he was actually enjoying it. I suddenly liked him even more.

'And Liv tells us you're a doctor?'

'I am.'

I was puzzled by this. Sasha couldn't care less what anyone did for a living, being unilaterally unimpressed by most people no matter what they did as a day job.

'Thank God. Come on then,' she said, grabbing his hand and heading in the direction of aforementioned booth. 'I've been making small talk with this woman who has been rambling on about jogging for the last half-hour and I'm ready to press the fire alarms to escape her. You can take over. And if you run out of things to say, you can always offer to stitch up her gob.'

Richard found this hilarious – we all did – and I felt a pang of gratitude. As far as ice-breakers went, it was perfect... until the moment that we reached the table and I realised that the jogger in question was Nate's new companion.

Oh. Bollocks.

I hadn't thought this through, but I'd more or less assumed that we'd sit at a different table. Nope. The banquettes sat eight to ten, and apparently all the members of our group were congregated at the same one.

A flush of red heat began to crawl from my chest, to my neck, then carried on upwards, and the rise in my body temperature made me wish I'd brought an extra can of deodorant.

Oh and Nate? Rabbit. Headlights. By now I was standing right next to him, so I leaned down to give him a kiss on the cheek, just as he tried to get up to do the same. The result was a skull/teeth collision that made me yelp. It was like a bad sitcom moment.

'Sorry! Sorry! Are you okay?'

'Absolutely, I'm fine. It was my fault.' I wasn't and it wasn't, but this was mortifying enough without making it into a bigger drama.

We managed a mutual cheek kiss without further injury, then decided to just go for it and rip the Band-Aid off.

'Nate, this is Richard. Richard, Nate.' It was like two silverback gorillas sizing each other up in a room with a buffet, chandeliers and decorative soft furnishings.

My turn next.

I turned to the woman sitting next to Nate. If she wasn't Nate's new girlfriend, I'd say she was pretty, with blonde hair pulled up in a ponytail, and yes, she looked great in a tiny silky halter neck hanky top thing that I'd only get away with if I wore it on my head.

But she *was* Nate's new girlfriend, so I settled for immature judgement and internal conclusions that her eyes were too far apart so she was obviously a complete cow who loved herself and was as irritating as a suspicious rash.

Just because we were in the midst of divorcing, didn't mean that I wasn't going to have the occasional wobble.

'Hi, I'm Liv.'

'Janet,' she replied. 'Pleased to meet you.'

Janet the Jogger. Brilliant.

There was a pause as we all internally debated who should sit where, then realised we were taking too long and it was turning into a moment of extreme discomfort. Sheer panic made me crack first and I plumped down in the space next to Nate. The poor guy now had his new girlfriend on one side of him and his soon-to-be-ex-wife on the other.

Richard sat down next to me, leaving a space on the other side of him and an excruciating silence that was filled a few minutes later when Chloe arrived.

I was always happy to see her, but never more so than now. She gave Sasha a huge hug and wished her a happy birthday, then handed over a gorgeous gift bag, before kissing her way along the table. She finally slid in next to Richard and they immediately started chatting about some staffing issue on the ward.

I zoned out, grateful that at least Richard was occupied.

'On a scale of one to ten, how awkward is this?' Nate whispered in my right ear.

'I'm off that scale and in treble figures,' I replied, checking in my peripheral vision to see whether Janet the Jogger was listening. She wasn't. Justin had apparently engaged her in an in-depth conversation about Lycra, whilst – out of Janet's eye line – Sasha was pretending to shoot herself in the head.

'She seems nice,' I said, still whispering so only Nate could hear.

'So does he,' Nate fired back. I wasn't imagining the gritted teeth, or the fact that he was knocking back his bottle of beer like he had a raging thirst. Maybe he'd jogged here with Janet.

This was such a bad idea. Why had I ever thought we could pull this off?

'This is such a bad idea,' Nate said, echoing my thoughts. That had always happened to us. One of us would be thinking something just as the other one said it out loud.

'There had to be a first time though. Maybe it's good that we've done this, got it out of the way and it won't be as awkward from now on,' I said, not meaning a word of it.

He took another slug of his beer, then met my gaze. 'Do you really believe that?'

'Nope, but I'll go with it if you will,' I said, trying to inject some amusement into the whole situation. I did that when I was nervous. There wasn't a job interview in my history that I hadn't kicked off with a bad joke.

Tonight? The really bad joke was on me.

Seeing him, watching him, noticing that Janet the flipping Jogger's hand was on his thigh, I realised that... I missed him. And by 'missed him' I meant 'wanted to blow this whole awkward party off and leave here with him right now'.

How could this be? I had no idea. Coming to my senses? Something dodgy in this wine? Jealousy? If it were, it would be the first time. When we were together, Nate had never given me any reason not to trust him, so I'd never had even fleeting moments of jealousy. I'd never checked his phone or called his work to make sure he was there. I'd just been... sure. Not smug.

Just sure that he'd never hurt me. How had I repaid that loyalty? These non-jealous boots were made for walkin'.

The next couple of hours passed in a fixed-grin, stomach-knotted haze of self-doubt. What had I done? Had I made the biggest mistake of my life? And would Janet the Jogger's fingers snap like dried out twigs if I prised them from my husband's thigh?

Husband. My husband. Soon-to-be-ex. But was that really what I wanted?

I pushed my hand into Richard's. Yes, it was. Nate and I didn't work. Of course I was going to miss him – I'd been with him for most of my adult life. But it didn't make me happy or leave me fulfilled. Otherwise, I wouldn't have spent the last few months with Richard having extremely enjoyable times, many of which made areas of my anatomy exceptionally happy.

But... Oh bugger, the whole hand / husband / thigh thing was making my teeth grind.

Just then the DJ struck up the opening bars of 'Proud Mary' and Chloe jumped to her feet. 'Yassss! Come on. My inner Tina Turner needs some action.'

I shook my head. 'My inner Tina Turner has blisters on her feet from these bloody shoes and doesn't think she can stand up, never mind dance.'

The shame. There was absolutely nothing wrong with my feet, but the thought of Janet the Jogger watching her boyfriend's soon-to-be-ex-wife shaking her wobbly bits had made me entirely too self-conscious to hit the floor. 'Lightweight,' Richard said, laughing. 'Chloe, I'm in.' Off they went, dancing before they even reached the designated area. Thankfully, he didn't seem to have noticed that I was distracted and more than a bit flustered tonight.

Right now, I wanted to be anywhere else but here.

The proximity of Nate and the tumble dryer of emotions spinning in my gut was too much, so I slid out and headed for the toilets. When I got there, I noticed a door that opened to a lovely little back courtyard with a few wrought-iron tables and chairs. I stepped out and to the right, leaned back against the wall. Fresh air. That was what I needed. And a moment of solitude.

'Yep, it's that kind of night,' said a female voice, to my right. It came from behind a curtain of platinum-blonde hair that fell to the chin of a heart-shaped face, where it stopped in a blunt bob. Stylish. Sleek. The kind of woman who laid out her clothes the night before and never left home without a matching bra and knickers. Not that I'm prone to rash judgements. Much.

'Cigarette?' she offered, holding out a packet of something long, white, with a gold band around the tip. Menthol.

'I don't...' I was about to finish the sentence, when I realised that I really, really wanted a cigarette.

At least if I choked to death I'd go with a minty fresh aroma.

She held up a lighter and I had a flashback to a night outside the school disco as a fifteen-year-old, trying desperately to impress the coolest guy in the school by smoking with him. It didn't work then – I choked and was mocked for months. I carried on smoking for the next couple of years just in case he changed his mind, but I finally gave up on unrequited lust when I got to university, went into nursing and decided I preferred my lungs to be fully functioning.

We'd just put this down to a minor blip. I lit the cig, didn't give in to an instant urge to hurl, and tried to hold it as if it were a matter of habit.

'You look like you're having as good a time as me tonight,' she said. Actually, she more spat the words out.

She was a stranger, I'd never meet her again and I was seriously stressing, so I went for it. 'My husband and I separated at the beginning of the year and he's in there with his new girlfriend.'

'Ouch. Has someone removed all the sharp objects from the table?' she asked with a wry grimace.

'Nope. We're all being very adult and civilised about it,' I countered truthfully.

'Urgh, I hate that,' she said, with a dry, dramatic eye roll that made me laugh. I liked this woman already.

'Me too.' I agreed. 'I'm much better with open hostility and immature petulance.'

She nodded thoughtfully.

'Anyway,' I went on. 'What about you?'

'My boyfriend is in there with his partner. It's a long story.'

It took me a moment. 'His ex-partner?' I clarified.

'No. His current one.'

'His business partner?' I tried again to make this compute.

'Nope, his live-in partner. Like I said, long story.' That sounded like the kind of saga I wanted to hear over a large glass of wine and some high-calorie savoury snacks, but I wouldn't get the opportunity, because she stubbed out what was left of her cigarette on the concrete floor, smoothed down her skirt, inhaled, exhaled, then forced a smile.

'Good luck with the sharp objects,' she said.

'Think you might need some luck too,' I added sympathetically. I'm not sure why I felt bad for her. She'd just basically admitted to shagging some poor unsuspecting woman's partner. But there was a vulnerability about her, a jaded acceptance that just made me feel sorry for her.

Nate would never do that to me. I'd never do it to him. I had a sudden longing for the security and feeling of certainty that had been missing since New Year. Nate was the most decent, loving, kindest guy I'd ever known. Yet I'd just delivered him right into Janet the Jogger's over-toned thighs. The thought made the red rash creep up my neck again, but this time it was pure anger, most of it directed at myself.

What the hell had I been thinking? How could I have quit so easily? What a fool I'd been.

Or had I? Didn't I have a gorgeous new boyfriend who made me very happy?

I stubbed out the cigarette in the ashtray of the nearest table, and was about to charge back inside when a coughing fit stopped me. My lungs were obviously unimpressed by the minty stuff. As soon as they resumed normal operation, I carried back on inside, still hopping back and forward over a fine line of doubt. Was it time for this nonsense to stop? Time for me to tell Nate that it had all been a mistake, and that he had to unhand Janet from his body?

That mental image made my hackles rise. If this was what jealousy felt like, I now understood why it made people do crazy things – like tell their ex they wanted them back after a few too many glasses of wine.

I bumped into Sasha as I charged back in.

'Whoa there, Speedy, what's up with you?'

'I've buggered it up, Sasha. I need to speak to Nate.'

She immediately grabbed my hands. 'Ah bollocks,' she said, coming straight to the point as always. 'Let me guess, you've seen him with that woman – who, by the way, just about bored my tits right off – and you've suddenly decided you can't live without him.'

It was spooky how she did that. Her pupils at school must live in fear of her mind-reading abilities. Over her shoulder, I saw Chloe gesture to me to come join her and Richard on the dance floor. They were dancing in perfect timing with each other, doing some kind of shuffle thing and pulling it off in a much more sexy fashion than I could ever manage. Anyone looking at the dance floor would think they were a couple. Maybe they should be. Maybe I should be with Nate and then Chloe and Richard…

Sasha snapped me back to the present. 'Sasha calling Liv, come in Liv.'

'Yes!'

'Yes what?'

'Yes, you're right. Crap, I hate it when that happens. I've screwed this up, Sasha.'

'No you haven't. It's just jealousy, pure and simple. He's been yours for so long that it doesn't feel right to see him with someone else.'

'But what if I should have stuck it out longer and we'd have been good again?'

'Have you been smoking?' She always struggled to stick to one point at a time.

'Yes, but... Fuck, I need to tell him how I'm feeling.'

'You can't.'

An uncharacteristic wave of bloody fury took over me. I was the calm one, the voice of reason, but Sasha was way overstepping here and I wasn't going to back down. 'Of course I can. Sasha, move out of the way.'

Sighing, but with an expression I couldn't quite place, she let go of my hands and stepped to the side, allowing me to scan the room.

It took a few moments, before I realised she was right. I saw Chloe and Richard, still dancing. I saw Sasha's boyfriend, Justin, chatting to the girl I'd cadged a cigarette off outside. I saw a whole room of partying, happy people.

But I didn't see Nate.

'He left five minutes ago.'

He'd left. He and Janet had jogged on.

And this was all my fault.

On New Year's Eve I'd closed the door.

Nate had just double-locked it and I no longer had the key.

3

Justin's 30th Birthday Party

August 2001

'Has everyone you've ever known turned thirty in the last year, or does it just feel that way?' Richard asked, coming up behind me and planting a kiss on my neck to punctuate each word.

The warm sensation of his breath made me smile. 'Indeed they are. That's what happens when you're socially inept and your friendship circle is the same one you've had since university. We're like a less funny, less attractive, lower-paid version of *Friends*. That's why I'm almost thirty and living in my mate's spare room.'

It took a moment to realise that he was unbuttoning the back of my dress, but as soon as I did, I slid away. It was tempting, but we were late already and I'd paid twenty quid for a blow-dry and I wasn't going to ruin it, even for a quickie with a guy who could turn me on with just a sideways glance. It was the very best part of our relationship, probably helped by the fact that we both worked shifts, so often only actually managed to get together a couple of times a week. Even after a year of dating, that still suited me just fine.

Justin's thirtieth birthday party was in a pub in the Merchant City, the more upmarket, grown-up area of Glasgow nightlife. We'd shifted there somewhere in our mid-twenties, when we no longer walked home carrying our shoes in sub-zero temperatures, or stopped for a kebab on the way back. Now we were much more likely to get a taxi home, fully shod, and I even took my make-up off before going to bed. Most of the time.

I had a momentary flashback to Nate folding his clothes before sex – he always did that – then shrugged it off. That was my old life. Nothing there to revisit. Our divorce had come through a couple of months ago, and I'd had a moment of acute sadness, a few tears, and several large glasses of wine with Sasha and Chloe. Then I'd pulled myself together and decided to look at it as the start of a new life. We'd survived relatively unscathed and we hadn't killed each other in the process of splitting. That was something to be grateful for.

'Are you ready, Chloe?' I shouted.

'I'm here,' she said from the doorway. 'Playing bloody third wheel again with you two. People are going to start thinking we are a threesome if we carry on like this.'

She laughed, because the truth was that she didn't give a damn about being single. Ever since Connor, the love of her early twenties, had hot-tailed it off to the States, she'd been pretty ambivalent on the relationship front. Rob leaving to go to Ibiza had barely made a dent, apart from a rueful, 'What is it about me that makes men want to leave the country?'

I'd shut that down with, 'Connor only left the country because you broke his heart.'

'Yep, and he wasn't slow in letting Stacey from Chicago put it back together again, was he?' she'd retorted, but she knew that if she hadn't ended things with Connor that they'd have gone the distance – in fact, that was what had terrified her into wanting a break.

Water under the bridge.

She still had us. It was an extra bonus that she got on so well with Richard, both in and out of work, so it was only natural that we did a lot of things together. All of them fully clothed.

The party was already packed, hot and smoky when we got there, and there was none of the civilised 'greeting at the door' thing – this was 'everybody in, grab a drink and get on with the celebrations'. Even the arrangements had been low maintenance. Justin had sent out an open invitation to everyone on his email list a week ago last Friday, announcing there would be a piss-up tonight and everyone was welcome. This was why he and Sasha made the perfect pairing: both daring, both bold, both liked to live on the wild side and neither could give a crap about conforming to etiquette.

We negotiated our way in through the crowds, and eventually spotted Sasha sitting alone amidst a sea of glasses at a corner table. Chloe and I headed over, while Richard detoured to the bar for drinks.

'Hey,' I greeted her.

'Oh thank Christ. I've been trying to stop people sitting here by loading it up with half-finished drinks, but it's making me look like the deranged loner, drinking away her bitterness in the corner.'

'And that would be untrue because...?' I teased. She didn't rise to it.

Chloe and I plonked ourselves down and checked out the room. A few guys I remembered from university, Justin's brother Jake, sitting with what I assumed were their parents, a gang of his workmates... My eyes rested on a female that I recognised, standing in that group of Justin's colleagues, chatting to another woman. White-blonde hair. Cut in a chin-length bob. I hadn't caught her name last time we met, but at least I'd know where to go if I wanted to borrow a sly cig.

Richard came back with a tray of drinks for the whole table, the conversations got going, Justin appeared, already fairly lubricated, which made Sasha laugh as she jokingly chided him, and we got on with celebrating yet another milestone in our group. The drinks flowed all night as Justin alternated between getting drunker at our table, and getting drunker while he worked the room.

A while later, I spotted him doing the Slosh – a traditional Scottish synchronised dance that looks a bit like line dancing and is performed to the backing track of a jaunty tune – with his Auntie Doreen. I nudged Sasha, 'He's having a brilliant time.'

'Doesn't he always,' she said. There was a hint of dryness to her words and I made a mental note to keep an eye on her in case something was brewing. I hoped I was just being hyper-vigilant and oversensitive. Tonight was Justin's birthday – surely even if he was irritating her in some way, she'd let it pass?

'Darlings!' Oh God. My inner child put its head on the table for a moment of escape, before I rallied and responded. 'Hi Mum.'

'Ida! I'm so glad you're here!' Sasha beamed.

'Wouldn't miss it, my lovely,' she cooed, enveloping Sasha in a hug so heavily perfumed it could take out a cardiovascular system. My mum was grappling fifty, and she dressed accordingly. If the fifty-year-old in question was Cher. There were fishnet tights, there was a black sparkly dress with transparent bits, and there was a hairstyle so large, a swift turn of the head could take out several innocent passers-by.

She finally released Sasha and shared her effusive greetings around the table. I was next, followed by Chloe, and then the grand finale, when she eyed Richard with blatant adoration. Oh yes, the grief and devastation over my break-up with Nate had been brutal, it had been dramatic, it had required that I visit her multiple times a week because she 'was struggling to deal with the loss', it had been a complete nightmare... and it had lasted until about thirty seconds after I'd introduced her to Richard, mentioned he was a doctor, and she'd hit him up with every symptom she and her dancing chums had experienced in the last six months. He'd assured her that she was healthy as a thoroughbred, and she'd clicked her kitten heels, decided she adored him, and would now struggle to pick out Nate in a line-up.

That was our Ida. 'Right, I'm off to mingle. Where's that gorgeous man of yours?' she asked Sasha.

'Up there doing the Slosh with his Auntie Doreen,' Sasha replied.

'Oh, I love a Slosh.' She immediately tuned into the music and her diamanté slingbacks tottered off in the direction of the dance floor, singing 'Beautiful Sunday' as she went.

I decided to deflect by turning the spotlight on potential bumps in my personal life. Time was ticking by and I couldn't help notice that my ex-husband and my replacement were not yet here.

'Where's Nate?' I asked. 'Isn't he coming?'

Sasha adopted the pursed lips of disapproval. 'I've no idea. To be honest with you I'm a bit pissed off. We haven't been able to get a hold of him all week and then he left a message on Justin's voicemail earlier saying he'd be late.'

A dozen thoughts rushed through my mind. Was he sick? No, he'd have called someone. Maybe he was having an emotional turmoil? Perhaps he and Janet had split? Was it wrong that, even after all this time, a tiny part of me cheered at that prospect?

My thoughts were interrupted by the screech of electronic feedback, then 'Ladies and gentlemen, I'd like your attention please.' It was Justin's brother, Jake, standing on the bar with a microphone. This would be good. It could be anything from an emotional speech to an announcement that there was about to be a session of strip limbo dancing. 'I'd just like to say happy birthday to my brother, Justin.'

A cheer went up, then he carried on.

'Bro, we were too cheap to buy you a present...'

Another cheer.

'So we got you something that came free instead.'

Sasha groaned. 'If it's come out of a skip and ends up in our living room I'll kill him.'

Jake suddenly pointed at the door, and as every head turned and bodies parted we could see that there was a new arrival to the party.

'Oh Jesus.' That came from Chloe, as she realised that Justin's gift came in the form of a six foot six inch pal, one who'd left a few years ago to go and live with his new girlfriend in the USA, one whom Chloe had loved, lost and had thought about every single day since. 'Is his girlfriend there? Dear God, tell me she's not,' Chloe prayed.

I had a hunch that her eyes were closed, so I checked out the scene at the door. 'No girlfriend,' I confirmed.

Behind Connor though, I saw Nate, closely followed by Janet the Jogger. Yep, she was still on the scene, still had thighs that could crack nuts and her favourite subjects were still her fitness routines and the nutritional values of beans. We'd been in the same company several times now and we managed to keep it 'civil with a pretence of friendliness', all of which was done while I held in my stomach and tried to keep my chin at a flattering angle.

So that's why he was late. He was bringing the surprise. It wouldn't be a newsflash at all if he'd organised the whole thing. That was the kind of thoughtful guy he was. A pang of something flipped my stomach. I missed him. Not all the time. Just fleeting thoughts.

In moments of deep retrospection (usually between applying shampoo and conditioner in the shower), I could admit that Richard and I had a great time, an uncomplicated relationship that suited us both perfectly, but we didn't have that deep connection that I'd had with Nate. However, we did have plenty of laughs, great sex, and because we were both in the same field, we understood each other's pressures and challenges. He got me. I got him. Maybe I just wasn't letting my emotional barriers down, but it hadn't moved to anything deeper. We didn't have a decade of shared history, and sometimes I missed that, missed Nate. Maybe there was enough of a distance from the break-up to start hanging out together again. We could be friends. It wasn't as if he and Janet the Jogger were inseparable – Sasha had been telling me for the last year that it was a purely casual thing.

Connor and Justin had a prolonged man-greet-man hug in the middle of the floor to whoops and cheers from the crowd, breaking off only when Justin shouted, 'Connor Smith is here! Time to drink!', and the revellers duly responded by storming the bar. At that moment, Connor's eyes found us and, arm still around Justin's shoulders, Nate and Janet following, they headed our way.

It took me a moment to realise that Chloe had stopped breathing beside me. I immediately felt for her hand and grabbed it tight. Connor. It was obvious that no one at our table knew he was coming, and that Chloe, most of all, was slipping into some kind of catatonic shock at the sight of him. Her biggest regret was that she hadn't realised until after he was gone how she felt about him, and she'd never had the opportunity to tell him. Until maybe now.

Chloe's hand was now gripping mine so tightly it was cutting off circulation to my fingers.

'Play cool,' I whispered, not sure if it was to myself or to Chloe. 'I've got you,' I added. She squeezed tighter and I tried not to yelp.

They were at the table now and the exclamations of surprise were only halted when Sasha punched Nate in the arm. 'So this is why you've been playing hard to get this week. I was ready to hunt you down.'

Nate laughed. 'I had to stay out of the way. I knew I'd crack.'

He was right. He'd always been hopeless at keeping secrets. Another pang. Okay, so I really missed him. We definitely had to get back on 'friends that hang out' terms. And I really hoped that Richard wasn't staring at my face right now because I was fairly sure it was flushing.

While the conversation was going on, I noticed the look that passed between Connor and Chloe. More than a look. They locked eyes, and all we needed was a slow-motion replay to make this a moment right out of a romcom. He leaned over, she leaned over, his face cracked into the biggest smile, hers did the same, her arms went up around his neck, his went around her waist, and he pulled her up like she was as light as a feather and kissed her, hard on the mouth, for way longer than any casual greeting between friends.

'If he does that to everyone, I'm first in the queue,' Sasha deadpanned. I ignored her, my heart ready to burst with happiness for Chloe. I had no idea how it happened. I wasn't even sure that it had. But somehow, right here, right now, her man was back and all was right in Chloe's world.

When they finally broke off, Sasha stepped in. 'I'm next,' she said, holding arms up to Connor, cracking the rest of us up.

She settled for a huge hug.

'What is going on? What are you doing here?' she asked what we were all thinking.

Meanwhile, I noticed that Chloe had replaced my hand with Connor's, despite the fact that barely a word had passed between them yet.

My heart soared again. I loved this. It felt like old times... With the obvious exception. I caught Nate's eye and he smiled sadly, and in that moment I had a real feeling that he was thinking the same as me. Did we let go too soon? Could this have been us?

Connor took a bottle of Budweiser that had just been thrust into his hand by Jake, then got around to answering Sasha's question.

'Nate called me last week...'

I knew Nate would be behind this. So thoughtful. And kind. And... Oh God, I had to stop thinking like this. The feeling of Richard's hand, running provocatively up and down my spine, distracted me. *Focus.*

47

'And, the thing is, Stacey and I split a few weeks ago, so I decided I needed a vacation. When he told me about tonight…'

Connor was staring straight at Chloe, but my thoughts were back on Nate again. Look at him, all bashful, not even trying to take the credit. It was almost as if he was embarrassed.

'And then he told me his news, I knew I had to come back.'

Aaaah, so brilliant and… Wait, what? What news?

It took the others a moment to catch up too.

Sasha got there first. 'You have news?'

A pause. Nate still saying nothing, but looking at me now, a strange expression on his face. Almost apologetic. What did he have to apologise for?

Janet delivered the answer with an excited yelp, as she thrust her hand into the middle of the gathering.

'We got engaged!'

4

Barbeque at Chloe and Connor's House

July 2002

'That's the sexiest smell ever,' I purred, as we walked down the path at the side of Chloe and Connor's house, and unclipped the gate to the back garden.

'It's Calvin Klein,' Richard replied, preening just a little. It was almost a shame to burst his aromatic bubble.

'I was talking about the smell of sausages on the barbeque,' I admitted, trying oh so hard not to laugh.

He was saved from dwelling on the embarrassment by a rousing cheer of greeting. Chloe and Sasha were sitting at a beautifully set table that could have been straight out of a John Lewis summer advert. How did she do that? My barbeques consisted of crumbling burgers and burnt sausages, with plastic plates, a few bottles of ketchup, that yellow relish with sweetcorn in it, and napkins left over from Christmas plonked in the middle of the table. Chloe's? Aesthetic perfection. If I didn't love her so much, I could really take a dislike to that level of domestic superiority. And that level of personal style too. Her vintage, fifties style summer dress, cinched in at the waist and flaring out to just below the knee, made my boot cut jeans and sloppy T-shirt look positively shoddy. Sasha, meanwhile, was rocking sexy white hipster trousers and a red off-the-shoulder Bardot top. For the sake of my own self-esteem, I really had to get scruffier pals.

Richard headed over to the barbeque, where Connor and Justin were standing, bottles of beer in hand, pretending to supervise the sausage-browning process. It was always the same. Chloe would have done all the planning, the organisation, the shopping, and been up at the crack of dawn this morning preparing everything. Connor and the guys would slap some chicken skewers on the barbie and then act like they were the second coming of Jamie Oliver.

By the time Richard reached the menfolk, Justin already had a bottle of beer out of the cooler and uncapped for him. When I first started dating Richard, I'd worried that there would be awkwardness between him and the guys. Nate and Justin had struck up an instant friendship when Sasha introduced him to us – I did a quick calculation in my head – must be nine years ago now. And obviously now that Connor was back, his loyalties would lie with Nate. It would be only natural if they were wary of Richard or felt some kind of emotional conflict, but thankfully it was clear that still waters didn't actually run particularly deep. It helped that Richard had that laid-back attitude, a sense of humour and an encyclopaedic knowledge of Scottish football from about 1985 until the present day.

I joined the girls at the table, noticing first Chloe's beaming smile. It had pretty much been a permanent fixture since Connor had come back the year before. His trip home for Justin's birthday party had turned into a permanent thing when he rekindled his life with Chloe. He hadn't even gone back to collect his stuff, just had it shipped over here and they'd lived happily ever after. Not great news for me on the home front, as I'd had to move out and find a place of my own. In the end, Richard solved the problem by suggesting I move in with him.

So far, it was working out great – although I was very aware it was a false reality because we were permanently on different shifts, so we were lucky if we got one or two nights off together in a week. I can vouch for the fact that absence makes the heart grow fonder. And it also means you don't get heartily sick of picking up someone's socks off the floor.

Sometimes I wondered if it would work so well if we lived normal lives, with normal shift patterns, or spent more than a couple of days together at a time. I was sure it would, but right now it wasn't an issue.

We were happy.

Chloe and Connor were now ensconced in their new house, complete with front and back garden and – I kid you not – a white picket fence, and they were happy too.

Nate and his fiancée Janet were happy. I couldn't help it if my eyes rolled when I had that thought.

Anyway, three out of four couples isn't bad. I just wished I could say the same for Sasha and Justin. Right now, her face was wearing the kind of expression that could quite easily end in crime scene investigators dusting down the white suits and face masks.

'What's up, my love? You look like someone stole your hot dog,' I joked, trying to cajole her out of whatever irritation was winding her up.

'Nothing. Nothing at all,' she replied in a voice that made it obvious it was something. That was Sasha. Tough exterior, didn't show weakness, easily prone to irritation, quick to snap.

I decided it was easier to seek answers elsewhere. 'Is she mad at us or Justin?' I asked Chloe.

'Justin. He's already hammered and it's only two o'clock.'

'Ah, yep, that would definitely piss her off.'

Sasha glared at us, brow furrowed, but I could tell she was mildly amused by this. 'You know I'm sitting right here and can hear you,' she said, trying to stick with irritation and failing.

I nodded. 'Yep, but you weren't being straight with me and I'm not emotionally equipped for drama today, so I just wanted to establish the lay of the land.'

'Why, what's up? Is everything okay?' Chloe now.

'It's fine, I'm just… Och, it was a tough week. We lost Charlie.'

Charlie Moss, twenty-two years old, had fought cancer for the fourth time in his short life and this time the bastard disease had won. He'd been with us for almost five months, defying his prognosis to become one of our longer-term patients, and we'd become… friends. He was one of the good guys, an optimistic, positive kid who would have had a great life in front of him. No matter how long I'd been doing this job, sometimes the sadness and injustice that we saw every day just got to me. This was one of those weeks.

Chloe reached over and took my hand. 'So sorry, lovely. I know how much you cared for him.'

'Thanks,' I said, squeezing her hand, before outwardly shaking off my sadness and forcing myself to adopt a happier demeanour. I wasn't here to bring everyone down, no matter how I was feeling. 'Right enough of my woes. Let's turn our attention back to Sasha shooting daggers at Justin. That was way more fun.'

With precision timing, Justin chose that moment to sway, then drop a bottle of beer on the patio, causing it to smash and shoot amber liquid everywhere. Oh God. This wasn't going to end well. I could feel Sasha's irritation levels shooting skywards.

'Don't worry about it,' Chloe cautioned Sasha. 'It's fine. It's only a bottle. Connor will clear it up.'

'It's not fine,' Sasha snapped back, then bit down any further reaction. Justin had always liked a drink, but over the last year or so he seemed to like it more and more. Sasha was a serial party animal too, but this was becoming too much, even for her. Every gathering, every occasion, every day ending in a 'y' over the last few months had ended in them bickering about the fact that he was seriously drunk. 'Someone change the subject before I go over there and commit a crime with a half-cooked kebab.'

'I will,' Chloe said. 'Wait till I tell you who I met this week.'

'Brad Pitt,' I said.

'George Clooney.' Sasha offered, making a valiant effort to play along while refusing to even glance in Justin's direction.

'That bloke who's in *Fast & Furious*,' I countered.

'Okay, so any answer I come up with now will be a complete anti-climax,' Chloe wailed.

'No, I promise we'll act impressed,' I assured her. 'Especially if it's Matt Damon.'

She dipped her finger in her glass of wine and flicked it at me as I ducked.

Thank God for these women. They always had a way of making everything seem just a little bit better. Except Sasha, obviously. But we kept her in case we ever had to volunteer someone to be a gangland enforcer.

Chloe took a dramatic pause, commandeering the moment. 'Remember the girl you found in the toilets at the millennium party?'

'Of course. Francine,' I replied. That wasn't an encounter I would ever forget.

'Yes! She's working on our ward. After what happened to her, she decided to apply for uni to study medicine, and she's moonlighting as a nursing assistant to support herself while she's studying. How cool is that? She is going to be a doctor and it's all because of that night.'

'That is pretty cool indeed,' I agreed, feeling ridiculously grateful that I'd found her in time. The alternative didn't bear thinking about. 'I'll pop down to the ward and say hi next time I'm on night shift,' I promised. I'd often wondered how she was doing. It would be lovely to see her.

'Yep, keep her sweet,' Sasha interjected dryly, finally staring over at Justin, 'because she might come in handy one day for detoxing my boyfriend.'

I was about to try to console her when a screeching sound made my teeth grind. Okay, so it wasn't exactly a screech but Janet the Jogger's voice had the same effect on me as nails clawing down a blackboard.

'Hi everyone!' Janet bellowed, and Chloe immediately shot me an apologetic glance. I hadn't known they were coming, but I shouldn't have been surprised. Nate and Connor had been best mates for the same length of time as Chloe and I, so it would have been ludicrous to make them choose to have one of us at a gathering and not the other. Anyway, it wasn't as if there was any bad feeling at all. In fact, Nate and Richard got on really well. We weren't exactly all going on holiday together or sharing Christmas dinner, but when we saw each other at social events it was all very amicable.

If I could just get my inner bitch to stop contemplating gagging Janet with her swingy blonde ponytail every time she talked about squats and lunges, it would be great.

I watched Nate stroll over to testosterone corner and had to admit he looked well. Janet was obviously good for him. They were just back from two weeks in Tenerife and he was tanned, with sun-lightened flecks through his chestnut hair. He had on cargo shorts and a white T-shirt that clung in all the right places. My inner bitch was pushed out of the way by my inner ex-wife, the one that had a sudden urge to run my fingers through his hair. Wow, where did that come from? I hadn't even wanted to run my fingers through his hair the last few years we were married.

My emotions were just all over the place this week.

Janet kissed everyone, me included, then pulled out another chair for her Lycra-clad buttocks. Did she ever wear real clothes? You know, ones made of fibres that didn't stretch and shine? That was my inner bitch again. I attempted to drown her with a large gulp of Chardonnay.

Just a few minutes later, the guys headed over to join us, all carrying various components of the feast. Connor was clutching a plate piled with chicken skewers in one hand and a large dish of burgers in the other. Nate had the box of beers and Justin had…

'Fuck, fuck, fuck!' he exclaimed, as he staggered to the side and somehow lost his balance, sending the tray of sausages that he was holding scattering across the lawn.

'Bloody hell,' Sasha hissed, furious.

Justin, grappling to pull himself up, obviously heard her. His response was definitely slightly slurred. 'What's up with you? Chill out.'

I closed my eyes, a premonition of what was about to happen flashing in neon in my brain. In the entire history of the existence of Sasha, never once had a demand that she 'chill out' or 'calm down' been followed by her responding, 'Good idea,' then kicking off her shoes, lighting a Jo Malone candle and having an interlude of relaxation.

'I'm not doing this here,' she warned, her tone deadly, but keeping uncharacteristically calm.

Justin was a couple of Budweisers past the kind of sensible judgement that would have stopped him from pushing her any further. 'Aye okay, so I tripped. What's your problem?' he spat.

See, this was the thing with Justin. When he was sober he was the sweetest, kindest man, one who was unfailingly good fun and lovable. But when he'd been drinking, he could be sharp and belligerent. Not a combination that Sasha tolerated.

We could all see that this was about to erupt like so many occasions over the last year or so, but it was Chloe who intervened and diffused it like the perfect hostess.

'Och don't worry. If Connor cooked them, they were probably underdone and would have given us all botulism anyway,' she said breezily, passing a look to Connor that was sure to be a telepathic apology.

As always, Connor got it and laughed. 'Racing certainty,' he agreed, picking up the sausages and tossing them in the bin.

Chloe was still displaying her hostess superpowers, in full

jocular mode as she waved to the empty chairs at the table. 'Come on everyone, grab a seat, eat and we'll try not to poison anyone with Connor's meat or my coleslaw.'

It was the perfect smooth-over to an awkward moment, and everyone did as they were told. Even Sasha.

Okay, awkward situation averted. Normal service resumed. Let's just have a pleasant afternoon, like any normal gathering of a love-struck pairing, a seething female, a blitzed bloke, and a former married couple and their new partners. Yup, just like any other day.

All we had to do was stay civil, keep everything neutral, stick to middle of the road, idle chat, and avoid the subject of grass-stained sausages. What could possibly go wrong?

'You know, I love it when we all get together like this,' Connor said, holding up his beer glass in a toast. Good. Positive move. Reminding the group what a good thing we had. 'I always missed it when I was... away.' He looked at Chloe when he said that and she leaned over and kissed him.

'Oh for Christ's sake – that makes it sound like you did a five-year stretch for armed robbery,' Sasha barbed, the resulting laughter elevating the mood even further. Excellent. We were winning. Showing our maturity. Taking strides forward.

Conner grinned too. 'It was four years and I was wearing a balaclava, so they'd no proof,' he shot back, before returning his attention to the rest of us. 'So I was thinking...' he carried on.

Suddenly a large dose of the fear gripped me. Nooooo, he shouldn't be thinking. Why would he think? It could only lead to some ridiculous idea for some future group activity and I was only just getting through on the basic 'barbeque and special occasions' level. Stop thinking. No more thinking.

'How about we plan a group holiday?' he finished, with an air of triumph at his genius idea.

'Yes!' Justin blurted. 'I'm in. Let's go all-inclusive for the free booze.'

'Pass me a fork, so I can stab myself in the hand,' Sasha muttered, but Justin was on a roll and coming back with a new idea.

'No, no, wait a minute! Malibu! I've always wanted to go to Malibu.'

'That's only because you've got a sordid addiction to reruns of *Baywatch*. Pamela Anderson doesn't actually patrol the beaches there,' I teased.

'Yes, she does. And there's only one way to prove my point. Malibu!'

We were still laughing when Chloe gave her thoughts. 'Oh, it would be great!' she gushed. Of course she would. She loved every one of us and wouldn't see past the joy of having all her friends in the same place at the same time.

I glanced at Richard. 'If I can get time off, I'm there,' he agreed. Oh bloody hell, even he was selling me out. So much for our telepathic coupledom. Read my mind. This. Is. Not. A. Good. Idea.

An image of Nate, on our last holiday together jumped to the forefront of my mind. He was playing football with some local guys on a beach in Estepona, top off, just shorts, laughing at something one of them had said, looking like an advert for sports deodorant or razor blades. True, he'd spent the rest of the night reading a book, and we'd only had sex twice in the fortnight, but my brain was currently in some default mode that weeded out the negative bits and made me remember only the good stuff. Did I want to watch Janet leering over him for a fortnight in bloody Malibu? Absolutely not. Was I having momentary, fleeting feelings of attraction to my ex? Yes I absolutely was. Therefore, could I stand it if they slipped off every afternoon for a quickie? No I absolutely couldn't. The thought of Richard and I, and Nate and Janet, lying on double sun loungers next to each other sipping pina coladas and discussing whose turn it was to go for the lunchtime ice lollies made me want to reach for Sasha's fork.

It was a terrible idea and – despite the fact that I hated to be the one that killed it – I couldn't let it happen. I had to speak up. Say it now.

'Actually, I'm really sorry but that won't work for us.'

It wasn't me who had spoken. Someone else had got there before me. My gaze flicked to Janet, who was shrugging apologetically, and I breathed a massive sigh of relief. *Well played, Janet. That was my very favourite thing that's come out of your gob since we met.*

'We, erm, already have plans for our holiday next year,' she went on.

'Oooh, tell us, tell us,' Chloe prompted, excitedly.

It was Janet's turn to look at her partner conspiratorially, and before they'd even had their telepathic conversation my premonition talents kicked in yet again and I knew. I bloody knew.

Fear and dread and resignation combined to make the skin on my buttocks tingle. *Don't say it. Please don't.*

Nate cleared his throat like he always did when he was nervous, excited or apprehensive. 'Em, yeah, so the thing is…' he began.

Don't say it. Don't fricking say it.

'We've set a date for the wedding. It's next October, so our holiday next year will be our honeymoon.'

Justin's state of inebriation suddenly seemed like a place I really wanted to be.

5

Justin's 32nd Birthday Garden Party

August 2003

'So are we going to talk about it?' Richard asked. Again.

'Here? Now?' I replied, lifting a sausage roll from the buffet as I passed it. Sasha had outdone herself, admittedly with loads of help from Chloe. They'd managed to lay on a feast for sixty people that would have a professional caterer weeping into their vol-au-vents. It had started off as a small gathering to celebrate Justin's birthday, and had ended up a full-scale garden party, complete with food, copious alcohol and a DJ. The sun had even chosen to shine – although it couldn't quite break through the little cloud above Richard's head.

'Why not? You won't talk about it any other time.'

It was the elephant in the room, the taboo subject for the last month. He'd been offered a position as a consultant neurosurgeon back in his home city of Manchester, a fantastic promotion that would absolutely solidify his career. He wanted to take it, wanted me to go with him and I wouldn't give him a decision. I couldn't. Call it cowardice, indecision, lack of clarity, sheer bloody-mindedness, call it reluctance to live 200 miles away from my friends – whatever it was, it was shutting down my life-changing decision-making skills and causing waves of panic whenever the subject was raised.

It was crunch time. Long-distance relationships didn't succeed in our line of work. The shifts, the demands, the pressures. As we'd experienced over the last couple of years, even with a partner in the same house it was difficult to get quality time together.

'You two look so serious!' Sasha commented as she appeared at my side. She was wearing a cream suit, with trousers that sat so low on her hips they had to be held up with nothing but prayer and optimism.

'I'm trying to persuade your friend to join me for a life of tropical bliss.'

'Where?' Sasha asked.

'Manchester. I might be using a bit of artistic licence with "tropical". I've been offered a job there. A promotion.'

'Congratulations! But she'll never go,' Sasha said with a weird but spot-on combination of blasé conviction.

'Why?' Richard asked, amused at her certainty. I decided to let them discuss me. Sometimes hearing someone else's take on your actions was enlightening. Unless it was my mother, in which case it was bound to be mildly disparaging with an edge of disappointment.

'Because she wouldn't leave Chloe and me, especially when you're going to be working long hours, so you'll barely see each other. And because I'll be clutching on to her ankle and she'll never manage to dislodge me. Biceps of steel,' she said, flashing a finely toned upper arm.

A new arrival to the group reacted first.

'Those pull-ups are paying off, Sasha,' Janet the Jogger said, clapping her hands like a seal. Sorry. Even after three years, I still couldn't control my inner bitch when it came to this woman. She was being perfectly nice and there was I, thinking evil thoughts. No wonder the Gods punished me by moving my boyfriend to another city. 'I've booked your next gym session for Monday, usual time,' she added.

Sasha at least had the guts to glance at me and I saw a mild apology in her eyes. She was working out with Janet? First I'd heard of it. Judas. Thirty pieces of silver and arse cheeks you could bounce a cricket ball on.

Yes, I was aware that I wasn't being completely rational. We were adults. We all got on well. If I'd met Janet under other circumstances we might actually be friends. Hang on, that was perhaps a step too far. I don't think I could be friends with someone who ended every conversation with, 'You know, you really do need to start working out – you'll be toned in no time and you'll ward off all sorts of mid-life health issues.'

'I'm just going to grab a drink,' I blurted, then realised that my words had come with an echo. Nate had arrived, was standing next to Janet, and he'd just said exactly the same thing at exactly the same time. That was cute when we were married but just plain uncomfortable now that we were divorced.

Richard, Sasha and Janet looked at us for a moment that just oozed awkwardness. We'd said it, so surely we had to follow through, otherwise it would just make it even more strange.

'I'll come with you,' I said, my voice a little higher than usual. 'Richard, I'll bring you back a beer. Sasha, Janet?'

'Wine,' Sasha replied, just as Janet said, 'Water.'

Of course. I could have guessed that.

Nate and I shuffled off towards the makeshift bar, set up in the far corner of the garden between the hut and the barbeque.

'Sorry, that was weird and I wasn't entirely sure how to make the best of it,' I admitted.

'Me either,' he seemed to be relaxing a little now that it was just the two of us. Sometimes I thought we spent so much energy focusing on making our new partners comfortable, that we forgot how well we actually knew each other. I'd accepted now that we'd never be best buddies, hanging out and swapping life stories and gossip, but at least we weren't bickering and point scoring.

'So how are things?' I asked.

'Yeah, good. You?'

Small talk. I'd seen his penis and yet we were acting like we'd just met in a bus queue.

'I'm fine. How are the wedding plans coming along?' I didn't actually want to know, but I was trying to be mature and cordial.

He shook his head. 'We decided to postpone. Janet's sister announced she was getting married the week before our date. Kind of stole Janet's thunder, so we're going to hang off for a while. We'd only provisionally booked it, so it wasn't a big deal.'

'Wow. Bet Janet wasn't thrilled.'

That would be the understatement of the year. Janet liked to be involved, be up front and centre, make an impact. I had no doubt at all that the wedding would be a grand spectacle, but at least now it wasn't a grand spectacle that was happening this year. I'm not sure why I was relieved about that.

'No, she wasn't delighted. But to be honest, holding off for a while isn't a bad thing. It was going to cost more than a Mercedes,' he said ruefully. 'Who knew weddings cost so much?'

'Not me,' I quipped. 'Change out of £500.' It was true. Nate and I had tied the knot in a tiny church in Luss, a stunningly beautiful village overlooking Loch Lomond, then nine of us – Chloe and Connor, Sasha and Justin, his parents and my mum, had walked through the gorgeous, cottage-lined, winding streets to a local hotel, where we'd feasted on all our favourite foods, then danced into the night. It had been beautiful, perfect, low-key and just exactly the way I'd always imagined it to be.

A little lump of nostalgia got stuck in my throat just as Justin's Auntie Doreen accosted us with a tray of tiger prawns. I paused to give her a hug of greeting (and thanks for rescuing me from flashback sentimentality). We were about to walk on when we were joined by one of Sasha's brothers, Lee – a lovely guy but as far departed from Sasha as imaginable.

Lee was a hippy, man-bun-sporting yoga guru, who stayed at home taking care of his twins while his wife worked in… Actually, I had no idea what she did because Sasha only ever referred to her as The Overachiever.

He had one of his children strapped to his chest in a papoose-type thingy. My knowledge of such things was limited. 'Hey guys,' he drawled, 'How ya doing?'

'We're good thanks, Lee.' I answered automatically, then realised I had no place speaking for Nate any more. 'All right mate?' Nate shook his hand, and if he noticed my inclusive reply he didn't comment.

'Yeah, I'm great,' Lee answered Nate. 'Thought you two would have one of these by now,' he went on, pointing to the baby. Clearly Lee wasn't big on current affairs.

'Lee, we're… erm… divorced,' I stuttered, hoping Nate would step in with some witty retort to diffuse the situation. He didn't.

'Oh… well… cool. Not be getting one of these any time soon then,' he said, as if he was talking about a new lawnmower or a food mixer.

Sasha appeared at my side and must have caught the last bit of the conversation. 'Sorry, I did tell him this many moons ago, but unless it's to do with yoga, kids or weed, he has no powers of retention.' She turned to her brother, 'I think your wife is looking for you. She just went inside.'

'Ok… well… cool,' he repeated, before wandering off in the direction of the house.

'Honest to God, there's no way we're related,' Sasha groaned. While she was speaking, I glanced back to see Richard and Janet chatting away. With no baggage between them, they'd always got on well.

'By the way,' Sasha sighed. 'Next time you two want to leave me stuck with your new partners, can you make sure I'm hooked up to an IV drip shooting straight tequila into my veins? I need a drink, maybe two or th—' Her voice tailed off and I immediately picked up on a new, twitchy vibe. 'Just for a change,' she hissed, gesturing towards the barbeque area, where Justin was deep in conversation with a woman.

'What change?' Nate asked, absolutely clueless. I didn't have the same rapid response. My eyes had to follow Sasha's gaze, until they fell on Justin, talking to a familiar blonde bob. I really had to find out her name so I could stop referring to her in my head as a highlighted hairstyle.

'I met her at your 30th birthday party,' I said, keeping my tone fairly nonchalant in the hope it would rub off on my pal with the irritated demeanour. It didn't.

'Yep, she works with him. Can't remember her name. She's just always there when there's any kind of occasion or night out,' Sasha said, and something in her tone made the skin on the back of my neck prickle. I decided to try to diffuse things with an opinion on blonde bob's character.

'She seemed nice. I sponged a cigarette off her.'

'You smoke?' Nate asked, shocked.

'That isn't the point here,' I retorted. I no longer had to account to him for the well-being of my lungs. 'Anyway, she's got a boyfriend. I remember her being raging because of something to do with him seeing another woman or something. I forget the details.'

Sasha's eyes narrowed on the woman now, like a crocodile coming up to the surface ready to snap at an unsuspecting floater on their holiday lilo.

'Don't you think there's something off in their body language?' she asked, not taking her eyes off them for a second.

'Whose body language?' Chloe asked, appearing at our side, catching the last comment but oblivious to everything that was going on.

I sighed as I answered her, realising this was only going to go one way. Sasha and Justin were notoriously jealous about each other, and the slightest suspicion could escalate from curiosity to open warfare in minutes, especially now that Justin's drinking had become an issue between them. 'Justin and the woman he's talking to.'

'I think there's definitely something off with them,' Sasha said, answering her own question.

I was sure there would be a perfectly innocent explanation. Unfortunately, Sasha was on a completely different page.

'Fuck it,' she said, as she marched over to join them. Nate, choosing wisely, spotted Connor standing at the bar, bunked out and made a beeline for him, while Chloe and I looked at each other, shrugged, then followed Sasha for health and safety purposes. Mostly the stranger's health and safety.

'Hi. I don't think we've met properly. I'm Sasha, Justin's girlfriend.' Even from a few feet away, I could see Justin's newly assumed expression of dread. This couldn't be good.

Chloe and I reached them just as the woman introduced herself as Madeleine.

'You work with Justin.' Sasha left that one hanging there, creating a hugely uncomfortable moment.

'I do,' Madeleine said, but there was definitely an undercurrent of hostility from her too. What the hell was going on?

'Sasha, leave it. Let's go and...' That was me – Miss Conflict Avoidance Champion 2003.

'No,' Sasha said, quietly. Bollocks. Only her friends would know that when Sasha got quiet it was the calm before the 'oh dear God, everyone duck'. 'I think,' she went on, the fakest smile I'd ever seen on her face, 'that I'd like to know what Madeleine and Justin were chatting about because it seemed very serious.'

In fairness to her, Madeleine, in her very elegant black crêpe shift dress and a Prada bag that didn't look like it came from a dodgy stall in Thailand, showed no signs at all of being intimidated. Actually, she seemed even more pissed off than Sasha.

'Fuck. No wonder I drink,' Justin muttered. 'Sasha, you don't want to do this. We'll talk about it later,' he added.

'Oh, I do want to do this,' she countered.

I decided to step in again. 'Sasha, this isn't the time. Come on, let's go and...'

'No,' she said, again barely above a whisper. 'I'm still really interested in knowing why Madeleine seems perturbed. Is something wrong? Something I can help with?'

The other woman's body language changed in an instant as she exhaled and said wearily, 'Really? You really want to know?'

Justin looked panicked, 'Madeleine, don't...'

Oh God, was this actually happening? This wasn't the time for confrontation. It was the time for small talk and musings about the weather.

'I'm here because I've worked with Justin for ten years,' she began, in a staccato, matter-of-fact, hint-of-vitriol voice. 'You know, Justin, your saintly, loyal boyfriend?' It was like a dam had burst and there was no stopping her. 'Well, for five of those years, I've been having sex with him. For four of them, he's been telling me he would leave you. For the same amount of time, he has been assuring me that you no longer sleep together. Yet, I come here, and, once again, you're playing happy bloody families, in your nice garden, with your nice house and your nice friends, and I think I've been a mug. A complete fool. Because I believed everything he said.'

I'm not religious but... oh sweet Jesus, this was a moment that required urgent divine intervention. A flash of lightning. A plague of locusts. A bloody big crater to open up and swallow us whole.

'Oh, and for what it's worth – he didn't want me here today because I'm fairly sure he's trying to cool things with us. I decided to come anyway. Nothing left to lose and a few home truths to share.'

She was getting louder and louder, and I was desperately trying to think of a way to put this genie back in its adulterous bottle. Not that I believed a word she was saying. It was ridiculous. Nonsense. Justin wouldn't do that to Sasha. Come on, they'd been together for years. Sure, they had their problems, but these long-term secret affairs were the kind of things you read about in books. If Justin hadn't wanted to be with Sasha, surely he'd just have called it a day? Why carry on? There were no kids to consider, no marriage contract to dissolve, or joint lives to rip apart. This was Sasha's house – left to her when her mum died a decade ago, five years after her dad. She'd come to an arrangement with her two brothers that they'd take the pensions and life insurance, and she'd have the house. Justin lived here, but he'd arrived with just a suitcase and could quite easily have packed a bag and left at any point.

Other people around us were surreptitiously paying attention now to what was going on and a glance at Justin's group of workmates told me everything I needed to know. Not one of them looked surprised. They knew. They all knew. That made me mad as hell. It all began to make tragic sense. The first time I met her she'd said she was having an affair with someone else's partner. Now it was becoming devastatingly clear that the lover was Justin, and the unwitting victim in the infidelity was one of my closest friends.

'True. Or. Untrue?' The words, spat out individually, came from Sasha and were aimed with lethal venom at Justin.

I could see that he was weighing up the consequences here. If he denied it, there was every chance that the ever increasingly agitated Madeleine would create an even bigger scene. If he admitted it, then he was whipping up the relationship equivalent of a nuclear fallout.

In the end, he realised he didn't have a choice. It was the moment at the end of every shite TV crime show, when the suspect admitted his crime, faced justice and the titles rolled.

'True,' he said.

The word was barely out when the sound of the slap echoed through the silence, the red outline of Sasha's palm searing his cheek.

'Fuck this...' With that, he turned and walked off, didn't even have the balls to stay and face what he'd done.

Sasha didn't respond or react. Nothing. For the first time ever, she was frozen, silent, still, as he left.

'Sasha, let's go,' I urged. How could he? Bastard. All I cared about now was getting her out of the centre ring of this circus.

But she'd finally found her voice and it was aimed at Madeleine.

'All these years you knew he was with me and you still had a relationship with him?'

'Yes.' There was a defiance there. A desperate bravado of someone on the edge of a precipice. At work, I saw many human beings pushed to beyond their tolerable level of emotional pain, and that's what I was looking at now. I recognised a woman who had been forced past her limit, who was distraught to the point of self-destruction, who saw no way out other than to walk through the fire.

I braced myself for a typical Sasha reaction – volatile, explosive, furious – but she surprised me.

'You still want him?' she asked Madeleine.

To my surprise Madeleine let out a low, bitter laugh. 'Pathetic, isn't it? But do you think I'd be here, humiliating myself if I didn't?' The words were bitter, but they were delivered with almost a plea for understanding.

'Then he's yours. Now get out. You might just be able to catch up with him. And if you do, tell him that his stuff will be cleared out of here tonight. I never want to set eyes on his cheating bastard face ever again. Or yours. Got that?'

A hint of a smile and then a flinch of something – shock, maybe victory, even relief – narrowed Madeleine's eyes, before she turned and walked, head held high, down the path that led to the gate. She had balls, I gave her that. They clearly filled the void left by her lack of scruples and empathy.

The guests who'd overheard everything made a show of resuming their conversations with the people closest to them, pretending that there was nothing to see here, nothing at all. Only we knew they'd be replaying this moment and discussing it in minute detail as soon as they were out of here. This would keep the office water cooler in gossip for weeks.

Right now, I didn't give a toss. All I cared about was what had just happened to someone I loved.

'Oh Sash,' I heard Chloe whisper, just as I felt Sasha's whole body deflate.

I thrust my arm around her waist, supporting her. 'Come on, love, let's get out of here,' I whispered, then watched in utter admiration as she smiled, lifted her head, and said, 'Let's carry this party on inside.'

With that, holding Chloe's hand on one side, mine on the other, she walked across the garden and into the house. That was an inner core of steel right there – but it was one that I knew would either melt or explode the minute we were out of the glare of strangers.

We were just about to go through the patio doors into the privacy of the house when, across the garden, I saw Richard turn, look at me, and smile as we locked eyes. He was blissfully unaware of everything that had just happened, and in that moment I knew. Just knew.

I was going to be needed here.

He was going to be leaving for Manchester. Alone.

6

The Stag Night

July 2004

'Isn't the whole point of a stag weekend the fact that it's supposed to be men only?' Chloe suggested, speaking just a little louder than usual to be heard over the background noise of the train. We were on our way from Glasgow to Edinburgh for what just might be the most bizarre event in my social history – my ex-husband's stag night. The wedding had been pushed to this summer, when no pesky siblings could steal Janet's thunder.

Sasha sighed, adopted a grave demeanour. 'Yes, but these are desperate times. Number one, Liv hasn't had sex in fricking months and Richard will be there – always good for a regret-free encounter.'

'Aw!' I yelped, a little outraged – but not too much, because it was basically true.

'And number two, Janet didn't invite us on her hen weekend, so we're doing this out of protest.'

That last part was definitely true. Janet had decided to invite her ten closest friends to a spa in Marbella for a long weekend and we hadn't made the cut. To be honest, I understood in my case. Who would want your soon-to-be-husband's ex-wife along to celebrate your impending nuptials? Yes, we made nice with each other when we were all together, but I didn't blame her for cutting me out of the loop.

The others had mixed responses to their omission from Janet's mini-break. Chloe was typically prosaic and focussed on the positives. 'She'd make us wear Lycra all weekend and there'd be a daily jog between detoxing and meditating. I'd rather be here with a large vodka and the potential for a midnight curry.'

Sasha wasn't quite as understanding. 'Cow. And after we totally welcomed her right from the very first time Nate brought her to meet us.'

'I seem to remember that you avoided her that first night because you said she was boring your tits off,' I reminded her, taking another sip of Chardonnay from the straw that was attached to a bottle tucked inside my bag.

It may be 10 a.m. in the morning, but I'd worked fifteen days on the trot, sometimes staying long after my shift had finished – NHS cutbacks combined with a norovirus outbreak had left us hopelessly short-staffed on the ward. It felt great to be able to switch off, even for just twenty-four hours, and even if it was at my ex-husband's stag night.

I had to admit, Sasha wasn't far off with her comments about Richard. It was almost a year since he had moved back to Manchester and I'd re-joined the world of the singletons, so I was looking forward to seeing him.

We'd met up twice (once when Chloe, Connor and I had gone down to visit him, and a second time when he'd come up to Glasgow for a conference and stayed over with me in his old flat – I'd taken over the lease after he left). If you added those two occasions to the number of times I'd had sex in the last year, the total would be… two. There had been a bit of a drought, mainly caused by the combination of endless unsociable shifts and free nights being spent with Sasha, to stop her stalking Justin or venturing on to some gangland network to hire a hitman. She'd been through every emotional stage in the last year. Anger. Denial. More anger. Grief. Despair. Self-Doubt. Anxiety. Courage. Determination. Blind bloody fury. On the outside she was functioning, but I knew it was a superficial veneer and it could crack at any moment.

Justin had begged, he'd pleaded, he'd promised her the earth if she'd take him back but she'd point-blank refused. If it had been a couple of one-night stands she might have found a way to forgive him, but five years of infidelity? There was no going back from that. We'd heard – and by that I mean we'd grilled Nate with such dogged intimidation that he had no choice but to tell us what he knew about his mate – that he was no longer seeing Madeleine, but that didn't matter. Sasha was done.

I wasn't though. A few weeks after he'd moved out, I'd arranged to meet him for a coffee in a little bistro next to his office. While all my sympathy and fury was on Sasha's behalf, there was no escaping the fact that he'd lied to us all. This guy had been like a brother for over a decade, and the whole time he was betraying my best friend. Even now I wanted to rant and rave and ask him how he could do it, but there was a bigger picture here. It was time someone pointed out what had been in front of us all for some time – Justin had a drinking problem. He was an alcoholic. Time to say it, tackle it and try to turn it around.

Right on cue, he'd turned up, by-passed the hot drinks, and ordered a large glass of red wine. It was more depressing than surprising. I knew what he'd done was horrendous, almost unforgivable, but I loved him and I wasn't ready to give up on him, especially when I suspected the root cause of everything was the liquid in the glass in front of him. He was defensive and aggressive from the moment he sat down.

'So... sent here to tell me what a prick I am?' he asked, his glare challenging me.

I shook my head. 'Sasha doesn't know I'm here.'

That surprised him. 'So what's the script then?' he countered.

I wondered how many drinks he'd already had today. This wasn't the lovely, funny, affectionate Justin that I'd always adored. This was the antagonistic version that usually surfaced after half a dozen drinks. There was no point trying to mollify him because it wouldn't work, so instead I got straight to the point. 'I think your drinking is out of control and I want to help you,' I said, then watched as his eyes narrowed in anger.

'I don't need any fucking help.'

'Justin, every month I've got someone in my ward, who can look back and pin-point the moment that they said they didn't need help, then drank themselves into a bed in palliative care. I care about you and I honestly don't think you'd have done the things you've done if you'd been sober. This is a disease, Justin. There are programmes, treatment centres...'

I didn't even get to finish the sentence.

'Ah, piss off Liv. Sitting there all holier than though when all of you take a drink.'

'Not every day,' I countered, then wished I hadn't because that sent him into orbit.

'Don't you dare judge me,' he raged. 'Christ, you're priceless. Why don't you just take care of your own car crash of a life and stop fucking worrying about mine?'

With that he got up, sending his chair toppling, and left.

Tears bristled behind my eyes. This wasn't him talking. It really wasn't. I knew that, but it didn't lessen the sting of helplessness that I was feeling right then. I'd tried. And I would try again. But for now, I was going to have to let him make his own way to the point when he realised he was self-destructing and chose to do something about it.

I hadn't told Sasha, and I figured it was better that way. I didn't want her to think I was choosing sides, when all I was doing was trying to help a friend that I loved, before he completely wrecked his life.

'Are you going to be okay, dealing with Justin being here this weekend?' I asked her, dreading the answer. Of course Justin was going to be here. He was still one of Nate's best mates.

'Absolutely. He's dead to me. I'm just going to act like he doesn't exist...'

Fair enough. Maybe a civil silence was the best way to go.

'... right up to the point where I snap and stab him with a cocktail stirrer.'

Or maybe not.

'You don't think you and him...' the hopeful lilt in Chloe's voice made it clear that she was going to suggest a reconciliation.

Sasha cut her dead. 'No. Never again. Not even if his dick has been washed in Dettol.'

Chloe surrendered immediately. There was more chance of us developing superpowers that could make this train go backwards than there was of changing Sasha's mind about this. On a relationship level, I totally agreed with her. Five years. That wasn't some meaningless fling, it was a double life and I was furious with him for doing that to my friend. That said, I'd still be there for him if he needed help, but I didn't expect him to call anytime soon. As soon as it was clear that Sasha wasn't interested in reconciling, and since that day I'd met him and tried to encourage him to get help, he'd cut off all contact with Chloe and I too. It was understandable. Inside Justin, somewhere far from his infidelity gene, was a good guy and he was probably mortified at what he'd done, but it was drunk Justin who was calling the shots.

Given Sasha's decimated life and my sexual drought, I'd have lost faith in the romantic process altogether if it weren't for the fact that Chloe and Connor were still blissfully happy. Even all these years later, I couldn't bear to think what would have happened if he hadn't come home that weekend. It was impossible to imagine now what Chloe's life would be like without him. There would be three single women sitting around this wine-and-snack-laden train table instead of two.

The wine was definitely going to my head by the time we reached the hotel in the Grassmarket area of the capital. The streets were packed with Australian rugby fans, having pre-game celebrations before playing an off-season friendly against Scotland at Murrayfield stadium.

We ditched our cases, then headed downstairs to meet the guys. A pub crawl wasn't the most original idea for a stag party, but the event had been organised by Justin, so we'd have been shocked if there had been any other plan.

All the usual suspects were already warming up their livers. Nate, of course. Justin – looking sheepish the minute he spotted us and seeking refuge with a couple of guys I didn't know. Connor. A few of Nate's friends and… where was Richard?

'He phoned this morning. He was called into work at the last minute so he's not going to make it,' Nate revealed. I tried not to let my disappointment show, but I was gutted on the inside. So much for my wild night of sex with an ex. And don't get me started on the fact that the painful removal of six months' worth of body hair had been a complete waste of time. I consoled myself by opening another bottle of wine and drunkenly asking the pub DJ to get a bit of Usher on. There was gyrating. Warbling. And a whole lot of miming along to 'Burn'. Like I said, it was a long time since I'd had a night out.

The next ten hours were a blur of drinking, dancing, singing and revelling in the atmosphere, despite the fact that Scotland got tanked at rugby. However, being a nation of good losers when it came to field sports, our commiserations looked a lot like our celebrations. By 2 a.m., half of Nate's workmates had disappeared because they'd copped off with a squad of Australian girls who'd travelled up from London for the game. Justin had got completely sick of Sasha making pointed digs and gone off into the Edinburgh nightlife wilderness. As the day had worn on and his alcohol levels had raised, he'd got more and more loud and developed a demeanour that was almost arrogant whenever Sasha was nearby. In short, he was being a dick to Sasha, while ignoring Chloe and me, so I was glad when he left.

The rest of us were back in the hotel bar now. I was happy. Drunk. Having fun. It had been a long time since I'd experienced those three things at the same time and it felt great. Sexy, even. Which presented an obvious problem given that Richard was AWOL and there was no one else here that could potentially fill his shoes.

My wine-fuddled brain decided that this was a good time to call it a night. Chloe was sitting on Connor's knee, smooching and laughing, so I didn't interrupt her. Sasha and one of Nate's remaining workmates had left ten minutes before, off in search of late-night food. At least, she said it was food. I had my suspicions it was probably a detour on the way to the One Night Stand Motel. And Nate... I couldn't see him anywhere. Probably just as well. I might blurt out something derogatory about Janet omitting our group from the hen night.

Definitely time for bed.

The lobby was fairly empty, the lift came in seconds, and I channelled Fergie from the Black Eyes Peas and sang 'Let's Get It Started' all the way to the fourth floor. There may also have been dancing – which explains why I had my back to the elevator doors when they opened, and took a few seconds to turn around and see Nate, sitting on a fancy velour Chesterfield chair by the floor-to-ceiling window of the landing, an incredulous grin on his face. Granted, Fergie from the Black Eyed Peas never swung her hands in the air while doing some kind of ill-advised pelvic thrust thing. Goddamn wine.

I'd forgotten how much I used to love his laugh back in the day, when we were young and I was intoxicated by this gorgeous man who was never the loudest, or the funniest, or the highest achiever in the group, but he was absolutely the sweetest, most laid-back and most decent.

'Still got it then,' he said, trying and failing to make that sound like a compliment. His amusement was contagious.

'Don't think I ever had it,' I replied, giggling. 'And if I did, it was only after a bucket of wine and it usually involved Take That.'

I plonked myself down on the chair that was opposite his, mainly because my wobbly legs were protesting at remaining upright. Through the window, the whole of the Grassmarket was still a beautiful blaze of lights, with people mingling along the street, lovers snogging in doorways and a group of men in rugby jumpers tossing an Irn-Bru bottle between them as they charged along the road.

There were a few moments of silence, which would probably have been awkward if I were sober, but in my current condition it was just the perfect space for my drunken self to formulate a response to the current situation.

'So are you going to tell me why you're sitting here? Shouldn't you be drinking yourself into a coma or doing something with strippers?'

'Nah, did all that last time.' That made me laugh again because it was so untrue. We both knew that for his stag night before we got married, he'd gone out with all the guys for a game of snooker and ended up in bed with me by midnight, watching old reruns of *The Sweeney*.

'Tell me what you're doing here then.'

He took a slug of his beer. 'Trust me, you don't want to know.'

'I do!' I had a sudden thought. 'So you are waiting for a stripper then?'

'Nope, no stripper.'

'Ah, right then.' I liked this game. Next guess. 'Are you having second thoughts? Is it because Janet didn't invite us to her hen weekend and we think she's a boot?'

One of my greatest failings is that I think I'm hilarious when I'm drunk. This was a prime example of that flawed personality trait. I knew I was being ridiculous. Of course he wasn't having second thoughts. He was Nate. He thought everything through a gazillion times and didn't do anything until he was absolutely sure it was right. I blamed the alcohol for my ludicrous suggestion.

'Yes. Not about the hen weekend. But about the second thoughts thing.'

'Oh.' Bloody hell. Somewhere in my inebriated haze, this had just gone from a daft, drunken quiz to a life-defining moment. I wasn't sure I was the right person for this job. Shouldn't it be a pal? I'd have thought 'ex-wife' would be pretty far down the 'appropriate confidante' list. Okay, right things to say in this moment?

'I'm sure it's just cold feet. Everyone gets them,' I offered.

'I didn't when I was marrying you.'

Fair point. I went back in for a second try.

'It's because you've been married before and it didn't work out. You're more cautious this time because you don't want to make another mistake.'

'Last time wasn't a mistake.'

Oh. That took the wind from my attempting-to-be-pragmatic sails. Somewhere inside, it made me warm and fuzzy to think that he didn't regret marrying me, even though it hadn't lasted forever.

I mentally swatted away the distraction. Back to the matter in discussion. My heart was breaking for him. What a nightmare. I kept going back in with more attempts at reasoning, while realising that the conversation was definitely having a sobering effect on me.

I took a deep breath and came up with my next possible explanation. 'It's the drink. It always makes you maudlin.'

'I'm not drunk.'

'Right. Look, it's just a temporary mind-blip. You'll wake up in the morning and you'll remember all the reasons that you want to be with Janet.'

There. That was a great line. I gave myself a congratulatory nod for that one.

'But tonight I just remember all the reasons I wanted to be with you.'

Ah, shite.

He stood up. 'I need to go.'

I knew exactly what he was going to do. He was going to call her and offload all this on her. He couldn't! Not a week before the bloody wedding.

I jumped to my feet, 'Noooooo. Don't do it.' Unfortunately, my body wasn't ready for the change in position, given that, while my brain may have sobered with the conversation, my bloodstream was still 95 per cent vino. The sway took me by surprise, the lurch forward almost floored me.

Until Nate caught me.

And then there I was, in his arms, looking up at that gorgeous face, swept up in the moment, feeling exactly like I did when I was twenty-one and every bit of me wanted to be touched by him. My arms went around his neck, my fingers went into his hair, his mouth was hard on mine. He groaned in a totally sexy way as his hands reached my arse and he lifted me. My legs went around his waist, my back was against the flocked wallpaper, and there were tongues. Probing, sexy, nipple-raising tongues.

We bumped off every wall and door as we staggered down the corridor, his legs probably straining under the weight. The key card worked first time (and in my blissful delusion I decided that was a sign) and then we were on the minibar, across the table, perched on the trouser press, straddling the sink, in the shower, and finally... oh God, the shame... on the bed.

That plan to have sex with an ex?

Right plan, wrong ex.

7

Chloe and Connor's Wedding

November 2005

The bridal party was camped out in a two-bedroom suite, with two make-up artists, three hairdressers and a waitress who very helpfully kept replenishing the drinks. Chloe's mum, Verity, and six aunts were already fully preened and prepped, and looking resplendent in outfits that were gloriously colourful and evocative of their Jamaican roots. With them sat my mother, who was also gloriously colourful because she had a policy of never leaving the house unless she was wearing at least five clashing shades of the rainbow.

I was the first to be ready, so I was sitting next to Sasha as she applied a final coat of lip gloss. We were both wearing gorgeous, one-shouldered, pale pink dresses, both of us with our hair pulled back in the kind of elegant chignon that I'd never be able to recreate by myself.

'Do you love me?' I asked her.

'Of course,' she replied.

'So you'd do anything for me?'

'Absolutely.'

I made a subtle head gesture in the direction of my mother.

'Then promise me on your life that if Ida goes anywhere near a microphone you'll take her out in a rugby tackle. And don't let her get up until someone supplies gaffer tape.'

'I'm on it,' Sasha promised, but I didn't have time to make her swear with the locking of pinkies, because she stood up and checked out her reflection in the huge, silver gilt, full-length mirror, perusing the dress with very vocal distaste. 'Pink. Honest to God. I haven't worn pink since primary school,' she groaned. 'I look like Bad Bitch Barbie.' Her comparison wasn't far off the mark. With her dramatic mane of ebony hair and trademark red lips, she did look like the evil villain in a Disney movie, crossed with a pageant queen who wanted to save the earth and put an end to world poverty.

'Sasha, stop your moaning, girl. No one will be looking at you because they'll all be blinded by the beauty of my gorgeous Chloe,' Verity chided with a raucous chuckle. Chloe's mum could get away with any amount of cheek because, firstly, we all loved her, and secondly, she and her sisters – accompanied, of course, by my mother – were the warmest, loveliest, most gregarious, naughtiest crowd at any party.

Sasha sighed. 'You're lucky I love you, V. I'm saving up the biting retorts until either you or Ida see sense and adopt me.'

'I'll adopt you, pet,' my mum offered. 'But only if you'll come with me to get Botox because our Liv point-blank refuses.'

I sighed and shook my head. It was her latest thing, one of many ideas that I filed under 'Are you sure she's my mother?' There was the naked yoga holiday. The single-and-ready-to-mingle cruise. The hair extensions that gave her the coiffure of Cher in her 'Turn Back Time' years.

'No problem Ida,' Sasha agreed, laughing. 'You'll be so happy that I'm yours. Although, obviously, you won't be able to show it because your face won't move.'

That earned another raucous chuckle from both Ida and the mother of the bride, who was – understandably – relishing every single moment of today.

Chloe was getting married. After all these years, she was finally getting hitched to the love of her life, the guy she'd met in university fifteen years ago and loved ever since. If there was ever a personification of sheer bliss, she was it.

All chatter faded away when she stepped out of the bedroom into the lounge, the seamstress who'd made her wedding dress walking behind her carrying her train. The white lace was cut in a perfect heart-shaped neckline, with a boned corset that flared into a mass of pearl-embellished tulle. On her head, a simple band of glistening diamantés. The cries that went up from Verity and her sisters could have been heard four floors away. The sight of her even made Bad Bitch Barbie stop moaning.

'Chloe, you look incredible,' I said, happiness and emotion choking my words. In my peripheral vision I saw Sasha's eyes mist over – an event that was up there with a solar eclipse and the sighting of a blue moon. I knew it must be hard for her. All those years spent with Justin, only to discover it was all a lie. And while she'd never been one to dream of her wedding day, she'd assumed – we all had – that they'd be together forever. She still wasn't over it. Two years later and she'd traded a long-term relationship for no-strings sex with whoever took her fancy. She claimed it was the way forward. 'No lies, no cheating, just the good bits and none of the crap,' she'd said.

'But wouldn't you want to have a relationship again if you met the right guy?' I'd probed, hoping to soften her approach. It didn't work.

'I'd rather remove my internal organs with a Hoover,' was the reply.

'Okay, people, let's move this along,' Chloe exclaimed, after her mum, each of her aunts and Ida had smothered her in hugs and kisses.

Although my mum did accompany her hugs with, 'Och, Chloe, love, you're stunning. This is a marriage made in heaven and it's going to last forever.' I thought that was beautifully poignant until she added, 'Unlike my Liv's,' and gave me a disappointed glance. I ignored her. If I challenged her it would only set her off on a rant that would rue my break-up with Nate, and then move on to her pain and suffering caused by the fact that I let Richard go too. There wasn't a person in the west of Scotland that she hadn't told about her daughter's 'gorgeous doctor boyfriend'. 'George Clooney couldn't shine his stethoscope,' she'd boast with glowing pride. It had taken her six months to admit to her chums at the bingo that we'd split up. I was considering getting her counselling for her loss.

I switched my focus back to the bride. When the mums and aunts had cleared the way, Sasha, Chloe and I converged in a group hug.

'Have a wonderful day, my darling,' I told her. 'I'm beyond happy for you.'

'Thank you,' she said, squeezing us tightly. 'Okay, bridesmaid instructions. Sasha don't be sad, because we all love you and your happiness will come back. But, in the meantime, even if you're really tempted, do not punch Justin. Especially in front of the minister.'

'Instructions understood,' Sasha confirmed.

'And Liv,' she finished softly. Aw, I was going to get a special comment just for me. 'Two things – do you have a battle plan to stop your mother singing?'

'I do. Either Sasha or I will wrestle her to the ground.'

Chloe seemed reassured by our strategy. 'Excellent.'

'The other thing?'

Perhaps a declaration of love. Maybe an acknowledgement of all we'd been through together in the fifteen years of our friendship. Maybe a...

'If you're going to have sex with an ex, make sure he's single.'

The others found this hilarious, as I flushed a deeper shade of rose than my dress. They'd never let me forget it. One drunken mistake. That was it. And no one would even have known if Nate hadn't called off his wedding. The morning after the stag night, I'd begged him not to tell Janet all the gory details. I'd also sworn him to secrecy about what happened, making him promise to tell no one, not even our friends. He'd stuck to his promise. Chloe reported (learned via Nate) that he'd just, really apologetically, told Janet that he was having second thoughts. Unfortunately, I hadn't kept my side of the secrecy deal. The combined interrogation forces of Sasha and Chloe had cracked me and I'd confessed all.

He'd appeared at my flat a few days later and told me the wedding was off. I'm not sure what he was expecting, but there was never any possibility of us getting back together. We'd been there. We'd tried. We'd somehow survived as friends with an episode of benefits. That was enough for me. Despite the odd wobble, I knew deep down that nothing had changed, so we'd decided to move on with friendship status intact. He'd reluctantly agreed, but I could see he knew I was right.

I was wracked with guilt for months afterwards, so much so that I'd ignored his calls and completely avoided him. What had I been thinking? Nothing. That was the point. Complete mind bloody blank. In the moment, it felt amazing – it was Nate, whom I'd loved for so long, but there was a new excitement there, a thrill, a... I stopped trying to rationalise it. I was a terrible person and that was the end of it.

Now, thankfully, that was all in the past and today I was going to think of nothing other than Chloe's happy future.

After a flurry of kisses and tears, we made our way downstairs, where Chloe's mum and aunts were waiting for a final glimpse, before they headed to their seats. We gave them a few minutes then followed them. The string quartet played the wedding march, as Sasha and I made our way up the aisle, lined with beautiful white roses, towards Connor, and his best man, Nate. I avoided eye contact. The symbolism of me walking up an aisle towards him was just too much. Instead, I glanced around the crowd at all the beaming faces. I loved a wedding. Especially if it wasn't mine.

I was almost at the front when I spotted Richard, in the second row of Chloe's side, three of her aunts on one side of him, a woman I didn't recognise on the other side. I sent up a silent prayer that it was one of Chloe's long-lost cousins. I'd missed him. Not enough to pack up my life here, move to Manchester and resume our relationship, but I missed those moments, the laughs, the love, and, yes, the sex.

I dismissed the thought. Today was all about Chloe and Connor. Nothing else mattered.

At the top of the aisle, we stood to the side and then watched as the exquisitely beautiful bride made her entrance to a chorus of cheers. I'm not sure that the minister knew what to make of it.

'Dearly Beloved...'

The beauty and emotion in the vows were enough to defy any mascara. Chloe and Connor were just meant to be together, end of story. Maybe that just wasn't in the plan for me, and perhaps I was okay with that. Perhaps. Okay, I admit it – days like this made me think it would be great to have someone in my life that I felt that way about.

'I now pronounce you man and wife.' Another cheer and it didn't stop until the bride and groom had danced – yep, danced – all the way back down the aisle and out into the reception hall.

The photographs took so long, my cheeks ached with smiling. Eventually, dismissed from the final shots of just the bride and groom, I headed to the bathroom.

I was at the marble sinks when a face I'd spotted earlier joined me. 'Liv, isn't it?'

'Yes,' I said warmly, trying my very best to be gracious.

'I'm Charlotte. My boyfriend, Richard, pointed you out earlier.'

'Ah,' I said, trying to take a mental video of this moment so that I could relay all the details to Sasha and Chloe later. Actually, not Chloe. I was fairly sure she'd be busy. First point to note? Given the evidence in front of me, I'd say Richard definitely had a type. Charlotte looked like... well, me. A little shorter, a little slimmer (damn her), but the same green eyes and long, red hair. We could be sisters. I wasn't sure if that was flattery or weird. If she noticed, she chose not to mention it. 'Lovely to meet you,' I lied. I'm a terrible person.

'And you. I was so worried about coming up here with him because I don't know anyone, but he said everyone would be lovely and they have been.'

'Of course. All newcomers are very welcome,' I said, with a smile that was intended to set her at ease. This was fine. It really was. So my ex had a girlfriend. I could deal with that. I could... With the help of a bucket of wine. I sent up a silent prayer that she didn't encounter my mother. Ida's reasons for living were firstly to find the fame and adulation that she didn't achieve first time around, and secondly, to see Richard and I get back together, so she could revert to bragging about him. There was no telling what she would do if she met this Charlotte-shaped flaw in that plan, especially after a few glasses of champagne.

I tuned back in to what Charlotte was saying. 'I know you, er, dated for a little while.'

Dated. For a little while. Is that the same as 'lived together for two years'?

Dr Richard Campbell could bloody pay for that bucket of wine.

'Ah, we did, but it was nothing. Really. We weren't at all right for each other. I'm delighted that he's met you. He looks happy.' I'm not sure any of that – except the last bit – was true.

She gave me a hug. 'Thank you. No wonder he dated you – you're so nice.'

So nice. That was me. Liv – the nice single one with the bucket of wine.

She toddled off back to her beloved boyfriend and I deliberately avoided glancing at them throughout dinner.

'What's up with you?' Sasha whispered at one point just before the speeches.

'I can't look over that way at Richard,' I said, gesturing to the table on my right. 'And I can't look left, in case I catch Nate's eye. So I'm only staring straight forward. Now I'm fairly sure Chloe's Uncle Bob…' I nodded at the rotund man at the table in front of me, 'thinks I fancy him. Pass the wine.'

She topped up my glass.

'How are you holding up?' I asked her. It couldn't be easy. Justin was already showing signs of overindulgence and throwing pleading glances in her direction. The only mercy was he'd apparently come on his own, with no new partner in tow. Unlike Dr Richard bloody Campbell. Not that I was jealous. Absolutely not.

'I'm okay,' she said, surprisingly sure. 'I couldn't give a toss. He's already half-wasted, and it just reminds me of every event we went to since the day we met. I used to think his wild ways were entertaining and fun, now they're just embarrassing and pathetic.'

'Good,' I said, relieved and, frankly, surprised at this new mature attitude. I'd been fully prepared to remove the butter knives from the table. 'You know, I've got some pretty impressive friends,' I told her, leaning over to kiss her on the cheek. 'Does this mean you're going to stop making effigies of him and stabbing them with kebab skewers?'

'Absolutely not,' she answered, deadpan. 'Have a bread roll.'

Despite the joke, I knew that she'd moved on and it impressed me. If she could look forward to a new future, I could too. No more going backwards. No more revisiting the past. Strong, brave, resolute.

Shame it only lasted for approximately four hours and another bottle of wine.

I was heading out to the lobby to ask reception if they had any blister plasters for my aching feet when I realised I was in the path of one Dr Richard Campbell, who was walking towards me looking exceptionally handsome. Damn him this time.

'Hi you,' he said, smiling that fricking adorable smile. 'We haven't had a chance to catch up.'

'No, we haven't. But I did meet Charlotte earlier. She's lovely.' If my teeth were slightly gritted, he didn't seem to notice. I instructed myself to get a grip immediately and stop being pitiful. 'Really lovely,' I emphasised. No gritted teeth this time.

'I meant to warn you about...' he couldn't quite finish the sentence, so he switched tack, '... but I didn't think I'd make it today and then I managed to get away at the last minute and...'

'Ah, there you are, handsome – I was wondering where you'd got to.' Charlotte appeared out of nowhere and attached herself to him like a strip of Velcro.

'Anyway, so... have a good night,' he said, bringing the discussion to an abrupt close.

'You too,' I gushed. 'Lovely to meet you again, Charlotte.'

It took me a good thirty seconds of resting my head in my hands while sitting on the loo to recover. On the way back, after stopping to check that, no, reception had neither blister plasters, an on-call chiropodist or – I was desperate – a roll of bubble wrap, I'd just about reached the doors back into the function suite when I heard, 'Hey.'

Nate. Clearly this was a hang-out spot for my exes.

'Hey,' I replied, and I couldn't help smiling. He was so handsome, with his wide shoulders and his chestnut hair, flecked with a tiny bit of grey now, flopping over his forehead. And I'd always been a sucker for a man in a kilt. Except Chloe's Uncle Bob, whom I'd been dodging since the wedding dinner.

'You're avoiding me,' he said, but it wasn't a reproach, more a gentle statement of fact. Today was the first time we'd been in the same room for almost a year and I'd been studiously keeping out of his way all day.

'I am,' I replied, hoping the smile softened the words. 'I'm still so sorry about you and Janet.'

A hint of sadness now. 'It wasn't right. To be honest, even if you and I hadn't...'

'Dear God, don't say it out loud,' I begged. 'The mortification could kill me.'

If there was a silver lining, it was that the excruciating embarrassment was taking my mind off my blisters. He took a slightly different angle.

'If we hadn't met that night…' he continued, with the emphasis on 'met' making me laugh. He was so easy to be with. And did I mention the kilt? '… I'd still have called it off. I'd known for a while it wasn't what I wanted, but we got caught up in the whole wedding thing and I bottled out and convinced myself it was right. It wasn't though.'

'How did you know?' I asked, genuinely interested.

'Because I never felt about her the way I felt about you.'

That stunned. Or stung. I wasn't sure which. For a few seconds I was speechless, until he carried on…

'Look. I'm not saying I feel that way about you now. I know it's over between us and I'm glad there are no bad feelings. This isn't an attempt to get you back, I promise. I just mean that when we got married I was so sure, and I couldn't wait to be your husband. I didn't feel that this time. Just took me a while to realise.'

I exhaled, relieved that this wasn't a build-up to a discussion about getting back together. We'd been there, done that, and got the divorce. Lesson learned. Even if I did miss him sometimes.

A grandfather clock in the corner struck eleven, and the lobby was filling with people wandering in and out of the wedding reception. I spotted Sasha and one of Connor's groomsmen heading in the direction of the residents' bar.

But back to Nate. I made another attempt to smooth things between us.

'For what it's worth, I'm genuinely sorry. And whoever ends up with you, Nate Jamieson, will be a lucky woman because you're a good guy.'

'You mean, apart from the fact that I slept with my ex-wife

on my stag night, called off my wedding and broke my fiancée's heart?'

It was wrong to laugh, but I couldn't help it. 'Yeah, but apart from all that, you're a catch.'

We moved to the side of the corridor to let a group of Connor's cousins past us.

'My ego thanks you,' he said, grinning. I realised we were close enough that I could feel his breath on my face.

That's when it happened again. That little bubble of excitement, of danger, and of really enjoyable bendy stuff being right there in front of me. This was the first time I'd been physically turned on in months. Months! I mean, what kind of life is that for a thirty-four-year-old woman?

But it was Nate. And I couldn't go on making the same bloody mistakes. I was better than this. Hadn't I made a vow only a few hours before to stop revisiting the past?

Did I mention he was wearing a kilt?

'I'm glad we're okay,' I told him, truly meaning it.

Then it happened. Coming from inside the wedding suite, was the unmistakable sound of my mother, belting out the opening bars to 'Pretty Woman'. Sasha and I had taken our eye off the ball and now it was too late. The only option was to hope Chloe was close enough to unplug the microphone.

'Ida?' Nate asked, grinning. She'd been his mother-in-law for many years and he'd always thought her spontaneous performances were hilarious. I stuck with 'mortifying and completely bloody unnecessary'.

'Indeed,' I replied, eyes closed, head shaking.

'Are you going to intervene?' He was also familiar with my attempts to stop her hijacking every event by finding a stage and bursting into song.

'Nope, it would be like standing in front of a runaway train – one that's singing Roy Orbison's greatest hits. So I'm going to ignore it and hope it stops. Actually, I'm just going to head upstairs to change my shoes. My feet are killing me.'

We hadn't broken eye contact the whole time I was saying that. 'Okay,' he said. How could one tiny word be so loaded?

Don't do it, Liv. Do. Not. Do. It.

'Want to come keep me company while I change?' I heard myself say.

Without breaking our gaze, he nodded slowly, sexily.

I did it.

Again.

8

A Late Night in Hospital

August 2006

The hospital ward was quieter than I'd expected it to be. I closed my eyes, trying to distract myself from what was happening.

Come on, Liv. You've got this. You've got it. Take a breath. Then another.

Over the years, I'd developed a coping mechanism for keeping my emotions under control when I was working. I was no use to a patient if I was crumbling or breaking my heart over the sadness of what was happening to them. When I was on the edge of losing it, I'd learned to channel my thoughts elsewhere, sometimes to a moment that I was planning for the future, sometimes to the past.

Tonight, I needed that detachment more than any other. I chose the past, drawing on every bit of focus I possessed to concentrate on the memory playing out in my mind.

Six months ago. Just after 9 p.m. in the evening. At the end of a busy shift. Sasha called just as I was heading to my car, looking for someone to vent to.

'You're never going to believe who I met tonight?'

'Don't make me guess. I'm so tired that if it's not Ida or Nate, I'm all out of suggestions.'

'Madeleine.'

Any particle of my being that had even a smidgeon of energy left, duly deflated. It was… I tried to count it up… almost three years since the split with Justin and the last thing Sasha needed was a reminder of it, because much as she adopted a Teflon veneer and claimed that she was over it, I knew that the memory was still red raw and prone to blistering.

'Where? Why? And what happened?'

'Frozen food aisle at Tesco. I know – not my most glamorous moment. But at least I was picking up a toffee pavlova. She was standing holding two pounds of frozen haddock.'

A bubble of laughter got caught in my throat. Only Sasha could tell a high-stress story and make it funny. 'So what did you do?'

'It went from daggers at dawn…' I could imagine that, '… then I shot over a couple of caustic comments and asked if they were back together.'

'Are they?'

'Nope. She said he never forgave her for telling me and it ended their relationship.'

Strike one for the good guys.

'And then what happened?' I couldn't bear to think. My money was on a violent encounter between a pavlova and a haddock that ended with two shamed faces being escorted from the premises.

'We went for a cup of tea.'

'No!'

'We did. She suggested it and I thought, fuck it, why not. I wanted to know all the details. I kicked him out so soon after I found out he was shagging her that I always felt I didn't know the whole story.'

'So tell me everything. Actually, hold that thought. Before you tell me, let's talk about what's really important,' I said.

'What's that?'

'Did you buy the pavlova?'

That made her cackle. 'I did.'

'I'll be there in twenty minutes to help you dispose of it.'

I'd gone, I'd eaten, I'd listened, I'd scoffed some more, then I'd gasped in astonishment at the conclusion of the story.

'So basically, he told her that he only stayed with me because he couldn't afford to buy me out of the house...' Sasha revealed.

'But it was never his house! That was your house from the start, your parents' house before that.'

'I know. He told her a whole load of bollocks. He promised her that we slept in separate rooms and that as soon as he could afford it, he was going to buy me out, sell the place and then set up a happy little love nest with her.'

Even now, after everything I'd learnt about Justin, I still found it difficult to believe that this guy we'd known, loved and trusted could be so duplicitous.

'But...' she paused, and I could see that she was struggling to say something. 'Madeleine still works with him – although, they don't speak any longer – and she says he's drinking himself into oblivion.'

So he still hadn't kicked the booze. I felt a pang of sorrow. I'd treated far too many people whose lives had been wasted because they had been unable to control their alcohol addictions. I may be mighty pissed off with Justin, but I would still be there for him if he were in trouble. We were family. He was just, right now, being the brother who'd gone way off the rails and who was refusing to let us help him.

'So what are you going to do?' I asked.

She shrugged. 'I'm not sure. I don't know that it's my place to do anything.'

We left it there, but it was hours before either of us fell asleep. It was one of those nights that I wanted to speak to Nate, to ask him if Justin was okay and if there was anything we could do for him. I totally understood Sasha's hurt and pain, but I still couldn't completely shut the door on Justin. He was a sick man. He just didn't realise it.

Next morning, I'd felt dreadful. Really, really dreadful. Vomiting, dizzy, exhausted. Chloe had popped up to my ward to return my box set of Quentin Tarantino DVDs, and couldn't hide the startled expression when she saw me.

Under protest from the unwilling patient, she took my temperature, checked me out and fired a dozen questions about symptoms at me. I'd answered, then tried to brush her off.

'I'm fine. It's Sasha's fault. She's obviously trying to kill me one pavlova at a time.'

Even saying the word 'pavlova' made me retch.

'I'll be back in a minute,' Chloe had said, then disappeared, only to return five minutes later brandishing a pregnancy kit. This had to be a bad joke. It definitely wasn't needed and who had one of those lying around anyway?

'You just happened to have one...?' I'd asked.

'We've been trying. I bought it for me.'

'Oh Chloe, that's amazinnnnn...' I had to make another dash to the loo.

When I'd crawled back out of the cubicle, I'd refused to take it. 'I'm not pregnant! Nate used a condom. I'm not some naïve teenager, Chlo. I'm a fricking nurse, for God's sake!'

'I'm not saying you are, but condoms are not fool proof.' She wasn't telling me anything I didn't know, but I was sure she was wrong. It was a ridiculous notion. Ludicrous. Even if there had been that tiny moment of exposure before we'd actually got to the 'putting the condom on' bit. It was a split second. I mean, the chances were practically zero.

Practically.

Five minutes and a whole lot of coercion later, the second blue line told me what it thought of 'practically'.

Fast forward to right now, back in the present, in a hospital ward, as a sharp pain on my right side made me groan.

Come on Liv, I told myself again. *Stay with it. You've got this. You have.*

Another memory. A week or so after the first one. I'd knocked on the door of the house Nate and I had lived in when we were married. I should have called to tell him I was on the way over, but I wasn't sure that I'd have the courage to actually do it. His car was in the driveway, so he was home. Every instinct was telling me to run, but this wasn't about me anymore. My stomach was churning as I heard his footsteps, then the lock turning and… Bugger, what if he wasn't alone? What if he had someone there, a woman, a new girlfriend? He had every right to do that. That would be an awkward conversation. 'Hi, hope you don't mind if I have a quick chat to my ex-husband – I just want to let him know I'm having his baby.'

Where would I even start with that? This was going to shock the life out of him. It had taken me hours to regain the power of speech after that blue line had shown up, and days before I actually believed it. I'd fretted, I'd had sleepless nights, and there had been a few moments of outright panic, before chinks of excitement started to drown out the doubts. Now I was all in. I hoped Nate would be too, but I was prepared to go it alone if he wasn't.

'Hi,' he'd said, unable to hide his surprise. He was in his standard uniform of grey cotton sports shorts and a varsity T-shirt. His hair was short again, now that the summer holidays were over and he was back at school. He'd be the teenage sixth-formers heart-throb, no doubt about it.

'Hi,' I'd croaked, because I seemed to have temporarily lost the power of my vocal cords. 'Wondered…' Cough. 'If we could…' Cough. 'Have a chat.'

He'd nodded. 'Sure, but only if you don't have some weird bubonic plague that will cut me down in my prime. You sound terrible. Have you got the flu?'

'Something like that,' I'd answered, appreciating his concerned expression. I followed him into the hall, biting my tongue not to comment on the beautiful wood panelling and gorgeous wallpaper above it. Nate hadn't the first clue about decorating, so I knew that must have been Janet's work. Before she jogged off.

We'd headed into the living room, and it was a small victory when, in the midst of a sea of new decor and furnishings, I spotted a print on the wall. It was only small. A black and white scene of a beautiful sunset over water, an image that I knew so well. We'd bought it on one of our first days together, when we'd jumped in the car and headed down to a village on Loch Lomond called Luss, the same village we'd later married in. We'd sat on the edge of the old wooden pier in the rain, and talked all afternoon, glad to be away from university and the rest of the world for just one day. I'd known then that I loved him, known that he was a keeper. Sad how things change. We'd spotted the print in a little gift shop and bought two, one for each of us – and we'd drawn our initials in a love heart on the back of them both. Then we'd walked through the grounds of the beautiful ancient church and stopped to read the words on a gravestone, about a group of men, Baronet James Colquhoun and four others, one only a boy, who'd drowned together in the loch in 1873. The sadness of the story made the moment even more poignant.

We'd strolled on through the deserted, winding streets, and it felt like we were the only people there. Just the two of us. All that mattered.

I've no idea when or how we lost that, but it was long before I'd packed the second print away and moved out of our home. It still lay in a box in my loft, with everything else that had sentimental value from my time with Nate. A decade of cards. My wedding photos. Every note he'd ever written to me.

'Do you want something? Tea? Coffee? Actually, I don't know why I asked that because I'm not sure if I have either of those things.' He was strictly a water, milk, beer guy.

'I'm fine, thanks.' Again, it was a struggle to get the words out as my larynx appeared to have constricted to the size of a straw.

There was a pause as he waited for me to explain and I waited to see if the ground would open up and swallow me. It didn't, so I knew I had to go for it.

'Okay. I have to tell you something…' I started.

'Oh Christ, is it Ida? Is she ill?' His genuine concern made my heart melt. I blamed the hormones.

'No, no, Mum is fine. She's indestructible in fact. As always,' I'd said. Ida had loved him, but she had eventually come to terms with the divorce thanks to Dr Richard Campbell. She still hadn't got over that split and I was going to have to break it to her that the Richard option definitely wouldn't be back on the table now. Although, perhaps the prospect of a grandchild would make up for it and Nate would once again take the 'favourite' slot.

The words got stuck again, until I'd blurted, 'I don't know how to say this…'

'You're ill?' he'd guessed, concern oozing.

'I'm pregnant.'

'You're…' Now it was his words that were stuck. I couldn't take my eyes off his face as I waited for the reaction. I knew him so well and I could always tell what he was thinking. And right now he was thinking…

'Wow. That didn't even make the top ten of things I thought you were here to say.'

'I know it must be a bit of a shock.'

'And is it… I mean, who… Erm, do you think…' He couldn't say it in case he hurt me.

'Yes, it's yours. Definitely.'

'Wow,' he'd said again. I wasn't sure if it was a delighted 'wow' or a horrified 'wow', so I didn't say anything for a moment. After a few seconds, I realised he was still just standing in front of me, looking at me, as if he were waiting for me to say something else. So of course, at that point I started to ramble.

'I know this is a huge shock and you'll need time to adjust and I'm not looking for anything from you at all. I mean, other than seeing the baby and being its dad. But I had to tell you because… well, it's half you, so even though we're not married anymore and we're never getting back together, I wanted you to know from the start so that you have time to come to terms with it and…'

'I don't need to come to terms with it,' he'd said, quietly.

Bollocks. Had I misjudged him altogether? Was he going to want nothing to do with me or the baby? It wasn't such a long shot. In all the years we were married we'd barely even discussed having a family, other than to throw out the occasional casual comment about it being something we'd do one day. Maybe now that he was older he'd decided that his life was perfectly fulfilled without kids and I'd just come and thrown a positive pregnancy test into his future.

'You don't?' I'd stuttered.

He'd answered by wrapping me in a bear hug. 'This is amazing news, Liv. A bit of a shock, but amazing.' I could hear the incredulous laughter in his voice. 'And no matter what, we'll figure it all out and make it work. It'll be great.'

I wasn't a crier, but tears had sprung to my bottom lids.

That, right there, was why Nate Jamieson would make an incredible dad.

There was no time for tears now. Not, here, tonight, while I lay in this hospital bed, using every technique I could conjure up to keep myself focussed and together, and to manage the panic and pain.

There was a knock at the door, then the midwife, Jane, popped her head around.

'Liv, you've got a visitor,' she said, smiling, before beckoning Nate in the door.

He strode over and immediately took my hand. I could tell from the slight sheen on his forehead that he'd been running.

'I got here as quickly…'

'It's fine,' I reassured him. 'We've got a little while to go yet.'

'I'll pop back in ten minutes and see how you're doing,' Jane said, before her head disappeared from view.

Nate's furrowed brow told me he was concerned. 'Are you okay?'

I nodded. 'I am. Although I might not be in about…' I looked at the clock that I'd been using to time my contractions, '… eight minutes, so you might want to brace yourself.'

'Don't worry,' he said. 'I've got you.' He put his hand on my stomach. 'And I've got you too,' he told my bump. Our bump.

I had no idea how the future would play out for us, but right here, right now, I was just grateful that he was the one holding my hand. We could do this. Just me, Nate, and our baby…

'Don't worry, I'm here!' came the screech that accompanied the whirlwind that blew into the room, followed by a concerned midwife.

'Liv, I'm sorry, I couldn't stop her.'

'It's okay, Jane,' I said, trying not to sigh. 'This is my mother.'

Jane gave me a look that I interpreted as 'rather you than me'. It wasn't the first time I'd seen it in my life.

'Right,' Ida proclaimed. 'Nate, budge up and give me room,' she said, dislodging Nate from his position by my side. 'In fact, is there anywhere you could get a cup of tea? Hospitals always make me thirsty. And I like to have a cuppa when I'm putting my make-up on.' At that, she pulled a cosmetic case from her bag and began touching up her visage. 'Liv, pull your hair back, darling, and I'll sort you out too. You could do with a bit of colour.'

Unreasonable. Self-centred. Demanding. Stroppy. Single-minded. Immature. With poorly developed decision-making skills.

After decades of dealing with my mother, bringing up this baby would be a doddle.

9

The Ceremony

May 2007

The pews were full and the organist was warming up his fingers with what sounded vaguely like 'All Things Bright and Beautiful'.

Sasha exhaled. 'Jesus… no offence,' she looked heavenward, 'but whoever wrote that song had never heard this organist at work.'

'Sasha! You can't say that in church!' Chloe chided.

Despite the solemnity of the surroundings, I dissolved into fits of giggles.

'Right, are we ready? Come on, little guy, we've got this,' Nate said, scooping nine-month-old Finn out of his pram. Yep, it had taken us a while to organise the christening. My heart panged a little. Nate was so handsome in his suit, and Finn couldn't have been more gorgeous in his little soft white trousers and shirt. Of course, there was a good chance that he'd vomit over them at any point in the proceedings, so I was keen to get things underway.

Sasha opened the door and gave my mum, standing up at the front, the prearranged signal. I'd indulged her. I couldn't help myself. More accurately, I couldn't face the sulking if I hadn't.

In fairness, Ida loved her grandson even more than she loved the spotlight. Just. So there she was, utterly resplendent in a cerise hat so large it could double as a satellite dish, standing at the microphone belting out Stevie Wonder's 'Sunshine Of My Life'. The organist appeared a touch put out that he'd been ordered to stand down. Ida didn't need a musical accompaniment. There wasn't an audience she couldn't wow, or a room she couldn't win over with that voice. At least, so she believed. This morning it was working. By the time she got to the chorus, the whole congregation was singing and swaying in their seats.

They said that when you became a mother, you understood your own mother so much more. I didn't, she was as much an enigma as ever, but I did find myself judging less and appreciating more. She'd been great with Finn. Of course, she wasn't for babysitting overnight, or handling the food shifts, but she took him out regularly and paraded him around at every opportunity. I was grateful for the break. Three months after Finn arrived, I'd gone back to work on half-shifts, then increased it to full shifts at six months. The hospital staff day-care centre was a lifesaver during the days, and Nate took over when I was on a back shift or a night shift. So far, we were working it out, but I knew that it wasn't Nate's idea of the perfect scenario.

He'd made that clear last week.

I'd just come home from work, tired and drained and desperate to sleep. Being back on full-length shifts was tough, especially when Finn wasn't sleeping through the night yet.

I was touched, though, to see that Nate had really made an effort. There was a lasagne in the oven, a salad in the fridge, and Finn was fast asleep in his cot. Nate hadn't stretched to washing, ironing or any of the other things that needed doing, but nevertheless I was grateful.

He dished the lasagne into two bowls, then scooped the salad up with huge spoons and shared it between us.

'So I've been thinking – and hear me out before you say no...'

I was aware that conversations that started that way rarely went well.

'Okay,' I promised. My fingers may have been crossed.

'School breaks up in four weeks and I'll be off for six weeks. How about if you and Finn move back into the house for the summer? That way, I could do the night shift and be there for him whenever he needs me, instead of coming over here at allotted times.'

On the face of it, it was a perfectly reasonable, some may say great, idea. But somewhere between fatigue and logical thinking, claxons were sounding in my head.

'And this would be temporary?' I asked. I knew him so well that I saw the flinch that told me there was something beneath this. 'Ah,' I said, understanding.

It took him a moment to decide the best way to play this.

'Look, Liv, I'm not going to lie to you – I do think about getting back together. We almost made it last time, didn't we? And the fact that Finn's here shows that we weren't really over.'

I was too tired to have this discussion, I really was, but letting it hang there would only prolong the uncertainty.

Of course I'd given it thought. In many ways it made perfect sense, tying everything up in a neat little bow, just Nate, Finn and me, our family.

It could be fantastic.

But what if it wasn't right? What if we got back together now – and let's face it, that wouldn't even be on the table if we hadn't had Finn – and then in two, or three or five years' time we realised that the problems we had seven years ago still existed? Would I walk away from the life that Finn had become used to? Or would I settle for a relationship that still left me unfulfilled, and spend a lifetime regretting going back?

I didn't know the answers, and until I did, until I was 100 per cent sure of what the right thing was, then I wasn't going to risk making the wrong move and screwing up my life, Finn's life, or Nate's life either.

He deserved to be with someone who adored him in every way, not someone who was there because it was the sensible place to be.

My head started to hurt as I tried to put together the right answer.

'I love you for thinking all this through,' I said. 'And in so many ways it makes sense...'

'But?' he said, with real sadness and I realised he knew what was coming.

So I explained everything. That I wasn't sure, that I didn't want to make the wrong decision for the right reasons, that I loved him, but I wasn't sure it was the kind of love that could sustain a lifetime together. And the whole time, I felt like Cruella de Vil, kidnapping puppies.

'Tell me honestly,' I asked him, 'are you 100 per cent, absolutely positive about us? Would you have been at my door, begging for us to get back together if Finn wasn't here?'

His hesitation was enough of an answer. He ran his fingers through his hair, already getting longer as we approached the summer holidays, and sighed. 'I don't know,' he said truthfully. 'But I feel like this life we're having is in limbo. We're not together, but we're not apart.'

I understood what he was saying and I could see now that it wasn't fair in the long term for either of us.

'Getting back together just to give us a label isn't the answer either. Look, I appreciate the offer to move back in over the summer, but I think it's best if we keep our own space. We'll work out a schedule for Finn. Let's set up a room in your house for him, so you don't always need to come here. That way, we can share the sleepless nights.' I hoped that would make him smile, but it barely sparked a reaction, so I went for sincere and truthful. 'I love you, Nate, I really do, and I want you to be happy.'

'Even if it's without you?' he asked.

I nodded, hating that I was hurting his feelings. 'Even if it's without me. And look, just to get this out of the way, if you start seeing other people I won't be upset.'

I wasn't completely sure that was true, but, let's face it, I was too knackered to get upset about pretty much anything at the moment. I felt better that we'd agreed a plan, even if it was a plan to change nothing.

Now, at the church, walking up the aisle to christen our son, I hoped that we looked like a couple that was figuring things out as best they could. It had taken us almost a year to finally get round to doing this, but I was glad that we had. Neither of us were particularly religious, but I looked at this as covering bases. Nate had been christened. I'd been christened. It seemed right that Finn was too. Besides, any reason to have everyone we loved under the one roof was nothing but a blessing.

At the font, the minister waited patiently, as Ida prolonged the final note of the song until her lungs must have been fairly close to collapse. He didn't even seem to mind when the congregation burst into an enthusiastic round of applause and Ida waved like she was the closing act on the main stage at Glastonbury. It was the same minister who had officiated at Chloe's wedding, so he knew what he was getting into with another event attended by pretty much the same crowd.

Beside him were Finn's godparents, the subject of tense discussion between Nate and I in the last few months.

Chloe and Connor were indisputable choices, as was Sasha. However, Nate lobbied hard to have Justin there too.

'He's been one of my closest mates for years, Liv. He's like a brother to me.'

'A brother who cheated on one of our best friends, trashed her life and lied to us all for most of the time he knew us,' I'd shot back. Alcohol had played a huge part, but ultimately, he was responsible for what he'd done to Sasha, and I couldn't stand the thought of her being upset by having Justin thrust in her face.

'I know, I know. But I'm asking you, Liv, let me have this. I think he needs it. He's not been great over the last few months and I'm worried about him. Let me give him something to look forward to.'

That one had touched my sympathy gene. I'd been in his company a couple of times in the last year and could see how he was deteriorating. Madeleine was right about the fact he was drinking himself into oblivion. He'd always covered it up to others with parties, fun and revelry, but since Sasha had told him to leave it was like he'd lost any kind of structure that he'd ever had and now he was just a maudlin guy with an undeniable alcohol problem. Not the best candidate for a godfather. But... Maybe this would help him. Give him a reason to sober up. I couldn't refuse.

'Okay, I get it. I do. I'd hate it if he wasn't there.' It was true. No matter how badly he'd behaved, he was still the guy who'd been family for all these years and I still loved him. 'I'm not saying no, but I'll need to speak to Sasha,' I'd sighed, dreading the conversation.

I'd braced myself for a reaction that could be anywhere between fury, irritation and exasperation, but in the end, it was far simpler than I thought it would be.

'I understand,' she'd said, with totally matter-of-fact candour. 'You do?'

She'd nodded. 'If I fucked up, I mean really fucked up, had an affair, wrecked my life, even if I lied to you, would you turn your back on me?'

I saw where she was going with this. 'No.'

'So it's good that Nate isn't turning his back on Justin. I'll never forgive him for what he did, but you should. It's not like he's galloped off to some happy-ever-after existence. He's going to need his friends...'

She didn't finish the sentence, and she didn't have to. He's going to need his friends to help him get sober. To support him if he keeps screwing up. To bail him out when he inevitably gets into some alcohol-fuelled situation that ends up with a stone bed in a cold cell.

Today I was glad that he was with us. Across the font, I could see that his eyes were bloodshot, his tie was askew, but there was a glimpse of the old Justin, the guy who'd been part of us for so long.

I said a silent prayer that somehow, the responsibility of guiding my boy through his life would touch something in him and make him get to grips with his demons before it was too late.

I didn't realise no one was listening.

10

An Old Flame Relights

July 2008

I had no idea how long he'd been standing at the door of the room.

I'd straightened up Molly's sheets, then checked all her stats and marked them on the chart that hung on the end of her bed. The whole time I chatted away to her, hoping that somewhere, in some recess of her mind, my unconscious patient could hear me.

'It's almost nine o'clock, so your family will be here soon, Molly,' I told her.

There were no set visiting hours in palliative care. It was important that families could spend as much time with their loved ones as possible as their time neared its end, so we worked around whatever situation presented itself. Sometimes, there was a partner, a son, a daughter, who wanted to be here twenty-four hours a day, and that was fine. Other times, there would be a mass of people, shuttling in and out, and we weren't too strict about keeping to the maximum of four visitors in a room. Sometimes there was no one sitting by the bedside at all. Just a life that had been lived and was now going to take its last breath alone. We never knew why. It wasn't our job to investigate someone's circumstances, but no one should die alone. The sadness of that pulled me to them every time, and I'd do everything I could to be holding their hand as they passed.

'I think your Trina is going to bring in that book you like – the Maeve Binchy one – and read it to you. I might pop in and listen in my break. I love a good story. Right, Molly, I'm just going to look in on everyone else and then I'll be back. It's a busy ward today, but don't think I've forgotten about you,' I told her.

As I turned to head out of the door, our gaze met and my grin was instant.

'Richard! Hey!' Not incredibly profound, but the surprise had momentarily frozen my powers of communication. Instead of trying again, I just hugged him, and was instantly gratified to realise that he smelled exactly the same as I remembered. I just hoped the fact that I'd automatically and without forethought sniffed his neck wasn't obvious to him.

'Good to see you Liv,' he said. 'You haven't changed a bit.'

'I'm sleep-deprived, knackered and losing the battle against wrinkles, but thank you. Your delusion is gratefully received,' I joked, squeezing him tight. No more neck-sniffing this time. Eventually I released him. 'What are you doing here? And I mean that in the nicest possible way.'

'Neuro conference. Latest treatment protocols for glioblastomas.'

Our hospital was still a centre of excellence for the treatment of brain tumours, so it wasn't unusual to hold seminars here.

'How long are you here for?' It would be great to round up the others and organise a gathering. Although Richard and I had only gone out together for a couple of years, Sasha and Chloe had loved him and I knew they'd be stoked to see him after all this time. Besides, it was great to have allies when attempting to extract gossip. The last I heard, he'd married Charlotte, the woman he brought along to Chloe's wedding.

'Leaving tomorrow morning,' he said. 'Don't suppose you've got a free night tonight? We could have dinner?'

For once, the stars were aligned. Between my shifts and taking care of Finn, nights out were rare these days, but Nate's school had broken up yesterday for summer, so he'd offered to have Finn stay over at his house for a couple of days to let me get some time to myself and some sleep. I'd jumped at the offer before he could change his mind.

'I was just thinking that. Nate has Finn tonight, so that works. I'll call Sasha and Chloe and see if they're free. They'd love to see you.'

A couple of lines at the top of his nose wrinkled into a facial objection. 'Much as I love them, I was thinking maybe just us? It's been way too long since we caught up.'

'Oh.' That took me a moment to process. 'Sure. Okay. Actually that would be nice. I can bore you to death with cute stories about my toddler and you can tell me how married life is treating you.'

'Divorced life,' he interjected, with another wrinkle of the nose.

'Oh,' I said again. 'I'm sorry to hear that.' Okay, inside I wasn't. I hadn't been sitting at home in a onesie, eating ice cream and pining for Richard over the last few years, but I'd definitely missed him.

He shrugged. 'It's a long story. It'll bore you to death before we even finish our starters. Listen, I'd better get back. How about if I pick you up about seven? Do you still live in my old flat?'

'Yes, and yes.'

'Great,' he grinned, reminding me just how bloody gorgeous he was when he smiled. 'I'll book a table at that little Italian we used to like.'

'Okay then. It's a date.' The words were out before I realised they could have a different significance if taken the wrong way. 'I mean, it's a plan,' I stuttered. 'Not an actual date. A plan. An arrangement.' Dear God, make me stop speaking.

He was still laughing when he kissed me on the cheek and then headed off down the corridor.

I was grateful that the rest of the day was way too busy to give it any thought, because the risk of mild panic was high. Single Richard. Single me. Undeniable attraction on my part, not sure about his. But he had come looking for me, hadn't he? Nope, had to stop thinking like that. However, there was no getting away from the reality that it was... I counted Finn's exact age and added nine months... Two years and eight months since I'd had sex. Two years and eight months! That wasn't a drought, it was a barren wasteland.

I checked in on Molly before the end of my shift, and saw her daughter Trina, sitting on the chair beside her bed, reading the Maeve Binchy book to her mum as promised.

'I'll see you tomorrow, Trina,' I said warmly.

'Bye, Liv,' she replied. 'Enjoy your night off.' Relationships were built very quickly in this ward and Trina and I had developed a lovely rapport.

At four o'clock, I got home and dumped my bags on the kitchen worktop. At five minutes past four, I went into full-scale panic mode. Richard was coming to collect me, so of course I'd have to invite him in and the house was a disaster. I'd put off all domestic chores for the last week because I knew Nate was having Finn from today, so I'd planned to catch up over the next couple of days. My eyes went to the fetching pair of red knickers dangling out of the overfilled washing basket and I winced.

I picked up the phone. 'Chloe? Mayday. Mayday.'

'What's up?' she said, clearly amused.

'Richard is in town, he's picking me up for dinner in just under three hours, the house looks like it's been ransacked, my hair's a disaster, I've no idea where my make-up bag is, I've got nothing to wear and it's so long since I shaved my body hair that I could do with a Flymo.'

She roared with laughter. 'Look, I can't come and help because I'm heading to the clinic...'

'Shit, I'm a terrible friend. I should have asked you how you're feeling about that first.'

'I'm absolutely fine. I'm just sorting out my hormone schedule for this round, so it's nothing to get stressed about.'

Chloe and Connor were just starting their second round of IVF. She'd been devastated when the first round failed, but in true Chloe style, she'd bounced back and was full of optimism that this time would be a success.

'Okay, well, you know I'm here any time if you need me,' I promised. 'Except tonight – tonight I'm going out and being a grown-up, if I can work miracles in the next three hours. Have you got a Flymo?'

She laughed again. 'Nope. I'm sure he'll be so blinded by your beauty and charm that he won't notice you've got legs like fur.'

'I'm hanging up now. Good luck at the clinic and I love you.'

'I love you too. Have a great night and call me with a full report tomorrow.'

I hung up and attempted to squash my panic by switching into super-clean mode. The laundry basket was half emptied into the washing machine, then tucked into the cupboard it was supposed to live in. The ironing pile was thrust in next to it. I loaded the dishwasher, emptied the bins, cleared and cleaned all the surfaces, made the bathroom presentable, then ran around the entire house with a Hoover – and I did the whole lot at double speed.

House transformed, there was just over an hour to perform the same level of repair and restoration on myself. It would be touch and go.

I pulled a brand-new shaver out of the depths of my bathroom cabinet, then jumped in the shower. Ten minutes later, and a whole lot of follicles fewer, I was back out, hair and body clean and smelling of coconut body wash. I slapped on some lotion from the same range, hoping that it wasn't coconut overload that would leave me smelling like a shot of Malibu. I blasted my hair with the dryer for a few minutes until it was just damp, then left it to fall into its natural waves. My make-up bag was located under the bed, no idea how it got there, and by some divine intervention, at the back of my wardrobe I found a favourite white, off-the-shoulder top. It was made of a crêpe fabric so it hadn't crushed in the couple of years since I'd last worn it. I threw it on, added a pair of dark-wash flared jeans that Sasha had once assured me made my arse look smaller, and strappy heels. I immediately saw the flaw in the plan and slapped a dab of red nail varnish on my toenails.

I'd just added a sleeve of silver bangles when the doorbell rang. Richard had clearly made a bit of an effort too. He was looking way too good in his black jeans, with a casual white shirt, and his wavy hair had been coaxed back off his face. He was a bloke who hated any kind of hair products or fuss, so this made me strangely impressed.

'Come in, I just need to grab my bag.'

Bag! Bollocks. Hadn't thought of that. The one I used for everyday purposes was the size of a holdall and could accommodate enough stuff for a weekend break for five. It was also full of motherhood supplies: wipes, Calpol, nappy bags, et cetera. I needed to make an emergency dash back to the wardrobe and find one that was more appropriate to the occasion. This required stalling tactics.

'There's a beer in the fridge, if you fancy a drink before we go,' I told him.

He nodded. 'Sure.'

I dashed upstairs, found a black leather bag from my pre-child days, and headed down to the kitchen.

He had a beer in hand and had poured me a glass of wine from a bottle Sasha had left in the fridge when she was over a few nights before.

'Wine okay?' he asked, making no comment about the fact that I was currently delving into my everyday tote, pulling out essentials like purse, keys, and phone, and tossing them in the clutch that I'd just brought downstairs.

'Yes, it's great, thanks.'

I'd wondered if this would feel awkward or unfamiliar but it didn't at all.

I pulled out a bar stool at the kitchen island and he did the same, so he was sitting facing me.

'So how're Chloe and Sasha then?' he asked fondly.

'Chloe and Connor are blissfully happy and starting their second round of IVF, today actually, so we're praying it works this time…'

'That explains why she wasn't in A & E when I popped down to see her today. Tell her I send my love. And Sasha? Did she and Justin ever work it out?'

I shook my head. 'Nope. A five-year affair is a tough one to come back from. Sasha was done with him as soon as she found out.'

'I get that,' he said. 'Just a shame though. They were a great couple.'

'Talking of which…' I hadn't been going to raise it until later, but I was dying to know. 'Charlotte?'

'Ah, yes. Not my biggest success,' he said ruefully.

'What happened? I mean, if you want to talk about it.'

I really hoped he did – the suspense was killing me.

'She got offered an incredible job in Dubai a year after we married and she took it.'

My chin must have come close to hitting the breakfast bar.

'To be honest, I didn't blame her. Between her job and my job, we saw each other for about ten minutes every second week. The only prolonged, quality time we actually spent together was our honeymoon, and even then, there were signs that we weren't compatible. She wanted to go on walking tours.'

'Oh that's criminal. Holidays are for sun loungers and pina coladas.'

His eyes crinkled as he grinned and my libido experienced a definite lurch. And I could see by the way he was looking at me that…

Focus. Focus. Back to the conversation.

'It's a shame though to let jobs wreck a marriage,' I said gently.

'If we'd loved each other enough we'd have found a way to make it work. We didn't.'

It was a good point. Hadn't Nate and I experienced a similar lack of conviction? And hadn't the whole 'long distance relationships don't work' thing been the very reason Richard and I had called it a day when he moved to Manchester?

I kicked off my sandals, and realised I was entirely comfortable and happy right here, in this moment.

'Do you want to talk about this anymore?' I asked him.

'Nope,' he said, laughing.

'Okay. So we have two choices. We could leave now and go to the restaurant...'

He nodded. 'Or...?'

'Or we could stay here, phone in a takeaway, and...' I didn't get to finish because he leaned over, and softly put his mouth on mine and now he was kissing me so slowly and sexily it made my bangles jangle.

We never did get around to phoning in a takeaway.

11

Sasha's birthday

October 2009

'I swear to God, if a waiter or waitress comes out of those swingy doors with a birthday cake, I'm flipping this table,' Sasha warned.

'That's what I've always loved about you, doll,' I told her. 'Your carefree attitude and general love of life.'

She scowled at me, making me laugh even more. 'Just tell me how long I have to stay here, pretending to enjoy the fact that we're celebrating my ancient age...'

'Sasha, you're thirty-nine, not 109,' Chloe chided.

'... before I can go call up my personal trainer and ask him to come round and plank on top of me?'

The people at the next table didn't seem impressed by our admittedly loud cackles.

'Right, pay attention, because I have news,' Chloe announced.

'Oooh, I love...' my words drifted off to silence when I spotted Nate weaving through the restaurant tables toward us. The panic was instant. 'What's wrong? Is Finn okay? Where is he?'

Nate was supposed to have him overnight tonight, so that

Chloe and I could take Sasha out for her 'advancing years' celebration. Whether she wanted to be here or not.

Nate looked totally flustered. 'He's fine, he's fine, don't worry,' he said, doing nothing to dispel my worry at all. 'I called Maisie and she came over to watch him.' Maisie was a young student nurse I'd met when she was doing a rotation on my ward, and who supplemented her earnings by babysitting. 'I hope you don't mind, but we went to meet her at your house and she says she'll stay with Finn until you get home.'

Bang went my late night on the town, but right now I was too concerned to care. 'Of course, that's fine…'

He cut me off with, 'And I tried to call you, but it was going straight to answerphone.'

'There's no signal in here,' I explained hastily. 'So what's happened?'

For the first time he paused and took a breath before he spoke. 'It's Justin.'

'What about him?' Sasha answered, alarm written all over her face. They'd been apart for five years, but time – and many group gatherings – had mellowed her fury and they'd actually managed to get on to a civil, almost friendly footing. The hostility had all been based on pain, but I knew there was a part of her that would always care about him – especially as we could all see that, despite his protestations, his drinking was still out of control.

'I don't know the details, but he's in hospital. A&E. Apparently, he got suspended from his job today for turning up drunk, went on a bender, got into some kind of fight and now he's in hospital. He managed to give the nurses my number and they called me, but he's not in a good way. I need to go. Liv, I'm sorry…'

'Don't be! Of course you need to…'

'I'm coming with you,' Sasha blurted.

Nate was clearly taken aback by this. 'Are you sure?'

'I'm sure,' she said.

'Oh thank God,' I said. 'We're coming too.' There was no way we were leaving my son's godfather in hospital without us by his side. He was family. Good times and bad.

Chloe nodded. 'Let's go. I haven't had anything to drink, so I'll bring my car. I'll follow you there. I'll call Connor on the way.' Connor was in London on business and due back on the last flight.

Nate's shoulders sagged with relief. He'd tried to do everything he could for Justin, he really had. Even after the affair, Nate had stood by him. Justin had moved into a flat in the city centre, right next to his office, and Nate would go there, take him to the gym as often as Justin would go. Like me, he'd tried to persuade him to get help, but Justin wouldn't even consider it. And even when Justin brushed him off or raged at him, Nate still went back for more. He'd been a great friend to him when most other people would have written Justin off years ago. Even his brother, Jake, had washed his hands of him after too many drunken fights and late-night arguments, and so had all the mates who used to love his partying ways when we were younger.

Nate – and to a lesser extent Connor, Sasha, Chloe and me – were all he had left.

We arrived at A & E and were shown straight into his room, thanks to Chloe's inside connections. This was her ward, and she automatically switched into work mode, getting a full update from the staff and checking all his stats.

Even without the information, I could see he didn't look good. He was conscious, but he had dressings on his head and face, one eye purple and swollen shut. His knuckles were covered in blood, his clothes dishevelled and stained deep red, and somewhere along the line he'd lost his shoes. This poor soul lying here was about as far from the young, gorgeous cheeky twenty-three-year-old we'd first met as it was possible to be. How had it got this bad? I felt a twinge of guilt. Why had I not done more to help him? I'd tried, we all had. It was too little too late to wish I'd tried harder, but that didn't stop me from wishing that I could press rewind and get the old Justin back. Beside me, I heard Sasha give an involuntary gasp, and I knew behind her deathly calm, her heart would be racing. And breaking.

Sasha went immediately to his side and took his hand. 'I'm... am...' He tried to speak, but his words were slurred and he was clearly struggling, so she stopped him. 'Don't say anything,' she said gently. 'We've got you. It's okay. It's all going to be okay.'

He closed his one functioning eye with a wince.

Only a few minutes later, the porter arrived to get him down to X-ray. Chloe went with him, keen to get answers as soon as possible. They were back in less than an hour, but it felt like ten, as we sat in silence on plastic chairs, my hand clutching Sasha's. Justin was out cold now, so Chloe gave us the run down on the results. 'Two broken fingers, three broken ribs, a broken nose and multiple bruising and soft tissue damage. But, thank God, his head seems fine, no skull fractures. They're going to monitor him really closely overnight for any signs of deterioration and do a CT tomorrow just to be sure there's no other head trauma. In the meantime, they're just getting a bed ready in the admissions ward, and they'll take him upstairs.'

Sasha gestured to the bed. 'Is he unconscious or sleeping?'

'Sleeping. His blood alcohol level is extremely high,' Chloe said, stating what we all already knew. 'So he's going to be groggy for a while.'

She'd barely got the words out when Justin opened his non-swollen eye, made a gurgling noise, then tried to speak.

'Oh Christ,' Sasha whispered, and I knew what she'd seen. When he'd opened his mouth this time we could see that his top four teeth were missing.

If there was such a thing as rock bottom, this was it.

Chloe, still in work mode, was the first one to speak. 'Hey you,' she said, gently and with a warm smile. She was a total pro, even now. An outstanding nurse. 'You had us worried there. The test results look good though. You're a bit bruised and you've got some injuries, but you're going to be fine.'

His eye suddenly became blurry with tears. On the other side of Justin's bed, Nate stepped forward and placed his hand on his friend's forearm.

'All right, mate,' he said, not swaying from their standard greeting despite the fact that Justin was very far from being allright.

He tried to nod his head but winced with the pain. Perversely, I knew it was a good sign that he was responsive and awake, albeit still groggy and a bit disoriented, but I was also all too aware that with this level and type of injuries, the next twelve hours would be crucial in establishing the exact extent of the damage.

His eye slid to the side and then began to ooze tears. 'Sasha?' he whispered.

Chloe moved out of the way so Sasha could step forward and take his hand.

'You are a fricking nightmare; do you know that?' She was hurting for him, but she knew that gushy sympathy wasn't the way to go with Justin. Her bedside manner needed work, but it had the desired effect.

He winced again as his shredded mouth raised at the edges. He murmured something, that none of us caught.

Sasha leaned in closer. 'What did you say?' she asked.

It took him a few seconds to find the strength to answer. 'Stay,' he said, before exhaustion or concussion claimed him and he closed his eye again.

'Will they let me?' Sasha asked Chloe.

'Let me go make a call and find out who's up in the ward and what room they're putting him in.'

She'd just left when the door opened again, and a doctor came in, reading a chart as she entered. It took a moment before she noticed we were there. 'Oh, sorry, I didn't realise...' The moment of recognition was instant for both of us, but I was the first to articulate it.

'Francine!'

'Liv!' I saw her compute the rest of the scene. 'Family?'

'It is.' I nodded. Family I'd chosen for myself, but family nonetheless.

'Okay. We'll take care of him,' she replied.

Francine. The young girl I'd found in the toilets a million years ago. Chloe had nursed her immediately afterwards and a couple of years later she'd told me that Francine had decided to train to be a doctor. She'd obviously done it. In a different time and place I'd be delighted for her.

'Chloe said you were a doctor,' I offered.

'Neuro,' she said. 'But today's my first day here. I've been working in London since I qualified.'

'I'm really pleased everything worked out.'

'Thanks. Me too.'

Our eyes met and we both knew we were talking about more than just her career.

With no need for more words, she flipped back into doctor mode. 'I just want to check on Mr Donnelly.' She was talking to me, but I could see that her mind was already on Justin. She was reading stats, taking pressures, lifting his eyelids and checking reactions and… 'I'm not happy with this,' she said, almost under her breath. Then to us, 'Listen, I'm going to have him taken up for a CT right now…'

'It was scheduled for tomorrow,' I told her, in case the notes hadn't been updated by the A & E doctor yet.

'I see that, but I want to take him up now, just to be on the safe side,' she repeated, calmly and kindly. She clearly didn't want to alarm us, but something was wrong here. She was obviously seeing something that the A & E doctors had missed, or something that was just developing. With this kind of trauma, anything was possible.

Anxiety began to twist my gut.

'Take him now,' Sasha blurted. 'Do anything. Anything you can.'

Francine rushed out of the room and within minutes, two porters arrived to wheel him out.

When Chloe got back, we filled her in on what had happened and she immediately made a call. 'Let me know as soon as you have the results,' she said to the person on the other end.

It was two hours before we heard. There was a bleed on Justin's brain and Francine had taken him straight to theatre to operate. I had a sickening tug of guilt that I hadn't spotted it, and I could see from Chloe's stricken face that she felt the same. In reality, not only could these things develop extremely rapidly, but we weren't in charge of his care, so hadn't examined him, leaving it to the staff who were treating him, all of whom I trusted implicitly. His level of intoxication would also have masked many of the typical symptoms of a brain bleed, making diagnosis even more difficult. Right now, that was no consolation though.

Sasha was grey as she listened. 'Can I stay here?' she asked.

Chloe nodded. 'I'll take you to the family room.'

'I'll stay too,' Nate said. 'Liv will you…?'

I knew what he was going to say. Someone had to go home and be with Finn, and let the babysitter away. Justin was Nate's best mate – he had to be here for him. I checked the time. Almost midnight. The operation would be several hours. I could keep in touch with him during the night and come back first thing in the morning.

'Of course, I'll go home and let Maisie away. Text me if you hear anything.'

'I'll take you,' Chloe offered. 'I'm on an early tomorrow morning too, so I'll be back at 7 a.m.'

She also knew there was nothing to be done for the next few hours and the best thing she could do was to go home and get some sleep before her shift.

Chloe and I guided Nate and Sasha to the family waiting room, got them tea and food, and then hugged them goodbye. Chloe stopped at the nursing station to say thank you and goodbye, then we headed outside.

We'd just started walking down the path to the car park, when a car screeched to a halt in front of us and Connor jumped out.

'Sorry! We ended up sitting on the runway for two hours and my phone died. I only got your message when we landed and I charged it up in the car. Is he okay?' He wrapped his arms around Chloe and hugged her. 'Are you okay?'

'I'm fine, but Justin's in surgery. He's in a pretty bad way. Nate and Sasha are going to wait until he's out of theatre, but I'm going to go home and get some sleep before my shift tomorrow.'

'Can I go in and see them?' he asked.

Chloe nodded. 'They're in the family waiting room. Ask at reception and they'll give you directions.'

'Okay, I'll see you back at the house. You sure you're okay?'

The tenderness in his voice was palpable. Three years they'd been married and they were more in love than ever – something Nate and I had never managed. Seeing them gave me hope.

'I'm fine,' she said softly, before kissing him and watching for a second as he ran in the direction of the entrance.

We climbed into the car and started off home.

'You know, I feel massively guilty that we let Justin get into this state,' I said, with a weary sigh. 'I feel I should have tried harder, or somehow forced him to get professional help.'

Chloe spoke without taking her eyes from the road. 'It's one thing saying that, Liv, and I know it comes from a good place, but the reality is he wouldn't accept anyone's help. I see this every weekend – people with serious alcohol problems making decisions that lead straight to a blue flashing light. The truth is, he'll seek help when he's ready. We can encourage him and support him, but we can't do this for him.'

I knew what she was saying was true, but that didn't make it any easier to hear. I also realised we were talking as if he would make a full recovery from the brain bleed. In truth, we had no idea, but it was what we needed to believe.

'I get that. But I do think we need to be around for him more. I'll talk to Nate and Sasha and see what they think. Maybe he could move into Nate's spare room until he gets his life straightened out.'

'I don't think it's a spare room he needs,' Chloe said, and I knew immediately what she was thinking. 'He needs to dry out and he needs professional help to do it.'

'You're right,' I said. 'I'll speak to a couple of the consultants on the ward tomorrow and see what they suggest.'

We spent the next few minutes in silence, both processing what had happened tonight. When I replayed it, a niggling thought popped into my head.

'Your news!' I blurted.

'What news?'

'Just before Nate came into the restaurant, you said you had news.'

She thought about it, then dismissed it. 'Och that can wait for another time.'

'No it can't,' I insisted. 'If you have anything to say, especially if it's good news, then right now we need it more than ever, because we need a distraction.'

'Oh, this is definitely a distraction,' she said, and I could see that despite the stress, pain and heartache of tonight, her eyes were glistening. There was only one thing that could cause that reaction.

'Stop the car! Stop the car right now,' I screeched. Thankfully it was late and the roads were empty, so she was able to swerve right into the kerb and pull on the brake. 'You're pregnant!' I squealed.

The conflict of tonight's emotions prohibited speech, so she could only nod.

'Chloe, that's amazing! I'm so, so thrilled for you.' I threw my arms around her and hugged her tight.

I didn't buy into the adage that everything happened for a reason. I'd seen too much needless pain and sorrow for that. But perhaps, just maybe, Chloe's news was a sign that there were new beginnings and good things around the corner for our self-chosen family group.

We just had to hope Justin made it through tonight. And that if he did, we could make him believe that too.

12

A New Arrival... or Two

June 2010

We'd given up trying to resist and had capitulated to an unshakeable force that could not be broken or stopped.

Yep, Chloe had arranged for a stage and a support band, and given my mum the full gig of entertaining the guests at the reception after her twins' christening. Twins! Joshua came first, and six minutes later, Jasmin entered the world.

They'd been warned that the IVF could result in multiple births and they were beyond delighted that it had happened. After all those years of trying, they now had two babies at the same time. Chloe hadn't slept or stopped smiling since.

Today perfectly captured their happiness. The music played, the drinks flowed and the dancing was in full swing.

Chloe's mum, Verity, and an ever-increasing group of aunties were already on the dance floor, shaking their stuff to Ida's favourite Diana Ross hits. I'd seen her set list and it had everything from Motown, to Dusty Springfield, to her beloved Cilla, to Shania Twain, Céline Dion and Mariah Carey. This was a performer who liked to share her versatility.

The ceremony had been beautiful, made even more special by a speech from Connor, in which he paid tribute to his incredible wife and thanked her for their children and the lifetime of happiness in front of them.

There wasn't a dry eye in the pews. Except for Sasha, whose toes curled in her stiletto heels at the emotion of the PDA.

'You deserve every single bit of this,' I'd whispered to Chloe outside the church. 'I couldn't be happier for you. Your twins are wonderful, your man is a keeper and they're all so lucky to have you. Oh, and your pals are great,' I'd added, making her chuckle as she hugged me.

'Dear God, two crying women. This is what hell looks like,' Sasha had drawled, before she got dragged into the group hug despite furious objections. We knew she didn't really mean it. It was all part of her unique charm.

With the formal part over, the celebrations could begin and this showed every sign of being as riotous as their wedding. Not that it would end the same way for me. I experienced an involuntary heart tug at the thought. I'd ended up in bed with Nate, a one-night stand, and nine months later Finn had been born. I wouldn't change the end result of that for anything, but I could guarantee tonight wouldn't go the same way. There was zero chance that Nate and I would hook up, because we had neither the opportunity nor the inclination.

There had been no repeat of the conversation we'd had soon after Finn was born, raising the possibility of getting back together. We'd both settled into our own lives, and while mine was still a sexual wasteland, I could honestly say that I was happy. Finn was thriving in nursery and would go to school next year. I'd been promoted to charge nurse on the ward. And Nate and I were truly good friends who were making the co-parenting situation work. We even hung out together with Finn once a week or so, when my shifts allowed. It wasn't a conventional situation, but it was working for us.

I had no idea what he did when I wasn't there and I was happy with that. Although, I did know that he'd spent a lot of time working with Justin to get him better. The op had taken so much out of him, but he'd recovered, a little weaker and shakier than before, and swore that it was the shock he needed to finally stop drinking for good.

We all believed him, especially when he'd checked himself into rehab for a three-month intensive programme. When he got out, he'd moved into Nate's spare room, and Sasha and Nate had worked together to keep him busy and make sure he got to work every day. His company, thanks to a progressive Human Resources policy, had reinstated him and even financed visits to a private counsellor. It had all been going so well until a few weeks ago, when – for reasons no one knew – he'd spectacularly relapsed, gone on an all-day bender and, after a night scouring the streets, Nate had found him, bruised and battered, on a piece of waste ground near Sasha's house.

They'd got him back into rehab and were supporting him through the relapse. Sometimes I thought it would be easier if we understood why he drank, if there was some dark episode in his past that he was hiding from, but that wasn't the case here. He'd grown up with distant, authoritarian parents, but he was definite about the fact that they hadn't been cruel. Apparently, he'd been a shy kid, and when he'd sneaked some booze from his dad's beer stash it had made him vomit the first time, and the second… But by the time he was a teenager, it gave him all the confidence he needed to have a wild, crazy social life full of friends.

We'd never guessed where his drinking was rooted, because by the time we met him, that shy, awkward kid was long gone.

Now, the sociable, sexy, fun-loving Justin was gone too.

However, Sasha was by the side of the man who remained, and she hadn't complained once. I loved her for it. This was a guy she hadn't been in a relationship with for years, one who had devastated her life in the worst way, and yet she forgave him and was prepared to invest time in helping his recovery. Sometimes I could see that the worry and emotional challenge of supporting Justin was taking its toll on her, but she would never admit it and never give in to it. That was an incredible show of character and I'd never been so proud of her. Of course, I didn't tell her that, because that would be classed as an 'emotional outpouring' and she'd be completely horrified.

Ida changed it up and launched into the opening bars of 'Hi Ho Silver Lining'. It was like a call to arms for every woman – and a few men – of a certain age, who immediately stormed the dance floor and broke into a dance called the Alley Cat, the non-traditional synchronised movement that was second only in popularity to the Slosh at such gatherings.

I was just about to throw coolness to the wind and join them, when I heard a familiar voice at my side. 'So there I was, looking for a cute redhead...' he joked.

'Keep looking because this one outgrew "cute" at least a decade ago,' I retorted, laughing. I'd barely finished when I was snatched up and hugged for way longer than a cursory length of time for someone you bump into at a christening. Not the most understated of greetings.

'How are you, gorgeous?' Richard asked.

'I'm great,' I said, my grin wide. His enthusiasm, as always, was contagious. 'How long are you up for?'

'Just until tomorrow. I was supposed to come up last night, but there was an emergency at work and I ended up in theatre until dawn. That's why I didn't make it to the church.'

'Chloe will just be delighted that you made it at all,' I told him. It was true. We all understood that work got in the way and that emergencies that forced a change of plan were an occupational hazard. It was great to see him though. I flushed just a little when I realised that the last time I saw him was that one-night stand a couple of years ago. Back then, he'd suggested again that we make it more of a regular thing, but I'd resisted. The last thing I needed was another complication in my life.

We chatted about the christening, the babies, Chloe's wonderful life, as the minutes sped by, until there was a natural lull in the conversation.

'I've missed you,' he said, and I could see he meant it.

'I've missed you too,' I replied, meaning it just as much.

'So why?'

'Why what?' I knew what he was going to say, but I was stalling in the hope of avoiding an awkward moment.

'Why do you refuse to keep in touch with me? I don't get it. I really don't.'

I sighed. Hello awkward moment. We'd already had this debate a couple of times before and I'd skirted around the answer, but obviously it wasn't enough. Time for brutal honesty.

'Because there's no point,' I answered truthfully. 'I'm a mum, and I need to be up here. Weekend jollies to Manchester are out of the question for me, and you get so little time off that it's a rare thing for you to be able to travel here. Long-distance relationships don't work, especially with jobs like ours and a child to take care of. So...' I repeated, 'there's no point. What would it be? Late-night phone calls? Raunchy emails? That would be as much as we could promise...'

'Raunchy emails sound pretty good to me,' he joked.

I ignored him and carried on. Time for the harshest part of the objection. 'And the whole time, it would stand in the way of either of us finding a relationship that actually worked for us. I'm a monogamous kind of girl. If we had a commitment – even a raunchy-email one – then I wouldn't look at another guy.'

I decided not to mention that between work and Finn, I hadn't actually had time to look at any man other than Richard for the last four years. That wasn't the point. And neither was it relevant that over the last few months I'd realised that my feelings for him had deepened with the passing of the years. When we'd first got together, he was a rebound guy, the one right after my split when I was still in a state of emotional conflict. Now that things were clearer I could acknowledge that in a different time, a different place we could be great together. But that time and place wasn't now, so I carried on.

'And I'd feel guilty that you were constricted by us too. You deserve to find someone great – preferably someone who doesn't work extended shifts, live in Glasgow, and have family commitments that leave her with approximately an hour and a half of free time a week. I'm not the person for you,' I finished, quite simply, realising that it would only complicate the issue if I told him how much I wished it could be different. There was no point in 'if onlys'. The reality was that he lived in Manchester and I was a single mum, who worked long, unpredictable hours and lived in Glasgow.

'Don't I get a say in that?' he asked.

'Nope,' I objected, with an edge of finality that made it clear it wasn't up for further discussion.

'So where do we stand on casual sex when we do happen to find ourselves in the same place at the same time?'

A wave of laughter almost made me choke on the glass of orange juice I'd been nursing since I got here.

'Casual sex is entirely acceptable,' I told him, feigning formality, 'except today when I have to take my son home and be a mum.'

I experienced a twinge of gratification that he looked disappointed.

'I see. So if we take casual sex off the table, am I allowed to just come hang out with you and your son?'

I thought about that for a moment. Finn had never been introduced to a date, because, quite frankly, I hadn't had one. However, he was used to people coming and going at our house and at Nate's place, so I was fairly sure that meeting a male friend of Mum's wouldn't scar him for life.

'I think that would definitely be something we could consider,' I replied, trying to be at least a little bit sexy. I was way out of practice.

Before Richard could reply, I saw Nate approach, holding hands with a giggling Finn, and I scooped my son up when he got to me. 'Finn, this is Mummy and Daddy's friend Richard.' Nate shook Richard's hand and gave him a warm welcome. Navigating the social niceties of meeting your ex-wife's ex-boyfriend, talking to aforementioned ex-wife, was a complicated one, but the guys had built up an easy friendship over the years so it was fine.

Finn burst into a chorus of the 'The Wheels on the Bus', as Nate chatted.

'How're you doing, Richard?' he asked.

'Great, thanks. You?'

'Yeah, really good.'

I felt incredibly lucky to have loved two such good men.

Nate turned to me. 'Listen, I was thinking I'd just take Finn home with me tonight. Would that be okay with you?'

Beside me, I could feel Richard trying not to smile.

'Why? I'm happy to take him home when he's sleepy and let you stay and enjoy the party.'

'I know,' he said. 'But Sasha is planning to leave at four o'clock to go see Justin. He's only allowed one visitor at the moment, but I thought I'd take her and see how he's doing. There's a park right next to the rehab centre that Finn and I can play in while she's visiting. Isn't there, buddy?' he cooed to Finn.

'Park! Park!' Finn, of course, replied. Nothing like a bit of emotional coercion.

'That's good of you to go with her,' I said honestly. He was a good friend to them both. 'And sure, if taking Finn with you is what works best for you, I'm fine with it.' I smothered Finn in kisses. 'I'll miss you, little guy,' I promised. It was true. I'd never get used to not having him there to kiss goodnight and then cuddle in the morning.

Not that Finn had the same pangs of sadness.

'Park!' was his delighted reply.

I leaned over with my free arm and gave Nate a hug, then

handed over our boy, and waved to him until he was out of sight.

Well, that put a whole new perspective on things.

For a start, I could have the champagne that I was about to procure from the passing waitress...

My bubbles were barely in hand, when Richard leaned in close, until the feeling of his breath on my neck made my skin tingle, and whispered, 'So without being presumptuous, can I enquire as to whether casual sex is now a possibility?'

I pretended to think about this for a long, drawn-out moment before eventually replying, 'I think we can definitely confirm that it is.'

13

Christmas at Connor and Chloe's House

December 2011

'Mama, mama, mama, mama, look!' Finn squealed, charging around the room with Fireman Sam and his bright red truck. It was this five-year-old's dream toy and he'd been beyond excited when Santa had come through.

The twins, Jasmin and Joshua, were just as hyper. They were eighteen months old and utterly adorable, already moving at speed and into everything. I had absolutely no idea how Chloe kept up with them. One had been hard work, but two? Yet, she and Connor seemed to have it sussed with a divide-and-conquer methodology that usually saw one parent darting one way, and the other chasing the twin who was going in the opposite direction.

I'd been delighted when she'd suggested having Christmas dinner at her house this year. I'd been working long shifts all month and I was back at work on Boxing Day, so it was bliss to have a day off with no cooking, no clearing up and all my favourite people in the same room. She'd even invited my mum. That thought went through my head just as the doorbell rang. It freaked me out when that happened.

Chloe headed off to answer it, and, yep, right on cue, I heard an exuberant, 'Darlings! Merry Christmas!'

Aw, it was lovely to hear Ida so happy. Maybe today would be one of those lovely family memories, and there'd be no drama, no barbs, just a warm, beautiful day full of joy and cheer.

That thought was blown out like a chip fire on Fireman Sam's watch, when Chloe came back into the room first, wearing an expression that was somewhere between shock, helplessness and apology. Bugger. What had my mother done now?

'Merry Christmas everyone!' Ida cheered. 'I'd like you all to meet my boyfriend. This is George.'

At that, a well-tanned, silver-haired gent of perhaps late fifties, sporting a pink polo shirt and a pair of well-cut navy chinos gave us all a wave.

'Did you know about this?' Sasha, sitting beside me, hissed.

'Not a bit,' I whispered back, barely containing my amusement. 'Should I call him Daddy?'

We were still giggling like teenagers when my mother made a personal introduction. It was tough, but as I shook his hand and wished him a Merry Christmas, I refrained from using any fatherly terms.

It was a shock, but my overriding reaction was to be pleased for Mum. She embraced life, she lived it to the full and she didn't give a damn. It wasn't ideal if you were her only child and came somewhere below cabaret, self-promotion and her tap-dancing squad on her priority list, but there was something to admire in a woman who lived every day like it was her last.

I could learn a lesson there. More and more lately, I felt like I was drifting through life, going through the motions. New Year's resolution – I must start being more like Ida. Not a sentence I'd ever thought I'd say.

'George, this is Sasha,' she said, introducing my chum next to me.

'And over there,' she said, pointing at the collection of blokes at the breakfast bar, 'is Justin. Sasha and Justin used to live in sin, but they split up years ago,' she said.

In my mind, I slapped my palm to my forehead in mortification.

'Next to him is Nate.' Nate duly waved over and I closed my eyes to shut out the horror of what I knew was to come. She leaned into George's ear to give him the sordid details, but it was in a stage whisper that the families two doors down could hear. 'He was my son-in-law, married to Liv, but then they split up. He's Finn's dad, though. One-night stand.'

'Sasha, smother me to death with that cushion right now,' I begged.

'And next to him is Richard. He's a doctor. And Liv cohabitated with him after she and Nate got divorced, but then they split up too. Not a great track record.'

'Hurry up, Sasha. Kill me. Kill me now,' I demanded.

'No way – this is fricking hilarious,' Sasha chuckled.

'And finally, that's Connor. Och, he's lovely. You're a clever girl, Chloe,' she said, and every ounce of teenage angst and insecurity came flooding back to me.

If there was a bright side, I could see that Nate and Richard were on a shared mission not to dissolve into fits of laughter. Richard's attendance was not at my instigation. In fact, I didn't even know he'd be in town. Our last conversation had been a curt one, the morning after the twins' christening, after I stressed once again that there was no point in us pursuing a long-distance relationship. He didn't agree, but I knew that it could never work, so I stuck to my guns. Although, I do confess to a stomach flip of delight when Chloe had called yesterday and said that he was going to be in Glasgow for Christmas, and that she'd invited him over. Richard and I could never come to anything while he lived in Manchester and I lived in Glasgow, but having his face in the same room still made me smile.

It was great to have Justin here too. He was still living in Nate's spare room, and Sasha hung out there a lot. Sasha and

Nate had made a pact to take care of him and it was a tough commitment. Justin had been in and out of rehab four or five times in the last two years, each time coming out and promising he'd conquered it, only for him to fall spectacularly every time. He no longer worked, realising that he couldn't cope with the pressure of his job. He still looked fragile, a little shaky on his feet, but he was sober and he was here and surrounded by people who loved him, so whatever Nate and Sasha were doing to support him was working.

As always, Ida injected a whole lot of raucous joy into dinner and George soon got to grips with who everyone was and the convoluted dynamics between us all.

I'd already arranged to stay overnight, so I put a happy but exhausted Finn up to bed at the same time as the twins. We broke out the board games, battled it out over Pictionary and Trivial Pursuit (with Sasha at one point threatening Richard with violence over a closely contested piece of purple pie), and it was close to midnight before the laughter subsided into yawns.

'Time to get home,' Nate said, looking at Justin, who nodded in agreement.

Neither Nate or Sasha had drunk alcohol all day – in fact, none of us had.

'Might just crash at yours, if that's okay?' Sasha said to Nate. 'Don't fancy going home to an empty house.'

'No problem. But only if you apologise to Richard about the threat to stick the Christmas tree up his arse.'

She rolled her eyes, then did an elaborate bow. 'Richard, I'm very sorry. I do not, would not, and never will cause you injury with a festive spruce.'

'Accepted,' Richard said, laughing.

It had been a good day, I decided, when I headed into the kitchen a while later. My mother and my potential future dad were gone, Sasha, Nate and Justin were away too, and Connor, Chloe and Richard had all headed up to bed. Thankfully, Chloe had a four-bedroom house to accommodate us all.

I was just pouring a glass of wine when I heard a noise behind me.

'I'll have one of those too,' Richard said, making me jump.

'Bugger,' I gasped, as the red wine spilled over my hand. 'I thought you'd gone to bed.'

'Nope,' he said. 'Just went to change out of my jeans into something with an elasticated waist...' he snapped the waistband on his jogging trousers, '... because I had three helpings of pudding and I think I've cleared the house of the green triangles out of the Quality Street boxes.'

I handed him his wine, and we headed over to the sofas a few feet away. One of the first things Chloe and Connor had done when they'd moved in – inspired by Connor's years of living in the USA – was knock down the internal walls and make the whole house open plan. It was gorgeous.

'We need to talk,' he said, his uncharacteristically serious tone making me laugh.

'What do we need to talk about Dr Campbell?' I teased.

'About when we're going to stop messing around and give this another try. Us. Give you and me another try.'

I couldn't keep having the same conversation and I didn't understand why he wanted to either. I'd assumed he saw other people, had other relationships in Manchester, and what we had was just a lovely consequence of his trips up north.

How many times was I going to have to tell him I didn't want a long distance relationship? Wasn't life busy enough? Did I really want to get myself back into a situation that would be hard to leave if it didn't work out? Did I want Finn to become attached to someone new?

'I didn't realise there was an "us",' I said, playing for time.

'Liv, there's always been an us. Look, nothing else works. No one else comes close. We've been dancing around this for years and it's ridiculous. I want to be with you. I really do. I'll move back to a Scottish hospital, I'll find a place to live until you're sure you and Finn are ready, and we'll make it work. I love you.

I want to be with you. I'll even call Ida "Mum" if it helps and I'll visit all her friends in person…'

He was making me laugh now and that was fatal, because I was a pushover for someone funny. Maybe it was time. Maybe Finn should have another man in his life, one who loved his mum and was around at home. Maybe… just maybe… we could be something.

I just needed to decide if I loved him enough to take the chance.

14

The Wedding

September 2012

'Are you royalty? A princess? Keeping it quiet that you're in line for the throne?' Richard asked, and I fully understood why.

Approaching the steps of the cathedral – yep, a cathedral – was a horse-drawn carriage, and when it stopped at the steps, I was pretty sure cartoon footmen would appear at any moment to carry in the Fairy Princess's twelve-foot train.

You had to hand it to my mother – she did things in style.

'Your dad and I married in the registry office, and had a fish supper on the way home,' she'd told me, when I'd commented on the, erm, elaborate spectacle. 'So this time, I'm doing it the way I want to,' she'd announced, hands on hips and oozing defiance.

There wasn't much to argue with there so I didn't.

Instead, I marvelled at the splendour of a blessing with 200 guests at the cathedral, followed by a reception for 300 at Lomond Grange, the same hotel we'd spent Millennium Eve in all those years ago.

I'd drawn a line at being bridesmaid, and Ida hadn't minded because she felt disinclined to dilute her limelight. Therefore, the only person in the wedding party other than the groom, was

Finn, who held his gran's hand as they walked up the aisle and gave her away, to the pre-recorded soundtrack of Ida singing 'Ave Maria'.

It was both glorious and ridiculously lavish too. George, it turned out, had made his fortune in property in the eighties and never married. Now, he was more than happy to indulge my mother's whims and pay for everything. Had my mum asked for the streets to be paved with gold, I was sure he would have done it. Instead, she settled on an opulent two-centre spectacle, with the wedding party being chauffeured the thirty-five-minute journey to the hotel in a Rolls Royce, while the rest of us followed in luxury coaches.

'Are you taking notes?' I asked Richard, when we were shown to our seats at the top table.

'Should I be?' he said, grinning.

'Absolutely not,' I replied, truly meaning it. I'd been married once. I had absolutely no intention of doing it again, even if I adored this man sitting next to me. He'd been living with us for three months now and it had been so much more than I could ever have hoped. He'd won me over with his offer to move back up north, and by an incredible stroke of luck, just a few weeks later, the head of neuro at our hospital had announced his retirement. Richard had immediately applied for the job and got it. Given that he'd worked there for years, they were delighted to have him back. So was I.

It had taken a few months to get everything organised and for him to work his notice period, but during that time, he'd come up as often as possible so that Finn could get to know him. By the time he was ready to make the move, we both knew that it was unnecessary for him to live anywhere else, so he'd moved straight in with us. On his first day in his new job, I'd kissed him at the door. 'Good luck. Don't break a leg. Or a head.'

'I'll try not to,' he laughed.

A thought struck me. 'I've just realised you'll be working with Francine. Do you remember her? The girl that…'

'You saved in your underwear. Yeah, I met her again when I was up to meet the board. I reminded her that she was once my patient. Strange how things work out sometimes.'

It sure was. Twelve years ago, I'd saved Francine's life. She'd then gone on to save Justin and countless others. What a loss that would have been to her family, to Justin and to all those other patients if she hadn't made it.

And while we were on the subject of strange happenings, I'd never have predicted that Richard and I would end up here.

Once upon a time we'd worked together and lived together. Now, ten years later, we were doing it again. Our disciplines rarely overlapped, though, so it wasn't too claustrophobic. Instead, it just made the logistics of running our new family so much easier. Finn absolutely adored Richard and loved having him around.

Meanwhile, I'd never been happier. And looking along the table, I could see that my mother was feeling exactly the same.

After the meal, George gave a beautiful speech that made his bride cry – a result that would no doubt horrify my mother because it would threaten to ruin her make up. She recovered to belt out 'My First, My Last, My Everything' and had the whole place dancing in their chairs. Then they kicked off the first dance to 'You Are So Beautiful', and I cried. Yes, unromantic, never getting married, oh my mother's so embarrassing... and at that moment it all went out the stained-glass windows and I cried tears of happiness for her.

I was definitely getting more emotional as I got older. However, age didn't seem to be having the same effect on my friends.

'Christ Almighty, every time I look at you, you're spouting water like a hose pipe,' Sasha groaned as she bumped across into Richard's vacant seat to be next to me. The top table had been cleared away and we were now at a big round table with Chloe and Connor, Nate, Justin, Sasha, and, of course, Richard, who chose that moment to come back from the bar with three ice buckets filled with champagne.

Justin had announced a few weeks before that we had to stop with the teetotal thing around him because it was making him feel guilty. Despite our protestations to the contrary, he'd insisted, and eventually we'd capitulated. There would be no getting falling-down pissed, or shots or hard spirits, but we were okay with a few glasses of champagne on special occasions.

'She's not letting me marry her,' Richard announced, 'so I just thought we'd have the champagne anyway, and I'll work on the vicar, the ceremony and the rest of the official stuff.'

'Good plan,' said Chloe, who was already giddy after two glasses of wine with dinner. She and Connor didn't get out much – it was tough to have a rampant social life with toddlers – so she was making the most of this child-free night, thanks to our babysitter Maisie and her friend Carly, who had come to the church and taken Finn, Joshua and Jasmin home to Chloe's house, where they'd be taken care of until 2 p.m. tomorrow. Bliss!

That gave us a serious window of opportunity to party and we did. We danced, we sang, we drank (with the exception of Justin) and we laughed all night. It was the closest we'd come to those thirty-year-olds we'd been a decade ago. Only we'd pay way more for this tomorrow morning.

'I'm just going to the ladies,' I told Richard, then squeezed past Nate on the way from the table. I had to give kudos to my ex-husband because he had been brilliant over the last year. He'd been supportive when Richard had moved in, and there was absolutely no sign of any jealousies or resentment. If I didn't know better, I'd think he had someone else and had moved on. I made a mental note to ask Sasha. She was the one who was with him most, because she'd now taken up a post as head of Business Studies at the same school as Nate, and out of school hours, she was always over at his house spending – purely platonic – time with Justin. Both Sasha and I were still friends with our ex-partners after all these years. That didn't happen often and I was grateful that we'd somehow managed it.

I was halfway across the lobby on the way to the toilets when I spotted the very person I wanted to speak to sneaking out the front door. I nipped into the ladies, then went to track her down. It wasn't hard. She was sitting on a bench to the right of the entrance, at the edge of the gravel drive. Thankfully, it was an unusually balmy night for September in the west of Scotland.

'Hey,' I said, sitting down next to her, 'Is everything okay?'

Poignant moments and introspective solitude weren't things I'd ever associated with Sasha.

'I'm fine. Just needed a minute.'

'For what?'

She shrugged. This wasn't like her at all. 'To clear my head. I'm fine,' she repeated. 'Are you having a good night?' She shifted gear halfway through that response and I could see she was really making an effort to shrug off the melancholy.

I wasn't letting her get away with that though. 'Is it Justin? Is something going on?'

Sasha's first instinct was always to keep her problems to herself, but I wasn't allowing her to do that this time.

She shook her head. 'Nothing more than you know already. The doctor says his liver tests will be back this week, but he's fairly sure he has cirrhosis.' Justin's liver function tests had been abnormal, so his doctors had ordered an ultrasound-guided liver biopsy. I was depressingly positive that it would show he had Alcoholic Liver Disease and had explained to Sasha that this was the umbrella term that medics used, encompassing cirrhosis and other alcohol-related disorders.

It wasn't a surprise, but that didn't make it any less heart-breaking. He'd just never overcome the need to drink. I'd lost count of how many times he'd fallen off the wagon in the last few years, only for Nate and Sasha to pick him up again. He was a shadow of his former self now. Skin and bone and sorrow. Since that night we'd almost lost him in hospital, we'd all tried so hard to help him, but the reality was that he had to help himself by stopping drinking for good. So far, he hadn't managed to do it, but we lived in hope.

'We'll all be there for him, you know that don't you? And for you too.' I reached over and took her hand. 'I know this will make you hurl or stomp off in disgust, but I love you. Just in case you were in any doubt.'

I waited for the reaction to this public declaration of emotion, but it didn't come. Instead, one solitary, bulbous tear ran down her cheek. There was something going on here, something she wasn't telling me.

'Sasha, what is it? Tell me!' I said, grabbing her hand for support. She didn't even try to shake me off. This must be really bad.

'I can't,' she said, her words strangled by emotion.

'Of course you can. Honey, there's nothing we can't deal with or fix. Unless... Oh no, Sasha, are you ill?'

Noooooo. How could Chloe and I have missed this? We were nurses for God's sake and our closest friend was sick and we hadn't even...

'I'm not ill.'

I sagged with relief, still clutching her hand. 'Then anything else we can fix or get over.'

She still wasn't speaking, so I decided to take a different approach that would bring down her distress.

'Look, if you don't tell me, I'll go get Chloe and we'll come out with pathetically sentimental declarations of love until you crack and tell us.' That was Sasha's idea of emotional torture – sure to work.

Or perhaps not.

She sighed, looked out into the darkness and shook her head. 'Not tonight. This isn't the right time to talk about it.'

'Yes, tonight,' I argued. 'Sasha I'm not going to be able to go back in there and enjoy myself for worrying about you. Tell me, so we can come up with a plan and then go back and gasp in awe at my mother's third costume change of the night.'

'I'm in love with Nate.'

She said it. Deadpan. No emotion. Just right out there.

My brain wasn't computing. 'You're in love with Nate? Nate who?'

I knew I was being ridiculous, but it was so outlandish I just couldn't grasp it.

'Nate that you were married to, Nate,' she clarified.

'Oh.' Not the most articulate response but a canon full of questions were exploding in my head. 'Since when?'

She shrugged, and I knew she would be honest. In all the time I'd known her, Sasha didn't ever lie to spare feelings. 'I don't know. I think I realised it a couple years ago. Maybe more. It was after Justin got sick and I went back to help him. Nate and I became… a team. We spent so much time together and I gradually realised that he was more than just the mate who was helping me take care of my ex-boyfriend. I'm so sorry, Liv.'

I inhaled deeply, filling my lungs with fresh air in the hope of clearing my mind. *Okay, get it together. Say the right thing.* I had absolutely no idea how I was feeling about this, but there was no judgement or disapproval, just surprise.

'Why are you sorry? Sasha, Nate and I haven't been together for twelve years. Apart from, you know, Finn, but that was a one-off…'

Bugger, I was so shocked I was doing the nervous rambling thing

'I guess I'm just really surprised because you two are about as different as two people can be. I never figured him for your type.'

'Me neither,' she admitted ruefully. 'I've thought so much about this and I think I get it…'

'Tell me.'

'I think it's…' she paused, struggling to put it into words. 'I grew up in a really chaotic house, with a mum who left when I was a teenager, and a dad I could never depend on, always fending for myself and fighting my own battles. Dad died when I was seventeen, and a few years later, I met Justin. He was a whole different kind of chaos. At least I thought so. Turns out he was pretty much the same. The drinking. The womanising.'

I started to see where she was going with this.

'And then Justin and I split up and I decided I didn't want another man in my life. Too much drama. Too much unpredictability. I was tired of it. I just wanted peace. But I couldn't turn my back on him when he hit rock bottom. I thought I was going to have to do it myself but Nate was right there, helping me lift him. Over the years since then, how I feel has become something else. I love that he's dependable, that he's decent; that he's solid and he'll stand by the people he loves. He doesn't want drama, or thrills, or adrenalin rushes. He makes me feel safe. Secure. Content. I've never understood what contentment actually meant. I've never had that before, and now that I know what it feels like, I don't want to let it go.'

The irony didn't pass me by. So many of the reasons that Sasha wanted Nate, were the ones that had made me walk away.

'Does he feel the same?' I realised that I really, really hoped he did.

Her mouth formed into a rueful, sad smile. 'I don't think so. Who knows?'

'Hang on – you haven't told him? Sasha, come on!' Here was the most direct woman I'd ever met and she was keeping this to herself?

'I can't put him in that position. Things have been over between Justin and me for almost as long as you and Nate have been apart, but I know Nate. He's loyal. And he's right to be. How could we even think of having a relationship when Justin lives with him? The slightest blip can send Justin over the edge – can you imagine what something like this could do? I can't risk even telling Nate in case it makes everything impossibly uncomfortable. Which it probably will, because he's never shown any sign at all of having those kind of feelings for me.'

She was right and I completely understood. I wrapped my arms around her. 'Sasha, I'm so sorry. You deserve to be happy.

I wish I could sort this for you. And for what it's worth, I think you and Nate would be wonderful together. I really do. You'd be great for him. I won't say a word, but if you need me to talk to, to rant to, anything at all, I'm always here.'

It had taken me a long, long time to find the person I should be with and make it work. It had taken Ida even longer.

After everything she'd sacrificed and given, Sasha deserved love.

I just hoped that Nate felt the same way too.

15

Make or Break

May 2013

'Are you sure about this?' Sasha asked me for the tenth time. 'I mean, you don't have to do it. You could walk away now, go back to your normal life and no one would even know you had this moment of temporary insanity.'

There was a lot of sense in her argument, but I was frozen to the spot. 'Nope, not moving,' I said, only to be rewarded with a roll of her eyes.

I had to do this. I knew I did. It was time. Once before, I'd contemplated staying with someone who didn't make me completely happy, and I'd walked away in the hope of finding more. It had been a risk, a gamble that had terrified me. Now I was about to take another leap of faith and I was just as scared.

The doors flew open and in rushed Chloe, Justin, Connor and Nate, with Finn, holding his dad's hand, running to keep up with them. I'd called the four adults earlier and warned them what I was going to do. Like every event in the last twenty years, they'd pitched up in a time of need.

We were in a little private enclave of a restaurant in the city centre, a fantastic tapas place that Richard had discovered a few months ago and it had become his favourite place to eat. We were there at least once a week now, usually with some of the others in tow. Chloe absolutely adored it too, even if we did tease her because Danny, the head chef, clearly had a massive crush on her. Every time she was there, he'd insist on sending out mouth-watering extra dishes, so we weren't complaining. Thankfully, Connor took it all in his stride and just enjoyed the Spanish gastronomic benefits of having a beautiful wife.

I checked my watch. It was still only four o'clock so there were no other diners in yet.

Danny had sent out a tray of tapas, but I was too nervous to even contemplate eating it.

'Christ, if ever I needed a drink,' Justin whistled, and Sasha eyed him with a lethal stare. 'Don't make me kill you with one of those potato croquet thingies,' she warned.

Justin laughed, and for a moment, their conversation distracted me from my tension. It was good to see the easy rapport they had now. And good to hear that the slight slur in his speech that remained after Francine had operated on his brain bleed a few years ago had almost completely gone. Touch wood, he'd been sober for five months now. He'd had another lapse at Christmas, but Nate and Sasha had scooped him up and worked with the team at the rehab centre to get him straight again, with Chloe, Connor and I helping and supporting them too. His liver disease was under control for the moment and didn't seem to be getting any worse. He was a shell of the man he'd once been, but I had to believe that he would beat this for good. We all did. Over the years I'd nursed countless patients who'd been alcoholics in their thirties and forties, and who'd recovered and gone on to lead long, happy lives. Despite the signs, I just had to remain positive that Justin was going to be one of them.

'Have we missed anything?' Chloe gasped.

I didn't answer quickly enough.

'HAVE WE MISSED ANYTHING?' she barked this time, and Finn's eyes widened with interest. At almost seven, he loved any kind of drama, excitement or disaster. I wasn't sure which category this fell into.

I looked at Nate, desperately seeking reassurance. He was sensible. Strategic. A voice of reason. He'd tell me if I were being a fool.

'Nate, am I being crazy?' I asked him.

After a long pause, he nodded his head. 'You are, but I wouldn't want you to be any other way.'

That really didn't help.

The door opened again, and in sauntered Richard, looking at something on his phone as he walked. He was already a couple of metres into the deserted restaurant before he stopped, glanced up, and saw the whole gang standing there, staring at him.

'What? What is it?' he asked, with just a hint of alarm.

Everyone turned to look at me now, and I opened my mouth to speak, only to discover it had apparently been subjected to some kind of numbing agent.

'I... I...' No good. Couldn't get any further. My heart was racing, my hands were shaking.

Eventually, it was left to the only sensible person in the room to intervene.

'Mummy, is it what you told me this morning?' Finn asked.

I managed to nod my head.

'Okay,' he said, taking it on board and deciding to run with it. 'Richard, my mummy wants to know if you'll marry her. And me,' he said proudly, and if it was humanly possible for a heart to burst with love, I'd need a sewing kit any minute.

Richard's whole face creased into the widest grin. 'I think I'd be very happy to,' he said, stepping forward to scoop up a cheering Finn.

I finally found my voice. 'Are you sure?'

'Of course. Thought you'd never ask.' It was the standing joke between us. He'd asked me to marry him a dozen times since we got back together and every time I told him I didn't see the point in marriage. Only, the truth was that I did. I was just terrified of making another mistake, for me, for him, for Finn. Now it was time to stop being scared and take the leap. I wanted to spend the rest of my life with this man. Now I would.

To a rousing roar of cheers and applause, he reached me in three steps and enveloped me into a hug with him and Finn, before finally pulling back.

'So when are we doing this?' he asked. 'Only it needs to be soon, before you change your mind.'

'Er, now?' I suggested, and before I could even process the look of puzzlement on his face, the door opened again and in charged my mother...

'Oh. Holy. Fuck,' Sasha whispered.

... dressed in a full-length nun's habit.

'They were all out of vicars' outfits at the dress-hire shop,' she announced, as George ran in behind her. 'It was as close as I could get.' She was the only one who'd been in on this idea from the start, a vital part of the plan, although she'd failed to mention that there would be costumes. 'So I'm here and ready. Let's get going,' she beamed, handing her oversized Gucci tote – the essential accessory for any nun – to George. I loved that he seemed to find her sheer bonkersness hilarious.

'My mum got ordained so she could conduct the ceremony,' I told my groom-to-be – that is, if he still wanted to be part of this circus that was our lives.

Before he had a chance to change his mind, Ida stepped up on to the raised platform that was used on the nights that the restaurant had live music. 'Would the bride and groom step forward please?'

On shaking legs, I stepped towards her.

And turned to see Richard coming right alongside me.

16

A Hospital Ward

December 2014

I passed out the plastic food containers to Nate and Sasha, then pulled up a chair to the side of the bed and sat with them.

'Hope it's okay,' I said, gesturing to the food. 'The staff canteen can be hit or miss. A bit like myself.'

My cooking inadequacies weren't exactly a newsflash, but at least that made the two of them smile.

'How long is your break?' Sasha asked.

'I can take a couple of hours because I'm on a split shift today. Ida and George are picking Finn up from school. Apparently, they have a hot date with crazy golf, Pizza Hut and a visit to Santa's Grotto at the shopping centre.' Christmas was only a few days away, but none of us were feeling festive. We were going through the motions for the sake of all the kids, but we were all consumed with worry about Justin.

I saw a flash of relief cross Sasha's face and I knew it was just the thought of having another person here, another layer of support. Thankfully, the schools had broken up for the Christmas holiday last Friday, so she and Nate had been able to spend as much time here as the medical staff allowed, in the three days since Justin had been admitted with extreme vomiting and disorientation. Even without the harsh light of the hospital room, the deep yellow tinge of his skin was unmistakable.

There was only one way to reverse his illness and that had been ruled out a few months ago, downstairs in the same building, in a discussion with the consultant who was overseeing his care. Justin had been in for two days for a succession of tests, and he was already showing signs of end-stage liver disease.

Nate, Sasha and I were there when the doc was on his rounds, and Justin had asked us to stay.

'What about a transplant?' Sasha had pleaded. She was right. It was the only hope, the only chance of coming back from this.

'I'm sorry, but that isn't an option in this case,' the consultant had said, clearly uncomfortable. Years of experience with similar situations told me what was about to come and I closed my eyes. What a waste. What a tragic, heart-breaking waste.

'But why not?' Sasha was getting agitated now, her voice rising.

The doctor had looked at Justin, met his gaze, then eventually filled the pause with, 'I'm afraid that's confidential and I'm not able to divulge the reasons...'

Justin had interrupted him with a bitter reality check. 'Because I'm still drinking,' he'd blurted. 'I'm sorry Sasha. Nate. I'm so sorry.'

Sasha had been the first to react, standing up so suddenly that her chair thrust backwards, then storming out of the room. I understood. She'd done everything she could for him for all these years and he'd sabotaged his only chance of beating this. She was angry and frustrated and hurting and devastated to see someone who had once been so vibrant and full of life come to this.

We all knew his alcoholism was a disease. An addiction. He wasn't deliberately being destructive and if he had the strength to fight it then he would have. He wanted to live. He wanted to beat it. But the disease had won again and it was understandable that Sasha found this too painful to bear and let frustration take over.

The doctor hadn't commented, just excused himself and gone on with his rounds.

Nate had reacted differently to Sasha. 'When?' he'd asked, needing facts and details.

Justin, his yellow eyes bloodshot with unshed tears, had lifted his shaking hands from the bed in an apologetic shrugging motion. 'Every day,' he'd admitted. 'Just a little, just enough to make me feel like I've got a reason to wake up.'

Nate had put his forehead down on the bed for a moment as he tried to process this. I'd stayed silent, realising it was important for them to have this conversation.

Eventually, Nate had lifted his head, then reached for Justin's hand. He hesitated before he spoke, choking on the words. 'I'm so fucking angry with you right now,' he'd said, but his tone was one of pure love and sorrow.

Justin couldn't reply.

'I thought we had this.' Nate's voice cracked on every word and I could see he was struggling to keep it together.

'I'm so sorry, mate,' Justin had whispered.

Nate shook his head. 'Don't,' he'd said softly. 'Don't apologise. We're still going to be here and this isn't over yet. Maybe if you stop now, buy some time, a transplant could be an option down the line.'

It was a long shot, but it was possible. And if there was one thing that a loved one sitting at the side of a dying person's bed needed, it was hope.

Now, three months later, that hope had faded. There was no transplant. He hadn't become a viable candidate again and now he was way too sick for it to be an option. His detox had been brutal and had taken so much out of his body, that I spent many nights sleeping in a chair next to him, just willing him to keep breathing. We all had. Over the last few weeks, his symptoms had escalated, with fluid gathering in legs and abdomen, until they were massively swollen and the pressure on his lungs made it difficult to breathe. His belly had been drained several times, and he'd been given intravenous fluids, but now his pain was being treated with morphine. The biggest risk now was that his damaged liver could no longer make his blood clot effectively, so the chances of a major bleed were frighteningly high.

The door opened again and Chloe came in, still in her uniform too. She gave everyone a hug and then sat on the one remaining chair. It was normally two visitors maximum at a bed, but the staff on the ward were flexing the rules because Chloe and I were just popping in on our breaks.

'Your lunch is there on the table,' I told Chloe. 'Lasagne and salad.'

She reached over for it. 'Thanks. How is he?'

Sasha shrugged sadly. 'The same. He was awake for a few hours earlier, but he didn't have a great night so he's exhausted. I think they gave him a sedative, too.'

She spoke softly, and I could see how exhausted she was too. In the months since she'd stormed out of his hospital room, despite her initial desperate fury, she'd never faltered in her care for him, not once.

The four of us sat with our thoughts for a few minutes. Sometimes, nostalgia took hold and we'd tell stories about the past, rewinding the clock to our favourite days and nights. Other times, we got lost in laughter, recounting the dramas, the disasters and embarrassing spectacles. And sometimes, like today, we were just still.

'You know, we never got to Malibu,' Sasha murmured.

Nate was the first to react. 'Malibu?'

'Yes. Don't you remember? We talked about having a group holiday – actually if I recall correctly, the plan was thwarted by your ex-fiancée Janet the Jogger…'

'Janet the Jogger!' Chloe smiled. 'I haven't thought about her for years.'

'Neither have I,' Nate admitted, making us all laugh.

Sasha went on, 'She announced that you'd set a date for the wedding that never happened...' she looked at me pointedly, making everyone chuckle again, 'and nothing ever came of our group holiday. But Justin was absolutely vehement that the destination should be Malibu.'

'Why?' Nate asked.

'*Baywatch*,' Sasha and I said at the same time, before she went on. 'He was fairly convinced he'd meet David Hasselhoff and they could become best friends.'

Nothing summed up the Justin we knew better than that story. Young, crazy, funny, wild and the most entertaining, incorrigible friend that anyone could have. So far from the Justin that lay in front of us now.

I nodded my head, smiling. 'I think that would definitely have happened.'

'Bloody Janet the Jogger,' Sasha muttered, stopping us from slipping into a maudlin conversation with a flashback to a better time. 'Seriously, Nate, what were you thinking?' she teased. 'She had a permanent camel toe in all that Lycra.'

That set us off and I hoped that somewhere, in his sleep, Justin could hear this. He'd find it hilarious too.

Chloe's mobile phone buzzed and she checked the screen. 'I need to go – we've got an RTA coming in. I'll come back up at the end of shift.' A road traffic accident. I hoped no one was seriously hurt. With another round of hugs, Chloe was gone.

I checked my watch. 'Listen, I can stay for another hour at least, so if you two want to go grab some sleep, or go home for showers, it's no problem, I'll be here.'

Nate shook his head. 'Thanks, but I'm okay. Sasha came in earlier this morning, so I've only been here for a couple of hours.' He turned to our friend. 'Sasha? Do you want to head home for a while?'

Sasha sat back in her chair and stretched. 'Not home, but I think I'll go for a walk, clear my head. Maybe just around the grounds.'

Nate changed his mind. 'Actually, that doesn't sound like a bad idea. Okay, if I come with you?'

Sasha stood up and lifted her jacket. 'Sure.'

Her strength never failed to amaze me. Since the night of Ida's wedding, she'd talked a few times about her feelings for Nate. She'd absolutely fallen in love with him, yet she still hadn't told him – not even a hint, despite being together every single day.

She pulled on her jacket, then her hat and gloves, and swapped her trainers for the boots she'd come in this morning. It was a typical Scottish day in December – below freezing, with a smattering of ice and a wind that could take your breath away. Nate reached for his parka and pulled it on too.

'Are you sure you don't mind?' he asked.

'Of course not. Take your time. Go for a coffee. If there's any change I'll call you.'

He leaned over and gave me a kiss on the cheek. 'Thanks Liv.'

'No problem,' I assured him.

He turned to Sasha. 'Okay, you ready? I'm warning you though, if you slip on the ice, don't take me down with you. I've got a low tolerance to pain and can be fairly pathetic.'

'Don't you worry,' Sasha retorted, 'I've got this. In fact, princess, I'll take your arm and make sure you don't accidentally trip and do yourself an injury.'

I honestly think that other than their love for Justin, their banter was the only thing that had kept them going over the last few years.

'After you, madam,' Nate said, his handsome face cracking into a rueful smile. He'd aged well. He was in his early forties but could easily pass for mid-thirties. For the first time, I saw them in a different light than Nate my ex-husband and Sasha, my lifelong friend. I saw them for how they related to each other, how they could be if they were a couple.

They looked perfect together.

More than that, I saw something else.

I watched as Nate's eyes followed Sasha, and I recognised something there.

That's when I knew that Sasha wasn't alone in having feelings for an old friend. He loved her too.

Because the way he looked at her, his eyes full of care and adoration, was exactly the same way that he used to look at me.

17

A Funeral

February 2015

The morning was beautiful. There was a thick blanket of snow on the ground, and icicles hung like diamonds from the trees. It was like every perfect winter scene ever used on a Christmas card.

And our hearts were breaking.

Ten years ago, when Justin was at the height of his party-animal popularity, there would have been hordes of people crushing into the crematorium. Now there were barely twenty of us.

Chloe and Connor moved into the pew first, followed by my mum and George, then Richard and me. Sasha and Nate sat in front of us, with Jake, Justin's brother, and his parents, who'd travelled down from Inverness. The only time I'd met them was at Justin's thirtieth when he'd celebrated like there was no tomorrow.

Now there wouldn't be.

They'd never been close; Sasha said his parents had always been distant, happy to live out their lives on a farmstead up north. But it was still heart-breaking that the booze had taken its toll and too many fights had caused an irreparable rift. Sasha had thought about contacting them many times over the last few years, but he'd refused to let her.

He didn't need them, he said. If they wanted him, they could make the first move. I wondered now if they regretted that they never did.

I saw Justin's mum's head fall, her shoulders shake with sorrow and I wondered if she knew, if she understood what Justin's life had been like.

Or his death.

He'd never left the hospital after that day we all sat together eating lunch from plastic trays. His condition deteriorated over the next two weeks, with him slipping in and out of consciousness, still disorientated and confused. In his final days, he'd been moved to my ward, and we'd sat with him, all of us, making sure he was never alone, spending every possible moment telling him how much he was loved. I'd nursed many patients, but to care for someone I loved so dearly in his final days had been both a privilege and a searing pain that would live with me for ever.

There had been so many 'what ifs'. What if we'd got him help sooner? What if he and Sasha had stayed together? What if he hadn't had that bloody affair? I wondered about her sometimes. Madeleine. I knew Justin hadn't seen her for years, not since he lost all control of his drinking, left his job and became a shadow of the man who was the big-shot finance guy. I wondered if she ever regretted the havoc she'd caused. But then, it was on Justin, more than her. He was the one who'd betrayed Sasha – Madeleine had just been the willing accomplice.

The closing bars of Snow Patrol's 'Run' faded, as the humanist funeral celebrant, a woman in her sixties, with a perfect grey chignon and a kind face, opened by talking about the man Justin was, about his love of life and the sadness that he was gone at such a young age.

'Now,' she said, 'I'd like to invite Justin's friend Nate up to say a few words.'

A sob caught in my throat as I watched Nate, his face pale and ravaged by grief, climb the steps and stand behind the lectern on the stage. It shouldn't have been this way. Nate should have been making this speech at his wedding, or birthday, or some other day of celebration, not at his funeral.

He cleared his throat and began to speak.

'There was no one else on earth like Justin Donnelly.' He stopped, the words catching somewhere between his heart and his throat. It was a few seconds before he could go on. 'We met when he fell in love with our friend Sasha, and she loved him right back. It was impossible not to. He was the guy who made everything so much better than it would have been without him. He cheered the loudest, he laughed the longest, he sang like a rock star and he was always ready to put on another song and take to the dance floor to show off his moves. That's what he called them – his moves.'

There was murmured laugh.

'Even when he and Sasha were no longer a couple, they remained friends, still loved each other, and I know it was one of his biggest regrets that he ever let her go.'

The tears were falling down Sasha's face now: silent, broken.

Nate stopped to steady himself, then went on.

'I won't talk about the challenges he had because we can't change what happened and that's not how he would want to be remembered. Instead, I'll use his own words. "Live fast, die young", he used to say, as he embarked on yet another wild idea. And we'd cheer him on because he was a force of nature that we all thought was unstoppable. We were wrong.'

He paused again, this time to wipe away a single tear that was rolling down his cheek. 'That's a sorrow that we may never learn to live with. Justin will always be a part of us. We, our group, you see, we're more than friends. We're a family who picked each other and, on any day, in any lifetime, I would pick Justin

Donnelly again. He was on this earth for forty-three years. We only wish he could have been here for forty-three more.'

So many tears were falling now, Nate, Sasha, Chloe, me…

I wondered if they would ever stop.

18

A New Dawn

January 2016

'I look ridiculous. I'm taking this off. Has anyone got a match? Anyone? I'll pay you to set fire to this dress.'

Everyone in the room knew Sasha well, so no one paid the least bit of attention.

Besides, she was oh-so wrong. She was wearing one of the most beautiful gowns I'd ever seen. The sleeveless bodice was overlaid with lace and cut into a V at the front and back, cinched in tight at the waist, and then the satin skirt flowed down to the floor. With her hair pulled back, curls tumbling down her back, she looked like a fifties screen goddess. One who was still muttering strenuous objections.

'I mean, it's white for God's sake. I've been having sex since I was fifteen.'

'Eh, do we need to know that?' Nate shouted from the sofa in the corner where the guys had congregated. Sasha had dismissed all that superstition stuff about the groom not seeing the bride on the big day. She reckoned they'd already survived so much that a bit of bad luck would barely register.

'Don't get jealous,' Sasha retorted, playfully baiting him, 'It was over so quickly I can barely remember it.'

The sound of Nate's laughter almost drowned out the fact that Sasha was still moaning. No matter how many times I saw them like this, it never failed to thrill me. It had been a sad six months after Justin died – half a year of healing and learning to live without him – before they'd finally acknowledged their feelings for each other. Nate proposed a couple of months later, and despite her acute objection to the marital contract, she'd said yes to make him happy. Already they were like a couple who'd been together for decades, which, in some ways, they had been. I couldn't be more happy for them. After everything they'd been through in the last few years, they deserved a lifetime of joy.

There was something in their chemistry that just worked, something that Nate and I had never managed to pull off. I often wondered if we were just too similar to light that spark. It was as if Sasha, in all her frank, fearless ways, brought out a latent part of his personality that made him laugh more, love more, and just enjoy life more than he ever had. And vice versa, his solid reliability took the edge off her abrasiveness and gave her… what was it she'd said? Contentment. That was it. Total contentment. I thought once again how ironic was it that the thing that had made me run from my relationship with Nate, was the very same thing that made it work for Sasha. Contentment looked great on her. Almost as good as that dress.

'Right are we ready?'

That was me. Chloe and I were joint maids of honour, but she was in charge of flowers, jewellery, dress and shoes, and I was responsible for timekeeping and getting everyone to where they needed to be.

'Let's go people,' I barked. 'We've a wedding to go to.'

'I can't believe I let myself be talked into this. Nate, I'll give you everything I own if you call this off and just let us live in sin. This dress is making me itch.'

He came over and kissed her. 'Nope, you're marrying me. End of story. More walking, less talking, Mrs Jamieson.'

The expression of disdain on her face had the rest of us howling with laughter.

His words, adorable as they were, made me glad I'd changed my name when I married Richard. After we split up, I never got around to reverting to my maiden name, and then when Finn came along, it made sense for us to have the same surname so I'd kept it. Now, after Richard and I had followed up our spontaneous wedding by legalising our union in a Glasgow registry office, I was Mrs Liv Campbell.

Sasha took a few steps towards the door, then spotted a partner in crime, newly delivered by his granny.

'Finn, what do you think of this dress?' she asked my son.

He immediately wrinkled up his nose. He was going to be ten later this year. If it didn't come as a football strip, a basketball kit, or with flippers and a snorkel, he wasn't interested. He'd already threatened to leave home because I'd prised him out of the Chicago Bulls top his Uncle Connor had bought him for his last birthday. I'd had to bribe him with football stickers to wear the suit we'd bought him for the occasion.

'I agree. Stick with me and take my mind off the fact that I look like I've escaped from a Disney parade.'

She held out her hand and he automatically took it and fell into step with her. The very best thing about Nate and Sasha getting together? My son adored her and it was absolutely mutual. There wasn't a time in his life that she hadn't been there, making him laugh, playing with him, hatching plans to get into trouble. Their relationship was everything I could ever want and I was so grateful that he would go through life with Sasha as his stepmum.

We made our way downstairs to the function suite on the first floor where the rest of the guests were already waiting. There were about fifty people in total, friends, family, work colleagues, all congregated in a flower-filled room, with one wall that was floor-to-ceiling glass and overlooked the waters of the Clyde and the hills beyond. It was utterly breath-taking. The perfect setting for the perfect day.

For the second time in his life, Finn walked the bride up the aisle. The last time, he was holding his grandmother's hand. This time he was listening to her, as Ida sang a pitch perfect, moving version of 'What a Wonderful World', leaving us all dabbing at our mascara before proceedings even got underway.

The celebrant, a humanist again, took a length of plaid fabric from the table beside him and tied their hands together, an old Scottish tradition called hand fasting, that signified that they were now forever bound together.

When Nate was called upon to make his vows, he spoke loud and clear, his gaze never leaving his bride. 'Sasha, every day I wake up and the first person I want to see is you. You're the last person I want to look at before I sleep. You're my friend, my love, and everything I could ever want. I'll be there for you always, loving you, laughing with you, until the end of time.'

'Sasha?' The humanist prompted.

Sasha didn't move, didn't say a word. It was as if she'd zoned out and lost the connection to what was going on altogether. My heart began to race. She was panicking. I could see it. For someone who didn't do public displays of affection, who had never wanted to get married, who had been through years of emotional trauma, it was all too much.

Nate could see it too. I watched as his brow furrowed in concern, as his gaze searched her eyes for answers.

I reached for Chloe's hand, as if by somehow joining forces we could will Sasha through this.

Just when we thought all was lost, she finally found her voice.

'Nate, I had a whole speech prepared, because I'm told that's what a bride does at something like this.'

The laughter gave her confidence, and she spoke just a little louder, a little clearer.

'But they weren't my words and they didn't feel right.'

That was true. She'd got them from an Internet website that gave thousands of examples of catchy vows.

'So I just want to keep it simple, to be true, and to say this. I will love you and Finn all my life. I may love him more than you sometimes, because he's way cooler.'

She winked at Finn when she said that and he dissolved into giggles, making my heart melt even more.

'I'll never lie, I'll never cheat, and I'll never walk away, no matter how tough it gets. And I know I should finish with a killer line, but I don't have one. So instead, I'll say this… I once heard a song that perfectly describes how I feel.' This time her gaze went to Ida, who was beaming with pride. 'Nate, in the words of The Drifters, and Ida, you're some kind of wonderful.'

'And so are you,' he whispered, before leaning over, and sending the order of the ceremony into chaos by kissing his bride.

Chloe and I cheered, clapped, cried again, then I squeezed the hand that was next to mine. As my husband turned to me and smiled, I couldn't help thinking we'd all found the place we were meant to be.

The bit in the middle...

So in letting Nate go, Liv had ultimately found a relationship that was everything she'd ever wanted. Nate had found his soulmate too.

But what if her decision had been different?

What if she had stayed? Given it another shot?

Would their marriage have been reignited, or would she have regretted hanging on to a love that belonged in the past?

And would her friends' lives have been changed as a result of her decision?

Would they have taken a different turn, missed a cataclysmic event, found a better path in the road?

Or are we all just pawns of some invisible force that has our destiny mapped out for us?

Back, in the opening moments of the millennium, Liv was about to take a step in a different direction...

WITH HIM...
FROM 1ST JANUARY
2000...

I

Shortly After Midnight

After salutations, hugs and promises of better things to come, we'd all ended up on the dance floor, with three hundred other revellers welcoming in the new millennium.

Sasha was dancing with Justin, her boyfriend of many years and Chloe was smooching with Rob, the guy she'd been dating for a year or so.

Nate moved in close. 'I'm going to go grab a drink. Coming?'

I honestly didn't want to be alone with him right now and have to respond to his bombshell about staying together.

'No, I'm good here. I'll catch up,' I said, ignoring his quizzical look. As soon as he moved off, Sasha ditched her beloved – who was more than happy to carry on with his dance moves alone – and shuffled over to me.

'Are you okay?' she asked, while doing her best Britney dance to 'Hit Me Baby One More Time'.

'Yes. No. I can't believe he's changed his mind and wants us to try again,' I managed to say while still dancing, although admittedly my timing suffered. This was why I would never get a gig as a Britney tribute act. Well, that and the fact I couldn't sing, didn't look like a pop star and my chances of fitting in a size-ten designer frock were up there with my long-held, teenage hopes of George Michael one day becoming my new best friend.

I could see Sasha wasn't impressed. 'It's pretty predictable. He always does this.' She had a point. Nate had backtracked on the decision to split a few times already.

Britney was still warbling in the background as Sasha, still dancing while dispensing emotional advice, came back with another argument for the prosecution.

'Liv, you know it's not working. How long are you going to give it? I love you, but you're wasting the best years of your life on a relationship that doesn't make you happy.'

'He does!' I argued. I'm not sure why, because we both knew that it was only semantics. He did make me happy – but he didn't make me blissful, intoxicated, thrilled, interested or excited about the future.

We were back to the old 'contentment' thing.

'You two are like flatmates. You need to get out there and live a little, otherwise you're going to wake up one day and you'll be thirty-five and regret the fact that you've spent half your adult life bored out of your buttocks.'

That made me laugh. I knew she was right, but wasn't this what marriage was about? Taking the crap bits with the good bits? Nate was a decent man, a good person, he loved me and he'd never deliberately hurt me. He was… safe.

'What's the evil one banging on about?' Chloe asked, laughing, as she shuffled alongside us.

'She's telling me all the reasons it would be crazy to try again,' I replied.

Chloe's eyes widened. 'Don't listen to her! Sasha, shut your mouth.' They had been friends long enough that this incurred a roll of the eyes, rather than a sharp rebuke. We were like sisters who bickered frequently but woe betide anyone who got in between us. Chloe was still advocating for Mills & Boon. 'Look, he loves you. You love him. Do you know how hard it is to find that?'

She had a point. But then, she had dumped the love of her life, who'd promptly taken off to the USA and never been seen since, so I wasn't worshipping at the heart-shaped temple of her deep romantic insights. Now she was dating Rob, who was perfectly acceptable, but I could see that her heart wasn't in it.

Sasha leaned in and I knew she was going to give me words of wisdom, clarity and spiritual guidance. 'Okay, so here's what to do...'

I braced myself to receive wise musings.

'... Get pissed, ignore the whole bloody thing and decide when you're hungover, that way the pain will barely register.'

Oprah should have this kind of insight on retainer.

I wondered if the other groups of women on the dance floor were having life-changing conversations while torturing their feet to the sound of Miss Spears bemoaning the fact that her loneliness was killing her.

She thought *she* had problems.

The music changed and we were subjected to the sound of Steps announcing that 'Love's Got a Hold On My Heart'.

I'd never had such a burning desire to unplug a speaker.

No more dancing for me.

I bailed out and left them to it. My eye caught Justin and Rob, who were now on their way to the bar in the corner of the room.

I was about to head back over to the table when I realised that Nate was already there, looking utterly handsome in his open-neck shirt. He was watching me come towards him and the expectant expression on his lovely face told me that he wanted an answer I wasn't ready to give.

Two choices – flee or face him. Flee or face him. Flee or...

Time to suck it up and face him.

I slid into the seat next to him and rested my head on his shoulder. Safe. There was a lot to be said for it. What if I walked away and never found another love that even came close to this one? What if my expectations were just too high? What if I realised it was a mistake somewhere down the road and he'd already met someone else and I couldn't get him back? That was exactly what had happened to Chloe. She'd ended a relationship with a guy she loved and she'd regretted it ever since.

Hadn't I done the whole 'till death do us part' thing? At no point in our wedding vows was there a get-out clause for 'if you just think it's all gone a tad stale'.

And surely the fact that I was still asking myself 'What If...?' meant that I wasn't 100 per cent positive that I was doing the right thing in packing my bags and calling it a day.

'Sorry,' he murmured. 'You don't need to give me an answer right now. We can talk about it tomorrow. Or whenever.'

I should have said there was no more discussion to be had, but that tiny chink of uncertainty had affected my vocal cords. The music had switched again and the DJ was slowing things down. Martine McCutcheon was obviously on the side of love as she began to belt out 'Perfect Moment'.

Not bloody perfect. Not even close.

But maybe this song was a sign.

I shouldn't give up yet.

I said nothing until the track ended, thinking it through, making my mind up.

We had to give it one more try. It was a new century, so perhaps we'd somehow find a new dimension to our relationship, one that made it work and shaped it into everything we wanted it to be.

Yep, we could do this. Or at least, we owed it to each other to keep trying.

Sasha appeared, dragging Justin behind her. 'Right, we're going upstairs so I can welcome in the New Year by shagging this gorgeous man.' He was laughing, his arms tight around her, obviously in agreement with this plan.

A spark of jealousy flared. Had we ever been like that? Surely, we must have been at the beginning? Of course we were. I just couldn't remember a specific example.

I emptied my champagne glass in one gulp, then grabbed the bottle.

'Yeah, I think we're going to do the same,' I said, smiling as I felt Nate's arm tighten around me. Safe. Content. Surely there was something to be said for that?

I didn't even want to look at Sasha's undoubtedly disapproving gaze, so I didn't. Decision made, I just stood up, kissed her cheek, then waved goodbye to Chloe and Rob as Nate and I passed the dance floor on the way out.

In the lobby, a very drunk man was reassuring two paramedics that he was absolutely fine and that there was nothing wrong with him that another drink wouldn't cure. As we waited for the lift, I watched them pack up and leave, no doubt entirely pissed off that their time had been wasted.

The lift was full, so we didn't speak until we got into the room.

'You changed your mind?' he said hopefully, as soon as the door was closed.

I took a swig of champagne.

'I did,' I said. 'I don't want to know what it feels like to be without you.'

And I'm a raging coward who just doesn't have the courage to do this in case it's a bloody huge mistake. I omitted to say any of that out loud.

'Thank God. I love you, Liv.'

'I know.'

'Two secs,' he said, as I lay down on the bed and waited for him, champagne in hand. Somewhere, along the corridor, Sasha was ripping the clothes off Justin. In this room, Nate was removing his own clothes, hanging up the jacket and then folding the rest in a neat pile.

By the time he joined me on the four-poster, the combination of alcohol and doubt were combining to make my anxiety rise.

I pushed it back down again.

'We can do this, Liv,' he said, with far more certainty than I felt.

I should have asked him why he thought that now, when we'd tried for a year and had failed spectacularly to get back on track. But I didn't.

Instead, after I'd wrestled my way out of my dress and cardiovascular-impinging support wear, we had sex. Comfortable, predictable, enjoyable, didn't-set-my-knickers-on-fire sex.

Afterwards, when his gentle snoring told me that he'd fallen asleep, I got up and wrapped the bed throw around me, then sat at the window, staring out at the moonlight and the jet-black outline of the hills in the distance.

What was I doing?

I was trying, that's what I was doing. I was being loyal and optimistic and strong.

Or weak.

It was hard to tell the difference.

Blue flashing lights coming towards the hotel snapped me out of my contemplation. No siren, but then we were in the country, in the middle of the night, so I guess they didn't need to alert other vehicles to their position.

Twice in one night the emergency services had been here, once for the pissed guy in the lobby, and now they were back, no doubt for the same guy, who'd probably drunk himself into oblivion by now. Just another Hogmanay.

Below our window, the gravel of the car park crunched as the ambulance came to a stop and two paramedics leapt out and disappeared into the building.

The lights, still on, were hypnotic, holding my gaze as the hand on the clock ticked down the minutes. They were taking a while, so not a false alarm or a harmless drunk this time. I said a silent wish that whoever they were here for was okay.

Twenty minutes later, they raced back out, pushing a stretcher.

They loaded it on to their ambulance and roared off, lights still flashing.

They were far in the distance by the time I closed my eyes and finally fell asleep in the chair.

It was thunder that woke me. Unfortunately, it was nothing to do with the weather and everything to do with the hangover caused by drinking a selection of cocktails followed by a whole bottle of champagne.

On top of that, I had raging cramp in my legs, caused by sleeping in a bucket chair with them folded beneath me.

Nate was still sleeping soundly on the bed, so I practically crawled to the bathroom, took two paracetamol from my toilet bag, knocked them back and then clambered into the shower.

Plan for today. Go downstairs, have breakfast, go home, and then get on with making this marriage work. Maybe if I requested constant day shifts it would help. It couldn't be easy being married to someone who was only there a couple of nights a week, and on those evenings, she was usually knackered because swapping between day shift, night shift and back shift really took it out of you.

Thunderous headache and dehydration aside, I tried to work out how I was feeling. Definitely a bit relieved that I wasn't going home to start looking for somewhere new to live and bicker over who got custody of the Tupperware tubs. Yes, definitely relieved. There was a bit of optimism in there too.

If I were being brutally honest though, there was a niggling doubt that I'd done the wrong thing and I should have stood my ground. Aaaargh! I couldn't have this internal conversation again. I'd been having it every day for the last year and I'd resolved nothing, so it was time to shut it down, stay put and make it work.

We could do this. We could. We had a true friendship and years of history – that had to be something worth saving. Although, I might have to bring up the whole 'folding of the clothes before sex' thing.

'Hey baby,' Nate said sleepily as I came out of the bathroom. The sheet had slipped down and his toned torso was on show – a throwback to his years playing football and rugby, maintained by his present life as a PE teacher and coach, keeping the current generation of teenagers off couches and on sports fields. 'So the Y2K bug didn't wipe out civilisation while I was sleeping?'

'Apparently not. Or if it did, it missed us.'

There had been countless scare stories over the last year about how mass computer malfunction caused by the dawn of the new millennium could wreak havoc, wrecking everything from the space program to my microwave, and destroy life as we know it.

Obviously I hadn't yet checked on my microwave, but I was going to take a guess that it was just dandy. Although, if it somehow managed to affect the hotel computers and wipe out our bar bill, I wouldn't complain.

'We need to be down in the restaurant within ten minutes if we want breakfast.'

'I'm starving,' he said. 'You?'

'I could eat something.' I couldn't, but I didn't want to come across as pathetic. I also didn't want to add any more pain to my aching head by trying to analyse why we were casually carrying on as normal, as if this was just another day, as if we hadn't just decided to salvage our marriage last night. We'd just reverted back to Liv and Nate, married couple, everything exactly as before.

He threw on jeans and a T-shirt, while I tied up my wet hair, then tracked down jeans, boots and a chunky jumper. We made it down with a couple of minutes to spare to find the others already congregated, the technicolour excitement of last night replaced by grey pallor and tentative movements.

'Hangover Central, I take it?' I asked in a muted voice.

Chloe winced as she nodded.

I slipped into one of the two empty chairs. 'Great, then I'll fit right in.'

'So are we deciding which one of you we like best and picking who to stay friends with, or does the fact that you were holding hands when you came in here mean that you're still together?' That was from Sasha, naturally.

'Honestly, someone should give the United Nations a heads-up about your skills in tact and diplomacy, Sasha,' Chloe said. 'There must be a warring nation that we could drop you in to stir things up more.'

The others laughed, before Nate answered.

'Still together,' Nate said, grinning at me.

I tried to return the gesture but it made the pain in my head hurt even more. I settled for a thumbs up.

Chloe cheered at half volume. 'Yay! I'm so glad. It's the right thing. Definitely is.'

Despite the confidence of her words, my gaze met Chloe's raised eyebrow and I knew what she was thinking: *Are you sure?*

This time I managed a half-smile and a nod, and her whole beautiful face relaxed. I could see she was happy about this. She loved Nate, but until last night she'd opted out of the discussions about leaving or staying because she said it had to be my decision. No judgement, no attempt to sway. Whatever I decided, I knew she'd be fine with it as long as I was happy.

I didn't even look back at Sasha, because I knew she'd be somewhere along the reaction that went: eye roll, shake of head, pursed lips of disapproval, shrug of 'well, hell mend you and don't come to me for sympathy when it all goes wrong'.

'Ida will be delighted,' Chloe went on. 'Have you told her yet?'

'Nope, but yes, she will.' Ida's reaction to my gentle warning that Nate and I were in trouble was to start wearing black and brush up on her repertoire of power ballads. Every time I'd seen her since, she'd go about her business while delivering a mournful version of Whitney's 'I Will Always Love You'. The happy news would get her back into primary colours and disco tunes from the eighties.

My stomach lurched as a plate loaded with a full English breakfast was placed in front of me. I ignored most of it and just took two slices of bacon, wedged them into the middle of two slices of toast, and washed it down with strong tea. I dipped in and out of the conversation going on around me until I heard Justin mentioning an ambulance.

'Yeah, I saw that. It must have been about 4 a.m. It came roaring up the drive with its lights flashing.'

'You were still awake at 4 a.m.?' Nate asked me.

'Couldn't sleep.'

A flinch of guilt shadowed his face. 'You should have woken me.'

'It was fine, honestly. I just sat at the window for a while.' There was no point sharing the truth of the angst-ridden, cramp-inducing night. We were moving forward. Onwards and upwards. If it didn't hurt to move my eyes, I'd have been rolling them at the overuse of mental clichés. 'Anyway, what was the ambulance here for?' I continued. 'Someone overdo the champagne?'

Justin shook his head. 'No. I was outside for a smoke this morning and the bellboy was telling me that a woman was hurt in the toilets. A head injury. Her friends thought she'd gone to bed, so they didn't go looking for her. Apparently, she lay there for hours.'

'God, that's awful. Was she okay?' Chloe asked.

Justin shook his head. 'No. The bellboy said she'd lost too much blood because she was there for so long. The poor girl died on the way to hospital.'

2

Sasha's 30th Birthday

October 2000

The phone rang just as we were stepping out of the taxi to go into the restaurant. Chloe. I skipped the small talk and went straight to the important stuff. What I really meant to say was it wouldn't be as much fun without her, but that came out as, 'Don't you dare call off tonight. That'll leave me with just Sasha and Justin and if I try to keep up with her drinking capacity I'll end up dead in a gutter.'

'Nope, just want to let you know that the ward is chaos, so I'll be late. Save me a seat. Two seats, actually.'

'Two? Did Rob change his mind about going to Ibiza?'

I was still finding it hard to believe that Chloe and Rob had split. He'd gone off to sell timeshares in the Balearics and left my friend fluctuating on the break-up scale somewhere between 'surprised' and 'he's such a dick, I had a lucky escape'. I was just glad she wasn't devastated. When her ex, Connor, had taken off to live in Chicago, right around the same time as she realised she should never have called it off with him, she'd been inconsolable for months. I still didn't think she was completely over it. Rob had been a great stand-in, but he was never a big love.

'No, not Rob. I'll surprise you.' And then she was gone.

Nate held his hand out and I automatically took it. Things were actually really good. Weirdly, in some way it was partly down to that poor girl who had died at New Year. I still thought about her. It was just another reminder that you never knew what was round a corner or through a door, or when your life could change or end. All you could do was move forward and make the best of every day. So that was what I was doing. Nate and I were making an effort and it was working. We were happy. We'd even decided to buy a new house, a slightly tatty cottage down by the river in Weirbridge, a gorgeous old village about fifteen miles from the city centre. It felt like a very grown-up thing to do and the renovation was keeping us both busy, giving us a purpose again. It almost felt like we were back in the days when we first set up house together, only this time around there was definitely less nudity. Not that we were still in the sexual wilderness. We were back up to a pretty solid once a week and it was fine. Good. Please someone stop me before I say 'nice'.

Sasha and Justin must have seen us coming, because they materialised at the door to greet us. There was a couple who definitely had sex more than once a week. The sexual chemistry sparked between them and they had the raunchiest relationship of anyone I knew. Sasha had offered details, but I'd declined, citing privacy laws and a desire to avoid mental images I might never forget.

Justin and Nate did that handshake, pat-on-the-back man thing, while I hugged her close, then handed over a gift-wrapped present. Hammered silver earrings that were so long they would skim her shoulders.

'Happy birthday, Sasha. You're old now. Really, really old.'

'I know. First one to thirty. Ancient.' The irony was that, thanks to a comprehensive moisturising schedule, disciplined nutrition and an unshakable gym routine, she looked like the youngest of us all.

'You look stunning,' I told her. 'I really don't think I can be your friend anymore. It's giving me a complex. If you have a mid-life crisis, can I tag along when you get everything rejuvenated and get all your high street cast-offs?'

'Absolutely,' she said, 'but I won't be hanging out with you anymore because I'll have new friends that I'll meet in the changing rooms at Prada. And the rest of the time I'll be busy with my new toy – a six foot four Chippendale who'll succumb to my every whim.'

'You've got one of those already,' Justin deadpanned, slowly rising on his toes to conceal the reality that he'd have to stand on a shoebox to hit 6 ft 4 ins.

Aware that a bit of banter could turn to bickering in seconds with these two, I diplomatically changed the subject. 'Chloe rang. She's going to be late,' I reported. 'She got held up at work, but she's on her way.'

Sasha steered us to a table and we slid into a curved, red leather banquette seat. She immediately stopped a passing waiter. 'Can we have two vodka tonics, two beers, and four Sambuca shots for medicinal purposes.' One gutter coming right up.

Nate sat on Justin's outside, while I sat on Sasha's, putting us at opposite ends of the banquette. We made general small talk until the drinks came, then split into separate conversations.

'So...' Sasha started, speaking in hushed tones so the guys couldn't overhear. I braced myself. 'Are we still in Delusion Town? Still trying to convince yourself that staying with him was the right thing to do?'

'Sasha, how many times?'

Really, how many? We must be going into triple figures on some variation of this conversation since New Year, all of them starting and ending with Sasha telling me I was doing the wrong thing.

'Loads. Until you see sense and realise you're wasting your time with a guy that you're not actually in love with anymore.'

'I am! We bought a gorgeous sideboard from Habitat this week. It'll look great once we've wallpapered the hall.'

My nonchalance pressed so many buttons she was going to need all four shots of Sambuca to get her blood pressure back down to normal.

'Right, that's it. I give up. I'm saying nothing else. You're on your own,' she spat.

'Good,' I replied, keeping the nonchalance going.

'But don't come crying to me when you're forty, still miserable, and you finally leave him only to discover that no one else wants you because you're bitter and twisted and your face is one big map of misery wrinkles.'

'Okay,' I agreed, pointedly. 'First, I won't have misery wrinkles because I'll be happy. They'll be laughter lines. And either way, if I need help ironing out my face creases, I'll go to Chloe instead. She's the kind of non-judgemental friend who would help me without blasting me with her opinion.'

'You don't need non-judgemental friends. They're completely overrated. You need someone to tell you the truth and stop you living a life of delusion and regret. I'm not taking you to the bingo when you're eighty and alone and can't even remember your last shag because you've completely fucked up your life.'

'When I'm eighty I won't need you to take me to the bingo, because Nate and I will be travelling the world, celebrating our lives together, one zimmer stroll at a time. However, your views are noted, appreciated, and duly ignored. Haven't you got guests to greet? Or people to socialise with?'

With a dramatic eye roll any fifteen-year-old would be proud of, Sasha slid out of the seat and went off to find new victims to torture.

I refused to give her opinions any significant consideration.

Were Nate and I in a windswept bubble of devoted bliss? No. But that didn't mean that we weren't doing great. Brilliant even. And did I mention that we were having sex once a week?

'Right you, come dance with me. Don't say no, because then I'll have to ask Sasha and she always wants to lead,' Nate said, laughing. He got up and was waiting for me by the time I did an arse shuffle out of the banquette. Whoever invented this form of seating had a twisted mind. They were the dining equivalent of a siege situation, relying on the people at the ends not to hold you against your will.

The music shifted up a gear and NSYNC said 'Bye Bye Bye'. I bloody hated dancing, but I gave it a shot, telling myself that I was Madonna on the inside, even if I was more Elderly Grandmother Line Dancing on the outside.

Nate sidled up close to me and kissed me on the lips. 'You okay?'

I nodded. 'Of course.'

'You and Sasha looked like you were deep in conversation there,' he said.

'Och, you know – talking about work stuff. She's on a mission to get her fifth years to picket the common room for a microwave and unlimited free condoms.'

That was actually true, but just not what we'd been discussing at that point. I figured a white lie was better than the truthful alternative. *She thinks I should leave you before I'm a dried-up old husk that couldn't buy a bloke on that new Internet thingy.*

He laughed. 'If Sasha ever moves to the same school as me I'm putting in for early retirement. Or emigrating.'

'We can't leave the country…'

'Because we've a new sideboard?' he joked, getting to the punchline a second before me.

'Exactly!' See that was the thing with Nate. We had simultaneous thoughts. We found the same things funny. It was just… easy.

He resumed dancing and I'm not exaggerating when I say he's seriously good. His hips move at the right time, he's got a cute shoulder shuffle action, and if I were sitting at the side of the dance floor right now, I'd definitely be watching him. In the early years, it used to make me want to sidle between his thighs for a bit of Dirty Dancing. Now, well, I still thought it was sexy. Definitely enough to make me wait another five minutes before going to the buffet for a mini steak pie or a chicken goujon.

We danced out the record, then called it a day when the track switched and Destiny's Child demanded that we say their name.

At the table, Sasha was back and fixing her lippy, using the mirror sewn into the inside of her sparkly silver clutch. I slid in beside her again, just as she lowered her bag, eyes fixed on the door.

'Holy shit, who's that?'

I followed her gaze. 'Chloe. She's been our best friend for many years,' I teased her, knowing full well she wasn't referring to our mate's arrival, despite it being indisputably spectacular. Chloe had poured her sextastic curves into a cream, column-style dress that was split down to the navel at the front, showing off her deep caramel skin and perfectly formed natural boobs. She'd pulled back her Afro on the sides, and added smoky eyes and a deep red lipstick. On anyone else it would be too much. On her it was glorious. Suddenly my plain black dress was woefully unspectacular.

'You're hilarious. No really,' Sasha barbed, oozing sarcasm. 'Who's the bloke, smartarse?'

'I could be mistaken, but I think it's a new doc at the hospital. A neurosurgeon. Dr Campbell.'

So that was the surprise Chloe had alluded to earlier. Well played on her part.

'I've only seen him in passing, never treated any of his patients,' I went on, 'but the hospital grapevine is alive with the sound of gossip about him. Single. Nice guy. A touch on the arrogant side, but then most surgeons are. Not a perv. No recorded moments of leeriness. And Maggie, the cleaner on our ward, says she's going to have his babies. Which might take medical intervention, because she's sixty-one.'

'I can see her point,' Sasha concurred, keeping her voice low so she wasn't overheard by our blokes. Not that she had to worry. Justin and Nate were once again embroiled in their usual conversation that involved the latest episodes of twenty-two men chasing a ball. If our circle was anything to go by, it was the favourite topic of the west of Scotland male.

Chloe headed our way, bringing Dr Campbell behind her. She introduced him to Sasha and me first.

'Chicas, this is Richard Campbell. Richard, meet Liv and Sasha.'

He flashed an exceptionally endearing grin, and I could see why Maggie the cleaner was contemplating babies at a time in her life when she should be contemplating retirement cruises.

'We've met?' he said, as he shook my hand. 'I recognise you.'

'I'm a nurse at Glasgow Central. Palliative Care ward. We've probably passed each other in the canteen.' I didn't say that we definitely had been in the same cappuccino queue in the staff restaurant as I didn't want to give any hint of stalker-like behaviour. The poor guy was probably self-conscious enough.

'Next time I'll say hello,' he promised. 'Good to meet you.'

'And you.' So far, the gossip seemed pretty much accurate. Nice guy. I approved.

He was already on to Sasha. Or rather, Sasha was on to him.

'Okay, I need details,' she announced before he could even speak.

This clearly amused him.

'Shoot,' he said, laughing.

'Where are you from?'

'Manchester.'

'Age?'

'Thirty-four.'

'Are you now, or have you ever been, married?'

'Nope.'

'Currently seeing anyone?'

'No.'

'How long have you been in Glasgow?'

'Ten months.'

'So you're a hot doctor. Why are you still single? What's wrong with you?'

'Sasha!' Chloe interjected, outraged. 'Enough!'

'No, it's fine. I can handle this,' Richard said, with far more good nature than Sasha deserved. She was truly a nightmare sometimes, but he was handling it well.

'Workaholic tendencies. Too busy to meet anyone. Live in hope,' he batted back.

Sasha was chuckling now too. 'Okay, you pass. You can stay.'

'Brain surgery is a doddle compared to this,' he added, as Chloe steered him to the safety of the men's side of the table.

'Are you two talking about football?' she asked, already fully aware what the answer would be.

Nate nodded. 'Busted.'

Richard slid right in beside him. 'Excellent. Sounds good to me.'

Chloe laughed as she left him there and came to join us back at the oestrogen side of the padded leather.

'Sit down and tell me what's going on immediately,' Sasha demanded.

Chloe obliged. 'Don't get your thong in a twist, Sasha. We're just friends. He moved here at the beginning of the year and hasn't really got to know anyone yet. He was at a loose end tonight, so I invited him along. Don't think he's really my type.'

'Because your type isn't good-looking, successful guys with a nice smile and a job that involves healing the sick?' I countered, laughing.

'Nah,' Chloe answered. 'I like them with just a bit more of an edge. Maybe he'll grow on me though.' I hoped so. If this guy couldn't fill the Connor-shaped hole in her heart, I wasn't sure that anyone could.

The DJ struck up the opening bars of 'Proud Mary' and Chloe jumped to her feet. 'Yassss! Come on. My inner Tina Turner needs some action.'

'My inner Tina Turner needs to visit the ladies, so I'll pass. Sasha, it's on you.'

Sasha groaned as she followed Chloe onto the dance floor, and I headed to the ladies, relieved to be escaping.

On the way, I spotted a door leading out to a gorgeous little courtyard and I felt the packet of Silk Cut in my clutch bag start to twitch. I hadn't smoked since I was eighteen, until a couple of months ago. One of the joiners who was working on the house stepped out back on his lunch break, lit a cigarette and I was immediately transported back to my teenage self, the one who was still full of huge ambitions for the future. I've no idea what possessed me, but I'd cadged a cig off him, and ever since then I'd been sneaking the odd one in times of stress or boredom. It was ridiculous. I was twenty-nine years old. A fully functioning adult. A bloody nurse. And I'd decided to take up smoking. Not every day. Just the odd one every couple of days, but still, it made absolutely no sense at all. That's why I'd decided that this was going to be my last packet. Absolutely. Definitely. Although I might have said that last week.

'Do you think I could have a light please?' I asked a striking girl standing alone in the corner. She had a glossy blonde bob, flawless make-up, and she was wearing a figure-hugging white dress that showed she didn't carry an extra ounce of body fat. Everything about her screamed 'impeccable grooming'. She was the kind of woman I aspired to be, but somehow, I still ended up rushing out to work with wet hair, wearing pants I turned pink in the wash back in 1998.

She held out a gold lighter and I lit the cigarette, already mentally running through the chewing gum/perfume/hand-washing system that would immediately follow so that Nate didn't realise I was smoking. He definitely wouldn't approve. Blonde bob then retreated back into the corner. It may have been a subtle sign that she wouldn't welcome small talk, but I chose to ignore it.

'Are you having a good night?' I asked.

'It's not one of my better ones,' she said, and there was no mistaking the bitterness in her voice.

'Oh.' I wasn't entirely sure where to go with that, but I get deeply uncomfortable in awkward silences so I broke into a nervous ramble to fill the void. 'That's a shame. I thought the music was really good though. And the food. Oh my God, the chicken satay sticks are amazing. I'd never tried them before but I'll definitely have them again. I think Iceland do them.'

I could see she was glazing over and I had an internal dialogue in the hope of getting myself under control. *Stop talking. Stop talking. STOP TALKING.*

But it seemed my anxious babble wasn't yet done.

'Are you a friend of Sasha's then?'

Of course she was, otherwise she wouldn't be here.

Put cigarette in mouth. Stop talking.

'I'm Madeleine. I work with Justin.' Ah, one of the modern-day yuppies. That figured. With their sharp clothes and impeccable grooming, they all looked like they invested heavily in their appearance and that white blonde hair didn't come from a bottle purchased down the chemist for a fiver.

'Ah, that's good. Have you worked together for long?'

'Seven years,' she said, and she didn't sound happy about it. In fact, either the smoke was getting in her eyes, or she was on the verge of tears. Poor soul. She was having a bad night and there I was making small talk.

'Hope you don't mind me asking, but are you okay?'

'I'm fine,' she said, shrugging. I thought she was going to finish there, but she didn't. 'Just boyfriend stuff,' she added.

'Is he being an arse?' I said, trying to make her smile. It didn't work. Her words oozed weariness and futility.

'Yup. Can't make his mind up between me and someone else.'

'Well, I bloody hope he picks you,' I said, trying to bolster her up again. 'You're clearly a catch!'

She finally smiled, but before she could reply we were interrupted by a new arrival. 'Nurse Jamieson, I don't believe the NHS endorses having a sly cig on a Friday night.'

Richard Campbell. Bollocks. Totally caught. I was going to have to make him promise not to mention this to Nate, Chloe or Sasha.

'It's for medical research,' I quipped back. 'I want to see how many I need to smoke before I feel really crap.'

'Interesting premise for a study. Mind if I join you? And by that I mean, can I cadge a cigarette because I don't actually smoke unless I've had a couple of beers and I'm looking for an excuse to freeze my arse off.' He had a point. It must be approaching zero on the temperature scale and yet here we were, standing outside in the cold for the sake of a vice that could kill us. I could see the flaws in this strategy.

Madeleine stubbed out what was left of her cigarette and headed back inside. I felt another twinge of compassion for her as she passed, and we shared a mutually sympathetic glance. Richard and I chatted for the next few minutes about his time at the hospital (almost a year now and, yes, he was enjoying it) and my friendship with Chloe (almost ten years now, and yes, she was fabulous) and I realised that if she didn't fancy him, she absolutely should. He was funny, and smart, and had that manner that put people at ease. He was… sexy. Not in an obvious 'muscle-bound gym-dweller' kind of way, but in a charming, cool, alpha male vibe that I could see would be seriously attractive. Not that I was attracted to him. Pfft. No. Absolutely not. I was married. And he was here with Chloe. Out of bounds on both counts. No, not attracted to him at all.

I cut off what he was saying with, 'I'd better go back inside. In fact, I'll just nip to the loo first. And we'll erm… keep this whole smoking thing between us?'

'Absolutely,' he agreed. 'Unless I ever need to blackmail you.'

'Just say the word and I'll give you everything I own,' I joked.

He opened the door for me and I headed to the ladies. Perfume. Chewing gum. Hand wash. And repeat: *I am not attracted to my friend's date for the night.*

Unfortunately, no one told my face this, and I blushed furiously when – de-smoked – I eventually joined the others back at the table and saw he was already there. In fact, he was next to Nate. My husband. The love of my life. I was attracted to him, not to some swarthy doctor. Another pfft. How ridiculous.

I caught his eye and he gave me a conspiratorial wink, sending the blood rushing to my face.

'Why are you bright red?' Sasha asked, in full suspicion mode.

'Think I'm just a bit hot. It was really warm in the toilets.'

Lies. Lies. Lies. I was a terrible person.

She sniffed. 'Have you been smoking?'

'Don't be ridiculous.' More lies. This was turning into an episode of *Crimestoppers*.

Clearly she'd had one too many Sambucas to pursue this line of enquiry, and thankfully decided to switch her interrogation skills to a situation that interested her far more than my possible nicotine habit. She leaned in close to Chloe. 'Tell me again why he's not your type?'

Chloe chuckled. 'Just not feeling it. Besides, I work with him – that makes it way too complicated.'

'Potential?' Sasha asked.

'Don't think so. Although I reserve the right to change my mind.'

'Permission granted. You'd be fricking nuts not to because he is entirely shaggable. Not that I'd choose him for a wanton one-night stand over Justin,' she clarified.

At that, she gestured in her boyfriend's direction. I followed the trajectory of her nod and saw Justin leading a chant as he did simultaneous shots with a whole table of colleagues, including Madeleine, the girl from the smoking session.

She still didn't look very happy. In fact, as soon as Justin had downed his drink, I saw her lean in and say something to him. Judging by his expression, it seemed that it wasn't a compliment on the mini steak pies.

Sasha was no longer gazing their way, so I didn't enlighten her. If riled, she could whip up a jealous outburst in a heartbeat and it was always completely unfounded. She had absolutely nothing to worry about. Justin adored her – he'd never cheat.

'Right, girls, this is how I see it,' she announced, taking the lead in our impromptu committee meeting. 'Chloe, you need to jump that doctor's bones. And Liv…'

I could hardly wait. 'Yes?'

'You need to come to your senses about your marriage, call it a day before you waste any more years of your life, or else the future burden is falling on Chloe.'

'What future burden?' Chloe asked, perplexed.

Sasha answered Chloe like she was passing on grave, tragic news, nodding in my direction as she spoke. 'You'll need to take this sad old husk to the bingo.'

3

Justin's 30th Birthday Party

August 2001

I checked my watch: 7 p.m. We should have left fifteen minutes ago. Sasha would go nuclear if we were late to Justin's party, but Nate was still on the phone to Connor in Chicago. The two of them had been mates long before we all met at university and they still spoke every couple of weeks on the phone.

Last week, Connor had called Nate to let him know that he'd split with his girlfriend, Stacey, and Nate had called him back tonight to see how he was doing. What was supposed to be a five-minute call had turned into an hour and a phone bill that would leave us skint next month.

Nate had tried to persuade him to come back for Justin's party, but Connor wasn't up for it. He and Justin had become good mates in the year or so that they'd hung out together back in the day, before Connor had headed off to the USA, but not the kind of friendship that would make you travel thousands of miles just for a birthday party. Besides, too many bridges had been burned, he'd said. We knew what he meant: Chloe. They hadn't kept in touch, not even once, since he went off to the States, and it was perfectly understandable that Connor would feel uncomfortable seeing her again after all this time. She'd dumped him. And then he'd reacted by getting over it all pretty quickly and leaving the country with his rebound girl. He hadn't been back since and we'd never made it over there. The truth was that every year I came up with a reason not to go – work, skint, moving house – because I felt it would be disloyal to Chloe.

Now, I'd be lying if I said I wasn't pleased his relationship with Stacey hadn't worked out. Chloe had long since stopped talking about Connor on a daily basis, but I knew she'd regretted calling it off with him since about ten minutes after she did it. I couldn't wait to tell her that Connor was single again, but I wanted to do it when we were on our own and away from work, and we'd been on opposite shifts all week.

I'd try to find the right moment tonight to let her know.

Nate finally got off the phone.

'Any luck convincing him to come back yet?' I asked, ever hopeful.

He shook his head. 'I think it would need to be something really special to make him come back and I know it's because he's not up for facing Chloe. I told him she was single, but he's never got over her dumping him, no matter how many times I tell him she regrets it. I don't think he believes me.'

'Argh, he's so bloody stubborn. Sad thing is, if he'd just bloody walk into a room, I think they'd clap eyes on each other and that would be it.'

Nate leaned down and kissed me. 'Eternal romantic.'

It wasn't the moment to say I hadn't felt a gush of romance in a long time. I shook that thought off. We were still good. The house renovation was taking forever, but we were enjoying it. I still loved my job. Nate had moved to a new school in an undeniably deprived area of the city, but he was relishing the challenge of initiating a new PE programme there. Life was working out just fine. We were happy. Content. I ignored the tug of irritation that pulled my gut at the thought of that 'c' word and reminded myself that I was lucky. A lot of people never got this.

After a mad dash in a taxi, we got to the pub only half an hour late. Sasha might forget murdering us and just go for minor assault instead.

I spotted her at a corner table and headed over. 'Hello gorgeous,' I greeted her.

'Hello latecomers,' she drawled. I shut up her dig by giving her a kiss, then we plonked ourselves down and checked out the room. There was a gang of Justin's workmates, a few other guys from university and his brother, Jake, was sitting with what might be their mum and dad.

My thoughts were blown away by Chloe's arrival. 'Hello, you shower of lovely people!' she chirped, sounding happy and carefree. I hated the thought that there was every possibility that I'd change that mood before the end of the night. How would she take the news that Connor's relationship had ended, but that he wasn't coming back? Gutted? Furious? Sad? Hopeful?

She leant down to start a round of kissing everyone, revealing Richard Campbell behind her.

'Hey stranger!' I exclaimed, my delight at seeing him bubbling to the surface. 'Long time no see.'

'I know!' he bellowed. 'I finally persuaded her that she couldn't show up at another party on her own so she had to bring me. It's not that I like her, you understand, it's just that I miss you lot.'

It was mutual. Since the night Chloe had brought him along to Sasha's party, he'd become a frequent addition to our gang and we really enjoyed his company.

I was still laughing when I got up to kiss him on both cheeks, closely followed by Sasha, who murmured in a stage whisper, 'Doctor, feel free to let your hands wander. Justin is pissed already – he'll never notice.'

'I would, but I'm not wearing gloves,' he jousted back, sending her into hoots of hilarity. He was one of the few people who could absolutely handle Sasha's in-your-face manner and dish every outrageous thing that came out of her mouth right back at her. I loved him for it. Just a shame Chloe didn't feel the same way. She and Richard had stayed firmly in the friendship zone despite all our efforts to persuade her otherwise.

'Not one nipple erection in his presence,' she'd say mournfully. 'It's just not meant to be.'

I was fairly convinced he didn't agree with that summation, but I'd yet to come straight out and ask him, hoping that he'd drop it into conversation with me first. We didn't bump into each other often, but we'd shared a few coffees in the staff canteen and I'd waited for him to say something about moving things to a different level with Chloe but he never did. Sod it, next time I was just going to come right out with it and ask him. If he was attracted to my friend he should tell her and soon. She was going to need something to take her mind off the discovery that Connor was single again.

Richard sat beside Nate, and immediately got into a chat about football, while Chloe sat in between Sasha and me, then immediately zeroed in on my face.

'What is it? What's up?'

It really spooked me that she could read me like that.

I decided to bluff. 'Nothing! Why would you think that?'

'Because you've got an expression that is somewhere between concern and pity.' This was why I could never play poker with her.

'Ladies and gentlemen, I'd like your attention please!' The announcement was accompanied by a rattling of a glass, and came from Justin's brother Jake, who was swaying on the bar top.

'Just as well we have a team of medical experts here, because it'll be a miracle if he doesn't take a header off there,' Sasha muttered.

She loved Jake, but as with everyone, she hid it behind a veneer of sarcastic bitchiness.

'I'd just like to say happy birthday to my brother.'

A cheer went up, then he carried on.

'Justin, we were too cheap to buy you a present...'

Another cheer.

'So we got you something that came free instead.'

Just at that, one of Jake's mates (topless) and my mother, Ida (thankfully not topless), galloped in from a fire exit carrying a long pole. Nothing surprised me. Not a thing. Not since she'd appeared at my school as a parent helper on the occasion of my Primary One Halloween party, dressed in a full country and western outfit, announced that she was Calamity Jane and treated the entire collective gathering to a full rendition of 'The Deadwood Stage'. With whip. Her arrival now with a pole didn't even register as a blip on the Ida-ometer.

'Strip limbo!' Jake bellowed, as the pub went wild.

'God, I love him,' Chloe chuckled.

'Good,' Sasha said dryly. 'You can visit him when he's in traction.'

Right on cue, Jake wobbled, fell off the bar and was only saved from certain fracture by the super-quick reflexes of a pal who managed to grab him and break his fall.

Interruptions over, and with me trying to studiously ignore the fact that my mother was shuffling under a pole with her knees at an angle that could lead to dislocation, Chloe lost no time at all in getting back to where we'd been before Jake's highbrow, spiritual speech.

'So what's going on?' she asked, one eyebrow raised.

I wasn't going to tell her. Not here. Not now...

Who was I kidding? One glance of her raised-eyebrow stare of intimidation and I caved. I'd be a hopeless spy.

'Nate has been speaking to Connor a lot over the last week or so.'

Her face immediately clouded and she took a large slug of her Southern Comfort and lemonade. 'How is he?' she asked.

Oh bugger. The only way was to tell her straight and Nate should be the one to do it so that he got the story absolutely correct.

Unfortunately, he was still analysing the latest developments in the world of men who chased rubber balls.

'He split with Stacey,' I blurted, then watched as her face ran a gamut of emotions that moved through surprise, pensiveness, relief and, as predicted, finished somewhere around hope.

'Is he coming back?' she asked, and I could see how desperate she was for that to happen. I'd give anything to tell her what she wanted to hear, but instead, I shook my head.

'I'm so sorry, Chlo, but he isn't. Nate tried to convince him it would be a good idea but he didn't want to.'

'Who broke it off?' she asked.

'I think it was mutual. It's difficult to get the full story. Nate's rubbish at getting to the bottom of stuff.'

She processed this news for a moment.

'Look, Chloe, I know you still have feelings for him...'

'I don't!'

We both knew she was bluffing, so I carried on, 'But he doesn't know how you feel. Maybe you should tell him. You could go there...'

She shook her head so strongly the huge pile of curls on top of her elaborate up-do quivered. 'No. If he wanted me, he'd come back. He'd fight for me.'

I didn't think it wise to point out that by refusing to make the first move, she wasn't exactly putting up a fight for him either.

She was still on a roll. 'Or at the very least he'd get in touch and sound things out. I know it was my fault that we split, but he moved on a long time ago and there's no going back.'

'I don't think you believe that.'

'I do. Or at least... I will.'

She rested her head on my shoulder for a moment and I could feel the tension in her neck. She deserved to be happy. She was the loveliest, kindest person and just because she'd made one mistake and let love go...

Would this have been me? If I'd left Nate that night, would I be sitting here now, two years later, wishing that I could get him back? Would I be devastated because he'd moved on and it was too late? I'd never know, and I was pretty sure I didn't want to find out.

'I think I've been in some kind of weird holding pattern, hoping he'd come back, Liv.'

I knew that was true. She'd been with Rob for about a year around the time of the millennium, but she didn't shed a tear when they split. Other than that, there had been a few short-term dating situations and that was it. It said everything that the longest relationship she'd had with a member of the opposite sex since Connor left, was with Richard, and that was purely platonic.

I was glad. I'd hate to see her settle for a guy that didn't drive her wild. And no, it didn't escape me that I may be projecting slightly there.

'Fuck it,' she said, lifting her head off my shoulder and physically shaking off her gloom. 'You know, it's his loss.'

'It is.' I agreed.

'I'm not going to sit here moping or waste any more of my life waiting for him to sweep back in and carry me off like Richard Gere in An Officer and A Bloody Gentleman.'

'I think you'll find that isn't the actual title of that movie,' I said grinning, before knocking back a couple of slugs of my vodka and tonic. Emotionally draining discussions always made me thirsty. 'So what are you going to do?' I added.

Her turn to take another large slug of her Southern Comfort now. She paused after she returned it to the table, clearly pondering the words that would perfectly describe her plan of action moving forward.

'I'm going to proposition Richard and see if he's up for being more than just good friends.'

4

Barbeque at Liv and Nate's House

July 2002

The sight of my mother made me grin. There she was, resplendent in a figure-hugging red dress, her ever-present heels, hair teased to perfection, wearing an apron with a nude, male, six-pack torso on it, while holding up a grilling fork.

'Right, love, I've put the Cajun chicken on the barbeque – got the recipe from that Naked Chef bloke,' she proclaimed. 'He could boil my eggs any time.'

I didn't rise to it. It was best not to – it only encouraged her. 'Thanks, Mum.'

Nate came out of the house behind me, carrying a case of beer and began to unload it into a large rubber ice bucket that was put into service whenever we had friends round.

'Are you okay?' he asked as he passed me on the way back to the kitchen for more beers.

I nodded. Then shrugged. Then shook my head. Which pretty much summed up the bubbling conflict of emotions I was feeling right now. Losing patients was an unavoidable part of my job and I accepted that. One of the reasons I went into palliative care was because I truly thought I could help people in the last days of their lives and I was positive I could deal with the emotional pressure that came with it. Mostly that was true, but every now and then I lost a patient I'd come to know and to care about on a deeper level, and Charlie Moss was one of those people. Twenty-two years old. Wrong. Unfair. Devastating. Just heart-breaking.

In all honesty, after the sadness of the last few days, I didn't feel like the glittering hostess. I could happily spend the afternoon under a duvet on the couch, with a flask of tea and some serious comfort food.

Today had been arranged for weeks, though, and I didn't have the heart to call it off. It was supposed to be a celebration of our house renovation finally being finished. A couple of weeks ago, we'd washed out our last paintbrush, inhaled our last lungful of dust and – after a day of near-divorce in IKEA's soft furnishings department – added the finishing touches to the house. It was done. Weirdly, since then I'd been a bit lost. It felt like the work in the house had been the purpose of the last year or two, and now it was finished, I wasn't sure what should occupy our free time.

Barbeques! That was the answer. Weekly doses of Ida's Cajun chicken. Not that such a concept was possible in Scotland. We'd been lucky to have a dry, sunny day today, but the weather was so unpredictable we could have anything from torrential rain to snow by next weekend.

I shook off the gloom and told myself to stop being pathetic. Charlie would be the very person who wouldn't be wasting his time sitting here reflecting on the sorrow. He'd be making the most of every minute and that's exactly what I should be doing too. Besides, my mates were on the way here and if anyone could cheer me up, it was them.

I realised Nate was still standing there, his face a mask of concern.

'I'm fine, really. I'll just go help Mum and check everything is organised.' I already knew it was, because I'd been up since

6 a.m. making sure we were fully prepared, but it got me out of a longer discussion with Nate, and I saw the relief on his face as I said it. In-depth, emotional conversations were up there with a trip to IKEA on his 'Things to Avoid' list.

Before I got very far, I heard the click of the garden gate and the voice from behind me immediately made me smile.

'Hello there!'

'Good afternoon, Dr Campbell,' I teased, as I let him wrap me in a huge hug.

It was easy to see why Dr Richard Campbell was the object of many desires at the hospital. He had that easy-going smile and contagious charm that just made him fun to be around. I'd still really hoped that he and Chloe would get together and become a couple, but they never had. I knew she'd considered it once, the year before, at Justin's birthday party, when she'd heard that Connor was single again but not coming home. She'd made some comment about drowning her sorrows by taking things with Richard to the level that involves seeing stuff that can't be unseen, but she'd bottled out before it happened because she said no amount of Southern Comfort could manufacture sexual chemistry between them. Thus, their friendship remained unblemished by misguided naked fumblings, leaving Chloe to keep her position as his chief friend and supplier of advice on his dating life, his work life, and any other part of his life she chose to voice an opinion on.

'What are you doing here?' I asked Richard, then realised that sounded rude, so immediately followed up with, 'Although I'm so glad you are! That came out completely wrong.'

Fortunately, my faux pas cracked him up. 'Well, thanks. You know how to make a bloke feel welcome.'

'Oh hush and stop being so sensitive,' I chided him, laughing. It had been ages since I'd seen him. He'd definitely established a friendship with all of us and he'd fitted right in, but Chloe was the link between us all and he only hung out with us when Chloe brought him along to a gathering.

He returned to my question. 'Chloe invited me over. Just so happened we were both off on the same day. That hasn't happened for a while, so I jumped at the chance to come here for some of Ida's cooking.'

'Ah, you are such a smooth-talker. She's over there wearing the torso of a male stripper. She'll be delighted to see you. If she makes any inappropriate innuendos, feel free to file a complaint on the way out.'

I watched as he headed off in Ida's direction and her face beamed as she saw him approach. She'd a real soft spot for him and every conversation she'd had with Chloe for the last year had included a plea for her to see sense and snap him up. It took a tough cookie to refuse Ida anything, but Chloe was standing her ground in the platonic zone.

Chloe arrived not long after Richard, closely followed by Sasha and Justin.

I immediately sensed Sasha's vibe and it wasn't a happy one. It didn't take a genius to work out why. Justin was heading towards Ida, Nate and Richard at the barbeque, and yup, there it was. Even from here I could see that he was swaying in the manner of someone who'd had way too many beers for this time of day.

This wasn't going to end well.

Sasha didn't lighten up at all in the next half-hour or so, and by the time the guys headed towards us with the food, Sasha looked fit to explode. Ida had the sausages and steak. Richard was clutching a large dish of burgers. Nate had the box of beers and Justin had…

'Fuck, fuck, fuck!' he exclaimed, as he staggered to the side and somehow lost his balance. Thankfully, Richard managed to steady him before the chicken skewers went scattering across the lawn.

Sasha closed her eyes for a second and I could see that she was struggling to hold it together. Chloe spotted it too, so she immediately jumped in with a diversion.

'Right, guys, I've decided we need something to look forward to, so how about a group holiday next year? I'm thinking Los Angeles. Not too hot for the ginger,' she gestured to me and I nodded in thanks for her consideration, 'and so much to do there for all of us. The flights are on sale this week, so I reckon we should book it and sort out accommodation later. Although, I'm thinking if we all chip in we might even be able to afford something in Santa Monica or Malibu. Please say yes, because I need to start the diet now if I'm going to get into a bikini.'

'I'm in!' I yelped, without any hesitation, desperate to join Chloe's argument-avoiding bandwagon. Besides, life was so much better when we had a beach and cocktails on the horizon.

Richard was next. 'Sounds good to me. I'll need to check I can get the dates that suit everyone, but I'm up for it.' I loved his sense of adventure – he was always game for anything.

'I'm in,' Sasha agreed, but with less enthusiasm.

'Partyyyyyyyy on the beach in Mal-i-bu. Baywatch baby!' Justin exclaimed, holding his bottle of Bud in the air and doing an impromptu dance. I made a mental note to make sure Sasha didn't burn his return ticket and leave him in LA.

So we were all in. Chloe, Richard, Sasha, Justin, me and… My gaze went to Nate, who was strangely quiet on the subject. No immediate acceptance.

My mum was uncharacteristically schtum too. What was going on? The only time I ever saw her speechless was when Tom Jones was on the TV.

'What am I missing?' I asked, eying them both with suspicion. If Ida and Nate were colluding, God knows what the outcome could be.

Nate tried to brush it off. 'Nothing. We'll talk about it later.'

Now I was absolutely positive something was going on.

'I don't want to talk about it later. There's nothing you can't say in front of everyone here.' It was true. There were no secrets in our group.

'No, it's…'

'He wants to start a family,' Ida blurted. 'Soon as possible. And, for what it's worth, I'd like a grandchild. Or two. Let's face it, love, you're not getting any younger.'

Sasha and Chloe slowly turned their heads to face me, both with eyebrows high, lips pursed and expressions of expectation.

Bollocks.

How many levels of wrong were in that outburst?

'Let me get this straight. You two have been getting together to discuss future options for my ovaries? Were you intending to include me in this little plan or were you just hoping that some Rambo sperm would impregnate me next time I brush past you on the way out the door?'

'Liv, don't… it wasn't like that, it was just…'

I wasn't having it. Not today. Not any bloody day. I wasn't prone to scenes or drama, but my womb was fucking furious and determined not to let this go. Ida first. I tried my best to keep my voice steady but firm.

'For what it's worth, Mum, I'm thirty-one. I still have well over a decade before I'm too old to carry on our bloodline. And when I do, I hope my future son or daughter hasn't been splashing in the shallow waters of the tact section of your gene pool.'

'As long as they have my voice,' she chirped, showing all the emotional awareness of the salad tongs sitting on the table in front of her.

'Hopefully they'll know when to keep it on mute,' I countered. My wine glass was empty so I took Sasha's from her hand and drained what was left in it.

The others were still resolutely silent. I was about to call Nate out too, when Chloe's hand reached under the table for mine and gave it a squeeze of support. I bit my tongue. This wasn't the time to tackle Nate. I'd do it at home, when we were alone, and I could be as shrill as I wanted to be. That wasn't a spectator event.

'Anyway, who'd like another sausage?' I offered, changing the subject.

'Me!' Sasha answered, before bailing me out by telling a story about some scandal at her school.

I gave her a grateful smile then zoned out so I could inwardly seethe about Nate and Ida's conspiracy.

This was their most outrageous stunt yet. Why couldn't Nate have been just like Richard, agreed to the holiday and we'd all be planning our tour of the stars' houses right now?

And as for Ida, I couldn't win with her. There was no insulting her, because she took no one else's thoughts or opinions on board. It was impossible to embarrass her because she had zero shame, and she was completely devoid of anything even closely resembling empathy.

In all honesty, her viewpoint wasn't a surprise, because she'd been going on about having a grandchild for years. It wasn't so she could care for it, cuddle it, bake cakes and pass on grandmotherly words of wisdom. Nope. It was so she'd have loads of photo opportunities and a child to stage-manage into the career she never had in show business. It was an eternal disappointment to her that my singing voice was in the same register as two camels indulging in foreplay in the middle of a dusty night in the Sahara.

No, Ida expressing her opinion was nothing new, but Nate discussing this with her without even raising the subject with me? He'd never mentioned it. Not once. If he had, I'd have told him that I absolutely wasn't there yet. I wanted to do so many things before I had children. I wanted to... to... I realised I had no plans or aspirations at all. None. I wasn't aiming for another promotion or planning to climb Kilimanjaro. I really had to get myself some kind of list of ambitions. All I knew was that having a baby wasn't anything I was looking to do in the short term. We weren't so much on different pages as in different bloody books.

I squared my gaze firmly on Nate. The irony wasn't lost on me. Here he was, announcing grand desires to expand our family when we'd slipped back down to fortnightly sex. At this rate, there was more chance of me winning the tombola at the village fete than there was of accidentally falling pregnant due to spontaneous intercourse.

A couple of hours later, the garden gate had barely closed behind our departing friends, when I charged right back on to the hot topic of the day.

'So were you planning on discussing any of this with me? You know, giving me a heads-up that you wanted to change our lives forever?'

I expected him to go on the defence, but he took the opposite route and went for enthusiasm and persuasion.

'Don't you think we're ready? It would be incredible. If we started trying now, we could get pregnant soon and then the baby would be born just before summer next year, and I'd have six weeks off to help you look after her.'

'Her?'

He smiled. 'Yeah. In my head, it's a girl.'

Holy crap. I hadn't even got my jeans off and I was already pregnant, giving birth next June, to a girl, and Nate would be on hand to change her nappies.

I felt a subconscious need to cross my legs.

What about my career? My life? I loved my job and had no desire at all to take time off to start a family. Not yet. Not for a long time to come. Shouldn't there be a consultation period before he started reading baby names' books and opening a Mothercare account?

'Does this baby that I'm giving birth to next summer have a name?' I asked, with a top note of sarcasm. Of course she didn't.

'Sophie.'

Oh for Christ's sake.

'Nate, I don't want to start a family.'

My mum bustled back out from the kitchen at that point. 'Of course you do,' she argued.

'Mother, you have permission to interfere in my life, except the areas that begin with me being naked.'

She tutted and rolled her eyes, then pretended to be busy clearing away more dishes.

'You don't want to start a family?' Nate repeated.

'No. At least, not yet. Maybe someday. I promise I'll let you know when I do.' Weariness sucked all the fury from my body. What was I doing? Wasn't this what I'd signed up for? When I'd agreed to stay with him at the millennium, wasn't I pledging the happy ever after, happy family and total commitment until the bit where death do us part?

Was I kidding myself on? Was my subconscious refusing to contemplate having a child because I was then irrevocably tied to Nate for the rest of my life?

Was Sasha right when she said I'd made a huge mistake?

And would I get my money back on all those IKEA soft furnishings if I told them I'd changed my mind?

5

Justin's 32nd Birthday Garden Party

August 2003

'Another year, another party. Thank God for you two or I'd have the social life of a hibernating bear,' I said, as I squeezed Sasha into a hug. Justin was next. 'Here you go, birthday boy – something that's even more death-defying than living with Sasha.' I handed over a card, which he ripped open to reveal a voucher for paragliding. He'd been talking about doing it for years, so I'd decided to make it happen for him.

'Yassss! You doing this with me, mate?' he asked Nate.

'No problem at all,' Nate replied, without hesitation.

Sasha rolled her eyes. 'Action Men Glasgow – planning an adrenalin-fuelled activity while clutching a bottle of beer and an undercooked sausage.'

Justin leaned over and kissed me on the cheek. 'Thanks. This is great. And I'll try not to kill your husband in the process.'

'Always a bonus, because I'm fairly sure our life insurance doesn't cover ludicrous Sunday afternoon activities,' I replied, grinning. 'Anyway, glad you went for intimate and understated,' I said, gesturing to the melee in front of us. There was a barbeque. There was a bar in the corner. There was music. There were at least, oh maybe sixty or eighty people milling around. It was a full-scale spectacle and I wouldn't expect anything less from Justin and Sasha. Any excuse for a celebration got the full treatment.

Sasha nodded in the direction of a few people gathered in the corner. 'By the way, just a heads up, keep Nate away from that group over there nibbling crudities like they're bloody rabbits.'

I laughed at her obvious disgust, but she scolded me. 'I'm serious! See that one there with the swingy pony tail?' I spotted who she meant immediately. Black Lycra jogging pants and an obscenely tight white T-shirt over a body that was no stranger to a work-out. I felt myself pulling in my stomach and sucking in my cheeks as she went on, 'Justin was telling me that she has the serious hots for Nate. Been flirting with him at the gym for years.'

'Who? Janet?' Nate scoffed. 'She does not have any designs on me at all. She's just friendly. Stop stirring things up there, madam,' he reprimanded Sasha, who responded with a wink. 'She'd seduce him in a heartbeat,' she hissed to me, making me chuckle. At the sound of my laughter, Miss Lycra Pants turned to look over and her eyes immediately locked on Nate. Maybe there was something to Sasha's claim after all. Not that I was in the least bit flustered. Nate was so oblivious to such things that a woman would have to be in her knick-knacks and nibbling his ear before he realised she might be interested in him. And even then, he wouldn't do anything about it. I'd never in my life experienced feelings of jealousy, and this wasn't changing that. I trusted Nate. Nothing to worry about. I shot the girl a smile.

'Anyway,' Nate added, 'she's seeing one of the body builders now and they're getting married. She was telling me she's already booked her hen weekend in Marbella next year.'

Hen nights in Marbella. That was the kind of flash stuff that

Nate couldn't be arsed with. I decided my husband wasn't about to be stolen any time soon.

My thoughts were interrupted by Chloe and Richard, who were next to arrive. They joined us while Sasha and Justin went to greet a crowd that had just turned up. I recognised them from the last half a dozen parties as Justin's workmates. A riotous bunch, right on cue they headed straight for the bar.

'I've never asked you – the year we all turned thirty, why didn't you have a party like the rest of us attention seekers?' Chloe asked.

She was gorgeous as ever today. Boot cut blue jeans and a white floaty top, with her ebony hair falling in loose waves over her shoulders.

Her question, however, made me shudder. 'That's the stuff of my nightmares,' I told her, honestly. 'Could you imagine? I'd be worried that no one would come, I'm rubbish at organising stuff like that, so it would undoubtedly be a disaster, and I'd have to keep an eye on my mother the whole time to make sure she didn't start a conga or a sing-song. Plus, you know the whole "centre of attention thing" makes me itch.' Ironic. I hated to be in the limelight in any way. No wonder Ida occasionally pondered whether I'd been mixed up with another child at birth.

Our conversation was interrupted by one of Sasha's brothers, Lee, who'd wandered over to join us. He was a lovely guy but as a hippy, man-bun-sporting yoga guru he had so little in common with Sasha she refused to believe they were related. Yet another child that may have been swapped at birth.

Lee had a child strapped to his front and another balanced on his yoga-toned hip. I didn't even need to glance at Nate to guess his reaction because he did exactly what he did every time he was with Sasha's nephews – he scooped hip-child up, threw him up in the air, and laughed as little Oliver shrieked with delight.

'Hey man, how's it going?' Lee asked Nate over the squeals of Oliver shouting, 'More, more, more!'

'Great,' he replied.

'Not got one of these of your own yet?' Lee said, trying to be funny. My ovaries slapped a hand to their forehead.

'Not yet. One day, Liv, eh? Hopefully soon.'

There it was. Nate's little dig. Just like all the other little digs and loaded comments he'd thrown out in the last year. The more he pushed, the more I resisted. In fact, my hackles now automatically went to a standing position every time he mentioned it. I wasn't ready. I loved my job. I was happy in my life. I didn't feel the need to move to the parenting stage yet. The batteries were well and truly out of my biological bloody clock. Why wasn't he getting this? Maybe I needed to be more upfront and clear. I made a note to find out how much a billboard up the high street would cost to hire.

That said, I got it. We were both only children and he'd always wanted a big family, but we both had to be ready. It wasn't a situation we could march into when one of us still had an adverse reaction to those Pampers adverts on the telly.

Richard had wandered off in the direction of the buffet, so I bailed out of the joys of parenthood conversation and turned my attention to Chloe, who – uncharacteristically – had a glum expression on her beautiful face.

'Och, cheer up Chloe,' I said. 'You look like someone has just kidnapped your favourite teddy bear.'

'They have. St John's Hospital in flippin Manchester.'

Ah, so we were still on that. Richard, her very best friend (present company excluded), had been offered a big-time promotion to a hospital in Manchester and she was absolutely bereft. They'd worked together day and night for three years now, socialised outside work, and built up the kind of relationship that most happily married couples could only aspire to. Without the sex of course. Her nipples still didn't react in his presence.

No matter how many times I told her we'd visit him, she was still devastated every time she thought about it. I'd miss him too. At too many gatherings to count, he and I had ended up being the last ones in the kitchen, putting the world to rights over Irish coffees and milky teas. He'd fitted right in with our group and we'd all grown to love him.

'What have I missed?' Sasha asked, re-joining us.

'Nothing much,' Chloe replied. 'I'm still feeling sorry for myself because Richard is going back to live in Manchester...'

'You really should have one last night with him and get naked. How can you know it's not for you if you don't try?' Sasha interjected.

Chloe just kept right on going as if Sasha hadn't said a word. 'And Liv is feeling sorry for herself because Nate and your brother are discussing the failings of her reproductive strategy.'

'Don't have kids,' Sasha said, with deep foreboding. 'Those two sproglings completely wrecked my hi-fi unit last week. I've told Lee not to bring them back until they're eighteen.'

'Aw, being around you just makes me feel warm and bubbly and hopeful for the future of humanity,' I teased her.

The fact that she didn't respond with a cutting retort made me realise that she was no longer listening. I followed her gaze until I realised it was lasered in on Justin, who was standing over near the bar chatting to his workmates. Actually, one workmate in particular. I'd spoken to her before. Outside, in the smoking area at Sasha's party. Madeleine, wasn't it? And I remembered something about... I racked my brain... a boyfriend who was also seeing someone else? Or had left her? Or... it was no use. My capacity for retaining gossip about people I didn't know was close to zero. This was why I had no interest in the world of celebrities and their antics.

Without the aid of a crystal ball, I could see what was going to happen next. Unlike me, Sasha had a fully developed jealousy gene. She would go charging over there, she'd escalate directly to Level One Bitchiness, she'd cause a scene, Justin would be furious and that poor girl would be left feeling like she'd been dragged into the epicentre of a tornado. We couldn't have a debacle like that in front of all these friends, their families and work colleagues. Sasha's headmaster was here. The prospect of hearing one of his senior guidance teachers calling her boyfriend a 'cheating fecker' (Sasha's 31st party, when Justin chatted too long with a waitress) or a 'whoremongering arse' (Justin's 30th – something to do with inappropriate limbo-dancing action) could be career ending.

'Back in a minute – just going to have a word with Justin…' she said, taking a step towards her target. How well did I know my friend?

Emergency intervention was needed. 'Hang on. I need you to help me first,' I hissed urgently.

She paused. 'With what?'

'With sorting out this one here,' I gestured to Chloe.

'I need sorting?' Chloe asked.

She didn't, but it was all I could come up with right at that moment.

'You do!' I exclaimed, despite having no idea where I was going with this. I was thinking on my raffia-wedged feet. And rambling. Oh sweet mortification, the toe-curling nonsense I came out with when under pressure. 'We think you should stop Richard from going. Take one for the team. I agree with Sasha – have a night of wild passion and see if it awakens something in you. Do it for us,' I added. 'We've very few friends and can't afford to lose any.'

I wished I could send her a telepathic message to tell her this whole conversation was manufactured to distract Sasha, but much as we occasionally had a psychological connection, it was more along the lines of buying the same bottle of plonk or forming the same opinion about a stranger.

Chloe roared with laughter at that. 'Liv, you're the one who can't be arsed socialising and, Sasha, you hate everyone, so I think you'd survive without him.'

'I don't hate Richard though!' Okay, we had Sasha's attention back. She was fully engaged here again.

In my peripheral vision I could see that Justin was still chatting to Smoker Girl.

Bugger. Come on. Surely he needed another beer by now? Or a pee? Anything to make him break up the cosy tête-à-tête before Sasha went storming over there.

Chloe, thank God, was running with it despite being unaware of the underlying subtext. She shouted over to where Richard was having an in-depth conversation with Justin's Auntie Doreen and Auntie Lily. 'Richard, can I borrow you for a second?'

The good doctor, ever the charmer, gave both women a kiss on the cheek and sauntered over to us. This gave me time to interrupt Nate's conversation with Lee – something to do with the highlights of the toddler stage – by hissing in his ear, 'Go grab Justin. Sasha's about to go nuts 'cause he's talking to that woman.'

Nate had enough experience of the Sasha/Justin dynamic to realise it was a priority action.

I stepped back into the conversation with Chloe and Sasha just as Richard reached them, clutching a plate of sandwiches and miscellaneous food items that suggested he'd already paid a visit to the buffet table.

'Okay, I'm mildly afraid to ask, but what can I do for you?' he said, holding a tuna vol-au-vent like a shield.

Chloe somehow managed to keep a straight face. 'Just want to run something past you.'

'What's that?' he asked, somewhere between amused and suspicious.

'These two think that I should ravish you in a one-off night of wanton lust, in the hope that it'll make you realise you can't live without me and you'll cancel the move to Manchester.'

'Would you be doing it because you've suddenly decided I'm your type, or just for them?' Richard asked, entering into the spirit of it.

'For them,' she said. 'But I do want to find a way to stop you from going, so maybe for me too.'

Richard adopted a furrowed brow, as he humoured us by pretending to give the idea serious consideration. 'Tempting. But I'd hate myself in the morning because deep down I'd know it was for all the wrong reasons. And then I'd have to leave anyway to escape the pain of rejection.'

'I much preferred it when blokes weren't in touch with their emotions,' Sasha drawled. 'Actually, Justin still isn't...'

The mention of his name made us all look in his direction, and to my relief, he was chatting to Nate now, with no sign of the icy blonde work colleague. Thank God. Spectacle averted. Jealousy genie back in the bottle. I'd never understand the volatile lack of trust between them. Sasha had been completely faithful since the moment they met, and of course Justin had too. He just wasn't the type to play around. Their relationship was stormy, but it was passionate too and I had total faith that neither of them would be stupid enough to do anything to jeopardise what they had. For as long as I'd known her, Sasha had been adamant that she didn't see the point of a marriage contract, but there had never been any doubt that – occasional bumps aside – they were both in this for life.

Sasha glanced over too, and when she saw Justin with Nate, her shoulders dropped from 'stressed' to her default setting of 'generally irritable'. Thankfully, it was enough to make her annoyance dissipate and her brain switch to less confrontational areas of concern.

'Chloe, will you come help me get the rest of the hot food out of the oven? Liv, I'd ask you, but you're... you're...' she was struggling to be tactful and then failed completely. 'Last time you dropped a lasagne and put the chicken on the same plate as the prawns. Set my OCD off for a week,' she blurted. 'No offence.'

'None taken.'

They wandered off and left just Richard, me and a plate of assorted treats from the buffet.

'Sandwich?' he offered.

'Absolutely. I plan to consume serious calories today. If I'm eating, I can't argue with Nate over my pregnancy.'

'You're pregnant?' he asked, surprised.

'Nope. That's why we're arguing. Pass me a ham and pickle please.'

His infectious laugh was one of the things I loved about him. I so wished I could tweak Chloe's libido and make her fall for this lovely guy. And no, pointing out that he was a complete catch didn't help – I'd tried that many times. I'd also tried listing his attributes – smart, funny, decent, kind, handsome, toned torso, great chat, and already willing to put up with the rest of our group. Nothing worked. He just wasn't Chloe's type. He wasn't Connor.

'I'm sad that you're leaving us,' I said. 'We'll miss you.'

'It's only a few hours away. I'll come back and visit. And you lot can always come down and stay with me. It's not like I'm cutting off all ties. Well, maybe with Sasha, but that's only because she scares me,' he joked.

'She scares me too, but it's too late for me, I'm in too deep. Perhaps you're right – save yourself and don't look back.'

He laughed at this and enveloped me in a hug. 'I'll miss you too,' he said warmly, before pulling back and...

I don't know how to describe it without sounding completely Mills & Boon, but he looked at me, I looked at him, and there was a moment.

That was the only way to describe it. A fleeting, momentary something that passed between us.

I had no idea if he felt it too, all I know is that it made my stomach twinge, my mouth smile and then it was gone and we were back to normal.

I searched his face for any sign of acknowledgement but there was none.

Whatever I thought that was, I'd imagined it. I must have.

Anyway, I was a happily married woman. My husband was right over there, deep in conversation with Justin and Lee, and he'd probably moved on now to discussing other parts of my reproductive system. If my fallopian tubes started burning I'd know why.

'So tell me about this argument with Nate then,' Richard said, genuinely interested.

'He wants to have a baby, I'm not ready yet.'

Richard thought about that for a moment. 'Then you should wait until it's the right time for you.'

I sighed, unsure whether to continue this conversation. We were standing in the middle of a lawn on a sunny day – hardly the right time for discussing innermost fears and feelings. So of course, I switched to my fall-back position of flippant humour.

'Oh I will. I've scheduled in deep, contemplative thought about my future for a week next Tuesday in between *The Bill* and painting my toenails during *Question Time*.'

He smiled, then paused, like there was something he wanted to say but this wasn't the time. Or perhaps the 'moment' thing had just freaked me out and I was reading too much into this.

'Just be you, Liv. You'll make the right decision. You always do.'

Did I?

I glanced over at Nate again, laughing now with an even bigger group of guys. I was right to stay with him, wasn't I? Sure, we weren't perfect, but we were making it work. No relationship went through the years unscathed. Look at Justin and Sasha – they stuck together despite the occasional derailment. Lee and The Overachiever made it work. And...

My eyes went off to the side hedge of the garden, where the blonde bob was standing alone, smoking, looking like she was balancing the world on her shoulders. There was someone who wasn't making it work. I felt a pang of sympathy. My mind went back to a comment she'd made about a boyfriend. I couldn't remember the details, but I just hoped that whoever was making her this unhappy got his comeuppance.

6

Liv's Ward

July 2004

I'd looked in on Jessie and Al every hour or so since I'd come on shift this morning. 'He's doing fine, love,' she'd say, and I'd give her a cup of tea or a glass of water and squeeze her hand.

We both knew he wasn't doing fine and we both knew that this was her way of getting through the day. She'd told me that they were born only five days apart, and only streets away from each other in a town called Renfrew. Their mothers had known each other and they'd gone to the same school. Over seventy years of seeing each other almost every day. Now, she still had plenty to say to him. She talked to him from morning until night, recounting every moment of their lives together, she brushed his wispy white hair, she shaved his face, she held his hand and she told him he was doing fine and they'd get through this.

I hoped that despite his unconscious mind, he could hear her. Al had been battling advanced prostate cancer for many months. It had metastasised, spread to his bones, lymph nodes and liver, and now infection had taken hold. His organs were failing and it was only a matter of time. Maybe hours, maybe days, maybe longer – but always with Jessie by his side.

'I'm going off shift soon, Jessie,' I told her, when I checked on her at 8 p.m. Today had been my fifteenth on the trot because we were hopelessly short-staffed on the ward.

If I were being honest, there was part of me that was glad of the escape. If I was here, then I wasn't at home and Nate and I weren't arguing. We'd bicker about everything. Whose turn it was to put the batteries in the remote control. Who'd overloaded the washing machine. Where we should go on holiday next year. The list was endless. But what we were really bickering about was still my reluctance to commit to starting a family. How long could we keep having the same argument? It had been years since he first suggested that we try for a baby, and I wasn't getting any closer.

So being at work was good, even when it broke my heart.

I watched Jessie's sad smile cross her face. 'All right then, love. Will you be here tomorrow?'

'I will.'

'That's good. It helps to have a familiar face. Al was never great with strangers. That's why I always talk so much, he says – making up for the fact that he could be shy. Imagine, a big strapping man like this being shy,' she said, and a little bit of my heart chipped off.

I made a split-second decision, then crossed the room and settled into the armchair at the other side of the bed. I was needed here. 'I don't have to leave just yet though. I'll stay and keep you company for a while.'

'You don't?'

'I don't.' The truth was I'd told Nate I'd be home for dinner for the first time this week, but he'd understand. No matter how different our opinions on so many things, he was a kind, big-hearted, thoughtful guy and I knew he'd do the same if he were here right now.

Jessie gave me another sad smile. 'Then that would be lovely, pet. I'm sure my Al must be sick of hearing just my voice all day long.'

'Oh I'm sure he isn't,' I assured her gently. 'Do you want to go home and have a break?' I asked her. 'I'll stay with him until you get back.' She'd been sleeping on a camp bed at the side of his bed for a week now, nipping home in the mornings for half an hour to shower and sort out food for the rest of the day. 'Maybe even get a few hours' sleep in your own bed?' I suggested.

She leaned over and adjusted the collar of Al's pyjama top as she spoke. 'No thanks, Liv.' I'd told her to call me by my first name when they'd arrived here from the general ward. This was no place for formality. 'I'd rather be here with Al. If I were home I'd just be wishing I'd stayed here with him. We've never been ones for doing things separately. Especially since the girls left home.'

Jessie's girls. She'd told me all about them. Hannah, who lived in London now, and Sarah, who'd emigrated to Australia after falling in love with an Aussie ten years before. The two girls were on their way. Hannah was flying in the next morning, Sarah in the afternoon. I was glad that Jessie would have them here. No one should go through this alone.

'You must have missed them when they first left home,' I said. Some family members preferred to sit in silence with their own thoughts, but Jessie wasn't one of them. She liked to chat and conversation passed the time.

'Och, I did, love, but Al and I had loads of things we wanted to do. Two cruises a year. He loved his ships. Put on ten pounds every time, mind you.' Her eyes glistened at the memory. 'And we went out for dinner every Saturday, sometimes on a weeknight too if the telly was rubbish. And we visited all the places around the country that we'd never seen. We enjoyed ourselves so much. We even visited Sarah every year in Australia and had lots of weekends down seeing our Hannah in London. We made the most of it all. At least we can say that.' Her voice cracked on the last word, so I let that memory sit with her, knowing that she'd need all of those thoughts to keep her going in the coming weeks and months.

'We'd just booked our next holiday the week before he got really sick. One of those huts over the sea in some tropical place...' Two tears were rolling down her cheeks now. 'Bugger, I can never remember what it's called. Al booked it all. One minute he was talking about the things we'd do and the next minute he was...' She was fighting to stay in control, struggling to get the words out. 'It was... this.' She had both his hands in hers now. 'Look at me, all these tears. He'd be telling me to dry my eyes, that it'll all look better in the morning. That's what he'd say when things went wrong. "Don't worry, Jessie, it'll all look better in the morning." He was right. It always did. But not this time. Not this time.'

'Your girls will be here tomorrow, Jessie,' I said softly.

She nodded firmly. 'They need to see him. He's a great dad, you know. He loves all of us. "His girls", he called us. He never let us down, not ever. He was steady as a rock.'

Steady as a rock. I could use the same words to describe Nate. I was all highs and lows and sharp turns and unexpected detours, and he was a constant line. The very thing that Jessie loved about her man was the thing I struggled with most. Different generation, maybe. Or perhaps just different expectations. All I knew was that if I'd spent a lifetime with Nate and I still had things to tell him and adventures to have when we were in our seventies, then surely that was a lucky life to have lived? Why was I wasting time with all this marriage angst, when Nate and I should just be getting on with enjoying every day and making the most of our lives together?

I stayed with Jessie until she fell asleep, holding hands across the bed with Al, then I slipped out.

On the way home, I'd usually make the same round of calls – Sasha, Chloe, Ida – but Sasha and Justin were on a two-week holiday in the Seychelles. Those two knew how to live. I used my hands-free keypad to call Ida first.

'Hello my darling,' she chirped. 'You must have been reading my mind! I was just about to call you.'

'Because you were missing me?' I joked, knowing that definitely wouldn't be the answer.

'No, love…' No surprise, and I couldn't help but smile at her bluntness. 'I just wanted to ask… All these online dating websites that are around these days – do you think the people who sign up for them just want sex?'

In my thirties, and she could still shock me silent.

'Are you still there, Olivia?'

'Yep, I'm just scared to find out what you want the answer to that question to be.'

Her raucous cackle made me smile. 'You know, maybe you're not the person to ask about these things. I'll call Sasha – she's much more switched on. Bye, darling, love you!'

Click. She hung up before I could even point out that Sasha was still on holiday. Not that it would matter – Ida would have Interpol track Sasha down just so she could ask if she thought Bill from Dundee, age fifty-five, GSOH, wanted to get naked on the first date.

In need of some sanity, I pressed speed dial to the next number on my list. Chloe. 'Hey lovely, how's your day going?'

'Sore,' she replied.

'Sore? Why what happened? Did you get hurt at work?' A feeling of dread rose from my trainers. Chloe had finally got her transfer to A & E and she loved it, but there was no denying the danger she faced there every shift. Drunk and high patients. Gang members being brought in, still fighting. Warring family members carrying on disputes even when both sides had bloody wounds from the altercation. And Chloe was in the middle of it all, facing every unpredictable outburst or action, in an environment that no amount of training could prepare for. She'd already suffered a mild concussion when a raging drunk had knocked her out of the way and she'd hit a wall at speed. And she'd been pushed to the ground by a furious father who felt his child wasn't being dealt with quickly enough. Yet, she loved her job, and hadn't regretted moving to A & E for a second because she said the positives outweighed the negatives all day long.

'Nope, I pulled a muscle trying to commando crawl out of the restaurant before my blind date realised I was leaving.'

My laughter came from both relief and amusement. 'Oh God. That bad?' Chloe had been tentatively back on the dating scene for a couple of years now, but none of her encounters had come to anything. I wasn't sure if she was unlucky or way too picky.

'Worse. He talked about himself for two full hours. Two! And for most of that he wouldn't make eye contact because he was too busy admiring himself in the mirror behind me. I'm seriously considering giving up.'

'You should speak to my mum – she's decided to try online dating. I'm trying to block that thought from my mind.'

Chloe laughed. 'Good idea. Although, maybe she's on to something. At least I could weed out the bores before I buy a new outfit and get my hair done.'

'Where did this date come from?' I asked.

'One of the porters in work. It's his cousin. Yep, that's what I'm reduced to – everyone I've ever met is trying to set me up on a sympathy date.'

I bit my bottom lip, then decided to just say what I was thinking. 'You know, babe, Nate was talking to Connor last week…'

'Don't say it!' she stopped me. 'I'm not going over to Chicago to track down an ex who is clearly so interested in me that I haven't heard a word from him since the moment he got on a plane a gazillion years ago. I'm desperate but not that desperate.' There was a pause and I knew what was coming next. 'Is he seeing anyone?'

I tried to remember what little information I'd gleaned from Nate after the last call. They'd spent nearly an hour on the phone and apparently fifty-five minutes of that was sports-talk, and five minutes was stuff that didn't involve a ball.

'Some girl that he works with – but I'm sure it's not serious.'

'Did he say that?' She was trying to sound nonchalant and failing miserably.

'No, not exactly, but...' In fact, he'd told Nate he'd been seeing this woman for a couple of months and it was working out well so far, but Chloe didn't need to hear that. Call me an eternal romantic, but I just still thought that if they saw each other again...

Of course, for that to happen they'd need to be in the same country. I wished for the umpteenth time that she would just jump on a plane, go there, and see him face to face. At least then she would know if there was a chance for them. And if not, she could move swiftly on and be completely open to meeting someone new.

'There you go then,' Chloe said with finality. 'Case closed.'

'Okay, well get some Deep Heat on the dating injury and have an early night,' I said, trying to cheer her up. 'I'll come find you for lunch tomorrow. I'm on another double.'

'Yay! It's mince in the staff canteen. That'll be the best date I've had this week.'

She was still laughing when I hung up and pulled into our driveway.

Nate was still awake and in the living room.

'Hey babe. Did you get my text?' I asked him.

'Yeah, I got it.' That surprised me. He was hopeless with technology and hated his mobile phone with a passion. Said it was too intrusive and he'd rather talk to people face to face.

Maybe it was the lighting, or just the emotional drainage of a tough day, but for a moment I thought he'd never looked more handsome. He was lying on the couch, in shorts and a T-shirt, a Christopher Brookmyre thriller lying open on his chest. This was when he was most relaxed. Exams over, sports tournaments and leagues finished, sixth years gone and another school year done. Although, in four out of the six weeks of the school holiday, he volunteered at a local sports centre three hours a day, running a summer camp for kids. It was just pure enjoyment for him.

Jessie's words were lingering in my mind. Al was a great dad. Nate would be a great dad too. Jessie would give anything for another day with her husband, and yet here I was, squandering my time with Nate, avoiding him, bickering, putting off starting a family even though I knew that he so desperately wanted one.

Maybe it was time to stop frittering away our time and start appreciating it instead. I climbed onto the couch beside him, wound my body around his and laid my head on his chest. If he was surprised, he managed to cover it up well.

'Rough night?' he asked, stroking my hair.

'A lovely couple. Been together their whole lives. He hasn't got long. Their family arrives tomorrow, but I didn't want to leave her alone until she'd fallen asleep. My heart was breaking for them.'

At work I stayed calm and professional, but I'd always been able to tell Nate how I really felt.

'Made me think though…' I hesitated, wanting to be sure, checking that this wasn't just a human reaction to a sad situation. No. I wanted this.

'I think maybe I'm ready to start a family.'

His hand stopped and he leaned up on one elbow, his face just inches from mine. 'Are you sure?'

I nodded. 'I'm sure.' I was. Why waste more time? Why not close down the fear? There was absolutely no reason at all for me to stall any longer. Nate and I were already a family, and now it was time to grow until we got to where Jessie and Al had been, in our seventies and still making the most of every day, with absolutely no regrets.

Nate didn't say any more. Instead, he pulled my top up and started to kiss my stomach, working his way from my belly button upwards to my ribcage, to my…

I blamed the twelve-hour shifts for the fact that I was asleep before he got any further.

7

Friday Night on the Town

November 2005

'I meant to say, Richard told me to tell you all he said "hi",' Chloe announced, as soon as the restaurant manager sat us at our table.

'Aw, tell him we still miss him. Did you see him or were you just chatting to him on the phone?'

'I had lunch with him. He was up for the day for some seminar over at the Southern General. We had a quick catch-up.'

'How's he doing?' I asked, flicking a napkin on to my knee.

'Great. He's met someone – a gynaecologist called Charlotte and he's been seeing her for a few months. They seem happy. He's saying it's nothing serious, but I don't know if I believe him. He had a bit of a twinkle in his eye.'

That made me laugh. Richard always had a twinkle in his eye. It was what made him great company to be around.

'Any regrets that you didn't give things a try with him?' Sasha asked, blunt as ever.

Chloe shook her head. 'None at all. Especially now.' She beamed just a little as she said that. It was still in the early stages, but she'd started seeing Danny, the guy who'd moved into the flat upstairs from hers. He was single, solvent, good company and the head chef in the restaurant we were sitting in right now. It had become our regular hang-out destination on a Friday night, although, like tonight, we'd come late so that Danny could join us when the kitchen quietened down.

'Nate, you heard anything from Justin today?' Sasha asked.

'Nothing. I called him a couple of times at work but he didn't get back to me. Why? Is everything okay?'

Sasha took a large gulp from the gin and tonic the waitress had just put in front of her before answering, 'Who knows? Who bloody knows whether everything is okay with Justin or not.'

It wasn't a question.

'Has something happened?' Chloe asked.

Sasha shrugged. 'I cooked him dinner for our anniversary last night – twelve years since we met – and he bailed. When he got home he said he'd been out for beers with the guys from work. I don't know... Just felt like something was off.'

It took me a moment to get past Sasha cooking a romantic anniversary dinner. That wasn't her style at all.

'You know what he's like Sasha...' I said gently. The truth was, none of this was a newsflash or out of character.

Justin was... just being Justin. He was one of my favourite people in the world, and I adored him, but there was no getting away from the fact that he drank too much. Always had. And for a long time now it had been at a level that most would consider a serious issue. I'd tried to talk to him about it a couple of times, but he'd shut me down, with absolutely no room for discussion, so I'd backed off. I didn't want to cause a rift, or alienate him. Instead, I just let him know that I'd always be there for him if he wanted to talk about it.

Sasha took a different approach. Somewhere along the line she had decided that it was just one flaw in an otherwise perfect package. She'd tried to rein him in and sometimes it worked and he'd stay relatively sober for a few weeks or months. This clearly wasn't one of those weeks, but Sasha refused to accept that he had a problem. He functioned, he held down a job that he was great at, he played five-a-side football every Thursday night, he and Nate went to the gym most days – that, she insisted, wasn't the behaviour of someone who had alcohol issues. He was just a normal guy who liked to enjoy himself.

We'd talked about it countless times over the years and Sasha's answer was always the same. He was just a good-time guy. Liked to live it up. And sure, that came with situations like this, but on the other hand, he was the guy that everyone wanted at the party.

'I do know what he's like,' she answered. 'But sometimes he takes it too far. This is one of those times. In fact, this is one of those years. He's fallen out with his mum and dad. Not that they were ever particularly interested in him. But he got wrecked at his Aunt Lily's funeral and his dad went crazy. They ended up rolling about on the ground after the wake. His dad's always had a temper and they've never been close, but still, not his finest moment.'

There was general astonishment around the table. This was the first we'd heard about the fall-out. Justin was always Mr Party and Sasha hated getting deep and gloomy so she hadn't mentioned it either. It made me wonder what else she'd omitted to tell us, but I didn't probe because I could see that even discussing this with us was setting her on edge. Sasha was guarded and she kept things to herself, but underneath that pissed-off exterior was a core of unswaying loyalty to her friends and to Justin.

The volume over by the door increased, drawing our attention and, of course – in perfect timing – there he was, hugging the restaurant manager and high-fiving one of the regular waiters.

'Nothing like an understated entrance,' Sasha drawled as he reached our table. Justin acted like she hadn't spoken, and instead greeted Nate with an exuberant back slap and an 'All right mate?'

Nate's face creased into a grin. Justin just had that effect on people. He was like the incorrigible child who made it impossible for anyone to stay angry with him.

He kissed Chloe on the cheek, then me, then went in for a full-scale smooch with Sasha, who visibly rebuffed him.

'Oh come on, you can't still be pissed off with me,' he said, trying to cajole her out of her fury.

'Of course I can. You're a fricking nightmare,' she retorted.

'I am,' he agreed. 'But I'm the love of your life and I adore you, so let me make it up to you.'

Sasha raised a cynical eyebrow. 'This had better be good.'

Justin's confident swagger suggested it definitely was.

He reached into his jacket and pulled out an envelope. 'I wanted to have these for you last night, but they got held up.' He put the envelope down in front of her, and she eyed it with suspicion for a few moments before picking it up, opening it, removing the documents inside and reading them. Despite herself, a huge grin replaced her scowl.

'Oh come on, put us out of our misery,' I pleaded. Sasha turned the documents around. Two tickets, first-class, to New York. She then flicked the itinerary open so we could see that too.

'And a week at The Plaza,' she said, saving us from trying to scrutinise the paperwork.

'Happy anniversary, baby,' Justin said, sitting down next to her and kissing her hard on the lips. Her hands curled around his neck as she returned the gesture.

My eyes met Chloe's and she shrugged and smiled. How many times over the years had this happened? Fight. Make up. Fight. Make up. Fight. Make up. If it were my relationship, I'd find it all far too exhausting and, quite frankly, couldn't be arsed with the drama.

There were more important things in life to worry about. Like... like... I tried to stop myself thinking about it, but it came flooding right into the forefront of my mind. Like... having a baby. Oh the irony. I'd put it off all those years and now the

Gods of Conception were having a laugh at my expense by refusing to let me get pregnant. We'd been trying for over a year now and nothing. If one more person told me a year wasn't long and I should stop stressing, I might punch them. Or get Sasha to punch them. Sometimes you had to utilise your friends' strengths and areas of expertise.

I reached for Nate's hand under the table and he automatically folded my fingers into his. I knew so many couples whose relationships cracked under the strain of trying and failing to conceive, but for now at least, it was still having the positive effect of bringing us closer together. We finally had a common goal, a shared mission, and his positivity and unfailing support every month made me love him even more. This was when Nate was at his best. Wild crazy lust and excitement? Eh, nope. Solid, supportive, catch you when you fall, stand by you no matter what? Absolutely. And maybe I was just swayed by the high hopes and crashing disappointments of the last year, but it felt like as I got older, the second set of qualities had become far more important than the first.

Danny sent out a selection of delicious tapas from the kitchen, before joining us just after 11 p.m. Chloe visibly beamed the minute he appeared and I was happy for her. She deserved this. Not that she needed a man in her life to validate her, but she was definitely questioning herself right before she met Danny.

'I mean, come on,' she'd groaned, somewhere between the blind date with the narcissist and a misguided fling with an accountant she met while jogging in the park. 'I'm nearly thirty-five and I've been in love once in my life. If you don't count my devotion to Usher and a brief lusting for Seal.'

Cue a dropped set of keys, a chivalrous neighbour, and something that came fairly close to love at first sight.

Now he was sitting with his arm around her, matching smiles, their body language in perfect synchronicity. It just worked. Hallelujah!

'Right, let's get out of here,' Justin said, tossing back a glass of Drambuie in one gulp.

'I'm up for that,' Danny agreed. Working in the hospitality trade, he was used to socialising in the early hours of the morning, when most people with 9–5 jobs were already headed to bed.

'I'm off tomorrow, so count me in,' Chloe chirped. 'Where shall we go?'

'Casino,' Justin answered. 'We can pick up a taxi outside.'

I didn't even have to look at Nate to know what he was thinking, and I was bang on the same wavelength.

'Sorry, guys, but I'm on back shift tomorrow, so we're just going to head home.' I was knackered and if it was a choice between partying until dawn or going home for a good night's sleep, with the possibility of an intimate encounter with my husband, I was opting for the latter.

'Are you sure?' Sasha asked. 'Och, come on, just for a little while.'

I shook my head, laughing. 'Last time I came for "a little while" I blew a week's worth of lunch and morning coffee money on the roulette table and spent the next seven days being way too familiar with the joys of the banana sandwich.'

I pulled on my jacket as we headed out the door, then hugged everyone goodbye when they flagged down a taxi. We strolled across to our car, on the other side of the road. I never drank if I was working the next day, so I came in handy as a designated driver.

Twenty minutes later, we were back in Weirbridge, and thirty minutes later, we were heading for bed. One a.m. I'd get a good ten hours; sheer luxury after the massive number of hours I'd been doing lately. Just for a change, the ward was still short-staffed and we were having to fill in the gaps, even when we were way over our standard hours for the week. There was no point complaining. The NHS underfunding and staffing issues were a fundamental issue that seemed impossible to solve. Thankfully I loved my job so that made the exhaustion and the lack of free time easier to bear.

'I've got a really bad feeling that Sasha and Justin are on a collision course,' I mused, as we stripped off for bed. And yes, he still folded his clothes, but it was one of those little irritations that I'd decided to let go. If that was the worst thing he did, then I really had nothing to complain about.

I pulled on a vest top and a pair of tartan pyjama bottoms. They were essential nightwear in the Scottish winter.

'I hope not,' Nate answered, but I could see he was concerned. 'I've tried to talk to him a couple of times, but he just brushes everything off.'

'Does he ever say if he's happy?'

'That's a weird question,' Nate answered. 'What makes you ask that?'

I climbed under the covers first and shivered as the cold cotton touched my skin. 'I don't know, it's just a feeling I've had for ages. Like there's something beneath his behaviour, something not right.'

'Maybe the fallout with his parents?' Nate suggested.

I shook my head. 'I don't think so. I know he didn't have the easiest childhood. He's said before that he wasn't close to his parents and that his dad was a real staunch disciplinarian. But this feels like it's something that's got worse over the years. Something I can't put my finger on, something that's making him unhappy, making him drink too much, party too much, live life on the edge.'

Nate's arms wrapped around me, spooning, and I felt his breath on the back of my neck. 'Have you asked Sasha?'

I nodded. 'Yeah, but she says there's nothing wrong. I'm just not sure I believe that.'

Nate's fingers found their way to my hair and he gently ran them through from root to tip. 'I'll try talking to him again and see if I can suss anything out,' he promised. 'But right now, I think you should stop thinking about other guys and concentrate on your husband,' he joked, and the husky sexiness in his voice immediately turned me on.

His hand slipped down, under my vest, and at the same time his kisses made a trail from my ear, to my neck, to my shoulders.

There was absolutely no chance that I was going to get that ten hours sleep after all.

8

A Late Night in Hospital

August 2006

'Oh my God, he's got my nose!' my mother screeched, fidgeting because she was desperate to hold him and I wasn't ready to relinquish my skin-on-skin contact just yet.

I know it's a terrible thing to admit, but I'd made Nate promise not to call her until after I delivered. That way, by the time it took her to get here, Nate and I would have some time to adore our new arrival. I'd pay for the fact that she wasn't in the delivery room to witness Finn's arrival until the end of time, but right now it felt like that would be a small price for the interlude of utter bliss we'd just shared.

We had our baby. Finn Jamieson. 7 lbs 10 oz. Born on 30th August. And utterly beautiful.

Nate had lain on the bed beside me, with Finn nestled on my chest, and we'd just stared at him, at his fingers, his face, his beautiful little mouth, his eyelids, closed as he slept. I wanted to just keep us there in that moment, keep him safe, protected, adored forever.

'I'm so in awe of you right now,' Nate had whispered to me, stroking his son's face as he spoke.

I turned to him, kissed him, then kissed the top of Finn's head. This was everything.

'I'm so glad you didn't go,' he whispered, and I could hear his words choking with emotion. I knew what he was referring to. Years ago, the dawn of the millennium, when I chose to stay with him rather than walk away. I couldn't even bear the thought of the alternative now – of not being here, with my boy and with Nate by my side. I couldn't imagine any other life would make me happier than I was right now.

We'd already been moved from the delivery suite to the maternity ward when Ida arrived and went into orbit.

'And my mouth! Oh my God, he's the spitting image of me.'

I was so glad I was in a room with two beds and the other one was empty, otherwise some poor, exhausted new mum would be getting treated to the full Ida experience.

She wrapped Nate in a hug, then leaned over and kissed me, gently pushing my hair back off my cheek. 'My girl, with her own baby,' she said wistfully. 'I'm so proud of you.' I had a little twinge of guilt that I'd delayed notifying her, right up until she added, 'And so lucky only to have eight hours in labour. I was twenty-six hours with you. There are bits of me that were never the same again.'

I covered Finn's ears. He'd have plenty of time to get used to his grandmother.

'Right, time for granny cuddles,' she said pointedly.

Reluctantly, I passed my sleeping son over, feeling a twinge of an ache as I did so. Was it always going to be this difficult to let him go?

Ida nestled him into her arms, and… sigh… of course she began to sing. She had form for this. She often boasted that she'd sung most of the younger members of our extended family into the world, and most of the older ones out of it.

At least she kept her voice low and gentle, as opposed to her normal decibel level that came close to cracking windows. I wondered if my son would grow up to have any latent, deep-rooted memory that the first song he ever heard was James Brown's 'I Feel Good', sung by his grandmother when he was just a few hours old.

Polly, the charge nurse on the maternity ward, popped in just as Ida was fading out the last chorus. I'd met her back when we were young, wide-eyed, Pot-Noodle-fuelled students. We were in the same halls of residence, although she was studying midwifery while I was in general nursing, and she'd slept over many a time on Ida's couch, so none of this was a surprise to her.

'How are you doing, gorgeous?' Polly asked.

'Oh, I'm great, love,' Ida replied, her gaze still on Finn, so she was unaware that the question had been directed at me. I didn't correct her.

Polly laughed, hugged Nate, then me, before cooing over Finn, still sleeping in Ida's arms.

'Thanks for letting Nate and my mum stay with me,' I said gratefully. Dads usually only got to stick around for a couple of hours after the birth, so I appreciated Polly bending the rules to let Nate linger and allow my mum in.

'That's okay. We were just in luck that the other bed was empty. We have someone coming up for it later this afternoon, though.'

'Okay, I'll kick them out before then,' I assured her, smiling.

I heard a bell ring in the distance and checked my watch: 2 p.m. Visiting time. The hours were just flying by.

'Great. But are you feeling up to more visitors? I think you might have some other people waiting to meet this little guy,' she said with a grin, just as Chloe, Sasha and Justin burst in the door, laden with balloons and gifts, and swamped us all in hugs and kisses, before converging on Ida and my boy.

'He's so handsome,' Chloe gasped, tears in her eyes.

Chloe and Sasha fussed over Finn, while Justin shook hands with Nate, and I realised something was jarring with me. Maybe it was the harsh fluorescent light, or perhaps he'd been on a bender last night, but Justin was definitely starting to show signs that his lifestyle was leaving its mark. He looked older than the rest of us, maybe five years, maybe even ten. His body still looked trim thanks to the daily gym workouts, but there was a bloatedness to his face, a red tinge to his cheeks, and his eyes seemed to be shrinking in size. I had no idea how Sasha could fail to notice, but perhaps the denial was just all-encompassing. It was all the more surprising, because if there was anyone on this earth who could face a challenge head-on, it was Sasha – a point proven by the fact that she'd just managed to gently wrestle Finn from a highly unimpressed Ida's grip.

'Hey, I'm your Auntie Sasha,' she said, with a sweetness completely unfamiliar to her. 'I'm the cool one. I'll be the one you'll call when you're in trouble, or falling out of a nightclub at 3 a.m., because I'll come and get you and I'll never tell your parents. Oh, and condoms. I'll buy your condoms, so don't ever be afraid to ask.' I was about to order her to stop corrupting his innocent mind, when her voice softened even more. 'And you'll need to forgive us, but you're the first baby in our group, because... well, I don't usually like babies and it's taken your Auntie Chloe a while to get going...' I realised there were more tears – all mine – and they were threatening to burst over my eyelids like water through a cracked dam. '... So we're going to completely spoil you. Not with, like, material things that'll make you a brat, but we'll be queuing up to spend time with you. I hope that's okay.'

I couldn't get over this whole new incredibly sweet person. 'Sasha, have you been struck by lightning? Alien abduction? Just a flat-out personality transplant?'

She stuck to addressing Finn. 'And don't listen to your mamma when she says things like that, because you know you and I are going to be the best buddies ever.'

'Eh, no, I think you'll find that he'll be my best buddy.' Justin moved in and gently lifted Finn from Sasha's arms and I had to bite my bottom lip to stop the tears again. Bloody hormones. 'Don't listen to Sash, mate,' he told Finn. 'I'll teach you the important stuff.'

Sasha snorted, teasing him. 'Like what?'

Justin paused, emotion on his face that I'd never seen there before. 'Like don't start sneaking drinks from your parents' drinks cabinet when you're ten, because that doesn't lead anywhere good.'

There was a stunned silence, before the moment was broken by Justin, who suddenly changed his demeanour and acted like nothing of any significance had been said.

'Right, Chloe, must be your turn,' he said brightly, handing Finn over. He was still sound asleep, completely unperturbed by all this activity.

Chloe came and sat down on the seat right next to me and just stared at him adoringly, gently swaying him a few inches from side to side.

'I could watch him all day,' she murmured, and I tried not to laugh when this made my mother purse her lips in disapproval. Granny wanted Finn back because then she'd be centre of attention again. The thought came without an ounce of bitterness. Ida's little foibles had stopped being a touchy subject to me right around the same time I turned sixteen, got a push-up bra and took my Take That posters down off the wall. She had a good heart and she'd do anything for anyone – as parents went, I could have done so much worse.

'You suit that, Chlo,' I said with a wink.

'Don't! I'd have one tomorrow, but I don't want to say that to Danny in case it scares him off. Oh, and he said to say he's so sorry he couldn't be here because he had lunch service, but he's managed to get cover for tonight, so we'll pop back later. He's dying to see this little guy.'

If it were possible for my heart to swell even bigger, it did just then. Finally, Chloe had found a great guy who adored her and she'd fallen madly in love. There had been times over the years when I thought she'd never get over Connor, or meet anyone who would match up to him in her eyes. I mean, she hadn't even been swayed by Richard Campbell and he was about as adorable as it got. Anyway, finally it seemed like she was on the road to her perfect life and this time I had a real feeling it was going to work out for her.

There was another knock on the door and then it slowly opened, and for a moment I wondered if I was still under the influence of gas and air. Or perhaps the epidural was causing some kind of strange hallucinatory reaction.

'So I heard there's a new kid in town?' said the voice.

Wide-eyed, suddenly terrified for my son's safety, I reached over and gently took him from Chloe's arms in case the shock made her drop him.

'Holy shit,' Sasha said, under her breath, but loud enough for it to reach us.

'No way!' Nate bellowed, striding to the doorway and enveloping the new arrival in a bear hug with loads of that man-back-slapping stuff. 'I can't believe you came!'

Neither could I. Nate hadn't even told me that it was a possibility or I'd have warned Chloe.

Nate finally released him and he stepped further into the room, and that's when we realised he was holding the hand of a very pretty blonde.

'Guys, this is Cindy. Cindy, this is Nate, Liv, Chloe, Justin and Sasha.'

'Good to meet you,' she said, in an accent straight from the Southern States of the USA, while smiling to reveal the most perfect teeth I'd ever seen outside an Osmonds' video.

The shocked silence was only broken when he reached the bed and leaned in to give me a hug. 'Congratulations Liv, I'm so happy for you.'

I wanted to say something sincere and heartfelt. I really did. But with all the tensions and toe-curling undercurrents in the room, I suffered a complete mind blank and went for something trite instead.

'Thank you, Connor. If I'd known that this would make you come back, I'd have had a baby years ago.'

9

The Christening

May 2007

I checked out my reflection in the mirror, thought about touching up the shiny forehead and the fading lipstick, then decided not to bother.

'I think this is the first time I've had make-up on since Finn was born,' I mused, to no one in particular. It was true. Finn was nine months old and I still didn't have enough hours in the day for superficial things like cosmetics and superfluous grooming. I'd fished the make-up bag from the bottom of the ironing basket this morning – absolutely no idea how it got there.

'And you need your roots done too. You're definitely letting yourself go,' Sasha added.

I swatted her with my under-used make-up bag. 'You're supposed to be my friend. Lie to me and tell me what I need to hear to salvage what little self-esteem I have left.'

'Babe, ignore her, you look gorgeous,' Chloe said.

'See!' I exclaimed to Sasha. 'That's exactly how you do it. Lie and leave me with my dignity.'

'I'm not lying!' Chloe objected. 'You do look beautiful.'

'Yeah, but she still needs her roots done,' Sasha deadpanned.

I gave up pointing out the error of her ways and took a sip of my vodka tonic. This was also the first time I'd drank alcohol since Finn was born, but I'd switched from breastfeeding to bottle last week, and decided I deserved to have a drink or two at my son's christening.

It had been a beautiful day.

Ida, dressed in a flamboyant, full-length dress of baby blue ruffles (she liked a theme) had sung us into the church ('Amazed' by Lonestar) and back out again ('You're The Best Thing That Ever Happened to Me' by Gladys Knight and the Pips). The godparents, Chloe, Sasha and Justin, had promised to guide my son throughout his life. Although, I did have reservations about that bit. In Sasha's case, God knows where she'd guide him to, and when it came to Justin, the destination would undoubtedly be a packed nightclub with endless happy hours and half-naked dancers on the bar.

Now we were back at Danny's restaurant for the reception, and Sasha and Chloe had joined me for an excursion to the very plush ladies' toilets.

'Danny's done an incredible job with the food, Chloe – everyone's raving about it,' I told her, then tried to catch her reflection in the mirror to gauge her reaction.

Chloe and Danny had been seeing each other for two years now, and I had a horrible feeling things were beginning to cool off. I really hoped I was wrong, but the fact that her eyes had just filled up with tears suggested that I wasn't.

'Chloe! What is it? What's up?'

She sniffed, dabbed her under-eyes with her fingertips, took a breath, then did her best to deflect with a self-deprecating brush-off. 'Nothing. It's fine. Come on, this is a christening – not the place for pathetic tears and self-pity.'

'Of course it is!' I corrected her, trying to cajole the problem out of her. 'Guaranteed, Ida will turn on the waterworks before the end of the day. Just ask her to sing any Céline Dion song and then watch them flow.'

Chloe realised we were going nowhere until she shared what was on her mind, and gave me a grateful smile. 'It's just... Danny. I feel... different.'

Even Sasha had now stopped fixing her face and turned to pay attention. 'Why? What happened?'

Chloe was clearly trying to stop the tears from falling again. 'I don't know. Something changed a few months ago and I can't even tell you what it was. How ridiculous is that? I'm a grown, intelligent woman and I've no idea why my feelings changed. I don't know if it's the hours he works. We get one night a week together and, even then, he's usually knackered. Christmas and New Year were a wipe-out because he worked right through. I knew what I was signing up for, but I guess I didn't realise how hard it would be.'

'Do you think that's all it is? The lack of time together?' I asked.

She hesitated. 'Maybe we've just got used to each other too. You know, the excitement of that first flush of love thing has maybe worn off...'

If I had a specialist subject, that was it. Hadn't Nate and I nearly divorced when our first flush of love and excitement wore off? Now I couldn't be more relieved that I'd stayed. We might be short on excitement and thrills, but what we had was solid, dependable. There was a lot to be said for that.

'Roughly how long have things been rocky for?' Sasha asked.

Chloe thought about it. 'Maybe a few months?'

'You want my theory?' Sasha asked.

Chloe was very definite. 'No. "Sasha-logic" is usually twisted and dipped in evil,' Chloe joked, trying to lighten the mood.

Sasha ignored the objection and carried on with her point. 'I think something shifted after you saw Connor again last year.'

Her analysis was absolutely accurate, but I was saying nothing in case Chloe felt ambushed.

'Don't be ridiculous! That's... that's... Oh God, you're right.' She took a step to the side, closed her eyes and rested her head against the cold wall tiles. 'Just leave me here to die,' she murmured.

'Absolutely not. You've just promised to guide my son through his life. I can't tell him that one of his godmothers was found in the corner of a lavvy between the loo brush and a bottle of Toilet Duck.'

At least that made her laugh.

'I knew the minute I saw him again that I still felt everything for him,' she admitted. 'So don't go claiming to be some kind of psychological love whisperer,' she warned Sasha. 'I just didn't want to actually admit it.'

'Why?' I asked.

'Because it's pathetic! Yes, I went out with him for six years, but we split up over ten years ago, and yet the minute he walks into a bloody room, I'm this giddy, love-struck idiot who feels like she's right back at university and madly in love with him. This is like one of those mid-life crisis stories where a frustrated wife gets a facelift, loses twenty pounds, tracks down her first love and runs off with him. Did I mention it's pathetic?'

'You did,' I confirmed.

I should really have been getting back out to the guests, but I was pretty sure Ida and Nate had it covered, and a best friend having an emotional crisis slash revelation was far more important.

Her whole body deflated. 'I don't know what to do. I really don't.'

Sasha spoke up. 'Is this a bad time to vouch for Danny and point out that last time you thought you were right to chuck a bloke, you regretted it for years?'

'Yes,' Chloe and I blurted at the same time.

I believed her when she said she had feelings for Connor again. There was a connection with Connor that she'd never managed to replace and it wasn't surprising that seeing each other that once, in the hospital after Finn's birth, when he was with Cindy, had rekindled her feeling for Connor and dampened how she felt about Danny.

I never got a chance to suss out if seeing Chloe had affected Connor too. Turned out he only had a few days off work, so it was a flying, four-day trip. They'd stayed in a hotel and visited us every day. I hadn't had time to get to know Cindy, but she seemed nice. In a South Carolina, perfect teeth, former pageant queen kind of way.

'Is he still with that one with the big teeth?' Chloe asked.

I nodded.

Don't tell her. Don't tell her. Don't tell her.

'They got engaged last month,' I told her. Damn it. I'd been waiting for a better time than standing in the toilets in a packed restaurant. Connor had called Nate on the night he proposed to tell him Cindy had said 'yes'.

The news made her go completely silent.

'Right, that's enough,' Sasha said, entering the conversation for the first time since the Toilet Duck. 'There's absolutely nothing you can do about it, Chlo. If he'd been meant for you, you'd have worked it out long ago. And so what if Danny isn't the right one? Someone else will be. Let's face it, you're a catch.'

I almost fainted at these uncharacteristic words of support and affirmation, until she followed it up with, 'You scrub up not bad, and you don't need your roots done.'

Even Chloe had to laugh.

'Honey,' I said, taking her hand, 'let's just not worry about any of this right now. Let's go out there, enjoy the party, and then... Are you off tomorrow night?'

She nodded.

'Right, my house, 8 p.m., I'll supply food, you bring the wine, Sasha, you're on the male strippers.'

'Done,' Sasha agreed laughing.

There was a reason I loved these women. Emotional crisis, weighed down with woes, exhaustion, or worries? We'd still find a way to go from tears to laughter.

We'd just opened the door of the bathroom, to step out into the restaurant, when I realised it had been a fundamental mistake to take ten minutes out of the party.

The restaurant had two dozen beautifully decorated tables in the main area. Then, there were two steps up to a raised platform that was reserved for extra tables, private parties, or in today's case, a buffet. However, the rows of delectable tapas didn't even come close to filling the space, so there was plenty of room left for Dolly and Kenny.

Actually, it was Ida and Justin, but they were belting out a version of 'Islands in the Stream' that definitely gave Dolly and Kenny a run for their money.

I locked eyes with Nate, who was standing across the room holding a wide awake Finn, making him giggle by dancing in time to the music.

My life had officially gone mad, but even in the midst of this bizarre country duet, seeing Nate with a giggling Finn melted my heart.

'Argh, bollocks,' Sasha sighed. 'I was away for ten bloody minutes and look at him.' There was total exasperation in her voice. 'I can't do this anymore. I really can't.'

My gaze flicked to her face, and I tried not to let my surprise show. It was so unlike her to admit she was running out of patience with Justin. Usually she'd put a face on it, cover up her irritation by planning the next party or holiday. Or she'd just brush everything off with a 'you know what he's like'.

I reached down and wrapped my fingers around hers. It was another testimony to how pissed off she was that she didn't pull away. PDAs weren't her thing. Today though, she held on as if she needed the support.

The song finally ended, and the stars took a bow as their audience clapped and cheered. Ida's grin was so wide it could have featured in a toothpaste advert. She just lived for the adulation of a crowd.

Justin held Ida's hand to steady her as she climbed back down to the main restaurant, then swayed his way over to us. When he reached us, it was obvious that he was already drunk.

'Don't,' Sasha said, putting her hand up to stop him getting any closer to her. 'Just don't.'

Justin's top lip turned into the snarl that only ever crossed his face when he was on the wrong side of a dozen beers. He followed that up by going right on the offensive.

'What's wrong with you?' he spat. 'Okay, go on. Tell me what I've done wrong now. Because it's not as if I ever do anything right, is it?'

We'd seen this before countless times so it didn't come as a shock.

Sober Justin – lovely, decent and respectful.

Drunk Justin – antagonistic, arrogant and verbally aggressive.

'I'm not dealing with you right now,' Sasha said, but before she could walk away, he challenged her again.

'Why? What the hell is wrong with you? Can't a guy just have a good time? Guess not. Well, pardon me for trying. Go on then, tell me how I've spoiled your day, how I've fucked up your life...'

'Justin, enough.' It took me a second to realise those words, firm and not to be argued with, had come from me. 'I'm telling you to cut it out. Go outside, get some fresh air, and cool down. Then come back and stop being a dick,' I added.

My intervention clearly stunned him into silence. I wasn't usually one for getting involved in my friends' disagreements, but he was going too far. I wasn't standing for him speaking to Sasha like that. Not today. Not any day.

'Fuck off the lot of you,' he spat, then took a step to walk away in the direction of the doors. At least he was doing as I'd asked. I had no idea how Sasha was feeling, but I was furious and it was taking every ounce of self-discipline I had not to tell him to go home, and then come see us again when he was ready to apologise.

Sasha got there first. Her next words stopped him in his tracks.

'No, don't go,' she said, and for a moment I thought that, as she'd done many times before, she was going to defend him or make excuses for him.

I was wrong.

'I need to say something first,' Sasha went on. 'I don't want you to come back in. I want you to go home, get your stuff and leave. And I want you to check into a rehab centre and get help. If you don't, then we're done, Justin. I can't live like this anymore, and neither can you.'

I wondered if the pleading in her voice would reach him, but no. His face twisted as his anger notched up a few more levels.

'Why the fuck do I need to go to rehab? There's nothing wrong with me. The only problem in my life is that I'm surrounded by boring bastards who've forgotten how to have a good time.'

With that, he turned, slammed open the door and stormed out.

Sasha watched him go, with a defeated shake of the head. On impulse, I ran after him and caught up with him twenty metres down the street.

'Justin! Stop. Wait.' I begged. Reluctantly, he turned around.

'Look, I'm just going to say it. We all love you, but we can't watch you doing this anymore. You need to get help. I know some really good doctors who can…'

'Liv, do me a favour will you?'

For a moment I thought he was buying into what I was saying.

'Just mind your own fucking business.'

With that he'd stormed off, flicking me a V sign as he went.

I dashed back to the restaurant, to find Sasha still waiting by the door.

'Did you get him?' she asked, her face stricken.

I nodded. 'I told him we would support him, find him a programme…'

'And?'

'He told me to fuck off.'

'Every time,' she said sadly. 'Every time I try to get him to sort himself out, this is how it goes.'

'Maybe he has to hit rock bottom before he'll accept help,' I said.

Sasha's complexion was grey now, her face etched with pain and worry as she spoke.

'I think he's already there.'

10

An Old Friend Returns

July 2008

I checked in on one of my patients, Molly, before the end of my shift, and saw her daughter Trina, sitting on the chair beside her bed, reading a Maeve Binchy novel to her unconscious mum.

'I'll see you tomorrow, Trina,' I said warmly.

'Bye, Liv,' she replied. 'Enjoy your night off.'

Trina visited her mum every day and we'd developed a lovely rapport. However, one of the hardest parts of my job was knowing that there was only one way this was going to end. For now, though, Molly was comfortable and Trina could spend a few more precious days with her, whilst I headed back to my own family.

It was four o'clock by the time I got home, almost twelve hours after I'd left it, and Nate was lying on a rug out in the garden playing with Finn. He was only coming on for two, but already he could muster a fair sprint, and was shrieking with laughter as he ran around his dad. That scene should have made my heart swell – and it would have if the rest of the house didn't look like it had been ransacked.

I shouldn't care. I absolutely shouldn't sweat the small stuff.

But a knot of resentment started to form in my stomach. The school term had finished for the year, so Nate had nothing on his plate at all, other than to look after Finn on the days that I didn't take him into the hospital day-care centre. Yet, still, he couldn't seem to bring himself to clear up the house, or do a bit of washing, or load the dishwasher. God, what a cliché I was. The wife who was pissed off with her husband because he didn't do the bloody dishes.

The truth, if I was being a bit more introspective, was that the real reason I was a powder keg of resentment went a bit deeper.

I felt like I was invisible.

There. Needy and pathetic as it sounded, that was the truth.

Every bit of me adored being a mum, and when I was in work I felt useful and valued. But with Nate?

Invisible. Actually, that wasn't fair. He saw me as a mum, and we were pretty much in tune when it came to Finn, but other than that?

We were housemates.

I couldn't remember the last time we'd had great sex, or roared with laughter, or even sat down and talked about anything deeper than the location of the nappy bags or childcare schedules.

Was this it? Was this the way it was going to be? And was I being ridiculously unreasonable to want more?

I'd tried talking to Nate about it a few times over the last year or so, but he either just glazed over, said all the right things, then changed nothing, or he booked a table somewhere for dinner, made a minor effort to be more tactile, initiated sex once or twice, then slipped back into his comfortable state of oblivion.

It wasn't that I was leaving it all to him. I'd tried too. I'd done the sexy lingerie, teased him into bed a few times, organised date nights and tried to stay positive, but eventually my ego couldn't take the fact that I was doing all the trying and I gave up.

I wanted to be here. I wanted to be Finn's mum and Nate's wife. But I also wanted a bit of fun, excitement, great sex and someone whose gaze didn't continually veer towards the sport on the telly when I was trying to talk to him.

I wanted to feel like I mattered.

Although, my son never left me in any doubt of that.

I pushed open the patio doors and squealed as Finn ran towards me and I scooped him up into a bear hug, his giggles going right to the top of his volume scale.

'Hi,' Nate said, 'How was your day?'

'It was fine,' I answered. I'd also long ago realised that 'fine' was always the answer he was aiming for when he asked that question. If I said it was crap and launched into the reasons why, he'd switch off before I'd even stopped to take a breath. 'Chloe has invited us over for dinner tonight. Says she's got a surprise for us. You okay with that?'

'Sure,' he said. That was the thing about Nate. He was so easy-going and happy to go along with any plan – just as long as he wasn't the one who had to organise anything.

'Okay, I'll see if Maisie can come watch Finn and if not, we can take him with us.'

Maisie was delighted to get the call, and promptly turned up at 6.30 p.m., half an hour earlier than planned. 'I'll give Finn his bath and leave you time to get ready,' she said. I could have kissed her. Every time we went out, I was invariably running at the last minute, slapping make-up on in the car, wearing clothes that I hadn't had time to iron.

Tonight I took an extra few minutes in the shower, half dried my hair, then left it to fall into waves, and put on enough make-up that Sasha wouldn't come out with her usual enquiry as to whether I was channelling a consumption victim from the 1800s.

From the back of my wardrobe, I dug out an old favourite white crêpe top, added a pair of jeans and sandals and I was good to go.

Chloe answered the door the minute we pressed the bell. 'Ta-da!' she exclaimed.

'Ta-da what?' I asked, laughing but confused.

'Look behind me!'

I did as she said. I could see a male outline, and for a second wondered if she and Danny had got back together. That would definitely have been a bolt from the blue, because she'd shown no signs of regret in the eight months since she'd asked him to move out.

I squinted to get a better look, and suddenly the surprise made sense.

'Richard! Wow! We haven't seen you for years!'

There were hugs (me), handshakes (Nate) and then clinking of glasses as Chloe dished out the wine.

'Congratulations! I heard you got married,' I said, trying to rack my brain for the details. Chloe had told me about it ages ago. I was disappointed that we couldn't all go, but it was a destination wedding. Maybe Bali. Or the Maldives. To someone called... Shannon. Or Charlotte. Or something like that.

'And divorced. It's a long story.'

'Oh bollocks, I'm sorry.' I was mortified. Foot well and truly inserted in mouth. I made a pathetic attempt to change the subject. 'What are you doing up here?'

'Neuro conference about new brain tumour protocols at the Southern General,' he said. 'So I tracked this one down – despite the fact that she made it difficult...'

'It was my day off,' Chloe explained. 'He had to go to the tortuous effort of leaving a voicemail on my mobile and waiting for me to call him back.'

'It was agony,' Richard said solemnly. 'But then she suggested dinner and drinks with you lot tonight and my pain was forgotten.'

I remembered why I'd always liked this guy so much and also why I'd despaired that Chloe wasn't interested in him romantically. He was fun, he was great company, he loved to chat...

'So tell me what's been going on with you,' he said, directing the question at me.

... And he was interested in others. I tried not to draw comparisons with Nate's indifference. Instead, I bored him to death with toddler chat and photographs for fifteen minutes until Sasha and Justin arrived.

Yep, they were still together. After the argument at Finn's christening, he'd stormed off, but when he'd sobered up the next morning, after spending the night on some co-worker's couch, a shred of realisation had compelled him to take a leave of absence from work and check into a rehab centre that specialised in alcohol and substance abuse. Proud to the last, he'd done it on his own, without letting me or anyone else in our group help him.

They'd released him a month later, and he'd come back detoxified, sober, and more highly strung than I'd ever known him. He was like a different man and I admired him for doing it – but I could see the toll it had taken on both him and Sasha. I just hoped that the longer he was sober, the more they'd find their way back to enjoying life and each other.

But not tonight.

The food was great, the chat hilarious, but there was an underlying tension emitting from Justin.

'Is Justin okay?' I asked Sasha, when we were in the kitchen clearing away the plates.

I could see she was weary as she struggled to formulate an answer. 'He doesn't want to go out anymore, and when I coax him into it, he just spends the whole time in this low-level state of bloody fury. It's like he resents everyone for having a good time, when he – in his mind – can't enjoy himself because he doesn't have a drink. I've tried everything, but nothing's making this any better. I just need to stick with it because I'm the one that made him go to bloody rehab in the first place.'

It was an impossible situation and my heart broke for her.

'It'll get better, Sasha.'

'Will it?' she asked, pulling a huge gateau from the fridge.

'I've no idea – I was just trying to be supportive and stop you comfort-eating that cake.'

At least that made her laugh. She headed back into the dining room with the gateau, while I finished loading the dishwasher with the plates Chloe was ferrying in. Table cleared, she grabbed some dessert bowls and followed Sasha.

I was almost done when I heard Richard's voice behind me.

'I've been sent in for dessert forks,' he said. 'Which is concerning me because I've no idea how they look different to any other kind of fork. If I take in the wrong ones, Sasha could turn nasty.'

I was chuckling as I opened Chloe's cutlery drawer. 'In our world they're exactly the same as every other fork, so don't worry,' I reassured him.

He counted out six, then saw that I was wrestling with a wine cork. He took the bottle out of my hands and tried to uncork it. He failed.

'That's what you get for trying to be the big strong bloke coming to the feeble little woman's rescue,' I teased him, just as I managed to pop the bottle and fill up my glass.

'I'd take offence,' he retorted, 'but I know you're kidding because you're the least feeble woman I've ever met.'

Perhaps it was the compliment, or maybe the wine, or even the sudden flashback to another time and place, years ago, when I'd felt a flush of something when I was talking to him, but I realised that, for the first time in a long, long, time, I actually felt... Oh God... I felt turned on. A bit giddy. Attractive, even.

He held my gaze for long enough to make his point, but not too long that it became inappropriate. I was married. My husband was in the next room. Richard was a dear and long-time friend.

But there, in that moment, I had the first real inkling that Richard Campbell was attracted to me.

And that didn't just go one way.

11

Sasha's Birthday

October 2009

Chloe, Nate, Finn and I stood outside Sasha's door, hatching a plan.

'Okay, so I think the first thing she should see is Finn's smiley face – that way, she's less likely to kill us,' I suggested, before turning to my gorgeous boy, in his favourite resting place on my right hip. 'What do you think, Finn? Can you have a big happy face for Auntie Sasha?'

Right on cue, he gave us his very best, utterly adorable grin.

'That's it! And what have you to say?'

'Happy burfday!' he cheered, clapping his hands.

'I actually think he's a genius,' I declared and Chloe nodded in agreement.

That's what friends were for: sharing delusions about children's superior intelligence and throwing surprise birthday celebrations for other friends who really, really hated birthday celebrations.

I know it was wrong, but I hoped Sasha would forgive us when she understood why we'd done this. Over the last two years it was like Sasha and Justin had had the joy sucked right out of them. They no longer socialised, because Justin didn't want to be around people who drank, even though we no longer consumed alcohol when he was with us. Still, it was understandable that he wanted to avoid all gatherings where he would have drunk before. Minimising the opportunities for his disease to be challenged was crucial for him and I was so proud of him for turning his life around and getting sober. The downside for Sasha was that this meant they avoided all social occasions whatsoever. Once a month or so, we'd drag her out for a girls' night, and it was almost like she'd been given a free pass to become the old Sasha again. I applauded her staying power, but how long could she sustain a life with no fun?

Meanwhile, Justin had turned his addictive personality back to work and the gym. He was putting in the hours, leaving for the office at the crack of dawn, then going to train, then coming home late at night and crashing into bed. Nate couldn't keep up with Justin's gym schedule now that we had Finn, but he went when he could.

Ironically, on the outside, Justin looked great again – like the old Justin, with the addition of a few grey hairs – but that was as far as the similarities went.

I didn't have the answers. All I knew was that we had to be there for them both, but we also had to make a real effort to give Sasha's life the occasional interlude of happiness. Her parents were gone, and she wasn't particularly close to her two brothers, so it was down to us.

I rapped on the door, and when she answered, Finn performed perfectly. 'Happy burfday!' he yelled, with a toothy grin.

I knew he was a genius.

Unsurprisingly, and not for the first time, Sasha's reactions ran through several emotions, which I read as surprised, irritated, apprehensive, then resigned – all disguised behind a huge smile that was reserved for Finn and that he responded to with a squeal of 'Auntie Dasha!' It was how he'd first addressed her and it had stuck.

'What are you doing here?' she asked, and not in a gushy overwhelmed way. More in the way you'd react to cold-callers trying to flog you double glazing.

'It's your birthday and we weren't going to let you ignore it,' I replied, before using Finn as emotional blackmail and backup yet again. 'Were we, Finn?'

'Nope,' he said. 'Happy burfday!' I'd forgotten to point out that it only had to be said once.

Almost grudgingly, she opened the door and let us in. I was fairly sure if Finn wasn't there, she'd have found some reason to send us packing. Justin was lying on the sofa watching American football, so Nate immediately went and joined him. I plonked Finn between them, then Chloe and I followed Sasha into the kitchen, and put our haul on the table.

'Spaghetti carbonara, pancetta tagliatelle, lasagne, chicken arrabbiata, focaccia, bruschetta and a banoffee pie for dessert.'

It was all her favourite foods, and the main courses were from her favourite restaurant. It might have been the aromas, but she definitely softened.

'Thank you,' she said, and I could see she meant it.

'Did you have plans? Did we spoil anything?' Chloe asked. It had been our big fear – that Justin had arranged something and we'd gate-crashed his moment. Or maybe that was wishful thinking on our part, a futile hope that Justin would make some effort to treat her to something special.

'Nothing,' Sasha said with a shrug. 'Justin only got home ten minutes ago, and he put the game on as soon as he came in.'

'Did he even remember it was your birthday?' I asked, astonished.

'Yes. That's why he's home early. He usually doesn't make it back until after ten.'

I don't know what shocked me more – the fact that she was admitting this to us or the fact that she seemed to be accepting it all. This wasn't Sasha. The woman I knew wouldn't stand for such blatant disregard. She didn't put up with being treated badly, she didn't let anyone get away with being an arse and she certainly wouldn't shut down her life for a guy who was being, quite frankly, a rude git.

But then, this wasn't Justin either. Was it? The Justin we used to know was funny, and crazy and made everyone's life far more entertaining. And that was all good until the alcohol stopped being a social thing and morphed into a demon he couldn't control.

Chloe and I met each other's gaze and I could tell she was thinking exactly the same thing. We had to support Sasha – and Justin – no questions asked. She'd chosen this and we'd be there for her, bringing her bloody pasta and trying to make life better, until things improved for them and they found their way back to a happier, emotionally healthier place.

'Plates?' I asked, and Sasha dug a stack out of a cupboard. We began to dish out the food, the strained atmosphere making it a pretty much silent affair.

'I don't even have wine…' she said, with an edge of exasperation.

'That's okay, we're both working tomorrow,' I answered. I didn't say that we'd all made a pact not to drink when Justin was around. We just hoped he would eventually see that we could still have a good laugh without it, and maybe it would encourage him to start hanging out with us all again.

We carried the food in on three trays, and Finn was delighted to see it coming.

'Happy burfday!' he cheered. I really needed to stress that it was a one-off deal.

Justin – a little grudgingly – switched off the TV and we all sat around the table. I tried to rationalise the situation in my mind. Sasha was miserable. Justin was troubled. The life they were living was so much less than it should be, but maybe this was just one of those blips in a relationship, one of those low points that they'd look back on in twenty years and be proud of themselves for getting through it.

And let's face it, I couldn't judge. It wasn't as if Nate and I were swinging from the chandeliers and basking in marital bliss. We were still firmly in flatmate central. Sex once a fortnight, lots of going through the motions, and don't expect gales of laughter or deep conversations. The biggest sexual thrill I'd had in the last year was a moment of frisson with Richard, which I was now fairly sure I'd imagined.

Sasha and Justin were clearly having problems, but they had an underlying cause that they could work on.

Nate and I had no excuse.

The tension was lingering until Chloe decided to spice things up with a bit of gossip.

'I had a pretty unusual conversation the other day,' she said, teasing out the mystery.

'Spill the details immediately,' I demanded playfully, desperate to make tonight fun.

'I got poked,' Chloe went on.

'You got what?' Sasha interjected, horrified.

'Stand down, Sasha,' Chloe laughed. 'It was on that new internet thingy… Facepage.'

'Facebook!' I corrected her, before going on, 'I joined that last year but it all seemed like too much work and just a bit weird to let the world know what you were doing every day. Some people were putting up pictures of their dinner. Seriously. Who wants to see that?' I didn't get it at all. Number one, who'd be interested in what anyone had for their tea, or what they were wearing? And number two, why would anyone think putting up pictures of their cat would be in the least bit interesting to anyone else? If I were down to my last tenner, I'd bet it on the whole thing being scrapped in no time.

'So what happened after you got poked?' Sasha asked.

'I poked him back.'

Nate, clearly puzzled, entered into the conversation. 'Poked who back?'

I was hoping Nate's contribution would encourage Justin to join the discussion, but he seemed completely disinterested.

Unlike the rest of us. Except, obviously, for Finn, who was more interested in his spaghetti.

Chloe paused, building up anticipation.

It must be someone good. Maybe she'd finally tracked down Usher.

'Connor!' she said, with a huge grin. If there was a list of potential pokers, Connor wouldn't even have made my top ten.

'Our Connor? In Chicago?' I clarified.

'Yup,' Chloe beamed. 'We ended up chatting for ages through the... argh what are they called?'

'The private messages?' I offered.

'That's it!' she said. 'The messages!'

Well this was news. Nate still chatted to him every couple of weeks or so on the phone, but invariably, he'd finish the call and I'd ask, 'What was Connor saying?' and the reply would be a shrug and 'Not much.' I'd now given up asking, so I knew nothing about the status of his love-life.

'Tell us everything,' Sasha demanded.

'Well, he's still engaged to Cindy, but they haven't set a date yet.' Despite an admirable attempt to conceal her irritation at this nugget of gossip, she failed miserably. 'And he's been promoted to Vice President of his division.'

I made a mental note to ask Nate exactly what it was that Connor did. I knew it was something to do with managing athletes, but that was it.

'We just chatted about... stuff.' Despite the fact that they'd only communicated over the Internet, there was a twinkle in her eye that I hadn't seen with Rob or Danny.

'Stuff?' Sasha asked with an edge of cynicism.

'Yes, and it was nice. We haven't had an actual conversation in over ten years, so it was good to chat, even if it was all typed. My fingers were aching afterwards.'

'Well, I'm totally impressed,' I told her truthfully. Maybe I'd check out that Facebook thing again myself. 'And next time you're poking him, tell him that we all send our love.'

The laughter lifted the mood and spurred a dozen different conversations, most of them funny, until we got to a point where – apart from the fact that Justin barely contributed and seemed to have an upset stomach because he kept disappearing to the toilet – it felt almost like old times.

Finn started to get sleepy as we cleared away the plates, so I lay him on the thick fur rug, with a pillow under his head and a swaddle of blankets around him.

We gabbed for another hour or so over coffee, then I used Finn as a reason for us to take off and get him back to bed. Justin hadn't said a word since dinner ended, so it was obvious that he was ready for us to leave.

Still, tonight was a good start. Baby steps. I was so glad we did it. Once Sasha relaxed she seemed to really enjoy herself and there was the occasional glimmer of our favourite sarcasm queen of bygone times.

We hugged at the door. 'Thank you,' she whispered. 'I don't think I realised how much I needed that.'

'Any time,' I answered, grateful that we'd got it right. It could just as easily have gone very wrong.

Justin was next, and I wrapped my arms around his shoulders and hugged him close. 'We love you, you know that?' I whispered, out of earshot, because that kind of emotional stuff had always embarrassed him.

It seemed to strike a chord. 'I know,' he said. 'Thanks for doing this for Sasha.' Not the time for me to point out that he should have been the one doing it, I decided. Like I said, baby steps.

Goodbyes over, we climbed into the car, and were a few minutes away before Chloe was the first one to speak.

'What do you think, Liv?' I knew she meant in general, but my mind was elsewhere.

'I think I just smelled alcohol on Justin's breath,' I replied.

12

Collision Course

June 2010

The hospital monitor beeped steadily, in sync with the whooshing noise of the ventilator.

'This is my fault. It's all my fault,' Sasha murmured as she stared, eyes dark, at the bed.

'It's not, Sasha. You could never have known...' I tried to console her, but I could see it was pointless because she wasn't listening.

Beep. Beep. Beep.

We'd been listening to it for days. Watching. Waiting. Praying. Neither Sasha nor I had left the hospital, too scared to go in case there was a change. Finn was in nursery during the day, until Nate picked him up after work, then Maisie sat with him while he was sleeping. That's when Nate would bring food and a change of clothes and stay with us until long after nightfall.

The hours were endless and nothing changed. The monitor would beep. We'd watch for something, anything. And Sasha would blame herself and I'd try to persuade her that it wasn't her fault.

I closed my eyes and the memory started playing, so I opened them again. It happened every time. Every time. But I was so tired and my eyelids dropped again, the need for sleep stronger than my power to stop us going back there to the moment Sasha had called...

Chloe and I were sitting at my kitchen table, drinking coffee while watching Finn navigate an overloaded spoonful of spaghetti to his mouth, when my mobile rang. 'Oooh, it's Auntie Sasha,' I told him, and his cheesy grin sent pasta sliding down his chin. 'Hello my love,' I answered chirpily. 'Where are you? Chloe and I are waiting patiently for our pizzas.' She was already half an hour late and we were famished. That's what happened when we put her in charge of collecting the food on her way here.

There were no niceties, just straight into the crux of the call. 'Is Nate home?'

The tightness of her voice was unmistakable.

'Yes, he just got back. What's up? What's happened?'

'Bastard,' she exclaimed.

'Who is? Nate?' I wasn't following this at all.

'No, Justin.'

'Why?'

'He called to say he's going to work out late with Nate at the gym, but I just drove past the Clydemont Inn...' I knew the place. We all used to go there regularly when we were young and sociable, before children and grown-up complications had got in the way. It had a gorgeous restaurant and a really popular bar. It had always been one of Justin's favourites. 'And his fucking car is in the fucking car park.'

'What is he doing there?' I asked, with a growing feeling of impending doom.

'That's exactly what I want to know,' Sasha spat.

'Oh God, Sasha where are you?'

'Sitting in the car park watching his car.'

No, no, no. This wasn't good. A pissed off Sasha, and a lying

Justin, in an establishment that sold alcohol. This could only end badly.

'Do. Not. Do. Anything. Do not go in there without us. We're on our way.' I slammed the phone down and made an instant plan.

'Nate, can you come look after Finn?' I shouted up to him. He appeared at the top of the stairs with a towel round his waist. 'Sasha's got a situation…'

'Is she okay? Is it Justin? Is he hurt?'

'No, no! Nothing like that. She's worried that he's in a bar. Look, we have to go right now. I'll call you and fill you in as soon as we get there.'

'Maybe I should go? If he's in a bar…' Nate began to object.

'No, Sasha's outside and we'll be better at talking her down,' I told him, feeling sure she needed the female contingent of our circle right now. She'd railroad Nate into anything and he was too nice to object – she needed the calm reasoning, support and restraint that Chloe and I knew how to deliver.

Chloe's car was last in the driveway so we took that and roared out of our street, anxieties rising.

Why? Why did he have to pull stunts like this?

Someone once said to me that alcoholism was a selfish addiction and much as I had compassion for anyone suffering from this horrendous disease, I knew they were right. Justin had put Sasha through hell over the last few years, and yet Sasha, the most intolerant, demanding, bolshy of us all, the one who didn't put up with crap or mistreatment, had stood by him and never wavered, to the massive detriment of her own life. On a human level, I'd never been more proud of her. But as a friend, I worried that she was giving 100 per cent and getting nothing back. Justin barely acknowledged what she'd done for him. He was still detached. Still living in his own head. Still blatantly disregarding everyone around him, especially Sasha. I loved him and I knew it was the disease that was making him behave like this, but if he'd started drinking again then I feared for his future with Sasha. She didn't deserve this life – she deserved so much more.

'Oh thank God, she's still in the car,' I said, as we pulled into the car park next to her twenty minutes later.

Sasha jumped out of her car and into Chloe's back seat.

'What's happened? Did you go in?' I asked.

She shook her head. 'I learned that lesson a long time ago. If he's drinking and I go charging in there, it'll end up in a full-scale war. I just want to wait until he comes out and see what state he's in, then deal with it.'

It was yet another sign of how much the last few years had changed Sasha. She was the one who'd have stormed the room and damn the consequences.

'Have you suspected he's been drinking again?' Chloe asked gently.

Sasha blew out months of worry and dread before she answered. 'I don't know. Sometimes. He's barely home, and when he comes in, there's fresh breath, deodorant, all the stuff he says he uses when he showers at the gym, so I never smell anything suspicious.'

I decided this wasn't the time to mention that I had suspicions a year ago at her birthday party. If I'd been certain, maybe I'd have said something, but I was too scared of being wrong and causing irreparable damage.

She went on, 'He's never been visibly drunk, but he's just always… angry. Wound up. Like the whole world's against him. Sometimes I really, really think he doesn't want to be with me.'

'But why would he stay then?' I said. 'He could leave any time.'

'I think he's scared to leave in case he falls off the wagon again and fucks his life up. When he's with me, he has a home, someone to care for him, someone there, stability whether he wants me or not. I think he's scared to be alone, but hates the fact that he has to stay and he resents me for it.'

The shock made me speechless for a few moments. Sasha always put a face on, always pretended everything was fine, that she was in control, handling her business... but this Sasha was being honest and vulnerable and I'd never wanted to hug her more.

While we were baring souls, I wanted to know some other stuff.

'I think if the positions were reversed and this was Nate and I, then you'd be telling me to leave him, that life's too short to stay in a situation that's so toxic. And yet, you stay. Is it just because you love him? Is it fear? Loyalty?'

She turned her head away for a moment, staring out the window at the door of the pub. When she turned it back, we saw the tears. In almost twenty years, this was the first time I'd seen her cry.

'My dad died when I was seventeen,' she said, then paused to steady her voice, turning her head so she was looking out the window again, talking to no one. 'He was an alcoholic. Had been my whole life. He was the fun drunk, just like Justin used to be. The kind drunk. The one who told you he loved you ten times a day. But he was also the one who forgot to come to school shows, who never turned up for parents' night, who couldn't have told you anything about our lives, who spent our food money on anything he could pour down his throat. That was my dad.'

My gaze met Chloe's. We had no idea.

'When I was sixteen, my mum decided she couldn't take it anymore. She'd stayed with him because of us, because of loyalty, because she had nowhere else to go. She'd given her whole life to his disease and she wanted just a little bit of happiness. So she left. Moved in with her sister. Lee and Tony were already out of the house, and she wanted me to go with her, but I couldn't. How could I leave him?'

She was choking on her words now, every one of them getting caught in a vacuum of pain.

'I stayed and I tried really hard to take care of him, but I couldn't. Without my mum, he fell apart, because he had no reason to come home at night, no conscience forcing him to make at least one or two good decisions in the day. I tried, I really did, but he wouldn't listen to me. He was lost. And he was dead in less than a year.'

We were all silently sobbing now, hearts breaking at the pain that seventeen-year-old had suffered, and that she'd kept inside for so long. We'd met Sasha when she was eighteen and she never told us any of this. She was a fierce, fearless, live for today and take crap from no one girl. We had no idea of the darkness that she'd come from.

'So I can't leave him. I just can't. A few years ago, before we realised how addicted he was, maybe I could have walked away, but not now. Because if I leave him when he's like this, it could send him right back to the bottle. And I can't watch someone else I love die like that. I just can't.'

I got it now. It made tragic sense. There was no judgement or arguing with this.

'There he is,' she blurted, and her hand went to the door handle, as our gazes swung to the pub entrance. There was Justin, walking towards his car, on the opposite side of the car park. No swaying, no staggering, no sign at all that he'd been drinking.

Sasha opened the door and stepped out, but she was too slow. Her call of his name got drowned out by a transit van driving in front of us, and Justin was in his car and pulling away before she reached him. He didn't even realise she was there.

'Jump back in,' Chloe shouted. We could see her weighing up whether to take her own car, but Chloe's was ready, the engine was running, and he'd be out of sight before Sasha even switched her engine on. She climbed back in and Chloe took off, turning left out of the space. It took us past the pub door and I only got a glimpse, a tiny glimpse of a familiar face who'd just stepped outside. Blonde. Her hair was long now, but I remembered it being in a bob. She worked with Justin. Madeleine. In the fading light of dusk, she couldn't see the disgust on my face.

I didn't have time to point her out to Sasha, because right then, as we turned out of the car park, through the same green light that had let Justin past, a Range Rover coming from our right didn't stop. The police would tell us later that the driver had been for a romantic dinner with his wife and had consumed a few glasses of wine. It was one glass too many to register the red light. He charged straight on through, hitting the driver's side of Chloe's car, spinning us around, across two carriages, until we finally came to a stop.

Then the screaming started. The other driver's wife, out of the car now, standing in the middle of the road while he stumbled out of his seat and sat on a kerb, his face a mask of shock.

'Sasha?' I yelled, trying to get my seatbelt off.

'I'm okay, I'm okay,' she groaned.

'Chloe's hurt! Help me,' I gasped, finally pulling the seatbelt off and climbing across the centre console to Chloe, pushing the airbag out of the way to get in front of her.

The side of the car was completely crumpled, the window smashed, the door caved in, and I could see her legs were trapped. She was unconscious, but what scared me most was the blood that was pouring from a wound on the other side of her neck. I pulled off my cardigan, made a pressure pad, and pressed it on, controlling the bleeding while making sure her head was stabilised, praying that her jugular, only millimetres away, wasn't about to rupture. She still had a pulse but it was erratic and her breathing was stilted.

'Come on, Chloe, come on, we've got you,' I repeated over and over. 'We've got you, we're right here, you're going to be okay, we've got you.'

Same thing, again and again, until the blue flashing lights arrived and took over, the firefighters cutting her out, the paramedics working on her lifeless body, the police breathalysing the bastard who caused it.

We had her. Four days later, still sitting beside her bed, we prayed that she knew it.

We had no idea where Justin was – Sasha had ordered Nate to tell him to stay away. Whether he was drinking or not, she wasn't ready to deal with why he'd lied to her. Nate said he didn't object. In fact, he'd seemed relieved that he didn't have to deal with this.

I blocked out any judgement about that.

Right now, all that mattered was Chloe.

And whether or not she had the strength to come back to us.

13

Christmas Day at Liv and Nate's House

December 2011

The doorbell rang and Finn went charging to answer it.

'Finn, what do you never do?' I bellowed.

He screeched to a halt, then rolled his eyes like he was fifteen, not five. I tried not to show how amused I was by this, especially as the effect was diluted by the fact that the five-year-old in question was wearing flashing reindeer antlers and a Santa suit. I'd always sworn I'd never be one of those parents who dressed their children in gimmicky outfits. Apparently back then I just wasn't in touch with my inner Rudolph.

'Open the door without an adult,' Finn answered, winning a point for the boy in the red suit.

Nate caught up with him, and I was a few feet behind, when Finn swung the door open, only for Ida to scoop him up and swing him around until he was squealing with glee. Glad we'd made a plan not to get him too overexcited today.

'Come in, Mum. I'm just...' I stopped.

Ida had stepped forward to kiss Nate and wish him a merry

Christmas, and there appeared to be a man standing behind her.

I didn't have time to lift my chin off the floor, as Ida made gushing introductions – 'Darling, this is my wonderful new boyfriend, George' – then swept into the kitchen with a very dapper George to fill two champagne glasses.

'Did you know?' Sasha, the next to arrive, asked me surreptitiously as we stacked a tray of mince pies and shortbread.

'I had absolutely no idea,' I replied. 'But hell, good for her. She deserves someone else in her life making a fuss of her.'

'You're only saying that because it takes the mother-heat off you.'

'Absolutely,' I giggled. I know. Sometimes I'm a terrible person. But it felt like Ida had been trying and succeeding in making me feel guilty since I was Finn's age, so if there was someone else giving her the adulation she needed I was all for it.

'How are things with you two?' Sasha asked, nodding over to where Nate was standing.

I shrugged, sighed. 'Same as they always are.' I didn't want to talk about this. Not today. I'd promised myself that I was going to have a wonderful Christmas with my boy, and create the perfect day of love and family, and then I was going to think about the future in January. It wasn't the most scientific of plans, but it was the best that I had.

'I think it's because we all turned forty in the last year or so,' Sasha said. 'Makes you re-evaluate life.' I knew it was more than that, but this was no time for deep and life-changing reflection so I went for flippant instead.

'That's pretty profound for you, Sasha. Have you been in at the liqueurs?'

'Yep, sucking the Baileys out of them to give myself a buzz,' she said dryly. I knew she was kidding. With the exception of Ida and her champagne, we were still an alcohol-free zone.

'Do you think all Santa's little helpers have messed-up lives?' I said, trying to lighten the mood.

'Absolutely,' Sasha replied. 'I think Mrs Claus is leading a double life as a high-class escort. How else can they afford all those presents?'

Our laughter made Nate glance over, but I didn't meet his gaze.

'Anyway,' I said, trying to make a festive design with the shortbread. 'Take my mind off my woes by telling me about your shite life. How's things?'

'I have no idea,' Sasha answered honestly. 'Ever since the... accident...' Both of us still struggled to get that word out. '... He still works long hours, and then hits the gym at night. It's almost robotic. I don't know what I'd have done without Nate dropping in over the last year. When he's with Justin, it's the only time I ever see a glimmer of the man I fell in love with. I've tried to get him to go back to a counsellor, but he says he doesn't need it. In fact, he says I'm the one that needs therapy. He's probably right.'

'Why would you think that?'

'Because I'm living in a loveless relationship, too scared to leave in case...' she didn't have to finish that bit. If the... accident... had any tiny glimmer of purpose, it was that Sasha and I had started being honest with ourselves and each other. It had definitely brought us closer together, bonded by a mutual apathy for the relationships we were living in. No judgement. No opinions. Just support.

'Not that he knows that, of course. I'd never tell him. But he can't be happy either.'

'Do you still think he's drinking again?' How many times had we pondered this question over the last year? No matter how vigilant Sasha and Nate were, they couldn't come up with a definitive answer.

'I still don't know. He's so secretive about everything that it's hard to tell. I don't remember the last time that I said something and felt like it actually reached him.'

'Do you think he feels guilt about the accident?'

Her answer was swift and definite. 'Absolutely not. He says that's all on me. Maybe he's right about that too.'

How many times had we rehashed this? Justin's explanation for that night was simple – after he'd said he was going to work late and go to the gym with Nate, the guys from work announced they were having a birthday celebration at the Clydemont and he'd decided to stop in there instead. When it was put like that, it was fairly plausible. It also, therefore, made sense that the blonde former-bob would be there too. But it had just never sat right with me. Or Sasha.

He was sticking to the story though, and adamant that he was still on the wagon.

The doorbell went again, and Finn thrust both hands in the air and cheered, almost punching a hole in Ida's beehive.

'Race you,' Sasha said, and I took up the challenge. The two of us skidded to the door a split second behind Finn.

'Who do you think this is?' I asked him.

'I think it's…' I opened the door, just as he hollered, 'AUNTIE CHLOE!'

At which point, and I've no idea why, but I burst into floods of tears.

'Liv! What's the matter with you?' Chloe said, her face flushed with alarm.

'I'm just… I'm just… I'm just…' I couldn't get it out between the sobs. 'So…' sob… 'glad…' sob… 'that you're here.'

At which point, Chloe promptly burst into tears and Sasha rolled her eyes and said, 'Come on, Finn, let's go get your wellies. The hall will be flooded in no time if these two get started.' Giggling, Finn trotted off with Auntie Sasha

'Sorry!' I sniffed, 'I didn't mean to make you cry, it's just that…'

'I know,' she sniffed back, but laughing through the tears.

Chloe's recovery had been long: it was months before she

was fully mobile again, and more than six months until she was cleared for work. The crash had left her with a scar that ran from her jawline, down her neck, to her shoulder. If you touched the right place on her face, you could feel the screw heads, just under the skin. That scar was mostly covered by her hair, but the limp was harder to disguise. Not too noticeable under normal circumstances, but when she was tired it became more pronounced. 'If that's all I've got to worry about, I'm doing okay,' she'd say when anyone offered sympathy.

As for Justin, she didn't hold any kind of negative feeling towards him at all. It was an accident, pure and simple. That's why she had no issue in being with the whole group on special days. There had been loads of them since that fateful night. We'd all made it to forty, and were grateful to have got there, but none of us felt inclined to stage the kind of parties that had been thrown a decade ago. How things had changed. Back then, Justin was the life and soul, the fun guy we all adored. Sasha had been madly in love. Chloe had just split with... I couldn't remember. Some bloke who went off to sell timeshares in Ibiza and was never heard of again.

But today deserved to be celebrated.

Last Christmas, she'd stayed at home, surrounded by her mum, dad, and aunties, who'd all flown over to be with her.

This year, we had her back. And I was so, so grateful.

We went on through to the lounge, and there were hugs, kisses, and 'Merry Christmas's' all round, right up until she got to my mother.

'My mum surprised us today with a little gift to herself,' I teased, making Ida's new friend flush. 'This is George, Mum's boyfriend.'

Chloe stopped, put her hands on her hips, and pursed her lips. 'Hang on, so, Ida, you came today and produced a boyfriend out of the blue that absolutely no one knew about?'

Suddenly, I didn't understand what was going on, and neither did anyone else. This was so unlike Chloe, who would normally be all gushy and delighted for any new relationship. However, now she was acting really pissed off. I couldn't tell if she was serious or not, but she certainly wasn't giving off happy vibes.

Ida, sensing a potential challenge, drew herself up to her full five foot height. 'Indeed I did,' she said, chin high, daring Chloe to object or criticise.

There was a pause, then Chloe dissolved into gales of laughter. 'Goddammit, Ida, you totally stole my thunder!' We were all laughing now, but we weren't entirely sure why. In my case, it was just pure relief that any potential conflict had been averted.

'Once, just once, I try to be the one to surprise people,' Chloe said, still chuckling, but now she was walking over to the patio doors that led from the living room out to the garden. She flipped the lock up, then used her body weight to slide open the door. 'I have something for you all too,' she said. I peered into the garden, thinking maybe a bouncy castle?

Nope, we'd have noticed that.

A new barbeque? An airplane flyover? Fireworks? I wasn't understanding this at all.

That's when I saw the shape, a person, coming from the side of the door, shaking a smattering of snow from his hair and stepping inside.

'Thank God,' he said, 'I was beginning to think you'd forgotten about me and I was going to freeze to death out there.'

Chloe threw her arms around him and rubbed his cold ears. 'Everyone, this is my new boyfriend. I believe you know him already,' she said, bursting with joy.

I was the next to squeal with excitement.

'Oh, happy flipping days!' I yelped, beyond thrilled to see him. 'Connor Smith, what are you doing here?'

'Just thought I'd come see this one for Christmas,' he said, his grin huge as he gestured to the woman he was cuddling. 'And maybe, if she'll have me, I'll stick around.'

For once, perhaps the only time in her life, Ida didn't mind being upstaged.

14

Ida's Wedding

September 2012

Chloe leaned over to whisper in my ear as Ida broke into a storming version of Diana Ross's 'Ain't No Mountain High Enough'. 'You know, we could have been her backing singers up there. I've totally got all the moves.'

'You have and you could,' I agreed, 'but neither Sasha nor me could hold a note if we were in a siege situation and our lives depended on it.'

I wasn't joking. Even Finn covered his ears when I tortured 'The Wheels on the Bus'.

Vocal failings aside, it had been a fantastic day. My mum and new dad had thought of everything and the hospitality had been perfection. It was every bit as spectacular as Ida had wanted it to be and I was thrilled for her. She deserved this happiness – and George deserved a medal and very large noise-reduction headphones. I'd grown incredibly fond of him. He was an easy going guy – of course, he had to be to live with Ida – and he seemed thoroughly decent and good fun. I'd yet to discover any skeletons or criminal habits, his friends and family were lovely, and he treated Ida like a goddess. He was definitely a catch.

'I hope you're taking notes,' I said to Chloe. Her wedding to Connor wasn't booked yet, but I had no doubt it was on the horizon.

Who'd have thought it? Almost fifteen years after they'd split up, a few pokes, a near-death experience, a broken engagement to a former pageant queen from South Carolina, then a typed conversation that lasted for months, had brought him back to her and it was quite clear he'd never leave her side again. Her only sadness was that she'd missed the chance to have a family with him. She was almost forty-two now and knew the odds of falling pregnant were slim to none. But the accident had taught her to keep looking forward, focus on life's positives, and make the most of every day, so that's what she was doing.

I wish I could say the same. It was getting harder and harder to keep up appearances with Nate, to lie next to him every night and know that I didn't want to be there.

The toughest thing of all was that he'd done nothing wrong. Absolutely nothing. He didn't let me down, or break promises, or treat me badly. He didn't make unreasonable demands and I'd rarely heard him utter a harsh word. He even put up with my long hours and unpredictable schedule without complaint. He had so much going for him and all of it would make him a great husband – for someone who wasn't me.

The truth was, this was all my fault, not his. Twelve years ago, when I decided to give our relationship another try, cowardice had fuelled that decision. Maybe optimism too, but mainly fear that I was doing the wrong thing, that I'd rue the day, that I'd never find another love, that I hadn't tried hard enough to save us.

Yet, I'd never regretted it. If we hadn't stayed together, I wouldn't have Finn and he was worth any lifetime of imperfect love.

'What are you looking all serious about?' Sasha asked, sliding in beside me. 'You've just become the stepdaughter of a man who has no other kids and who appears to be richer than several small counties. Slap a smile on your face and let's start planning how we'll spend your inheritance.'

Luckily my cackle couldn't be heard over the chorus of 'Ain't No Mountain High Enough'.

'You are the most shallow person I know,' I retorted.

Sasha laughed. 'You won't be saying that when we're in the presidential suite of a five-star hotel in Bora Bora.'

I loved her. I just did.

'Listen, I just wanted to say thank you,' she said.

That caught me off guard.

'For what?'

'For not minding that Nate spends so much time at our house these days. It's honestly the only thing that keeps me sane.'

It had happened gradually over the last year, all part of a strategy Chloe, Nate and I had worked out to give Sasha some more moments of happiness.

Despite the fact that Justin was still adamant that he wasn't drinking and had no desire to, she could only truly relax when she knew that Justin was okay and that he was with someone she trusted. Therefore, Nate had taken to hanging out at their house more and more, letting Sasha have a break to shop, to spa, to spend time with Chloe and me.

It was a two-pronged approach. We also hoped that having Nate around more would help Justin find a new way of existing that didn't come with a black cloud of irritation and bitterness sitting right above his head.

Actually, it had been good for Nate too. He and Sasha were working in the same school now, and they'd both been off for six weeks of summer, so they'd spent loads of time taking Finn to the park and chilling out. Finn loved having his Auntie Dasha around, and it made the summer so much more entertaining for Nate.

So Sasha was happier, Nate was happier, I just wasn't sure that it was working on the third party of the equation.

'How's he doing?' I asked, gesturing to Justin. 'All okay?'

She nodded. 'I think so, but I'm making myself crazy with worrying every time he leaves the table, so I'm just going to let it go and enjoy tonight. And plan what to do with my best friend's forthcoming fortune.'

'That sounds like a great plan to me,' I said, raising a toast and laughing as she clinked her glass of orange juice against mine. Our lives were not working out, we had problems to solve, but right now we had music, friends and dancing, and that was all we needed.

It was way after 3 a.m. when we broke up the after-party in the residents' bar and Nate and I headed upstairs to – by complete coincidence – the same room we'd stayed in when we'd welcomed in the new millennium.

In the suite, I plonked on the edge of the bed and pulled off my shoes, while Nate removed his clothes, folding them perfectly.

A memory took charge of my brain and made my vocal cords articulate my thoughts.

'You did that back then too,' I said.

His expression told me he had absolutely no idea what I was talking about.

'You folded your clothes. Hogmanay 1999, when we stayed here. You folded them exactly as you're doing now.'

I didn't mention that back then there was a slight difference because we were about to have sex. That definitely wasn't on the cards for tonight and hadn't been for a long time.

He placed his socks, in parallel lines, on top of his neatly folded trousers. 'I can't believe you remember that.'

I folded myself into the bucket chair by the window, the same one I'd slept in that night. 'I remember everything. I remember we decided to separate, and then you changed your mind at the last minute and asked me to stay. I remember agreeing. I remember coming up here and having sex, and then spending the night sitting in this chair, terrified that I'd made a mistake. I remember blue flashing lights, coming to take away a poor girl who'd fallen and died on the way to the hospital. I remember the next morning, having breakfast and vowing I was going to make it work.'

Nate was sitting on the bed now, in just his boxers, his body still perfectly toned, thanks to daily sessions with Justin in the gym. Gorgeous. Handsome. Sexy. Yet not one iota of me wanted to be naked with him. That said everything.

'And have you?' he said.

'Have I what?'

'Have you made it work?' he asked. That took me by surprise. I hadn't planned to have this conversation tonight; it just seemed to have happened. And I definitely didn't expect Nate to have any interest in discussing it. I don't think we'd had a conversation any deeper than the choice between spaghetti hoops and fish fingers since Finn was born.

This suddenly felt like a runaway train and my foot was nowhere near the brake.

I should say it now. Be honest. Get it over with.

But today had been a celebration of love and, just like twelve years ago, I couldn't bring myself to make it the day I walked away.

'No.' I replied honestly. 'But I still hope I will.'

15

A Time to Go

May 2013

'I'm starting to hate this bloody hotel,' I told Sasha, as our car tyres crunched to a stop on the gravel of Lomond Grange. Exactly a year after we'd celebrated her wedding in this very venue, my mother had announced that she and George were treating us all to an anniversary weekend here, all expenses paid. We couldn't say no, but my stomach was in knots. This was like some kind of prolonged relationship torture, played out with complimentary slippers and a minibar.

Chloe and Connor were coming down together after she got off shift, and Nate and Justin were coming straight from a football match. Finn was having a sleepover with his best friend Alfie, so Sasha and I had headed down for a couple of hours at the spa. And when I say spa, it didn't mean that we indulged in all the extortionate treatments and pamper services. No. It meant we lay in fluffy robes at the side of the pool, sipping overpriced Prosecco, eating smuggled in chocolate and setting the world to rights.

Within half an hour of checking in, we were doing three of

those things, and I finally felt the knot of tension that had been raising my shoulders up for months, start to loosen.

'Right, here's the chocs,' Sasha said, pulling a box of Quality Street from her bag. 'Don't eat all the purple ones or I'll…'

'I'm going to tell Nate that it's over,' I blurted, cutting her off.

Without saying a word, she opened the box, pulled out a purple one and handed it over to me.

Time was up. I knew now that I couldn't put it off any longer. There were lots of reasons. Turning forty a couple of years ago had been a time of both reflection and of looking forward to think about the life that was in front of me. Seeing my mum, and Chloe and Connor so in love made my heart pang for the same thing. Mostly, though, I wanted Finn to see what a great relationship should look like, how two people who adored each other acted when they were together: the laughs, the happiness, the love. How would he ever know what kind of relationship to aspire to if he'd had no experience of how great a healthy marriage could be? Not that he ever saw arguments or anger because there were none – but neither did he see gregarious love, uncontrollable hilarity, or the unbridled happiness and chemistry of a couple who adored each other.

Maybe this would be a huge mistake. Perhaps all those fears from years ago would come true. Maybe this was it. Maybe there wasn't another love out there for me. But I couldn't live with myself if I didn't try.

Sasha waited until I'd swallowed the hazelnut.

'I think you're crazy,' she said. I was grateful for her timing – a few seconds earlier and there was every possibility that the combination of her reaction and a large nut could have choked me.

'You've been telling me to leave him for nearly twenty years!' I argued, stunned at her response.

She nodded, uncharacteristically pensive. 'That was before.'

'Before what?' I didn't understand.

'Before I realised what it must be like to have someone who is solid, who is there for you, who is a thoroughly decent guy and who doesn't come with any of the complications that men who are wrestling with issues can bring. Hanging out with Nate so much over the last few months has given me some insight into that and I think you should hang on to him with both hands and never let him go.'

If she'd announced she was living a secret life as a stripper, I would have been less shocked than I was right now.

Sasha. The unconventional one with the wild streak, trying to persuade me to stay with a man who she once said had the capacity to bore us out of our buttocks.

Despite my surprise, I knew she had a point. I recognised the positives of being with Nate – they were the reasons that I'd managed to stick it out for over twenty years – but there was another issue that had now come into play.

'I get all that,' I told her. 'But there's a problem...'

'Then get over it,' she said.

'I can't. I've got feelings for Richard.'

It was her turn for the astonished expression.

'No way.'

'Way.'

'Oh my God, Liv. Since when?'

I shrugged. 'A while. A couple of years maybe...'

'A couple of years! And I'm only finding this out now?' she screeched. Two passing swimmers glanced up to see what was going on and I gave them an apologetic grimace.

'I didn't want to admit it to anyone. Especially myself,' I told her. 'Actually, I think I've probably been attracted to him since we first met a gazillion years ago, but over the last while we've been chatting on Facebook and he's gone from being someone I've always loved as a friend to someone I can't stop thinking about.'

'And he doesn't know?'

I shook my head. 'Of course not. I'm sure it's not reciprocated anyway. But just the fact that I'm feeling this way, shows that I shouldn't be with Nate anymore. It's not fair to him.'

She thought about that for a moment, before admitting, 'You're right, but I still think you're crazy to let him go. So what happens next?'

'I need to tell Nate.'

She popped another chocolate in her mouth.

'When.'

'After we get home tomorrow. I don't want to spoil the anniversary dinner for my mum tonight. She'd be raging and she can bear a grudge for a long, long time.'

I expected more comment, more discussion, more input on Sasha's part, but she was strangely reticent to talk about it any further. Instead, she topped up my glass. 'Bugger it, let's just drink too much and worry about it all tomorrow,' she declared.

It was irresponsible. Immature. But I couldn't think of a better plan.

Dinner passed without incident, other than my mum giving a speech that lasted twenty minutes and then snogging George in full view of a packed, very posh restaurant.

When we got back to the room, I dropped my clothes, pulled on my pyjamas and climbed in to bed, already feeling the effects of a hangover kicking in. That's what all-day drinking did to me.

Clothes folded, Nate climbed into bed and I waited for the arm to stretch around me. A night in a hotel was usually a sure-fire occasion for our monthly sex.

His arm didn't come.

'Are you okay?' I asked him, puzzled.

'Yeah,' he replied. 'Of course.'

Something was off, but I couldn't put my finger on it.

I should just roll over and go to sleep. Yep, that was the plan. Absolutely. Good idea. Yet, suddenly I knew that I had to tell him and it had to be now.

'Remember last time we were here?' I started, trying to ease in gently, still not sure I was going to say what had to be said.

'After your mum's wedding?' he asked, and I could hear his breathing, slow and steady.

'Yes. We talked about us and...'

I paused, the words stuck in my throat. It took a few seconds for them to be released and they came tumbling out.

'I'm so sorry, Nate, but it's time for us to do what we should have done thirteen years ago, and let this marriage go. I'll always love you, I truly will,' I added genuinely. 'But that's not enough to sustain a lifetime together.'

Oh God, I'd said it. I'd told him. Thirteen years later I'd finally found the courage to say goodbye to this good, decent man and now my stomach was clenching as I waited for his reaction.

Eventually he spoke. 'I know things haven't been great over the last few years, Liv, and please don't think it was because I didn't love you...'

My heart sank. He was about to argue, to tell me all the reasons that we should try again, that we could make it work, and I just couldn't let him. We couldn't keep having the same discussion over and over. One of us had to be the one to end this and leave no room for doubt, and clearly that was going to have to be me.

'I'm so sorry, Nate. I've tried, I really have. And every moment of our lives together has been worth it because we have Finn. You're an incredible dad and watching you with him is one of the very best parts of our life. But other than our son, what do we have?'

He didn't answer, so I ploughed on.

'This can't be all there is, Nate, and you must know it too. We haven't had a marriage for years. We've got a friendship and a great co-parenting relationship, but we're not a married couple. We don't laugh together, we don't bare our souls, and even the sex...'

I planned to leave that one there because I didn't want to make him think I was taking pot-shots at him. Especially when he was sitting there looking like the front cover of *Health & Fitness*.

'What's wrong with the sex?' he asked, sounding slightly exasperated.

'It's not that there's anything wrong with it, but come on, Nate, what are we down to now? Once a month. It's perfectly enjoyable, but it's a long time since there was that passion, that "have to have you now, can't get enough of each other" stuff. Be honest. When was the last time you looked at me and felt an urge to ravish me right there and then?'

He had the grace to look slightly sheepish and refrain from answering.

'It's not the way it should be, Nate. We both deserve that kind of love and passion in our lives. I can't come to terms with the thought that this is all there is – this amenable, co-operative friendship. I see Chloe and Connor, hell I even see how flushed with love Ida is, and I want to feel that again. I want to wake up and be thrilled to be lying next to someone.'

He didn't reply. I let the pause linger and then I decided that we were too far gone to turn back.

'Look, Nate, let's not discuss it tonight. We'll talk about it all tomorrow and we'll sort everything out in the best way possible for us and for Finn. I'll do this any way you want. I'm so sorry, Nate,' I said again, 'but I just want more. For both of us.'

He lifted his gaze until it met mine and I waited for an argument that didn't come. For the second time today, I was shocked beyond words by an unexpected reaction.

'So do I, Liv. It's taken me a long time to realise it and to accept it, but I agree with everything you've said. We tried. It didn't work. It's time to call it a day.'

16

Chloe and Connor's Wedding

December 2014

It was about as different from Ida and George's wedding as it was possible to get. Chloe had gone for complete informality. Seven of us – Sasha and Justin, Nate and I, Ida and George, and the late arrival of Richard, had congregated at the registry office, wept tears of joy when they finally, after almost two decades of knowing each other, made their vows. Afterwards, Finn's friend Alfie's mum came to collect him for football training and a sleepover, and the rest of us had headed to Danny's restaurant for an incredible meal. It seemed like a strange choice, given that he was Chloe's ex, but despite splitting years ago, they'd remained friends and he'd insisted on making this his wedding gift to them.

'To be honest, I beg you to accept,' he'd said, when we'd eaten there a few weeks ago and she'd shared the good news. 'Because I'll be cooking fecking turkey dinners for the whole of the month of December and it'll save my sanity if you let me create something spectacular for you.'

Spectacular it was. To honour Chloe's heritage, there was jerk chicken and fried plantains, ackee and saltfish and coco bread.

To honour Connor's heritage, there was Angus beef, and crisp roast potatoes, haggis and neeps, and a thick whisky sauce. And for dessert, there was a mango cheesecake and a huge apple crumble. The latter wasn't particularly Scottish but it was Connor's favourite.

Despite the fractured relationships sitting round the table, it was a wonderful day, all tension put to one side to celebrate Chloe and Connor.

Only the very perceptive would see that Sasha and Justin could barely look at each other, or that Nate and I no longer had that unspoken easiness of a married couple. We'd been separated for over a year now, and it had been hard but made bearable by the fact that we knew we were doing the right thing and we'd stayed on good terms throughout it all.

None of that mattered today. We ate, we drank, Ida sang 'Endless Love' and made Chloe cry, and it was almost a surprise when Connor announced that it was time for them to leave for the airport.

It had been our wedding gift to them. We'd all contributed to return flights to Jamaica, where Chloe and Connor would do all this again with her family. My sore heart was bursting with happiness for them. She'd got her happy ever after and she deserved every moment of this.

We hugged them tight before we waved them off in a taxi and trooped back inside the restaurant. I'd have been happy to call it a night, and I could see the strain showing around Sasha's eyes too, but Ida had other ideas.

'I've ordered another round of drinks and they're on the way,' she announced. At Justin's insistence, we'd abandoned our teetotal policy for the day. Ida, still commanding the room, rounded on Richard. She'd always been fond of him – we all had – and now, looking back, we could all see that those years of wishing he and Chloe would get together had been a waste of time. There had only ever been one man for her. I was pleased about that for very secret and selfish reasons.

'Right Dr Campbell, I need your opinion,' Ida announced and I held my breath. She was such a drama queen that anything could come out of her mouth. 'I'm thinking of getting a boob job.'

There it was. My mother. What a gem. Thankfully Richard had known her long enough to handle her perfectly.

'Ida, I'm a neurosurgeon. That area is way outside my expertise.'

Ida took this on board and regrouped. 'Facelift?' she asked.

'Nope, not my department either.'

'Mum! You do not need a facelift!'

'I know, my darling,' she answered solemnly, 'but I just love the look on your face when I say stuff like that.' She then dissolved into hoots of laughter and offered up another toast. 'To Chloe and Conner. And love. And boob jobs.'

I think she'd had one too many glasses of champagne, but she was happy and George was obviously thoroughly entertained by her, so I felt no right to judge.

One round of drinks turned to two, then three, and my head was decidedly giddy when I nipped to the loo. I was on the way back out when I almost collided with Richard, coming from the gents.

'Well hello there,' he said, and I didn't think he looked handsome at all. Nope, not at all. It was the alcohol that was driving that particular attraction bus and, talking of which, there seemed to be a marked difference in our states of sobriety.

'How come you look completely sober and yet I'm seeing two of you?' I asked. And for the record, both of them were handsome.

'Because I'm driving down early in the morning and going straight to work so I've had no booze today,' he said.

That explained it. Like us, he never drank if he was working the next day.

'A man of impeccable habits,' I joked, badly. It wasn't my finest moment, but he indulged me by laughing anyway.

'I just want to say I'm sorry to hear about you and Nate. I hope you're doing okay.' I'd barely mentioned it when we had our occasional chats on Facebook, feeling that it was somehow being disloyal to Nate. Instead, I'd deliberately kept our conversations sporadic, and firmly in the non-personal, frivolous zone.

'I am. We both are. To be honest, it hadn't been working for a long, long, time but it just took us a while to realise it. It's all been completely amicable and we've managed to split everything without killing each other.'

It was true. Nate had moved out, to a lovely rental flat near Sasha and Justin. It made sense. When he wasn't with Finn and me, he'd be with Justin, either at the gym or hanging out at their house watching sport. Sasha had said many times how grateful she was for the support. Nate had turned the second bedroom in his new flat into a room for Finn, and we'd pretty much managed to keep similar childcare schedules as when we were together. Finn was at school during the day, and had activities afterwards, so if I wasn't working, I'd collect him, and if I was, then Nate would do it. If there were any clashes, Ida and George would pitch in to help. My mother was definitely a less selfish, kinder version of herself since she got married and became a grandmother. Not that we were allowed to address her with the 'G' word.

It helped that Nate had the same school holidays as Finn too. It had been an adjustment for Finn at the start, but he soon came round to the idea of two rooms, two sets of toys, and loads of one-on-one time with each of us – although we still hung out as a family at least once a week too.

'We're making it work and I think it's going to be fine,' I added.

'I'm really glad. It's good to see you happy,' he said, holding my gaze, forcing my internal emotional barometer to explode with a full-on adrenalin surge.

I wasn't imagining it. There was a connection.

Or maybe I was wrong and it was just me who felt it.

I had a sudden urge to shift the conversation away from me, in the hope that this ridiculous teenage flush would subside.

'Anyway, enough about my dramas. How's work? How's Manchester? And has Charlotte still not returned from Dubai and begged you to take her back?'

'Well, there's a story there,' he said.

'She did?' I could feel my eyes widening and my heart thudding with horror.

'No, she didn't,' he said, chuckling. 'Last I heard she was marrying an obscenely wealthy plastic surgeon. Shit, I should have passed his name on to Ida.'

'Don't you dare!' I warned him. 'She'll come back with double-G boobs and she'll do her back in. So what's the big story then?'

'I'm moving back up here. There's an opening at Glasgow Central. It's a post they filled a couple of years ago, but it didn't work out, so now they've offered it to me.'

I felt flushed again. Richard was returning to my hospital. I'd see him in the corridors. In the staffroom. On consults in my ward. I was going to have to get over this pathetic crush I had going on, otherwise I'd spend a fair part of my working day with a beaming red face. Of course, I could always just tell him, but the thought of that made me want to hide under a duvet until the end of time, so it probably wasn't an option.

He was still looking at me strangely and I felt like there was some other meaning there. Or maybe I was completely imagining it.

'Oh, that's great. It'll be good to see you more,' I stammered, fairly sure that my red face had now notched the room temperature up several degrees.

I caught a hesitation, as if he was unsure of what to say next, then he obviously decided to go for it anyway.

'So I was thinking that…' Another hesitation. '…That since I've just lost my best friend in the world to the love of her life…' Another hesitation. Long enough for me to reflect on how cute that was. He and Chloe had been like brother and sister since the day they met and I loved that he cared so much for her. 'Maybe we could…' my heart rate increased and I was fairly sure I could hear it in my ears, '… hang out sometimes. I'd love to get to know Finn better and I'm absolutely down with superhero movies at the cinema.'

I could feel my face smiling, then my head got in on the act and began to nod.

'I think that would be great. I mean, Finn would really love that.'

And there we were, standing grinning at each other, and I realised that he was just a little bit flushed too.

'Have you seen Justin?'

The voice instantly snapped both of us from our mutual gaze-a-thon. However, Sasha was way too wound up to notice anything suspicious.

'No. He hasn't come this way.'

'And I was just in the gents and he wasn't in there either,' Richard added.

'Fuck,' she spat. 'He's a selfish bastard, he really is.'

Her fury sobered me up immediately. This wasn't good. 'What's happened?'

She sagged against the wall, all fight out of her now. 'We had an argument at the table. I saw him texting someone and asked who it was and he just exploded. He's been like this for weeks. Months. Said it was none of my fucking business and that he couldn't do this anymore…'

I didn't understand. 'Do what?'

She threw her hands up helplessly. 'I don't know. I really don't know. Then he got up and charged away and I assumed he was going to the toilets to calm down…'

Richard shook his head. 'He's definitely not in there.'

'Fuck,' Sasha repeated. 'So he must have left.'

'Come on,' I said, 'Let's go back in and get our coats and I'll come home with you.'

She shook her head. 'It's fine. Nate has already offered to share a taxi home with me. I just hope...'

She didn't need to finish the sentence. *She just hoped that whatever it was didn't make Justin have another drink, then another.*

'He'll be fine, Sasha. It's been... how long?'

'Maybe a year?' she answered, and I immediately remembered. He hadn't come home from work and Sasha and Nate had scoured the city centre for him all night. Next morning, they'd found his car in the same car park as the night of Chloe's accident, only this time he wasn't in the bar, he was in a room and he was wasted. They'd sobered him up and he'd sworn it was a one-off.

'I'll walk you out then,' I said, hugging her. 'I hope he knows how lucky he is to have you.'

'I don't think he even notices,' Sasha replied and I could hear the pain in her voice.

We'd just stepped back into the restaurant when we saw the unmistakable flash of stationary blue lights outside.

'What's happened?' I asked the closest waitress.

'Och, it's terrible,' she said. 'Someone got knocked down by a van, right outside. I don't think it looks good. There's police and ambulances and everything out there.'

I knew. And when I looked at Sasha I could see she knew too.

With Richard running behind us, we charged outside, over to the group of first responders. The medics were congregated around a figure on the road, the police talking to a van driver who was clearly in shock.

'Keep back,' a burly policeman shouted, but he wasn't quick enough to stop Sasha barging through to see Justin, lying on the road, unconscious, blood oozing out around him, being loaded on to a stretcher.

The paramedics were working furiously, but one of them looked up when Richard dashed forward and said, 'I'm a doct—'

'We've met,' the paramedic replied abruptly. I recognised him from Chloe's A & E ward. He must have been working there for a long time if he remembered Richard, but I was just grateful that he did. 'Could do with your help on the way back.'

With that, they raised the stretcher and loaded it into the ambulance, Richard climbed in the back, and then they were away.

'We'll follow them,' I said, whistling to hail a passing taxi. It pulled over and stopped. 'You get in here and I'll be right back – let me just go grab our stuff.'

Sasha was visibly shaking now. 'Get Nate, Liv. Please get Nate.'

17

When the Last Party is Over

February 2015

I'd wondered if she would come.

There were only seconds until the start of the service when the door opened and she slipped in, taking a seat at the end of the pew claimed by Justin's work colleagues. She hung her head. As she should.

In the corner of my eye, I saw that Sasha had seen her too, and I reached over and put my hand on hers. She raised her chin, stared forward, didn't falter.

Just as she hadn't faltered the night she'd learned the truth.

We'd raced to A & E, only minutes behind the ambulance, but already Justin had been rushed through so that they could work on him. We were asked to sit in the waiting room, and this wasn't a time to bend the rules. There was nothing we could do through those double doors. We had to let them work, to save him.

The seating area was unusually quiet, maybe a dozen or so people with ailments that could wait. We moved to a semi-private corner, with two rows of six chairs that faced each other, tucked in to the left of reception, almost out of sight, but close enough to hear when the nurses called for us.

We were silent.

Sasha stared straight ahead, blocking out the world and the pain, while Nate and I sat, staring at the double doors to the treatment rooms, praying for them to open and for someone to tell us it was all going to be okay.

It was the doors at the entrance that opened first.

She walked in and went straight to the desk. 'Excuse me, I'm looking for Justin Donnelly. I think he was brought in here?'

'He was.'

It wasn't the receptionist who answered, but Sasha. The woman with the blonde hair turned, saw us, and her expression told us everything that we never wanted to know.

'I'm sorry, I didn't realise…' She started to back out to the doors, to make an escape, but Sasha spoke again.

'Come sit.'

'I can't, I…'

'Come sit,' she repeated. There was no anger, no malice, more a traumatised resignation to the truth.

After another moment of hesitation, the woman did as she was beckoned, taking the seat across from Nate.

'Madeleine,' I said, as her name came to me. 'You work with Justin.'

She nodded, and I saw that her face was deathly pale with worry. 'Is he okay? Is he hurt or…?'

'Stop,' Sasha said quietly. 'How did you know?'

'What?' Madeleine asked.

'How did you know we were here? And please don't lie. Not tonight.'

Madeleine's whole body deflated, like every ounce of strength had been sucked from it. For a split second, I thought that she was going to get up and walk out, but she stayed and she spoke.

'He texted me and asked me to come and pick him up. Told me to get him at the corner of Bothwell Street. By the time I got there, some of the street a bit further along was cordoned off and it was obvious there had been some kind of accident. The police there wouldn't tell me much, just that a man had been struck by a van and been brought here. Justin wasn't where we were supposed to meet so I texted him, called him, no answer. I knew. I knew it was him. But I didn't realise that you would be here too. I didn't know he was with you.' For a moment I thought she was going to break down, but she was made of steelier stuff.

'You've always known,' Sasha said, cutting right through to the truth.

'I'm sorry,' Madeleine said again, and I wasn't sure what she was apologising for now. For tonight? For more?

How many times had I met her over the years, at parties and celebrations? She'd always been there, like a shadow in the background. Snapshot after snapshot lined up in my mind. Outside in the smoking area at Sasha's thirtieth. At Justin's party the following year. In Sasha's garden a couple of years later when... the memory was like a sucker punch to the gut... she'd been talking to Justin and Sasha had been on her way over to confront them and I'd stopped her. And then a couple of years ago, the night of Chloe's accident, when she'd come out of the pub just as we were driving away.

I realised she was apologising for way, way more than just tonight.

'How long have you been seeing him?' Sasha asked, her voice still calm and cold.

'Look, I think I should go, so I'll...' She started to stand up, but Sasha stopped her again.

'He's really badly injured,' she said. 'They haven't told us anything yet, but it looked about as bad as it could be. I've no idea if someone is going to walk through those doors over there and tell us if he's alive or if he's dead. I think you loved him. And if you did, then you'll want to know.'

Every shred of colour drained from Madeleine's face.

'All I ask is that you tell me the truth. Because I need to know who he'll want when he wakes up. *If* he wakes up.'

My gaze met Nate's and I could see he was as stricken as me. So he hadn't known. Not that I thought for a moment that he did. He would never have stood by and let Justin do that to Sasha.

'Seven years the first time,' Madeleine said. 'Then we didn't see each other for a long time when the drinking...' she paused, unable to say it. 'And then when he came back to work after he'd been in rehab.'

'All the nights he said he was working late or the times he said he went to the gym without Nate...'

'With me,' she said.

'At the Clydemont Inn?'

'Sometimes. I share a flat with my sister and she didn't approve, so we'd go there.'

So that night, Chloe's accident... I could feel a crushing wave of rage rise from my gut and I clenched my teeth to stop it exploding. This wasn't the time or the place for recriminations. This was Sasha's time, not mine, and I was incredibly impressed by her brutal honesty and composed calm.

'What I don't understand is why didn't he leave me and come to you?'

'Honestly? I think he was scared,' she said. 'With you, he knew where he was, what his life looked like. If he'd left you for me, everything was unknown. We would need to find a house, to uproot and start over again. He wasn't sure if his friends would forgive him. And I think he wondered if I could cope if he started drinking again. Sometimes he would test himself, have one drink, maybe two, then stop. Then there were the times that he couldn't control it. He always knew that he was just one bad night away from self-destruction, and he didn't know whether I could pick him up, support him if that happened. I didn't know either. So he stayed with you. I think he felt it was safer, because he thought that if he left you, or you left him, there was every chance he would lose any restraint he had left and he would just drink himself to death.'

Every word she said made sense. The times I was sure I could smell alcohol. The anger, the subdued behaviour, the resentment, the detachment. He didn't want to be where he was, but he wasn't strong enough to leave. Sympathy and anger fought for dominance as I tried to process how I felt about what he'd done. What a tragic, tortured existence for a man who was once the brightest light in any room.

Sasha met her gaze. 'So why did you put up with that?'

'Because I love him. And because he told me he couldn't live without me in his life.'

'Relatives of Mr Donnelly?' a nurse shouted from the double doors.

Sasha, Nate and I stood up.

'Come through please.'

We'd only taken a couple of steps when Sasha turned back and showed more courage and compassion than most people possessed.

'You can come too,' she said to her partner's mistress.

Justin spent the next three weeks on a life support machine, all hope gone. His injuries had been too catastrophic to come back from.

On the twenty-first day, his parents and Sasha gave permission for the machine to be switched off.

Sasha had held Madeleine's hand as he stopped breathing, then, when it was over, she'd let it go and she'd walked away.

She hadn't seen her again until Madeleine slipped in the door of the crematorium, just as the opening bars of Snow Patrol's 'Run' brought everyone to their feet.

After the ceremony, the mourners dispersed, heading in cars to the wake at a local hotel. Nate, Richard and Connor walked ahead of Chloe, Sasha and I, their feet leaving deep imprints in the snow for us to follow.

A question had been on my mind all day, a decision that I wasn't sure I could have made.

'Why did you let her come?' I asked.

Without explanation, Sasha knew what I was talking about.

'Because I'm grateful to her,' she said quietly. 'If I hadn't known about her, if she hadn't told me the truth, then I'd still be wondering if I could have done something different, loved him more, saved him from himself. Now I know that he made the choices. So I won't mourn what we had, because it was never true. Instead, I can say goodbye, and I can move forward. I can finally live my life the way I want to, with no guilt or regret. She gave me that.'

In front of us, the guys had stopped to wait for us. As we got closer, Nate turned, held out his hand to Sasha.

Move forward with no guilt.

I saw now what she meant by that.

And I hoped that she never looked back.

18

Nate and Sasha's Wedding

January 2016

The guests were all gone, Finn was sound asleep in a family room with his granny and George, and the rest of us were back in the same room the bridal party had used to get ready that morning.

'Can I burn this dress now?' Sasha asked.

'Absolutely not,' Chloe said. 'You should preserve it and wear it every year on your anniversary, just to remind yourself of today.'

'I'd rather just burn it and look at photos,' Sasha drawled.

Nate, sitting next to his wife, his arm casually round her shoulders, shook his head in mock exasperation. 'Don't listen to her. I'm going to get it mounted in a glass display case and put it in our front room.'

'This is going to be the shortest marriage in history,' Sasha sighed.

It should be strange, this scene in front of me, but it wasn't in the least. In fact, there was a deep feeling that everyone was exactly where they should be. It had taken Nate and Sasha many months to acknowledge their feelings for each other. After Justin's death, they'd been an inseparable force, sticking together as they both found a new way to live. Turns out it was together, and I was delighted for them. We all were.

I felt Richard's hand stroke the back of my neck and I had an almost irresistible urge to kiss his face off. That happened a lot. The first time we'd hung out after I'd split with Nate, he told me he'd been in love with me for years. So I hadn't imagined it. We'd been together since that moment. I knew the honeymoon phase would subside eventually, but it was showing no signs of it yet.

On the other sofa, Chloe and Connor were sprawled out, shoes kicked off, Connor's tie and jacket long abandoned.

'What time do you need to leave for the airport in the morning?' Chloe asked.

'About six,' Nate answered, 'Which is about... Oh, four hours from now.'

Sasha rolled her eyes. 'We can sleep on the plane. Otherwise I'll just get relentlessly bored and force you to talk to me.'

'Sleep sounds good,' Nate quipped. 'I love you, but I can't have a seven-hour conversation all the way to New York. I'll be out of interesting chat by the time the plane leaves the landing strip at Glasgow airport.'

I laughed, my delight for my ex-husband's happiness brimming over.

Behind me, I felt Richard's breathing change and I realised he was falling asleep. He'd worked through the night last night on an emergency admission and I knew he was exhausted. I was just glad he had some time off now, deliberately planned so we could spend the rest of the week doing fun things with Finn before he went back to school.

'So I've been thinking,' Sasha said, and the rest of us groaned.

'Will this end up with any of us being publicly humiliated or jailed?' I asked.

'Probably both,' she confirmed, laughing, before returning to her announcement. 'I've been thinking that obviously the next few months are out, because he's made me do this whole wedding thing and now he's forcing me to go on a honeymoon...'

Nate didn't rise to it.

'But maybe later in the year we could all go on that group holiday we've talked about for ever. I mean, I know it'll be totally weird, because you used to be married to him...' that one was directed at Nate and me, 'and we always thought you'd end up hooking up with him...' that one was for Chloe and my sleeping fiancé. He'd asked me to marry him while we stood on the sideline at one of Finn's football games, in minus degree temperatures in the drizzling rain, with feet so cold I could barely feel them. I'd snuggled into him for a heat. 'Marry me', he'd said suddenly, no fuss, no frills, no grand gestures. It was perfect. 'Only if you buy me better wellies,' I'd replied. He'd grinned that gorgeous grin of his. 'Deal.'

We'd decided to slip off to the registry office sometime soon and just do it with no fuss.

Sasha's voice snapped me back to the moment, 'But still, I think it'll be great. Who's in?'

My hand shot into the air. Right then I couldn't think of anything I'd love more than a foreign jolly with two best friends, a soon-to-be husband, an ex-husband and his best mate, who'd disappeared to America for ten years then came back after he poked my pal.

Like synchronised swimmers, Sasha and I realised at exactly the same moment that Chloe and Connor hadn't answered and both our heads swivelled to stare at them with blatant hostility.

'Oh, come on – you must be past all that romantic solitude rubbish by now,' Sasha said, words dipped in disapproval. 'I was over it by the time dinner was served today.'

A glance shot between Chloe and Connor, before her mouth broke into the giddiest of smiles.

'What? What is it? What are we missing?' I asked, my grin already replicating Chloe's even though I had no idea what was going on.

'I can't tell you…'

'Oh yes you bloody can. It's my wedding day – that makes me the boss all day. Now tell us what's going on?' Sasha said.

Chloe glanced at Connor again, and a silent question was asked and answered.

'Aaaaargh, okay then,' Chloe gushed, before pulling her clutch bag off the table in front of her and taking a piece of paper about 10 cm square from it. 'I didn't want to say anything before now because your wedding was coming and this time should be all about you…'

She took a deep breath and I could see her eyes were glistening as she turned the piece of paper around and held it up so we could see it.

'Meet the Smith twins. Coming July 2016.'

My eyes narrowed in on the image and there they were, two tiny little people wrapped in each other in their mother's womb.

I squealed so loudly I woke up Richard, before I jumped from the couch and gently landed on my pregnant pal.

Sasha was right behind me, slowed down by the satin princess skirt.

'Congratulations, you two. Connor, this is amazing…'

'It is indeed,' he agreed as I hugged him tightly.

'Oh Chloe, I'm so happy for you. I can't believe it!'

'Neither can I,' Sasha screeched. 'Because you're forty bloody five!'

Chloe nearly choked with laughter. 'I know! I still can't believe it. I honestly thought our time had passed, and then… well, blue line on a stick. The doctor told me the chances of this happening naturally at my age are tiny. How lucky are we?'

Over the last twenty years we'd all been through heartache and hurt, through times when we'd never felt happier, to periods where we were in so much pain we felt broken. And it had all brought us to today.

A wonderful wedding. Two babies on the way. My gorgeous son. And me, lying here in the arms of a man who had finally made me feel everything I'd been missing for so many years.

As days went, it didn't get much better than this.

WITH OR WITHOUT HIM

2017

EPILOGUE

Saying Goodbye

August 2017

It was the kind of scene that was usually only seen in movies.

The burnt orange sun was setting on the horizon, its fading rays sending shards of red across the surface of the sparkling blue ocean.

Behind us, on the beach, there was a long line of houses, some of them on stilts, all of them designed to capture one of the most beautiful views on earth.

No matter what direction we looked in, there was no one else to be seen. It was just pure peace, beauty, perfection.

'I wish we were staying in one of those,' Sasha piped up, ignoring the view in favour of eyeing up the multi-million-pound houses behind us.

We were in Malibu Colony, one of the most expensive and exclusive strips of real estate in the world.

'Unfortunately, we didn't have fifty grand a week to spare,' I told her. 'Besides, we're not exactly slumming it.' I'd found an Airbnb in one of the condo communities a mile or so along the coast, and it was perfect for us. Three bedrooms, with a one-bedroom apartment next door that was also available. We'd snapped them up and relocated the whole lot of us here for a fortnight. Richard, Finn and I were sharing the larger apartment with Chloe, Connor and the twins, while Nate and Sasha were enjoying the child-free peace of the flat next door.

Ida and George had chosen not to stay with us – I think it was below my lovely-but-rich stepfather's normal holiday standards, and they'd ensconced themselves in a stunning hotel in Santa Monica called Shutters on the Beach.

Ida said it was so glorious they were never leaving.

She did, however, keep her promise to sit with the kids for this one day, while the rest of us came to the beach to bring closure to an unfulfilled dream.

Richard held my hand as we walked towards the shoreline, all of us barefoot and carrying our shoes. We'd chosen here because we knew it would be peaceful and the perfect place to pay tribute to our friend. There was also a fairly good chance that one of the homeowners would take issue with the fact we'd sneaked on to their beach, and attempt to have us removed, which Justin would have found hilarious.

We stopped a few feet back from the water and sat down on the sands, all facing into the candle that Chloe had bought that morning in Walmart.

'A candle?' Sasha blurted incredulously, before loud, uncontrollable guffaws took over. 'A candle?' she repeated, trying to speak through peals of laughter. 'I thought we were going to light a fire?'

Chloe didn't find Sasha's reaction quite so hilarious. 'I was going to make a bonfire, but then someone told me it was against the law to make a fire on this beach, so I changed my mind. I've no idea if it's true, but I can't risk getting arrested – the twins would starve.'

'So you got a…' Sasha held it up so she could read the front, 'strawberry cheesecake flavored candle.' That set her off again, and it was a few seconds before she could add, 'Fuck, Justin would love this.'

We all knew she was right. He'd find it hysterical.

We'd all had tasks to fulfil for this outing, and mine was next. I opened the cool bag, pulled out six bottles of beer and handed them out. This was a celebration of the best of Justin's life, of his happiest times, and they never came without a beer in his hand.

Sasha was next. She opened the bag she'd been carrying and took out a beautiful bronze urn and placed it next to the strawberry cheesecake candle. We weren't scattering his ashes – Sasha said she didn't want to leave him behind somewhere he didn't know anyone. We'd just brought him to the place he'd always dreamt of coming to and then we'd take him home again.

Sasha raised her bottle up into the centre of the circle and the rest of us followed.

'To Justin Donnelly,' she said. 'Since he passed I've done a lot of thinking and I want to remember him as the guy he really was, the one before his demons got a grip of him. So here's to the real Justin – the most infuriating, but utterly lovable man there ever was. The guy who started every party and finished most of them days later. Who loved us all and was loved right back, even when he was driving us crazy.'

She cleared her throat, determined to keep it together.

'The man who took it too far every time… even when there was no coming back from it. Justin, you'll never be forgotten by any of us. You'll live with us always. And baby…' she stopped, breathed, gathered. 'You made it to Malibu. To Justin…' she finished.

We clinked out bottles together and echoed the toast. 'To Justin.'

'Right, I believe I'm up next,' Richard said, reaching over to switch on the boom box he'd been tasked with lugging all the way from the UK. It had been Justin's favourite thing all through university and Sasha had found it, still working perfectly, in the loft.

Richard slipped a cassette into the slot, turned up the volume, and one of Justin's favourite songs back then, House Of Pain's 'Jump Around', blasted from the speakers.

'Right you two, you're next,' Sasha bellowed to Nate and Connor, who immediately jumped to their feet and grabbed either end of the long pole they'd had to stick out of the sunroof on the way here.

Suddenly, Sasha reached over and turned the music down so she could be heard.

'Hang on, before we do this can I just check everyone is wearing swimwear under their clothes, because too many of us have seen each other's naked bits in this group already.'

There was a chorus of exclamations to the affirmative.

'Excellent,' she chirped. 'Then, ladies and gentlemen, let's get on with a solemn tribute to our long-lost friend. I give you... strip limbo.'

I've no idea if spirits exist, if they can see the loved ones they leave behind, but I'll always choose to believe that as we limboed, danced, and sang long into the night, Justin was sitting up there watching, laughing his head off, joining the party, and I know he'd have loved every wild, crazy minute of it...

Especially the bit where the cops came and asked us to leave.

AFTER THE LAST WORD
WAS WRITTEN...

Writing this book made me sit down and think about all the crossroads I've encountered over the years. I still don't have the answers to what would have happened if I'd made different choices.

What I do know for sure is that family doesn't need to be related by blood. It's the friends you choose to go through life with, the ones that surround you and walk beside you every day.

But as for the other stuff?

I'm choosing to believe that no matter what path we take, what decisions we make along the way, we still end up exactly where we were meant to be, with the people we're supposed to be with.

That's why, at the end of both storylines, Liv goes home to Richard and Finn.

Chloe and Connor got together at different times, but the outcomes in both worlds were the same – they found their way back to each other, and their twins, no matter what year they were born in, completed their family.

Sasha and Nate were in touching distance for half of their lives, but only came together when it was right.

Justin's life was a troubled one, but in both stories he found a group of people who would sacrifice so much to take care of him.

And Ida... well, she never did become a singing superstar, but if she'd found fame and fortune, then perhaps she wouldn't have met the man who would make her happy until the last chorus had been sung.

But then, what about Francine? What about the lives she went on to save? Would those souls have survived anyway? Or did her passing cost the lives of others?

Who knows?

Back in the real world, I find it reassuring to go with the belief that it's all predetermined, that we'll somehow find the people whose lives we're destined to share – our soulmates, our lovers, our friends, our children – no matter what we do, where we go or what choices we make.

There's no right or wrong move.

No mistakes. No missed chances or regrets.

Just different roads that take us to where we're meant to be.

All we have to do is keep walking towards the happy ever after.

ACKNOWLEDGEMENTS

Thanks as always to the wonderful, inspiring and endlessly supportive Caroline Ridding, and to Melanie Price and the fabulous team at Aria.

Thanks too, to my lovely friends, Kirstine and Lyndsay, two endlessly patient nurses who answered all my medical questions. They're both brilliant, so any mistakes are mine.

Thanks to Jan, who always gives me her honest opinion. To my godmother, Rosina, who is endlessly supportive. And Gemma, who I met at a crossroads and I'll always be glad I took the path she was on.

And finally, to my guys, J, C & B. I never forget how lucky I am.

Love,
Shari xx

Looking for another wonderful Shari Low read?

Then turn the page for a sneak peak at
The Story of Our Life...

I

Spring 2016

At the church

Fifteen years ago, I walked up the same church aisle.

Back then, the first person I saw was Annie, my gloriously indomitable grand-mother, in dramatic purple and a hat that resembled a frisbee, disguising her tears because she was born of a stoic generation that was disdainful about crying in public.

Next to my grandmother were my parents. My father, resplendent in his best morning suit and golfing tan, no doubt keen to get the formalities over with so he could squeeze in nine holes in before dinner. Meanwhile, the woman who gave birth to me was preening, loving the attention being mother of the bride brought her, while breezily overlooking the fact that she'd shown no interest whatsoever in her daughter's wedding. When I called her to tell her we'd set a date, she'd said, 'Oh right, Shauna. Let me write that down so I don't forget it. I think we were planning to be in Spain that weekend. I'll check my diary.' Still, she'd made it. My gain was the Marbella Golf Club's loss.

In the rows behind the star attractions, a sea of smiles beamed at us as we walked down the aisle. Steps behind me, were my best friends, Lulu and Rose in matching pastel elegance. Was it okay to call them 'best friends' at our age? Did that belong back in the days of teenage territorialism? Okay, so my 'closest' friends, their grins masking hangovers that were crying out for a dark room and a box set of Grey's Anatomy.

Rosie, a hopeless romantic, had been on board with the wedding from the start, but Lulu had been resistant, listing all the reasons I should wait and keep my options open. I was only 24. My catering company was growing and would demand lots of attention. I was an independent woman with a flat, a job I loved, a bank account that was (just) in the black. And besides, a piece of paper didn't matter to a relationship. Marriage was an outdated institution. Married women inevitably dumped their friends in favour of nights in, pandering to their men while gaining five pounds a month and neglecting their roots – hair, not ancestry.

Not for the first time, I ignored her.

And the reason was there in front of me. Colm. My gorgeous Colm. Standing there at the altar, in a suit that fitted him to perfection, showing not a trace of nerves. His expression radiated enjoyment, like this was a party he'd been looking forward to for ages and now he was thrilled it was starting.

I was too.

I wanted to dance towards him, sashay and pirouette into his arms, skip straight to the kissing and cheering part.

I saw flowers, and light and love. I saw promise. Commitment. Belonging. Delight. Contentment. Lust. Excitement. The realization of dreams. An incredible future.

I saw happy ever after. Until forever.

But that was then. Before everything happened. Before time, like a well-worn yet inevitable cliché, took its toll. Before my heart was broken. Before one of those closest friends betrayed me. Before my husband slept with another woman.

Before death.

Fifteen years ago, I walked up the aisle in white.

This time, I'm wearing black.